GOD'S EYE
THE NORTHWOMEN SAGAS

SUSAN FANETTI

THE FREAK CIRCLE PRESS

God's Eye © 2016 Susan Fanetti
All rights reserved

This is a work of fiction. Names, characters, places, and incidents are a product of the author's imagination. Any resemblance to actual persons, living or dead, events, or locales are entirely coincidental.

ALSO BY SUSAN FANETTI

The Night Horde SoCal Series:
(MC Romance)
Strength & Courage, Book 1
Shadow & Soul, Book 2
Today & Tomorrow, Book 2.5
Fire & Dark, Book 3
Dream & Dare, Book 3.5
Knife & Flesh, Book 4
Rest & Trust, Book 5
Calm & Storm, Book 6

The Pagano Family Series:
(Family Saga)
Footsteps, Book 1
Touch, Book 2
Rooted, Book 3
Deep, Book 4
Prayer, Book 5

The Signal Bend Series:
(The first Night Horde series)
(MC Romance)
Move the Sun, Book 1
Behold the Stars, Book 2
Into the Storm, Book 3
Alone on Earth, Book 4
In Dark Woods, Book 4.5
All the Sky, Book 5
Show the Fire, Book 6
Leave a Trail, Book 7

PRONUNCIATIONS AND DEFINITIONS

To build this Viking world, I did a great deal of research, and I mean to be respectful of the historical reality of the Norse cultures. But I have also allowed myself some creative license to draw from the full body of Norse history, culture, and geography in order to enrich my fictional representation. True Viking culture was not monolithic but instead a various collection of largely similar but often distinct languages, traditions, and practices. In The Northwomen Sagas, however, I have merged the cultural touchstones.

My characters have names drawn from that full body of history and tradition. Otherwise, I use Norse words sparingly and use the Anglicized spelling and pronunciation where I can. Below is a list of some of the Norse (and a few Estonian) names and terms used in this story, with pronunciations and/ or definitions provided as I thought might be helpful.

NAMES (in order of appearance in the story):
- Oili (*O-ee-lee*)
- Åke (*AW-kyuh*)
- Vali (*VAH-lee*)
- Leif (*LAFE*)
- Einar (*A-nar*)
- Knut (*kuh-NOOT*)
- Jaan (*YAHN*)
- Bjarke (*BYAR-kyuh*)
- Thorvaldr (*thor-VAL-der*)
- Nigul (nee-*GOOL*)
- Jakob (*YAH-kob*)
- Eivind (*A-vind*)
- Solveig (*SOL-vay*)

TERMS (in alphabetical order):

- Hangerock—an apron-like overdress worn by Viking women.
- Jötunn—(*YOH-tun*) one of a race of giants
- Karve—the smallest of the Viking ships, with thirteen rowing benches.
- Skause—a meat stew, made variously, depending on available ingredients.
- Thing—the English spelling and pronunciation of the Norse *þing*. An assembly of freemen for political and social business.
- Úlfhéðnar (*OOLF-hyeh-nar*)—a special class of berserkers who took the wolf as their symbol. They were known to be especially ferocious and in some sagas are identified as Odin's elite warriors.
- Völva (*VUHL-va*)—a seer or mystic

To my Freaks: warrior women, every one.

Special thanks to Lina Andersson, who helped me out with understanding the various and fascinating cultures, histories, languages and stories of ancient Scandinavia.

Skål!

PROLOGUE
THE EYE

SOME YEARS BEFORE

By the time she had six years, Brenna had grown used to the way people stared and then looked away. She'd become numb to the space that always formed around her as she walked through Halsgrof with her mother and father while they did their trade and made their offering to the jarl.

Now that she had ten years, she was learning to make sport of people's fear, to turn on them the eye they so dreaded and pull a face so that they might spend a sleepless night or three, waiting to see how she had cursed them.

The few souls of her own tiny village were less fearful but not much more warm. Even those who'd known her from her birth thought there something fantastical about her, something they could not understand. Some thought her a boon, others a bane, but none thought her simply a girl. Only the people who shared her blood spared her from their fear.

Her mother and father called it awe, that thing that turned people away from her, but Brenna thought that point too fine to split. Fear or awe, it meant friendlessness.

Brenna bore the Eye of the Gods. She herself had never seen it very clearly—her parents kept no looking-glass, and her reflection in water was of only a girl—but it must have been a fearsome thing to behold.

"Usch, Brenna," her mother said, combing back a loose blonde tress and tucking it into Brenna's braid. "You must go off on your own for a while, love. You know Sigurd will not trade with me if he sees you." She pressed a small piece of hacksilver into Brenna's hand. "Go get your sweet. But stay in sight of the docks and listen for your father's call."

"Yes, Mother."

Her mother patted her head and gave her a loving smile, and Brenna wandered off on her own, tucking the hacksilver into her sleeve. She wouldn't spend it. The sweets-monger was the worst place in Halsgrof for her. All the children loosed from their parents congregated there. And children turned their fear into cruelty.

But she let her mother think that she got to enjoy a treat; it eased her mind, and Brenna knew that her mother felt people's crude fear almost as keenly as she herself did.

She had expected to be sent off, she was on every trip to town, and she had a place she went to spend that time. That night, at home, she would return the bit of hacksilver to her mother's leather pouch. They could not afford to spend even that small sliver on sweets, especially imaginary sweets.

Giving a wide berth to the sweets-monger and to the crowded square before the great hall of Jarl Ivar, Brenna walked to the farthest edge of town, where the woods began again. If she stood on a rock and rose up on her toes, she could still see the docks. Her father's voice was big and booming, and she knew she would hear his call when it came.

There was a tree here, an old, gnarled tree, whose roots and trunk had grown in such a way as to make something of a snug little nook, almost a cave. She'd found it several months ago, and no one else in the world seemed to know of it. She had padded the ground inside with mosses, and she always found it just as she'd left it, as if even the woodland creatures understood it to be her den.

When she tucked herself in, she thought she was well hidden, though no one had ever come upon her so that she might know for certain that she would not be seen.

Until she heard her father's call, Brenna would sit in this snug, safe burrow. She would close her eyes, and she would tell herself stories. Stories of Brenna the Shieldmaiden. Brenna the Voyager. Brenna the Great Jarl.

Names she preferred to the ways she was known: Brenna the Witch. Brenna the Strange. Brenna the Cursed.

Just lately, her stories had begun to include strapping young raiders. Berserkers with fantastical pictures etched into their bare chests. She didn't really understand why. Her father had been a berserker in his youth, but she didn't think the way she felt when the young men were in her stories had to do with her father.

She had gotten well into a story about leading a raid across the sea when the crackle and thunder of heavy feet tromping into the woods broke through her reverie. It appeared that she would have a chance to know if her den were as secure as she'd thought it to be.

Her heart thumping, she hunkered low and peered through the laced roots of her tree. A man was dragging a boy—older than she, Brenna thought, but yet too slight of shoulder and smooth of cheek to be a man—into the woods. The boy resisted, his dark hair flying, but the man was much bigger, and he threw him to the ground.

"On your knees!" the man shouted, and the boy clambered to his feet.

"Father, please!"

"No more words from you! You have spoken your last word, boy. I said on your knees!" As he spoke, the man drew his axe—not a fighting axe, simply a tool like most working men carried on their belts—and swung it at the boy's knee.

The boy howled in pain and fell to his knees, his hands grabbing at the one his father had hit. Brenna, secreted in her wooded nook, gasped and covered her mouth. She expected a gush of blood, but there was none. The axe was clean as well. The man must have hit his son with the flat or the back. Small mercy, that, but a mercy nonetheless.

Brenna felt sick and scared—and she felt an emotion that seemed new to her, an anger bigger than she'd known before. It felt like fire in her joints. It made her fists clench, and it made her body want to come up from the ground. It made her want to stand. It made her want to do much more than that.

But she was just a girl, sitting under a tree, nothing remotely like a weapon on her. She looked around her for a rock or a stick, but there was nothing apt nearby.

Then the boy made a strange, strangled noise, and Brenna returned her attention to him. His father had him by the head—no, by the tongue. He had pulled the boy's tongue out and had it pinched between his fingers. Though the boy struggled, the man must have been very strong. She didn't understand why the man would be holding his son's tongue like that.

Then Brenna saw the knife, and she understood.

She was standing before she'd realized it, and she was walking toward them, a little girl, small for her age, no armor but the light wool of her summer hangerock.

"STOP!" she called, moving steadily toward them. "STOP."

The man did stop, and he turned toward her. The change in his attention loosened his hold on the boy, who pulled away and then tried to run. But his hurt knee collapsed, and he fell and could only scrabble backward to a tree.

The man leered at Brenna and advanced on her, raising the hand that had held his son's tongue. "Little girls should not be alone in the woods. They might get—"

14

He stopped, and his eyes went wide. Brenna knew that he had come close enough to her to see her eyes. To really see them. To see especially her right eye.

She pulled herself up as tall as she could and made her shoulders as broad as she could. Her heart raced and her knees shook, but she made her voice steady and deep and said, "Do not harm him."

The man made a ward sign, and then he turned back toward town, his son forgotten. He didn't run, but he came as close to that as he could and still preserve any dignity at all.

Brenna turned to the boy, who still sat at the base of the tree, his mouth bleeding and his knee swelling. She smiled and went to him, meaning to help him stand, or offer to get aid from town. Meaning to help him.

But he turned wide, scared eyes—both of them bright blue—on her and made the same ward sign that his father had.

She'd thought she was inured to that fear, but this time, she felt badly wounded by it. A tightness closed in around her heart, and she turned away.

She walked back into town and sat at the docks until her parents were ready for the journey home. She didn't look to see if the boy ever came out of the woods.

And she didn't bother to tell herself a story.

~oOo~

"Oof!" Brenna landed hard on the ground, and her already aching tailbone complained sharply.

"Sword out, daughter. This you must remember. Sword and shield, both are protection, and both are weapons." Her father shifted his shield and held out his hand. He pulled her up and then took a step back, brandishing his sword. He had advanced her training to real, honed swords only the week before. "Again."

Brenna made herself ready and circled, following her father's movements. "I want to learn the axe," she said and blocked her father with her shield.

"Good! Now attack."

Remembering to come around the side rather than step forward, Brenna swung her sword, aiming for his shoulder on his sword side and remembering to slash, not stab. But her father parried her easily.

"The sword is the first weapon, and the most important." He moved, and she parried. "When you are skilled with the sword, then you will learn the axe." She took a big step sideways and almost made contact, forcing her father to turn into her move to block her. Grinning, he nodded and added, "As long as you keep up your work, and your mother has no more cause to find us out." He waved his shield. "Enough for today. She will be home before the sun sets, and we both have work to do before she arrives."

He nodded toward the house, and Brenna followed, knowing that the first work they had to do was clean their swords. Her father insisted that they be tended to after every use, even though little blood had ever been drawn in her training.

As they sat at the table and honed and polished the heavy blade, Brenna grumbled, "She should be proud that I want to be like her."

Her mother had been a great shieldmaiden. In the stories, she was known as Dagmar Wildheart, and it was said that she had fought trolls and even giants of Jötunheim. Brenna knew that the stories were bigger than the woman who'd birthed her, but there was truth in her greatness nonetheless. She had seen with her own strange eyes her mother fight off raiders, with the ferocity and strength of a berserker.

And yet she would not hear of her only daughter picking up sword and shield and following her path. It was all Brenna wanted, and it was the only path to fulfillment available to her. She would never know love, never build a family. She had thirteen years now, and she knew already that no one would ever love her like a woman.

People shrank from her; in fear or in awe, they shrank from her. Those in awe of her might leave a gift on the doorstep in search of a boon from the magic they thought her to have, but none would ever come close enough to know her.

So Brenna would use that fear, that awe. She would be a great shieldmaiden, like her mother and her grandmother before her. She would do so against her mother's wishes, because her father could deny her nothing.

"You know well why your mother wants another path for you."

She did. Brenna had had four older brothers. Three had died raiding and had achieved Valhalla. One had been lost to a childhood fever. Dagmar Wildheart hadn't the heart to lose another. She wanted to keep her only surviving child, born late in her life and later in her husband's, safe.

But her only surviving child had been born different. Not much different—Brenna felt like a girl, a young woman, and she had no special powers she'd ever been able to discern— but different in a way the people of her world couldn't accept.

They thought she bore the eye Odin, the Allfather, had sacrificed for his wisdom. They thought she had seen Asgard.

They thought she had brought the sight of the gods to Midgard with her.

"There is no other path for me."

Her father nodded. He was training her because he agreed, and because he would be proud for her to fight. He and her mother had not married for love, but they had fallen in love fighting side by side.

But as he stood and carried his sword to hang it at its place on the wall, with his back to her as if he didn't want to see her face when he said it, he added, "Your mother thinks you would make a good healer. She is speaking today with Oili about taking you on as apprentice."

Brenna stood up. "Father, no!" Oili was an old woman who lived in the woods, even farther from the heart of the village than they lived. Everyone went to her for healing and remedies, and everyone made sure that she was safe and warm and fed, but no one ever went to her to keep company. No one ever chatted with her when she came to the river. No one invited her to break bread at their table. More than merely a healer, she was a völva—a witch, a prophetess—and they feared her. They thought her a necessary and powerful being, beyond concerns of good or evil, who helped them because they made her offerings.

Her parents, too, believed in Oili's power, and now Brenna wondered if her mother felt fear, or awe, of her after all. Why else would she seek to doom her own daughter to a life like that?

The idea that she would be locked forever into the shackles of life as the village mystic made Brenna feel sick at her stomach. "Please, Father. I cannot."

He turned and faced her, then came back to the table and took her sword from her hands. "Your mother and I will speak on it tonight. For now, there is work to be done."

~oOo~

That night, Brenna lay in her narrow bed and listened to her parents argue. The animals just over the wall from where she lay stirred restlessly, unused to such harsh sounds. One of the young sheep bleated and stuck his snout between the slats of the wall. Brenna scratched its velvety black.

"Gunnar, I will not! I will not lose another child!"

"You would have her be a crone? You think you will not lose her that way? She wants this, Dagy. She is the daughter of warriors. We should let her walk the path of her choosing. Let her be feared for the power she truly has, not over silly superstition."

"And you are so sure it's superstition?"

"Dagmar, no. Do not. She is a girl. *Our* girl. We would know by now if she were more than that."

"Would we? She has only just come into her blood. What if more than her womanhood flowers now? Shouldn't she be with someone who understands what that means? Who can help her use her power wisely? The God's Eye, Gunnar. If they who say it are right…"

"It is no god's eye. It is *Brenna's* eye. Our daughter. Her eye is only…colorful. It is beautiful."

"Too beautiful for a human to bear. It holds all of sea and earth and sky. It holds Yggdrasil itself. The eye of the Allfather. You know the stories. You know what they say."

"The stories also say that Dagmar Wildheart fought in Jötunheim and fed for a week on the heart of a giant. How did it taste, wife?"

19

Brenna heard a sweetly mocking tone come into her father's voice, a tone that was familiar. Normally, her mother would laugh and bat his seeking hands away.

Instead, her mother said, "Gunnar, stop. I cannot. I cannot have her go off to die the way our sons died. I cannot."

She was crying. When Brenna heard the susurration of her father soothing her mother with whispers, she knew that she was lost. Her father had been a renowned warrior, a fearsome berserker, but he was no match for his woman's tears.

But she could not be apprenticed to Oili. That could not be her life, doomed so young to live alone in the woods forever.

When her parents finally slept, Brenna left their home. She took only the sword and shield her father had been training her to use.

She hoped to return someday, but she knew not when.

PART ONE
THE SWORD

1

Brenna shrieked and leapt forward, over the body of the Estlander who'd just fallen to her sword. The ground all around her was littered with bodies. The liquid heat that always filled her joints and muscles in a fight throbbed and surged. She had known that frantic fire since before she'd ever picked up shield or sword, and she had come to know it as bloodlust. Battle rage.

Power.

The raiding party had landed too close to the site of an earlier raid and had had to move inland to find spoils worth taking. The Estlanders, broken and weary as they were from fighting the raiders and losing, again and again, were yet putting up a vigorous fight. They'd had time to prepare during the raiders' inland trek. But they were villagers, with not enough warriors to combat the seasoned party. Only a few were left on their feet, and the dirt had gone muddy with the blood of their dead.

"SHIELD WALL! SHIELD WALL!"

Brenna heard the call and abandoned her charge, turning instead toward Calder, the raid leader, and running to take her place with her fellows. As she ran, she saw a second wave of resistance charging into the village. Reinforcements— soldiers, dressed all alike, so they were from a nearby lord. Men who were trained, who were fresh, who had not been fighting nonstop while the sun moved through the sky toward midday. With that quick, running glance, Brenna knew that there were considerably more fresh soldiers than there were wearying raiders.

That a lord would send his men in such quantity against their war band told Brenna that they had trekked close to the seat of his power. In her experience, lords considered the villages on the edges of their territories expendable—distractions that kept the raiders occupied and away from the true treasure. She had wanted to trek inland for some time, but Jarl Åke and his sons preferred the easy pillage of the shores.

Brenna had never argued otherwise. She avoided attention to every extent she could, preferring to let her sword and shield speak for her.

She locked in with the others just as a volley of arrows flew into the sky and then thundered down onto their heavy alder shields. Then another volley rained down. An arrow slammed into Brenna's shield and made her arm sing. And then the new warriors charged, trying to break through the wall.

"BRACE!"

At the command, Brenna dug into her crouch and locked her shoulder. The impact of the mass of men falling on them at once was great, but the wall was not moved. Unshielded berserkers, men who fought with no protection but their weapons and their inner fire, leapt up and brought their axes down on the bodies of the men trying to breach the shield wall.

"OPEN!"

A space was opened in the wall, and another shieldmaiden slammed her axe into the face of a soldier who'd lost his helm.

"CLOSE!"

They closed the wall over his dead body, and the berserkers leapt up again, slamming brutal blows down on the soldiers, breaking pointed swords with mighty axes.

Again, Calder, Jarl Åke's eldest son, shouted, "OPEN!" just as the soldiers surged. At least ten soldiers fell into the breach and were surrounded by raiders as Calder shouted and the wall closed again. Brenna came face to face with a soldier no older than she. She saw terror in his eyes—and shock that he faced a woman.

And then she shoved her sword up, into the soft meat under his chin, and his eyes died with the rest of him.

When the odds were more balanced, the shield wall came apart, and raiders and remaining soldiers fought freely. Brenna yanked the arrow from her shield as she leapt backward, clear of the scrum. It was to a shieldmaiden's benefit to let her foe see she was a woman; whenever they fought across the sea, there was always the surprise that caused a missed step, some hesitation, something that gave her the upper hand.

Her own people expected women to fight. These savages kept their women weak and helpless, using them like little more than broodmares.

One of the soldiers surged toward her as she jumped away, bringing his sword forward with skill and intent. He barely blinked when he saw her face, and she barely managed to block the sword aimed at her neck. She did, though, throwing her shield up, and the force of her block surprised him. Using the half-second of his surprise, she slammed her bare head into him, catching his chin and mouth. His teeth opened her forehead, and her vision ran red with her own blood. As he reeled, she stepped out, bringing her longsword around in the way her father had taught her years before, and slashed the soldier across his back.

Unlike the villagers they'd been fighting, the soldiers wore mail, and her blow injured this one, but not mortally. He fell, and she raised her sword for the killing blow—

—and was knocked to her knees, her breath gone, by a blunt blow at her back. She spun on her knees, forcing air into her lungs, through the pain, and tried to bring her sword up, but there were two soldiers on her now, and one of them blocked her while the other hit her again, in the head this time, with his iron shield.

Her vision fragmented into shards, and she fell back, unable to make her body move. Her shield fell from a hand that had gone slack. With the sense she had left, she prepared to meet the gods in Valhalla.

At her first chance, she would ask Odin if indeed she had been given the eye that he had sacrificed for wisdom, and, if so, why. Because she had not, in all her twenty-one years, felt a power worthy of such a gift.

She had, however, felt its burden every day of her life.

And then a great roar split the air, and both soldiers fell dead, toppling over to their sides like felled trees. In the space they had left stood a bare-chested giant. A fellow raider. A berserker, soaked in blood, a bearded axe in his hands, dripping gore.

She didn't know him by name; he was not of her clan. The jarl she served had allied with another for this raiding season, and they had all converged on the day they'd embarked. This man raided for the other jarl.

He turned and killed another soldier who had advanced on them, then leaned down, holding out a massive, blood-drenched hand. She took it and let him pull her up, closing her eyes until the world stopped spinning.

When she opened them again, he was staring down at her with bright blue eyes, and the world around them had gone quiet. She looked around—the soldiers and villagers were dead or captured. The air stank of blood and offal. The man she'd wounded moaned, struggling to his knees; she drove her sword into his back and ended his struggles.

The berserker had not released her hand, and Brenna turned back and found him yet staring down at her. His face was bathed with blood, it dripped thickly from his beard, and his blue eyes glowed in that dark mask. She pulled her arm, but he seemed unwilling to let her go.

It did not occur to her that he wanted her as a woman; no man ever had. Her eye and its supposed origin held them all at bay, even the men acclaimed for their brash courage. None would take the risk that they might be ensorcelled.

But the berserker wanted something.

"Thank you," she said, deciding it must have been that. She pulled her arm again, and this time he let her go, so it must indeed have been thanks he was after. Her hand freed, she wiped the blood from her face and bent down to claim her shield.

"You are Brenna God's-Eye," he answered. As if she didn't know.

She nodded and walked away from him. There were spoils to collect.

~oOo~

They made camp deep in the woods, and Calder sent out a party to scout for the lord's hall. Though they had killed most of the villagers, Calder had ordered several of the women, three young men, and one of the soldiers be held captive: the soldier for information, and the young men for labor. And the women to service the raiders.

Raiders after a battle were a wild lot. Brenna understood the fiery need for violent release that didn't simply end when the targets ran out. She felt it, too. Other shieldmaidens might mate with a comrade, if that was their wont. It wasn't possible for Brenna, and she didn't know if she would have partaken even had it been. The rutting she saw was brutal and vile, even among comrades, and it stirred her not at all.

As the men fell upon the new slave women, Brenna stood and walked into the woods, her sword and her shield on her back. She closed her mind to the screams and wails behind her and walked until she heard them no more.

The women were captives. They were slaves, with no rights to any possession, not even of their own bodies. She understood the ways and laws of her people.

But she hated it. Killing in a raid, she understood. She had killed women and men both. She had killed priests and shopkeepers, soldiers and farmers, rich and poor. The violence of a raid fed something in her that was always hungry.

Plundering villages, she also understood. Such were the spoils of victory.

But she had once been a slave. She could understand killing another human being, but she would never understand treating one as anything less than a human being. Ways and laws be damned.

Keeping her eyes and ears sharp for trouble, she followed the stream they'd camped next to until the water began to burble noisily and then rush. She preferred busy water to still; she could not see her reflection in water rushing past. She always seemed to get caught in the reflection of still water, and she hated it.

She had had occasions to look into a glass; she had done so only once. What she had seen had upset her too much ever to look again.

Not because her eye was so terrible, but because it wasn't.

All she had seen, peering into the glass, was a girl. A blonde girl with long, wild hair trained into thick braids. A girl with one clear blue eye and one eye that was more than that. She had seen brown and green and blue and even yellow in her right eye. The brown seemed to cross through the center and radiate out in lines across the bottom, like the roots of a tree.

She understood why people said what they did.

But it was just an eye. The head it was in was the head of a girl. A shieldmaiden making her name, but no more nor less than that.

And yet, she was alone and would always be, because everyone else saw Yggdrasil in her eye. They saw the world tree. They saw the world, and they said it was Odin's eye she bore.

It would have been easier to bear if it had frightened her, too.

So she stayed away from her reflection and let herself imagine it was much more terrible than it really was.

It was a waterfall she had heard—just a small one, about as tall as two men, but the water rushed over the top with force. She approached the bank just downstream and prepared to wash her face and hands.

Then she noticed a shadow in the fall and realized that she was not alone. She brought her hand to the hilt of her sword and froze, and scanned the area for others.

But for the body in the waterfall, she seemed to be alone. Her hand still on her sword, she searched the area more closely and saw, on the bank just at the waterfall, soaking in the spray, the leather boots and bearded axe of a raider.

A friend, then. Or at least an ally. Brenna relaxed and moved downriver again, leaving space for privacy. He was no threat to her.

As she washed, stretching out on the grass and pushing her face and then her head into the chill current, she took a long draught of the fresh water. She could feel the fire leaching from her sinews, bringing her calm. A sharp sting reminded her that she had cut her forehead on a soldier's mouth. It was her only injury, and for that she counted herself fortunate. Five raiders had gone to Valhalla in the fighting with the soldiers.

She pulled back, throwing her head to clear the water from her face, and then sat up, cross-legged, setting her sword and shield at her side.

"You bleed still."

Brenna jumped and grabbed her sword at the voice so near. Standing a few feet away and behind her was the berserker who'd saved her life. It had been he under the frigid waterfall. He was clean and dripping water, his hair and beard nearly black with wet, and his leather breeches soaked. In one hand was the undyed wool of a rough tunic; in the other, his axe.

Their people were not small people, but this man was nearly a giant. He was tall and broad, muscles like boulders swelling his arms, his chest, his neck, his shoulders. His beard was dark, long, and thick. His head was shorn at the sides, leaving the top to grow long. It had been tightly braided earlier, but now it lay in a loose, wet hank down his back. The skin across his chest and over his shoulders was decorated in elaborate tattoos.

He glanced at her sword hand, gripping the hilt. "I am no threat to you, Brenna God's-Eye."

Although she had found a kind of camaraderie among her fellow raiders, people rarely spoke to her one on one, except to give orders, make requests, or negotiate for trade. She spent her winters alone. Brenna didn't know how to keep company. Not knowing what to say next, she said nothing. She dropped her hand from her sword and turned back to the river, expecting him to walk on.

He did not. Instead, he sat down at her side. "I can make a paste that will stop the blood and make the scar less. The herbs here are not so different from home."

She was about to protest that the wound was not so bad, when blood dripped from her brow and landed low on her cheek. The river water had opened it again. She wiped the blood away and said nothing.

Undeterred by her reticence, he opened the bundle of his tunic, in which he had a collection of mosses and flowers. Brenna recognized some, but she knew little of healing. She had diligently avoided learning any of that, always fearing that she'd somehow end up the crone in the woods her mother had meant her to be.

He tore pieces of some and then scooped up mud from the bank and mashed it all together, softening it with water. When he turned and brought his hands toward her face, meaning to touch her, Brenna flinched back, and he paused. But he did not drop his hands.

"I mean you no harm. Did I not save your life today?"

He had. With a deep breath for calm, she remained still and let him smooth the paste on her forehead. It was cool and soothing, and she closed her eyes, trying to remember when she'd last been touched so gently. She could not.

"You saved me once," he said, close enough that she felt the breath of his words on her face.

31

Brenna opened her eyes and met his. She was sure that she had never raided with him before, and she was sure she had not saved him today. She furrowed the brow that he was tending.

"I think not."

He smiled. And then he stuck his tongue out at her.

She was about to pull away, offended, when she saw a small nick in the side of his tongue.

The boy in the woods, all those years ago. The first time she'd ever felt the fire of battle rage. That, she remembered, and remembering, she recognized his bright blue eyes.

But he had been like all the others—fearful, even as she gave him aid.

"You were afraid of me."

His ministrations completed, he sat back, then leaned to the river and washed his hands in the clear water. "I was young and stupid and under the thumb of a stupider man. I'm sorry for that."

"Why? Everyone is afraid. I am Brenna God's-Eye."

"You are. And a magnificent eye it is. Why be afraid of a gift like that? It seems to me a great honor."

Again, Brenna looked away, turning her attention to the water before them. She didn't want it to be true. It wasn't true. She was nothing special, and she didn't want to be. They said her valor as a shieldmaiden came from her eye. It did not. It came from her heart. She wasn't magical; she was strong.

But none of that mattered. People believed what they wanted to believe. Brenna sighed. There had been a moment, just a flash, when she'd felt something new with this man. He'd treated her like a person. But he was the same as the rest, even if he no longer feared her.

A small fish jumped out of the current, flipped, and fell back. She had a thought that she would go back to camp for a fishing spear.

"You saved me. More than my tongue. I left that day and never returned, and my life has honor it would never have known had I stayed. I wanted you to know that. I wanted to give you thanks. I am Vali, and I am at your service."

With that, he stood, picked up his bundle and his axe, and headed back to camp.

2

Vali returned to camp and brought his bundle of gathered herbs and mosses to Sven, a raider whose mother, like Vali's, had been a healer, and who tended to their wounded. Then he pulled his tunic on over his head, fixed his belt and axe over it, and sought a place to rest. The camp was made and reinforced. Other than the guards stationed around the perimeter and the scouts still away, the raiders were at their leisure to refresh themselves.

A newly dressed deer was spitted over the main fire. After days of drinking only rationed water and eating salt cod and leiv bread on the boat, the thought of meat and mead made Vali's stomach rumble. He wasn't the only one; the whole camp was calmer than when he'd walked off to find a place to wash, and many of his fellows were sitting watching the animal roast, as if it were entertainment.

The captive women, bound with rope by their necks and hands, had been tied together at a stake and were cowering in a cluster. Several were barely dressed any longer, and the summer season was aging into winter chill, so they huddled for warmth, he guessed, as much as comfort. But they had been left alone, the men distracted by the promise of hot, heavy food. Vali was glad.

He didn't like this Jarl Åke, or his son Calder, who was leading this raid. Both men were brutal leaders and had fostered brutality among their clan. Jarl Snorri, to whom Vali had long ago sworn fealty, would not have allowed the savagery that had gone on today. He would have taken the captives, yes. He would have taken all the survivors captive, in fact, not slaughtered women, children, and old ones and left them to rot in the dirt. Snorri would have taken them as slaves for trade. And he would have made the women work. He would not have left them to the violent whims of men drunk on bloodlust.

But Snorri had allied with Jarl Åke for this raid, and Åke's son had been made leader over all the raiders. Vali hadn't understood the alliance, but once they'd arrived and had moved so far inland, and now that they were camped and scouting for the castle of the ruler of this place, he thought he understood better. This was no mere raid. More was happening.

He knew not what, and it wasn't his place to know. He followed his jarl. Freemen had a voice, and often a vote, in clan decisions, including raids, but to go against the jarl was dangerous business. Vali had never seen a reason to take a risk like that.

There had been one reason he had been glad to know they were allying with Jarl Åke: Brenna God's-Eye fought for him. She had changed Vali's life, and he had thanked the gods for the chance to tell her so.

Her name was known far and wide. The shieldmaiden who bore the eye of the Allfather, the girl who had sold herself into slavery and then had been freed when she'd singlehandedly saved the jarl's wife and children during a failed insurrection.

The stories varied in the details, whether she had fought five men or ten, whether she had fought them off with one of their own swords or with a spit from the cooking fire. But the stories all said that she fought with the power of all the gods. They said she glowed. They said she rose up like a giant above her foes and drove them to the ground.

He knew the stories to be true. He remembered the small girl who had saved him, who had faced his beast of a father down and sent him skittering away with only the power of her voice and her fantastic eye.

And now, with his own two unremarkable eyes, he had seen her fight. She did glow. She did rise up above her enemies and smite them down. But not with magic.

With inner fire. With will. With spirit.

Such a marvelous creature she was.

Vali had watched her these days since the two parties had become one at Geitland. When they'd been gathered in Åke's great hall, and then when they'd embarked in their longships, he'd kept her in his sight as much as he could.

It wasn't difficult to do. She was always off on her own, along the edges of the group. Jarl Åke had named her personally as he'd spoken his words to send them off in the good will of the gods, and Vali had seen her drop her head at that.

People no longer tried to ward her away, but no one made any attempt to speak directly to her, either. She was treated as an icon of reverence, someone too powerful to touch. She moved through and around those near her as if she were invisible, when the opposite was true. Everyone noticed her, but no one made eye contact with her if they could avoid it.

She rarely spoke. She never smiled.

No—once, he thought, she had. On the sea, on a bright day of good wind after a hard night of storms, their ships had regained proximity with each other and sailed nearly side by side. Vali saw her at the prow, her arms around the carved dragon head, her fair hair blowing loose from its plaits. He thought he saw her smile then, turned away from all those she knew and facing the adventure ahead.

Whether she had truly smiled then or not, it was the first time he'd known he wanted more than merely the chance to thank her. He wanted the chance to know her.

She had been cold to him at the bank of the stream, but he wasn't deterred. He owed her his life. His father might not have killed him that day in the woods; he might only have rendered him mute. But he would likely have killed him in short time.

It was more than simply his breathing body he owed the shieldmaiden, however. He was a man of honor, a warrior with renown of his own, and he would not have been had not the courage of a small girl with a strange eye shaken him to his toes.

His friend Erik sat at his side and handed him a horn of mead. As Vali nodded his thanks and took a long draught, Erik elbowed him, grinning amiably.

"Your sorceress returns."

Erik nodded toward the far edge of camp, and Vali turned and saw Brenna walk in, past the spitted deer, and to a basket of leiv bread. She picked up two flat, round loaves and walked back the way she'd come, her full skin of water rocking at her hip, still dripping. She must have filled it at the stream. As always, people stepped out of her way, as if a force around her pushed them all two or three steps back.

Bread and water. While the air was redolent of roasting meat, and sweet mead flowed freely.

"Be careful, my friend," Erik said at his ear as Vali swiveled his head to watch Brenna walk just out of camp and settle herself alone at the base of a tree. "She is beautiful, but many women are beautiful, and no other poses such a risk. Who knows how she might bewitch you. That is no mere shieldmaiden. That eye." He shuddered. "If not the gift of Odin, then the judgment of Mimir. In any case, a man could be unmanned. I would not risk so much."

Vali thought her eye lovely, not fearsome. Bestowed by the gods or not, it made her more beautiful to him. The eye no one noticed was lovely, too: a blue clear like summer sky.

She *was* beautiful, with a long, graceful neck, high cheekbones, and full red lips. Her fair hair was long and wild. On the day they'd left Geitland, the mass had been tidily trained in elaborate braids, but the ensuing days, with a rough sail and a tough fight, had loosened strands and left a halo of pale fire around her head. When the sun shone behind her, she did seem to glow indeed.

Though she had been small when he'd first seen her, now she was tall and strong, the power of her body obvious in the snug confines of her boiled leather breeches and tunic. She carried herself straight as a sword. She was magnificent.

Erik had gibed at him relentlessly since they'd first stood in Jarl Åke's hall and Vali had laid eyes on Brenna. He supposed he hadn't been subtle, drawn as he was to keeping her in sight, even as others looked away.

"Then I am more man than you," he said with a grin and stood, taking Erik's horn from him. Ignoring the protest of his friend, Vali went and refilled both horns and then carried them through the camp to the tree where Brenna sat.

As he approached, she looked up and glared at him with her bewitching eyes. The paste he'd made to heal her wound had hardened and paled, and it cracked slightly with her scowl.

She was among the raiders who painted their faces before battle, and she had landed on the beach that morning with her eyes lined heavily in black, the lines radiating from her storied right eye like rays of dark light. The effect had been eerie and had heightened the sense that it, that she, was more than human.

But her wash in the stream had cleansed most of that away, leaving smudges of grey that made her appear weary.

39

"Water is a paltry quench after a fight like today's." He crouched before her and held out a horn.

She didn't take it. "You need not serve me," she said, her hands in her lap.

Still holding out the horn of mead, he sat. "I'm not. I would like to join you."

She frowned. "Why? What is it you want?"

"Only your company. Need you no friend, Brenna God's-Eye?"

"No."

Vali disbelieved that strenuously. Perhaps no one in all the worlds needed a friend so much as this girl sitting here. Having experience with that feeling himself, he smiled. "Well, I do. Drink with me."

Though she still glared, she finally took the horn, casting a suspicious grimace into its contents before taking an experimental sip. As if he might have poisoned the mead.

After a moment's quiet, she said, "If you seek a boon—"

"I do not. Except, as I said, your company. Perhaps some conversation."

At that, she stared, her suspicion replaced by something that looked more like alarm.

But she was saved from the ordeal of talking to him by the sound of an actual alarm: the blow of a horn that meant the enemy approached—at a charge. They both stood, and Vali, in a move of instinct and habit, put his body in front of hers.

She scoffed loudly and stepped around him, her sword and shield already in hand. He pulled his axe from its ring on his belt as the horn blew again.

Their people were people of war and battle, and the camp before them had shifted from leisure to readiness fluidly and nearly instantly. As warriors and shieldmaidens abandoned their rest and prepared to fight, Brenna stalked forward, toward the heart of the camp. Vali kept step with her, picking up a racked spear as he passed it, without breaking stride.

There was no enemy in sight yet, but they could hear the thunder of galloping hooves. On horseback, then. No shield wall could withstand an onslaught of riders.

As if to answer the drumming hooves, raiders began to beat their axes and swords on their shields. Brenna did not. She took her place just behind Calder, and she bent her head forward and was perfectly still, staring ahead, shield and sword at the ready. Those around her made extra space, and she seemed to radiate focus and menace.

Vali, the biggest of them all, stood at her side. He carried no shield, but he drummed the spear into the ground in time with the beat that had taken over the camp, so heavy and loud that the air shook.

Horses broke through the trees, bearing archers at the front, firing as they cleared the tree line. Arrows began to rain down on the camp, and shields went up. Vali crouched for cover and scanned the scene, looking for his first target.

The archer at the center was clearly their most skilled shot. He'd gotten three arrows off and had already nocked a fourth when Vali stepped out from the cover of the shields and charged forward, setting his feet and then hurling the spear with all his might. It sailed past the line of archers and impaled the man riding behind the center. The man he'd aimed for.

41

That man wore a gleaming chain across his chest and a crimson cloak, and he'd been protected by their best archer. He was important.

And he fell dead from his black horse just as the archers, too close now for attack, pulled off and let the swordsmen through.

"VALI!" he heard Erik call. Knowing why his friend would hail him at such a time, Vali glanced back just quickly enough to set his aim and then held out his hand. Erik threw a second axe, and Vali caught it.

And now he was ready. As the first wave of mounted swordsmen came upon them, he bellowed and raised both of his axes.

Scores of riders had descended on the camp. When fighting on foot against riders, unseating them was vitally important— without killing the horse, if possible, but sometimes killing the horse was the most expedient path, and then that horse was meat.

The raiders were outnumbered, and expediency was crucial. So Vali went for the nearest horse first, burying an axe into its leg. When it came down, shrieking, he swung the other axe and separated the rider from his sword arm. Like the soldiers earlier in the day, these men wore mail tunics, so as the man fell, Vali sank his axe into his neck for the killing blow, and a great gout of hot blood sprayed Vali in the face.

He shook the blood from his eyes, and, with the preternatural sense that came with battle rage, spun just as an Estlander had raised his sword. Vali blocked him with one axe and buried the other in his exposed side.

In the efficient style he had learned and honed since he'd first begun training, Vali charged and spun, hacking and slicing his way through four more men, his throat roughening with his war cries, and no foe dealing him more than the most glancing blow.

Bloodlust, battle rage—these were the ways his fellows described the sing of their blood through their bodies, the heat of the fight in their minds, and Vali understood these. But for him it was more than that. He became something else, something other than human. Every impact of his axe gave him more power, not less, as if he took his foe's life force into his own body. It fed a bestial hunger that heightened his senses and shrank his focus. Nothing existed but the fight.

And yet, today, he found himself sparing a glance every now and then for Brenna. His eyes seemed always to find her at once, as if he had already known where she was without seeking her out. She fought with fire and fury, using shield and sword with precision and might greater than one woman's body should hold.

He didn't allow himself the luxury of admiration, not then. He sought her, saw her, understood that she needed no assistance, then focused his senses again on his own fight.

Soon he'd created a pocket of quiet in the chaos, killing all those near him. His focus flared outward, seeking more fight. The horse he'd hobbled, nearly severing its foreleg, screamed its suffering. Before he moved on into the battle, meaning to join Brenna, Vali took the time to open the horse's throat and give it ease.

An Estlander fell on him while he was still pulling his axe through the horse's neck. Vali had just time to duck from the blow, which sliced into his back, opening him, but did not cleave his head from his body. Too drunk on the fight to feel pain, he saw his chance for a killing blow and tried to lift his dominant arm, but he found that it weighed much more than it should have. The axe that hand held fell to the ground, sinking into the earth made sodden by the horse's ocean of blood.

He had never lost his axe. In all his years of fighting, no man had ever disarmed him. Few had ever wounded him.

He was confused by that for just a moment, and then he remembered he had a weapon and an arm left. But when he raised that arm to block the next blow from his enemy, the impact knocked the axe from his hand as well.

The Estlander smiled. He had blackened his teeth, surely in an effort to terrify. But Vali was a berserker. His greatest weapon was his fearlessness, and even as death stood before him, he saw only a man with black teeth.

And then an otherworldly shriek lanced through Vali's head, and a spirit glowing with bright fire rose up above the Estlander and brought a mighty sword down. The Estlander's head dropped heavily from his shoulders and rolled downhill, losing its helm along the way. His body crumpled, first to its knees, and then dropped forward.

Vali's body mirrored it. He fell to his knees and then forward, into the deepening, still-hot pool of horse's blood. His face sank in, and he knew enough to hold his breath—though why he bothered, he wasn't sure.

Brenna, his glowing spirit, caught him by the arm and dragged him out of the blood. Ignoring the battle around them, she crouched near his head and peered into his face. With one hand, she roughly wiped the blood from his eyes and nose.

She wasn't gentle, and her hand had been coarsened by war and work. But Vali felt nothing but pleasure in the touch.

"It seems we're fated to save each other, Brenna God's-Eye."

He didn't know whether he'd given those words voice or had merely thought them, and he doubted that she had saved him from anything but a speedier death than he now faced, but she gave him a brusque nod and then leapt up and rejoined the fight.

Vali lay with his face in the bloody mud and waited for the Valkyries to carry him away.

3

Blood had so soaked the earth that Brenna's boots sank to her ankles with every step. Then, of a sudden, while the raiders separated their dead and wounded from the remains of their vanquished foes, the twilight sky went near full dark and opened up, driving sheets of frigid rain down, as if the gods sought to cleanse the earth themselves.

Torches guttered out in the torrent, and the raiders finished their work in the dark, leaving the dead soldiers to the elements and bringing their own close. They had lost seven more, five men and two women. Of the shieldmaidens on this raid, only Brenna and one other yet survived. Twelve raiders lost in all, and six wounded gravely. Brenna couldn't recall a raid when they'd lost so many.

Among the gravely wounded was the berserker Vali, who seemed to wish friendship with her, for reasons she had not yet discerned. His back had been opened, rending his woolen tunic nearly in two. The gash was deep and long, from his shoulder to nearly his waist. When she had pulled him out of the deep pool of blood, she had seen the white gleam of ribs. She didn't believe any man could survive such a wound.

With their dead as well tended as they could be in the storm, Brenna went to the healer's tent and ducked inside. Candlelight flickered with a near blinding brightness after the deep dark of the night storm outside.

The healer and his two helpers—one of them a captive woman, Brenna noticed—looked over as she entered. The healer and the raider both nodded without meeting her eyes. The captive woman, though, let her glance linger, her brow furrowing as she noticed Brenna's right eye. And then she looked away.

But there had been something different in that woman's glance. Though she was a captive, and rightly anxious, still there had been something more normal in her curiosity. It gave Brenna a moment's pause.

Then she saw Vali, lying on his stomach, his bare back exposed. The healer was sewing the gash closed with a bone needle, making large, rough stitches with coarse black thread. Brenna's own flesh tightened as she imagined the pain.

If the healer were taking such care, though, then there was a chance Vali would live.

"How is he?" she asked, surprising herself and the healer, too. He looked up at her in shock, his eyes lifting no higher than her mouth.

"There is no offal in his blood. He might yet live if the bleeding stops."

Healers tasted the blood in a wounded torso to determine the severity of a wound. The taste of offal meant that vital workings had been rent, and there was little a healer could do in such a case. Vali had been fortunate, then.

"See, Brenna God's-Eye?" Vali gasped from the ground, his voice weak and hoarse. "We are fated to save each other."

She hadn't known he was awake. It would have been a mercy had he not been, as the healer speared his ravaged flesh and pulled the rough-spun thread through again and again, sealing the long wound. The pain must have been enormous. Brenna knew something like it; she bore a savage scar on one thigh and another across one shoulder, and both of the wounds that had caused the scars had been sewn together. She, though, had been made to sleep by the healer both times and knew only the pain upon waking.

And yet, with his face turned toward her and away from the healer, still covered in a dark mask of blood, he smiled. "Will you sit?"

Brenna turned and considered the opening of the tent. The rain was too heavy and the night too dark for Calder to call the raiders together to discuss the next move. But she wasn't sure what she would do in here, sitting in the way of the healer.

Yet she couldn't make herself refuse him. She sat at his shoulder. The healer paused his sewing, his mouth agape. When he started again, Vali groaned.

"Is the pain very bad?" she asked, fighting a sudden urge to lay a comforting hand on his shoulder.

His smile grew, and his eyes met hers. "It was. And then you sat with me."

With that, he closed his eyes. Brenna sat quietly while the healer sewed. Then she noticed that each time the needle pierced his skin, Vali's hand twitched. Following an impulse she didn't understand, she leaned forward and set her hand in his, wrapping her fingers around the hard, broad mass as best she could. His fingers closed over hers, and he was still.

Brenna felt deeply confused.

~oOo~

"To have such a force arrive in the same day, the seat of this lord must be very close." Calder turned to Leif, his closest advisor. "None of them will speak yet?"

Leif shook his head. "Four died in the night. Two are near death. Only three might speak, and they are staunchly silent."

49

Calder shook his head. "And no word of the scouts?"

"No." Leif took a deep breath and let it out. "We can assume they're dead."

One of the scouts was Leif's own son, Einar, only fourteen and on his first raid. Both were young, barely men, but Halvar, the other, was at the end of his third raiding season.

The morning had broken bright and clear, and those raiders who could were seated in the middle of camp, planning their next move. Brenna sat on the edge of the group, but close to Calder. She knew her place as protector—and as talisman. She had once saved Calder's stepmother and younger siblings, and he didn't like her far from him on a raid.

He had never said as much. Calder, like all the others, kept personal distance and rarely spoke directly to her except to issue an order. But he called her close when he needed her, and he sought her, even met her eyes, when he had a problem to solve.

He did so now. As always, she simply gazed steadily back and let him take from that whatever he needed. Whatever mystical power she had came from the people who projected it onto her from their own superstitions, their own needs.

Such was her role and her fate, she'd come to understand: to be the proxy for the fears and desires of others.

Taking what he needed from Brenna's fixed gaze, he turned back to the group. "We need to know who the cloaked man was. He was important. We might have learned much from him, had Vali been temperate."

"Because he fell so quickly, the soldiers lost focus. They were on horseback. We were greatly outnumbered, and we were weary already. We might well have been overrun if Vali hadn't taken down their leader."

Brenna turned to the speaker—a short, bull-necked man pledged to Jarl Snorri, with close-cropped, flaming red hair and a full beard. Brenna had seen him talking with Vali, but she didn't know his name.

"Erik speaks true," said another, answering the question Brenna hadn't asked. "We owe our victory to Vali's spear."

Calder seemed irritated by the dispute of his own opinion, but he let it stand. He turned back to Leif. "We need to know, or we lose this chance. We cannot take the time to send more scouts. Our time is now. How many soldiers have we slain?"

"Two hundred and twenty," came the answer.

"Two hundred and twenty," Calder repeated. "We have been outnumbered at every turn and yet victorious. The gods are with us, and we must take what they've offered us. We must strike before the lord here can gather allies and reinforcements. Make the soldiers talk."

He turned and stormed off toward his tent.

Brenna wondered why they would strike. They had raided well the day before, taking much plunder, and they had vanquished two attacks as well. That would afford them the space to refresh and recuperate. They should pull in, bury their dead, protect the camp until their wounded could sail, and then return home.

Moreover, the summer neared its end. They needed to be home.

Instead, Leif stood. "Knut, Oluf, come. The rest of you, take the time to make yourselves ready. We have not seen the last of blood here."

Brenna watched the three men walk toward the captive soldiers.

She didn't like not understanding, and on this raid, it seemed she understood very little.

~oOo~

Vali was asleep when Brenna went into the healer's tent after the meeting. She had stayed long the night before, well after his back had been closed, until his hand relaxed and freed hers. They hadn't spoken again.

She had found peace, sitting there quietly as he rested, holding his hand.

Another of the wounded had died while the raiders met, and the healer was preparing his body for removal as Brenna crouched at Vali's side and laid her hand on his brow. He was warm. Too warm.

When the body had been carried out, Brenna turned to the healer. "He's hot."

Without looking at her, the healer nodded. "Yes. Corruption in the wound. I'll prepare a poultice, but he is in the gods' hands." He stopped and met her eyes directly. "If he matters to you, you might use your influence."

She had none. But it was pointless to say. So she simply turned back to Vali and watched as her hand, without her intention, smoothed over the stubbled skin of his shorn scalp. Her fingertips combed lightly through his long hair. It was stiff with blood.

He stirred and groaned at her touch, and his eyes blinked open. "Brenna..." he rasped, seeing her. "Are you real?"

52

It was rare that she heard her given name only, without the addendum that made her both less and more than she truly was. Something fluttered in her belly. Hearing only 'Brenna,' she felt for a moment like the girl she knew she was. She felt real.

"I am."

He smiled and closed his eyes. Brenna sat with him, watching the healer make his poultice and listening to the screams of the soldier Leif and his men had chosen to make speak.

~oOo~

Brenna sat with Vali while the poultice was applied and held his hand as the hot, acrid-smelling cloths made him tense and moan. She didn't understand the draw she felt toward him. It was physical, something deep inside her that knew ease when he was close. His pain pained her. The thought that he was dying made her chest feel tight.

She knew him not at all, and yet she was comforted by his presence, and by the idea that her presence comforted him.

Perhaps it was only that no one else in years had spoken to her as simply another person. No one else in years had sought her company. Not since she'd left her parents' home in the thick of night.

When the healer was done with him, Vali slept again, his breathing harsh and irregular. It seemed to Brenna that his color was wrong, but she didn't know, and she couldn't find the will to ask. She knew nothing of healing and wished she knew less than she did, so she put her trust in the man who knew.

The blow of a horn pulled her attention from the man sleeping before her. Two short blows and a long. An envoy approached.

Before Brenna stood, she leaned forward, realizing only at the last chance that she had meant to kiss Vali's cheek. Pulling back abruptly, shocked at herself, she stood and hurried to the tent opening. The captive woman stood near the open flaps, and their eyes met. Strangely, the woman gave Brenna a kind smile. Brenna hurried past without returning it. She wasn't sure she remembered how to smile.

Grabbing her sword from the rack outside the healer's tent, she slung it on her back and took her place behind Calder as three riders, the lead bearing a flag rather than a weapon, approached. They stopped at the edge of the camp, where the raiders had erected a spiked fence.

Calder stepped forward. Brenna and Leif did as well. In a haphazard approximation of their tongue, the envoy raised his voice and said, "My lord Prince Vladimir seeks...seeks...p-parley. He asks that you ...steal ...er...you...you *accept* this...in-invitation. My lord seeks peace."

Calder looked over his shoulder, first at Leif and then at Brenna. Then he grinned back at all the raiders assembled.

He faced the envoy party again and, in the Estland tongue, in an accent that seemed, to Brenna's untrained ear, fluid and flawless, Calder answered.

She didn't understand the words, but she could read the reaction. Calder had accepted the invitation.

One of the riders behind the envoy, a grey-haired man in polished leather and a rich cloak, urged his horse forward and dismounted. He was stoic, but Brenna saw fear in his eyes and knew he had been offered as a hostage to ensure the safety of the raiders at this parley.

Calder took the man by the arm, said some words in the Estland tongue, and then turned to Knut. "Our guest. Bind his arms and keep a guard on him."

~oOo~

They had captured enough horses alive that they could all ride to the castle. They left enough raiders back to keep the camp safe, and the rest followed the envoy party to the castle of Prince Vladimir. The ride was short, only a few hours.

As they came through the gates, the people within, commoners and soldiers alike, stopped and watched—not in greeting, but in curiosity. And fear.

In all her years as a shieldmaiden, Brenna had never been so deep into raided territory. She shared these people's curiosity. But not their fear.

As she dismounted, she realized that she had not seen anyone make a ward sign. People stared, or they looked away, but not at or from her particularly. They had not marked her as different. Not yet, anyway.

Calder spoke with a small man with a long, pinched nose and hair as black as the darkest night. He wore a jeweled crown and a grand cloak trimmed, even in this waning summer afternoon, with fur and fixed over his shoulders with jeweled brooches. Arrayed at his sides were men in gleaming armor.

The prince, Brenna guessed.

He turned, the cloak swinging, and Calder followed him through tall oaken doors. Brenna and the rest followed Calder. The armored soldiers followed them.

She didn't like having the soldiers at their backs, and she rested her hand on the hilt of her shortsword. A glance at Calder and Leif showed them to be likewise prepared for trouble. All the raiders rustled with readiness.

They found themselves inside a hall, much like the great halls of their own jarls and chieftains, but made of stone, and bleaker and colder for it. Rather than the rich warmth of the wood and fur of a great hall, this room echoed and chilled, despite the many people filling it. It seemed all the grand lords and ladies of this realm had assembled for the parley.

In the middle of the room was a long table laden with food and drink. Calder stopped at the nearest end of the table and waited. The prince turned and spoke, rattling off long streams of gibberish beyond Brenna's comprehension.

Unable to understand the words being spoken, she used the time instead to scan the room. A dozen soldiers had followed them in. Another dozen lords were assembled along the sides, with women and even children in attendance with them. A woman wearing an elaborately jeweled crown held an infant at the far end of the assemblage. Six servants stood by. And the prince, still babbling.

They, on the other hand, were twenty. Assuming that Brenna was right about the general incompetence of the women for fighting, then the odds were good. It bothered her that there were children here, but she had not made that decision.

The prince finally stopped and stretched out his arms in a gesture of welcome. Two servants moved to the table, in the middle of which sat a large tray with a domed cover. As they reached for the cover, Brenna was not surprised at all to hear the heavy *chunk* of an iron bar being dropped over the doors. They were barred on the inside, but the delay in heaving it up could be deadly in a fight. They were effectively locked in.

But so were the Estlanders.

At the same time that sound rang against the stone walls, the cover was lifted from the golden tray.

The heads of their scouts rested on a bed of greens and fruits. Seeing his son's head dressed like a slaughtered boar, Leif roared.

At once, the lords pushed their ladies into the shadows behind them and threw their cloaks back, pulling shining swords into their hands.

Brenna knew little after that but the slash and bash and blood of the fight.

~oOo~

When only women clutching children were left of the prince's people, as well as the prince himself, Brenna pulled back. But Leif, in his rage of grief, did not, and Calder did not stop him—or Knut and Oluf, who helped their friend slay every woman and every child. The stone walls resounded with screams.

Then, as they reached the far end of the hall, spraying blood, Calder, holding the prince, called out, "ENOUGH!"

All that remained was the crowned woman holding a now screaming infant. Calder said something to the prince in the Estlander tongue. The prince nodded, whimpering.

Then Calder turned to Leif. "His wife and his heir. Brenna God's-Eye!" he shouted without turning her way, and Brenna came forward.

"Hold him at the end of your sword. Kill him if he so much as blinks."

She did as she was told, and Calder stepped away. He went to the woman and wrested the child from her arms. As the mother screamed, Calder took the babe by its ankles and slammed it into the nearest wall. Its wails ended abruptly. Knut silenced the woman by opening her throat.

The prince made not even a peep.

It had happened quickly, and was so beyond Brenna's expectation that she didn't understand until Calder dropped the small body to the floor and returned to grab the prince by the throat. As he dragged the prince through the hall, past the tray bearing the heads of young Einar and Halvar, past the bodies of the prince's family, guards, and inner circle, Brenna stood where she was and stared at that small broken body. Its mother had fallen so that her arm covered it, as if trying to protect her child even in death.

Brenna's vision swam, and she blinked and turned away.

"Brenna God's-Eye." Leif spoke at her shoulder, his voice rough and quiet. "We have duty elsewhere."

She nodded and turned, following him and the others through the hall. Calder had the prince outside, still holding that thin neck in his large hand. He was speaking rapidly and forcefully in the Estlander tongue. Brenna took her place behind him, not understanding anything but that—her place. Her role. Her fate.

He stopped speaking and drew his blade across the prince's throat. The stunned crowd gasped—commoners and soldiers alike. Some screamed. Then Calder threw the dying body forward and spoke again.

This time, when he stopped, the people before them dropped to their knees.

~oOo~

Calder evacuated the people from the castle and barred the gates, then left six men to stand guard. The rest returned to camp. They had lost two more men in the fight, and they carried their bodies with them. When they arrived, Calder stalked to the hostage, who had always been a sacrifice, and buried his axe in the man's chest without even a pause. Then he stalked off toward his tent, alone.

Brenna knew—she thought she knew—that all would be explained eventually, but she was numb and tired and didn't care. The sight of the babe on the bloody floor in its mother's arms would not leave her.

She had seen dead children. She had killed women. It was Jarl Åke's, and his son Calder's, practice to kill most villagers, neither of them wanting the bother of keeping a large cargo of slaves. Preferring death to slavery, Brenna had few qualms about killing.

It was not new. It was expected. But that death, the cold brutality of it, had struck Brenna somewhere new. It made her sick.

She went straight to the healer's tent, setting her sword and shield outside it. The healer wasn't there. Only the captive woman tended to the wounded, alone. Brenna wasn't surprised to find her unbound and unattended; slaves often had free run of the camp. There was nowhere they could go for escape, and should they try, they would be killed before they could do much damage.

Vali had been washed; his face, beard, and hair were free of blood. His color seemed better, and when she knelt at his side and laid her hand on his cheek, he was cooler. For the first time since she'd stood in that stone hall and stared at the bodies on the floor, Brenna felt a slice of calm.

"He...strong, your man. Like bear. He live, I think."

"He's not—" The words 'my man' died in her mouth as it dawned on her that the captive had spoken. Brenna stood and turned to her. "You speak our language."

"A little, yes. My…brother? He…" Words failed her, and she made a pantomime that Brenna understood as a boat on water.

"Sailed?"

She smiled. "Yes. Went far. He teach me. I…called Olga."

"Brenna." She patted her chest. Speaking to this foreign woman made Brenna feel a bit more grounded and a bit less strange.

"They all say you 'God's-Eye.' That this?" She tapped her own cheek below her right eye.

Brenna's guard went up, and she scowled. Even Estlanders were obsessed with her eye. She'd had a brief delusion that since the people of this place did not have a god who'd given up his right eye for wisdom, perhaps they wouldn't find her so terrifying.

Olga realized her mistake and dropped her head. "Excuse. I not mean…"

Ignoring her, Brenna turned and sat at Vali's side. The poultice had been removed, and his stitched skin was bared to the room. It looked better, not so swollen, and the seam was closing. She laid her hand on his shoulder, just to the side of the wound, and then lightly stroked the length of his long, strong back.

Caught up with watching her hand move over the contours of his muscles, she didn't notice that he had woken.

"I missed a battle, it seems." When she jumped and yanked her hand away, he grunted. "Please. Your touch…soothes."

After a doubtful hesitation, she returned her hand to his skin, and he sighed.

"By the look of you, I missed a whole war. Are we well?"

"We defeated the prince." She said no more; she didn't know if they were well. She didn't feel well. Behind her, the captive gasped, and Brenna remembered that she could understand them. All the more reason not to speak on what had happened at the castle.

"How do you feel?" she asked.

"Like someone tried to cleave me in twain." He slid his hand out and brushed it against her leg. Even through her leathers, she felt that touch deeply. "In this moment, though, I feel well."

"Vali—"

He cut her off with a sigh and a smile. "You said my name."

"Yes." She didn't understand why that had pleased him so. What else would she have called him? "Vali, I don't understand you." It was what she had intended to say before he'd cut her off; now she meant it even more.

"You will, shieldmaiden. In time. For now, will you stay with me?"

Brenna nodded, still stroking his back. After a few moments, weariness settled over her shoulders and, without thinking about it, she shifted and lay down at his side, facing him.

"Rest, beautiful Brenna," he murmured.

She closed her eyes, not noticing that she had wrapped her arms around his.

4

"Is she injured?" Sven cast a raised eyebrow on Brenna's sleeping form.

Vali smiled. "No. Only sleeping."

The healer redirected his eyebrow to Vali. "Well, you are a fortunate man to have the God's-Eye turned so well on you. By all rights you should be in Valhalla tonight."

In truth, Vali did feel better when Brenna was near, but he thought it at least as likely that the cause was worldly as otherworldly. He understood his mind—and his body. Currently, lying on his stomach was causing him discomfort for more reason than the gash in his back.

Then Sven knelt at his other side and began laying the pungent, all-too-recently-boiling strips of a fresh poultice on his back, and the great share of his attention went toward containing that pain. He didn't want to groan too loudly or tense his arm, lest he wake Brenna and end this sweet closeness.

She had his arm clasped in both of hers, and her forehead rested on his shoulder. If only he could have rolled to his side and pulled her close. At the moment, the one thing he wanted more was Sven's immediate and bloody death.

"Must it be so hot?" he muttered through clenched teeth, as quietly as he could.

Sven chuckled. "Now that you're complaining, I know you'll survive. And yes. The heat draws, as well you know." He finished and stood. "Shall I wake her and send her on?"

"No. I want her here."

"It's a dangerous path you seek, my friend." Sven spoke quietly. "Not only is she the God's-Eye, but Calder keeps her close. If this alliance breaks..."

He didn't finish, and it wasn't necessary. Vali understood. If the alliance broke, he and Brenna would be enemies. And it could well break. Snorri and Åke had been bitter foes not many years before, and Vali had seen traces of that contempt among the raiders old enough to remember. It was also true that Calder kept Brenna close, almost as if she were his charm—and perhaps she was. But it didn't matter.

He smiled at the blonde head sleeping so close. "I know. Heal my body, Sven. Leave my heart to me."

~oOo~

By the time the sky began to lighten toward morning, Vali felt well and strong enough that lying quietly on his stomach had become a torture of its own. He needed to move, and he could feel in his body that he would be able to. Not without pain, but pain was no deterrent to him.

The deterrent was Brenna, who'd slept motionless for hours, her brow smooth with peace and comfort. There was little in this world or any other that would cause him to disturb her rest.

Having already slept the better part of a full day, and feeling his body reject the infection and begin its mending, Vali slept little while Brenna did. Instead, he watched her, and he thought.

The captive girl helping Sven spoke their language, it was how Sven had known she would be of use, so no one said much inside the healer's tent about what was going on outside it. Vali knew little of what he'd missed except that a 'prince' had been beaten. He itched to know more, and he hated that he'd been lying helpless while battle had raged.

Lying at his side, Brenna still bore the marks of that fight. Dried blood spattered her face, streaked her hair, grimed the creases of her hands. She hadn't washed before she'd come to see him.

He liked that—the thought that she'd come straight here, to check on him, to stay with him. She felt the pull to be close, too. He liked that very much indeed.

In the years since Brenna had chased his father off and galvanized Vali to seek a life of his own, he had thought often of the debt he owed the girl. Then she had become the famed shieldmaiden, and he had asked the gods to give him the chance to repay the debt. It had been his request with every offering. He had not thought more of her than that—a great debt owed, a gratitude that would outlast repayment.

Then he had seen her. And then he had spoken with her. And now he was getting to know her.

What he wanted now with her was everything. Lying here with her, so intimate and yet so chaste, his blood boiled with the need to have her. All of her. Always.

But for Sven's snores, the tent was quiet when Brenna woke. The day was beginning in gloom; the watery grey light Vali could see through the gaps in the tent told of heavy cloud cover. Summer was nearing its end. The sail home would be miserable if they didn't get underway soon.

She stirred and stretched, taking a deep, luxurious breath. When she let it out, the air danced over Vali's skin and made prickles rise up. She opened her eyes.

As soon as she focused on the arm she held, she went rigid. Her head came up, and her eyes met his—the peace in which she'd slept was gone, replaced with shock and dismay.

Knowing what would happen next, Vali was prepared, and when she jumped, pulling her arms from his and trying to sit up, he rolled to his side and grabbed her. His wound complained mightily, but he ignored it.

His movement changed her focus, though, and brought it back to him. "Be careful! You're too hurt."

Heartened that she thought of him even now, he smiled. "Do not run away, Brenna. That would hurt me more."

"I…I…didn't mean to…I'm sorry."

"I am not. You slept well?"

She looked down at her arm, where he held her, and she nodded. "How do you feel?"

Vali let go of her arm and moved his hand up to cradle her cheek. The threads in his back stretched uncomfortably. "Much better. Your touch restores me."

It was the wrong thing to say, and he understood why as the words left his mouth, but it was too late. She flinched, jerking her head clear of his touch, and stood before he could stop her. She looked down on him, her marvelous eyes dim with disappointment.

"Brenna, hold. I didn't mean—"

She turned and left the tent before he could finish.

~oOo~

Vali tried to rise and follow her, and he managed to sit before it occurred to him that he was in no condition to chase her down. Sven had woken in the meantime and leapt to his feet while Vali struggled to get his knees under him.

"Usch, fool. You'll tear out my hard work! Lie down." He didn't have the strength to resist as Sven muscled him back to his pallet. "Look. You bleed again. Fool."

"You said that already."

"Well, it deserves saying twice."

Now that Vali was down again, Sven crouched at his side. As he dabbed at Vali's back, his head swiveled. Though they were alone, he checked the tent conspiratorially, as if there were some nook or cranny in the simple space in which an eavesdropper might lurk. "Calder has called everyone together. After yesterday—"

"What happened yesterday?" Vali snapped. He was tired already of convalescing. He was not a man who lay idly back while battles were fought and women walked away from him.

"The parley was an ambush. Yet we prevailed. Our people killed the prince and all his family, all his attendants and their families, his best soldiers. Then Calder closed the castle. He is expected to claim this land in his father's name."

"What?" They were raiders, not settlers. They had neither the resources nor the skill to take over a princedom, and the season was too ripe to bring more people and supplies over.

Moreover, this raid was an alliance. Calder had the lead, but he overstepped to think he could claim territory in Åke's name when Jarl Snorri had sent warriors as well. Vali pushed himself up again. If anyone could be said to lead Snorri's men above any other, it was he. "I need to be there. Help me stand."

"Vali—"

"Help me stand," he repeated, and Sven sighed, stood, and helped him to his feet. Vali gritted his teeth against the pain.

Sven shook his head. "You are a stubborn fool."

~oOo~

A camp of such size was never truly quiet, not even in the dead of night, but as Sven helped Vali through the tent opening and into the grey morning, their surroundings were as close to quiet as could be. Everyone who could be was gathered near the center fire, sitting, crouching or kneeling where Calder stood.

Sven handed Vali a spear to use as a stick, and with that, Vali made himself move forward on his own power. Every step was an agony, but he stood tall and joined the others, with Sven at his side like the worried mother of a babe taking his first steps.

Brenna, sitting near Calder, saw him and stood, her face a perfect image of shocked worry. She took two quick steps toward him before she remembered herself and stopped, then smoothed the notice from her face. He hadn't missed it, however, and it made him glad to see that her first thought was for him, even if it was against her judgment.

He refrained from smiling or otherwise acknowledging her. To get close to this woman the way he wanted, he would need be patient and perhaps a bit stealthy. She obviously feared the pull between them. And she obviously hated the fear.

He understood that. But he also understood that she felt the pull, and he wouldn't turn away from that. So he would leave her to her wariness for now and focus on the more pressing matter at hand.

Erik stood and came to him, but Vali waved off his help. He needed to appear stronger than he was—as strong as he should be.

"Vali," Calder called, seeing him. "Friend. It is good to see you on your feet so soon." His expression belied the sentiment his words had expressed. Calder, too, understood that Vali was Snorri's strong right arm in this raid, and no doubt knew why he would fight so hard to be present now.

"Calder. I am sorry I could not join you in battle yesterday. I hear we had a great victory." The pain had turned his body to iron, but he fought hard to make his voice steady and strong.

Not missing the way Vali had stressed the word *we*, Calder lifted an eyebrow. "Yes. And now we discuss the future. Come and talk with us."

Erik had vacated a crate when he'd stood and come over, and now Vali gratefully made his way there. If he'd had to stand, or worse, sit on the ground, he might not have made it. Easing himself down to the slatted wooden surface was challenge enough. "What about the future?"

"We have beaten this Prince Vladimir and all who owe him fealty. His lands are ours. As leader of this raid, I claim this territory in the name of my father. We will settle here."

"This is not your father's raid alone, Calder. Half the men sitting here raid for Jarl Snorri Thorsson. The spoils will be split among us all. But none of us here is a settler, and we have no supplies to make it so."

"We need no *supplies*, Vali." Calder made his contempt writhe around the word. "If you had fought with us, you would have seen. We have a castle full of riches and all the land and resources we could want."

Erik stepped forward. "You think a prince has no friends who would avenge him? We lost many in this raid. We could not hold off a foe who was well prepared for us."

Calder turned and scowled at Erik, but then Leif, Calder's closest friend and advisor, stood. "They speak true, my friend. It is not so easy as to hang our shields at the door. But summer is near its end. The Estland winter is as harsh as our own. That will keep them at bay and give us time to work out these differences and make a plan for a settlement. We should return to the jarl." He looked out at the group. "Both jarls."

After a long look at his friend, Calder nodded. "Well enough. But we cannot abandon this holding. Who will volunteer to hold the castle during the winter?"

Vali stood immediately, clenching his teeth to keep from shouting with pain—and saw that Brenna had stood as well. Several other men and the one other remaining shieldmaiden also stood. Vali had stood for three reasons that had come to his mind at once: because he needed to assert a strong claim for Snorri, and because he knew the voyage home would be torturous and possibly fatal for him, and because, unlike many of his fellows, he had no one waiting for him at home.

That Brenna had also stood made a fourth compelling reason. The most compelling reason.

Calder's attention went directly to his shieldmaiden. "Brenna God's-Eye? No. You are needed."

Vali saw him meet her eyes, then shift his focus slightly downward. What must it be like to live with no one willing to look directly at you?

She shook her head. "We are invaders, and he was a prince. You need strong fighters to keep this holding, even in winter. And I would be away at home in any regard. Here I can do good. Here is where I best serve your father."

70

It was the most Vali had heard her speak at one time.

Leif, still standing, put his hand on Calder's shoulder. "I will stay as well. This is where my son Einar, the last of my family, achieved Valhalla. I will stay."

To Vali's watchful eye, Calder seemed to have deflated. He was a great warrior and the son of a storied jarl. He likely had been groomed for his whole life to lead, but he had not expected to lose his closest advisor and his pet shieldmaiden to his plan. He stared at Leif, then looked out over the rest of the raiders, clearly trying to formulate a response that would right his course.

Vali scanned the group as well and saw that those who'd stood, thirty or so, were fairly evenly divided in their fealty. He had been paying attention to Calder and Brenna, and had not noticed the way the other volunteers had announced themselves, but he would not have been surprised to know that there had been a kind of intention in the even divide.

Erik had not volunteered, and Vali would have objected if he had. Erik had a woman and three small children at home.

But Orm had volunteered. Orm was a strong warrior despite his advancing age. Vali and he were not close friends, but they were loyal comrades.

At last, Calder said, "Very well. Leif will have charge of the castle. We will ride there today and bring all the spoils we can back to the ships. Those of us headed home will bring this great news and much treasure to our people, and we will return at the new summer's dawn." He clasped Leif's arm. "Thank you, my friend. My brother."

Calder walked off, and with that, the group dispersed. Sven came up to Vali.

"You got what you wanted, fool. Now back to bed with you."

"I should ride to the castle. It should not be Calder's people only."

"Orm rides with them. And others. You would die if you tried, and how will that help anyone?" Sven pulled him toward the tent he had grown to hate.

But in truth, he couldn't say he would be sorry to lie down. Pain had become a beat at the base of his skull.

~oOo~

He was just settled, again on his stomach, when Brenna came into the tent. He was the only patient left who'd survived but was not yet completely free of the need for care. Sven glanced at her and then turned and gave Vali a smirk. Without even devising a pretext, he left the tent.

The captive woman had been put to work elsewhere. Vali and Brenna were alone.

"Why would you stay?" she asked, standing in the middle of the tent and glaring down at him.

He rolled to his side, stifling the groan that wanted to be made. "You think I could survive a voyage on the sea?"

"How will you survive the ride to the castle?"

"The ships won't depart for a day or two more. I'll be stronger. And a few hours' journey on horseback cannot compare to a few days' journey by sea." He met her eyes and held out his hand. "Brenna, come."

She didn't move. Not even her eyes. He made it his mission in that moment to hold her eyes as long as she held his. She should be seen. She deserved to be seen.

"Brenna."

"You're not strong enough to fight. You won't be a help here."

He'd be the judge of that. The proud part of him wanted to be offended by her assertion, but he smiled and let patience quash pride. There was likely a reason other than her lack of faith in his ability that had prompted her to say such a thing. "I will be by the time a fight might come. Why are you angry with me?"

Her aggressive posture faltered, and she dropped her eyes— for a moment only, and when she looked back up, his eyes were right where she'd left them. Her surprise in that was clear. "I do not understand you."

She turned and left, and Vali dropped to his stomach with a sigh full of relief for his back and frustration for his heart in equal measure.

~oOo~

Two days it took to move the treasure from the castle. Every raider who had died in battle and every raider who'd chosen to stay the winter in Estland meant that much more weight could be carried back, and Calder used every spare ounce.

Vali leaned on the spear that had become his walking stick and watched more precious metal and stone than he'd ever seen in his life move through the camp to the shore. Even without the land, this raid would have been immortalized in the stories. Calder's name would resound across all of Scandinavia.

It was true, and Vali wondered what it would do to the alliance when Calder took the acclaim meant for them all.

He turned and watched Brenna, helping strike a tent. The day before, she had taken a chance to wash thoroughly and re-braid her hair. She was so clean that he thought she must have stripped to her skin, or near that far. He wondered if she'd stood in the waterfall, as he had that first day. His loins ached at the thought. Oh, to behold her like that.

For six months, at least, he had her. More time than that, probably—perhaps nearly a year. No matter what happened to the alliance at home, here in Estland, they would be isolated until winter broke. They would be their own alliance.

He would make it so.

~oOo~

For at least the tenth time since they'd embarked on the journey to the castle, Brenna, who'd been riding at the fore, abreast with Leif, slowed her big golden steed and pulled up alongside Vali.

"We should stop and rest. You're pale."

"We should ride on. I am well." He was not well; in fact, he wasn't sure he would survive the ride after all. He could feel blood seeping down his back, and the pain was exquisite. But the truth was that he would not be able to regain his mount if he succumbed to the temptation to dismount and rest. He'd barely made the saddle in the first place.

"Vali, don't be foolish."

He'd grown weary of being called a fool. "If I need a nurse, I could do better than you, I think," he snapped, regretting it instantly.

Her expression closed. With a terse nod, she kicked her horse and trotted forward, leaving him to his sour thoughts and hot pain.

~oOo~

"Gods, woman! If you're trying to kill me, I will see you join me!"

The captive jumped at his roar, weak though it was. "Excuse. Please excuse. Finished now."

He grunted and lay back down. He'd made it to the castle, a monstrous heap of stone. He'd managed to dismount and then to use his own legs to enter a barren, cold space where the floor was still stained with blood.

After that, a black, blank void in his mind, and then he'd woken here, in this cold room, lying face-down on a soft bed, with the woman who'd been helping Sven sticking needles into his back. Again.

"You can't kill her. Olga is the only one who speaks both tongues."

The laughing voice behind him was Leif's, and Vali went on his guard—for all the good that could do him, helpless as he was. Again. Where was Brenna?

"Leif."

"Vali. I come to make sure you are well. We need you, my friend." He walked around the bed to the side Vali could see and then crouched down so that they were eye to eye. "We are allies here. Allies and equals. No leader among us. Be well. There is much to do here."

Vali nodded, and Leif patted his arm and stood. As he went to the door, Vali, unable to stop himself, called out, "Brenna. I would like to see her."

At the edge of his vision, Leif stopped and turned back. "May I offer you some advice?"

Vali didn't want advice from anyone, but he was curious what Leif might say, so he remained still, neither encouraging nor rejecting further comment.

"The God's-Eye is special to Jarl Åke. He sees her as a gift from the gods. She saved his family. He attributes his success and power to her fealty and says often that Odin himself sits where she does. He will sing her praises when the bounty from this raid is known. You take on more than the Eye of the Allfather if you get close to her. You are sworn to Jarl Snorri, and Åke will do anything to keep her."

Leif's words made Vali wonder if Brenna had been more than a slave and then a shieldmaiden to Jarl Åke. A jealous ember flared in his belly at the thought of that old man lying with her, but he sought to tamp it down. By his guess, she had near twenty years; she had had seven or eight years when she'd saved him in the woods, and eleven years had passed since then. She had been a shieldmaiden of note for several of those.

Even with the fearful reverence with which she was treated, men were men, and she was beautiful—and a woman with needs of her own. It was folly to believe that no one before him had sought to taste the fruits of her body—especially not the jarl to whom she was beholden, one who was known to have fathered many bastard children, in addition to his twelve heirs.

Of course Åke had had her.

The ember flared hotter, and he only stared. There was nothing he wanted to say; Leif had said nothing he hadn't

76

known already, and now he had to contend with his helplessness while the image of Åke grunting over the treasure that was Brenna took over his mind.

Finally, without another word, Leif turned and left.

~oOo~

Vali woke later and found her sitting at his side, staring out the tall, narrow window in the stone wall. "Brenna." His throat was dry, and her name came out a croak.

Without answering him, she stood and walked out of his field of vision. Then he heard the sound of pouring liquid, and she returned with a golden cup. She slid her hand under his head and helped him drink. Then she sat again in the chair, setting the cup on a table near the bed.

"Olga said you are 'strong like bear' and have not yet succeeded in killing yourself."

She had tried to affect the captive's accent—she'd made a joke, though she hadn't smiled. Vali laughed as much in delight at her attempt as he did at the humor in it. Then he grunted as the laugh shook parts that had been shaken enough for a goodly while.

Tired of feeling helpless, tired of feeling frustrated, Vali decided there was little to lose in full speech. Never mind patience and stealth. "Brenna. You feel it, too, this pull between us."

When she moved to stand, he shot his arm out and grabbed her knee. The pain mattered not at all compared to the need he felt to make something happen. Unable to chase her, he would have to hold her. "Run from me no more. I want to be with you. If you don't feel as I do, then say it."

Her stunning eyes went wide and dark as their black centers flared open. He held them with his own. "I don't understand you," she whispered.

That was hardly a rejection, not with his challenge in the air between them.

He smiled and released her knee. "So you say. Here I lie, open to you. Let me help you understand."

5

Brenna hated the castle. The stone walls and floors held the cold no matter how large a fire was built, and the many rooms and heavy doors isolated each person from the others, and blocked out the world, as if they'd all been imprisoned. Though she had lived a life without friends or even true companions, she had only been alone when she'd sought it out—and then, she'd been surrounded by the world.

Here, in these stark stone cells, she felt more alone than ever she had before. The ceilings were tall and the rooms vast, yet she felt hemmed in, so much so that she woke gasping most nights, when she could sleep at all, clutching her chest as if the walls had fallen in on her.

The low wooden halls and houses of home, filled with people and animals, were warm and snug. No one was ever really alone in a longhouse.

As had become usual in the few weeks of their residence here, long before dawn, Brenna gave up the fight to rest in her tapestry-covered dungeon. She pulled her sleeping shift— an item of clothing she'd found, along with many others, in a heavy chest in one of the rooms—over her head and dropped it on her pillows. Then she bound her breasts and dressed in leather breeches and a heavy woolen tunic. The unyielding and bone-deep cold of winter hadn't arrived yet, but nights had lately begun to greet the morning with a kiss of frost.

After she pulled her boots on, she worked her tangled mass of blonde waves into one thick, simple braid, snug against her scalp, then trailing down her back. Before she left the room, she picked up her belt and slid the scabbard of her shortsword from it, leaving her dirk as her only weapon. She would need no greater protection. After an early fight that had resulted in the deaths of all of the prince's remaining soldiers and of two more of their own, these weeks had been quiet, and she didn't mean to leave the castle grounds. She needed only to see the sky, to feel the air.

Before she lifted the heavy iron handle that would release the hasp and let her pull the door open, she picked up a fur throw and settled it over her shoulders. Once in the corridor, she moved quietly, but even the sound of her breath seemed to echo off the stone walls. Stealth was nearly impossible in a place like this, with massive doors creaking open on iron hinges and stone surfaces returning even the softest sounds.

Along the corridor and down the sweeping, dark stairs she went, completely alone all the way. An enormous edifice, the castle had housed only the prince, his small family, and their servants. When the raiders had combed through it, collecting the treasure, they had come upon room after room that had been richly appointed but obviously unused.

So much space, so many riches, and the people who lived outside the castle had less than the poorest farmer at home. Less even than some slaves. Olga had explained that the prince had taken all of their harvest and rationed back to them food they themselves had grown. Their rations had been meager. Each year, while they'd merely subsisted, they had watched carts full of crops rolling away from them, toward the nearest town, to be sold and enrich the prince.

After the ships had left, laden with gold and silver and jewels, Leif and Brenna and the others had set back the stores they would need for the winter and then opened the bounty that remained to the villagers. That decision had turned the tide of sentiment toward the raiders, who could now roam the nearby countryside and be greeted with waves and nods.

They were under no delusion that their settlement would remain peaceful forever, of course. Prince Vladimir surely had allies, and they would answer his death and try to reclaim his lands. But they had not yet, and, as she stepped out into the night and her breath plumed up in a thick puff of white, Brenna guessed it would be a long while before any foe took up a siege.

Orm and Knut had watch. They sat at the fire in the middle of the grounds, relaxed and talking amiably. Both looked up when she came out of the castle, and both returned her nod, but neither invited her to join them. Just as well—she wouldn't have known how to have a casual conversation. Aside from her parents, the only person she'd ever spoken to about anything other than plans, strategy, and tactics was Vali.

Vali. He'd been on his feet for almost two weeks, and he was almost as strong again as she'd ever seen him. He was a marvel of a man. Four days after he'd taken what should have been a mortal wound, three days after an infection had laid him lower, he'd mounted a horse and ridden for hours. The ride had nearly killed him again—and then mere days later he'd been back on his feet. For the past week, he'd been on full duty.

Brenna had been more comfortable with him when he was abed and she could leave him behind when she felt awkward or strange around him. He said he was open to her, but still she didn't understand him. He said he wanted to be with her, but why? To what end? She had spent a good portion of the days since he'd been out of bed devising reasons not to be around him.

But she felt lonely when she wasn't around him. She liked him very much. More than that, she admired him. He was strong of body and mind. He was forthright. He was goodhearted. The reason he had been so badly wounded was that, in the heat of battle, he'd taken the time to put a horse out of its misery. And he seemed to sincerely like her. Her. Brenna. He looked her in her eyes and held there. He didn't call her 'God's-Eye.' He talked to her.

He tried, at least. She struggled to know what to say and had never been able to offer him more than the most perfunctory answer to a question he'd asked, and she didn't know what things to ask of him. Conversation was simply beyond her. If there was a muscle somewhere in her that had to be flexed in order to chat with another person, that muscle had atrophied long ago.

They would both be better off if she continued to avoid him.

After taking her fill of the night air and sky, she crossed to the stables and went in. Here, she felt more at home; the smells of straw and wood and animal were familiar. The rustling sounds of the sleeping horses gave her calm. The calm brought a pleasant sleepiness that eluded her in the castle.

Not all of the horses were sleeping, she saw. The big golden head and rich creamy mane of the mare she'd taken for her own dropped over a stall door. She turned in Brenna's direction and nickered softly. Perhaps she had grown accustomed to these late-night visits.

"Freya. No rest for you, either?" Brenna went to her and rubbed her soft nose. Freya pushed past the caress and nosed at Brenna's furs. "Forgive me, love. I have no sweets for you tonight."

The mare huffed as if she understood and was disappointed. Estlander horses were similar to the horses of home— massive, densely-furred beasts with broad chests, thick legs and wide hooves. This was the most beautiful of any horse she'd ever seen, with a coat so golden it seemed to glow and a mane so pure and creamy one might think it would taste sweet. Brenna supposed she was as much a slave to beauty as any other, because she'd seen the mare and fallen in love straightaway.

Perhaps that had something to do with why she could not dig Vali out of her head. He was not beautiful; that was the wrong word. Perhaps he wasn't even handsome. His features seemed too rough for that word as well. But he was…compelling. His huge, heavily muscled body. His straight nose and heavy brow, like his face had been carved from stone. His rich, dark beard. His serious blue eyes.

At night, while she fought to find rest in her luxurious stone cell, her mind would conjure him and make her all the more restless.

Freya had dropped off to sleep with her nose snug between Brenna's arm and side. Brenna leaned her head against the mare's face, feeling sleep finally move over her as well. She opened the stall and stepped in, making Freya chuff a protest as she backed her up.

In the stall, she went to the far corner and settled herself into the fragrant straw, wrapping her furs around her. Freya came over and nudged her gently, and Brenna rubbed her nose again.

Then they both slept.

~oOo~

The next morning, Brenna, Leif, and Vali sat in the hall with any of the other raiders who were free and inclined to be part of the discussion. Not everyone was interested in planning. Many preferred to live and work and be pointed in the proper direction when it was time to fight. Thus, of twenty-nine raiders who'd stayed behind and survived, thirteen were assembled around the heavy table that had, the first time they'd seen it, held the heads of their young scouts.

Even weeks after that day, Leif always scowled when he looked down at the dark wood.

Olga, their former captive and now in charge of the servants who'd stayed, sat across from Leif. Next to her was Jaan, a young farmer from the village. Everyone had focused intently on the end of the table, where Tord, Sigvalde, and Viger were giving their report of what they'd found in the world beyond. Despite the fate of Einar and Halvar, they had had no choice but to send scouts out again. They needed to know exactly how far away trouble might be. If such could be known at all.

They already knew that the central town in this region was a day's journey by horse and cart. They also knew that that town and its market hosted the people and trade of two other princedoms. That much, Olga and other villagers, with Olga's interpreting help, had been able to tell them, as well as the names of these other royals: Ivan and Toomas. What none of the peasants seemed to know, however, was exactly where these princes dwelt and what threat they might be. The scouts had ridden out to learn.

"The farthest is a hard day's ride northeast," Viger offered. "A blue flag with a white beast flies."

Olga spoke in her native tongue to Jaan, who nodded and turned to Leif. "Toomas." He brought up his fists in a pantomime of fighting. "He…" he turned to Olga and spoke; then Olga turned to Leif.

"Toomas make much war here. Jaan say in town men know to be…apart them?" She held up her arms and widened the distance between her hands. The men here knew to avoid Toomas's men.

"He was an enemy of Vladimir?" Brenna asked. Jaan's head jerked in her direction. The men of Estland did not expect women to do anything that Brenna or Astrid did. After weeks here, the villagers were still more shocked by women who wore breeches and bore arms than any of them seemed to be about Brenna's strange eye.

After that moment of shock, as Olga nodded and spoke a word, Jaan nodded, too, and answered Brenna with his eyes on Leif. "Yes. No…friend here."

"That is not encouraging," Vali said. "He wants this holding and is likely to be prepared for war already, then."

Sigvalde answered him. "The castle was quiet. There was no war in the air there—but there was light snowfall already. If they plan to strike, we do not think it will be until summer."

Leif stroked his beard. "And the other? Ivan?"

"Due south," Sigvalde responded. "The holding is small and poor. We could advance on it and take it, too. This Toomas is the threat."

"Please," Olga interjected, and the others gave her their attention. She might have been their slave for a brief time, but she had become integral to their peaceful settlement here. Although Leif was attempting to learn the Estland tongue, no one else had yet tried, and they relied heavily on Olga to bridge the gap between them and her people. Realizing how much trust they'd already given her, upon her agreement to stay and assist them, they'd made her free just more than a week after they'd moved to the castle.

She was the only of the raid's captives at camp who'd remained alive. Calder had ordered all of the others killed before he'd set sail. He would have had Olga killed, too, but that Leif had asserted their need of her.

With everyone's attention on her, Olga met Leif's eyes. "Will you make war south?"

Leif glanced around the table, then shook his head. "No. I believe Sigvalde meant that Prince Ivan is no threat to us, not that we should raid his lands. We respect the winter, and our task is to strengthen this holding for our people."

Olga's smile at that was so full of relief that Brenna cocked her head, curious.

"Our plan remains the same, then," Vali said. "Use the winter to prepare for trouble. We should stay alert, but perhaps we can enjoy some peace." With those words he brought his eyes to Brenna and smiled.

He always looked her in the eyes. It made her feel restless and hot. She wasn't so naïve that she didn't know why her body felt as it did, or why her mind brought him to the fore in such vivid detail when she was alone. But she didn't understand why she was drawn to him. She didn't understand what it would mean if she gave in to those feelings, if she gave him what he seemed to want, what *she* seemed to want. She didn't understand why he wanted it. Wanted her. She didn't understand how to be wanted. She hated not understanding.

So she got up and left the table. If they could enjoy some peace, then she would do so. She would ride—away from the cold stone castle and away from Vali and things she didn't understand.

~oOo~

It was the first time she'd ridden off alone here. They had agreed to stay in pairs when they left the castle grounds until they understood the extent of any threat against them. Now they had the knowledge they'd needed. They were safe. So she could finally get away and be alone out of doors.

Since Jarl Åke had freed her and she had become a shieldmaiden, Brenna had always left Geitland for the winter. The close crush of people there during the dead months had made her feel more of an outsider. So she had spent her winters in a small hut in the woods, not too far from her jarl, but far enough to be spared so many people, all of whom dropped their eyes or flinched back when she approached.

She had never gone back home. Geitland was far from Halsgrof, but she had the resources, should she have desired to make the journey. She had not.

She missed home. Always. Never again in her life had she truly had a home. But she had gotten word of her father's death the year after she'd left. Only her mother was alive, the mother who had wanted to make her even more of an outcast than she was. The mother who had feared so much to lose her last child that she had forced that child to run. The competing emotions of shame and anger had kept Brenna far away.

Riding out now, alone, focused only on her thoughts and the world around her, Brenna felt the pull of homesickness more strongly than she had in years. This world, this tiny farming village, was the world of her childhood. The sights and smells and sounds were familiar and beloved.

She sat astride Freya at the top of a gentle rise and scanned the huts and reaped fields of the village. She could smell the wood smoke that wafted from chimneys and the aromas of meals being prepared in those fires. The people here had plenty for the first time in ages, because the raiders had opened the stores.

There was food left at the castle, beyond what Brenna's people had held back for themselves. No one had taken more than they'd needed. They had been orderly, even shy. A few had come back, asking for a bit more. None had been denied. In this way, they had made the villagers allies, even though the story of their brutal sacking of the coastal village was well known here.

Nudging Freya forward, Brenna moved through the village, nodding at those who were outside at their work. She had come out to find peace, but instead, she'd found an ache she'd thought had been healed. So she urged Freya into a trot and rode on, headed to the river.

Here, far upstream from their camp, the river was wider and deeper, its current steady and smooth. She dismounted and turned Freya loose to graze at what was left of the grasses, and she sat under a tree on the bank. Its leaves had turned a rich, fiery red and fluttered steadily to the ground with every breeze.

Alone was something Brenna understood. Her parents had loved her, and she'd been happy in their home, but she had known of her difference from a young age, and she had felt her otherness keenly since. As she'd grown, as she'd begun to understand why people kept apart from her, she'd only felt it more keenly. Eventually, she had embraced it, deciding that she preferred her own company to any other. She had learned how to use others' fear or awe to her advantage. She held solitude before her like a shield.

Here in Estland, that was changing, and she didn't understand why. She felt lonely now. Vali was part of it, she knew that much. He had stoked a fire in her that she'd smothered long ago. But he wasn't all of it. It was this place, too. These people. So much like home and so different, as well.

The Estlanders noticed her strange eye but didn't fear it. There was nothing in their traditions, she guessed, that made her especially remarkable. When they wouldn't meet her eyes, it was simple respect, not reverence. They didn't meet Leif's eyes, or Vali's, either. Unless they had been addressed directly.

Oddly, these people's lack of fear made Brenna feel more lost. Her own people, for her whole life, had treated her like something beyond human, to be feared or to be revered, but not to be known. Only to these people, these strangers, was she just a woman. Powerful, but human.

She'd been wrong. It couldn't be homesickness she felt.

She had no home at all.

6

When Brenna had been gone long enough that the sun had moved into the western sky, Vali couldn't hold back any longer. He hadn't liked her riding off alone, no matter if the castle was free from threat for the time being, and no matter that she was a famed shieldmaiden and the God's-Eye.

She was a woman, and here, in this place, she was only that. These people did not feel the reverence for her that kept her free from trouble at home. They did not know the stories here. And if she'd ridden out farther than the village, then she was only a woman alone.

He prepared his horse and rode out after her. With no true sense of where she might have been headed, he followed a hunch. He had noticed in her an especial affinity for the water, greater even than most coast-dwelling seafarers, such as they were. She would grow still, for just a moment, even at a water barrel. So he set out for the river beyond the village.

Although she'd been with him for long stretches of each day that he'd been trapped in bed, as soon as he was on his feet, she'd made it her daily mission to find somewhere to be that was away from him. It had been days since they'd been alone together.

He was vexed beyond measure. While she'd sat at his sick bed, he'd gotten her to talk a bit. Nothing he'd learned about her had abated his fascination. Quite the opposite. In fact, it was wrong to think of what he felt as fascination. The pull he felt toward her came from a deeper place than that.

She'd spoken about her time in Geitland, and with every sliver of information she'd shared, the legend of the God's-

Eye reconciled more with the truth of Brenna, the woman. He knew that she felt much like he did when she fought: like she was swallowed up by something bigger than herself. He knew her versions of battles she'd fought. And he knew her version of how she'd been made free, the night that raiders had beset the town and she, a slave girl tasked with care of the jarl's children, had saved them and their mother.

Vali thought of it as 'her version' rather than the truth, because he suspected that, as the legend had embellished the stories, she had dimmed them overmuch. The truth lay in the dark space between. Brenna was a bold and brave warrior, and he'd come to know her as an intelligent and thoughtful strategist, and as a compassionate person. But as a woman, she was shy and self-effacing.

What she wouldn't talk about was her family or how she'd become a slave. The stories said that she had given herself over to slavery, and she had confirmed that much. Beyond that, she had only offered stony silence.

He knew that that was at the core of her avoidance of him now. They had, in her mind, exhausted the story she had of her life with Jarl Åke. He had pushed too hard to know about the child he'd once met, and now she was running from him again.

But he was well enough now to chase her.

~oOo~

His hunch had been correct; he found her standing under a tree at the riverbank, watching him approach. She had her horse by the reins and her hand on the hilt of her shortsword, but when she saw it was him, she released them both and crossed her arms.

The aging afternoon had turned brisk with a sharp breeze coming from the north, and Brenna's thick blonde hair was blowing loose from her braids in wispy strands. Her cheeks were rosy with the chill. He noticed that she had not brought a fur with her. She had walked straight out of the hall and to the stable, apparently.

She watched him silently as he rode to her and dismounted. As his feet hit the ground, the still-weak muscles in his back tightened sharply, and he clenched his jaw, trying not to react otherwise. She must have noticed, because she gave him a cocked eyebrow.

"If there were trouble at the castle, you would have sent someone else for me, so why are you here?"

He tied off the reins and freed his horse to graze with hers. The beasts bumped noses and wandered off together a short distance.

"To be sure you were safe. You should not ride alone, even now."

She scoffed. She had a way of making a simple exhale of breath sound like a terrible insult. "You think I'd fall prey to a farmer?"

"I think even the great God's-Eye can only fight so many farmers at once, and farmers often know how to fight. Many of our own warriors are farmers."

He'd intentionally used the name she hated; he was irritated and tired of sparring with her. Her expression went dark, and she turned back to the river without answering him.

Closing the distance between them, he stood at her side. "I believed we were becoming closer, but you avoid me again. Have I been wrong about how you feel?" He knew he hadn't. He'd caught her eyes often enough, even as she skittered away, to know she still felt that pull. But he wanted her to say it.

She sighed. "I don't understand—"

Impatient, he cut her off. "Yes, I know. You say it again and again. I would help you understand me. But you seem to want to know nothing about me. Yet I know, I can see, that there is something between us. I feel it, and I see you feel it. Tell me that I am wrong, tell me to leave you alone, and I will. If not, Brenna, then tell me what you want of me."

She walked a few steps closer to the bank, so that her boots were just at the edge of the water. Crouching down, she put her hands into the current and pulled out a fistful of shining, rounded pebbles. Then she threw them all in so that they rained lightly into the stream, the ripples swirling in the moving water.

"My parents were farmers. We lived in a tiny settlement near Halsgrof."

He had assumed that much; they had first met in the woods outside Halsgrof. But she was speaking about her childhood, and he stayed silent and let her speak as she would.

"My father told me once that I was born with my eyes open, facing the world, and the midwife nearly dropped me when she saw my face. She wouldn't stay to help my mother finish with the birth, so my father took care of me and her. Before night had fallen on that first day, our neighbors all knew I bore the Eye of the Allfather.

"My parents had four sons before me. The first three died in battle, and the fourth died of fever. I came later, the way that I am. Some people said I was a gift from the gods, and some, their judgment."

She stood and turned, her eyes burning into his. "Do you know what I am, Vali? I am a person. I was a little girl, and now I am a woman, and that is all that I am."

He took a step toward her. "I know that."

"Why? Why do you know it when no one else has ever known it? Even my parents believed it. My mother wanted to apprentice me to a völva, someone who could 'teach' me to use my 'gifts' while she taught me the healing arts. She had made the arrangements. She thought I belonged in the woods, a crone, telling prophesy. That is why I left home in the middle of the night. I was thirteen. Åke took me into his home as a slave because he believes the gods gave me to him. But it's not true. All I have ever seen out of either of my eyes is the world before me. The same world you see. And no one has ever seen me that way."

"I do. Brenna, I do. I see you." He took two more steps. She hadn't backed away, and he was close enough that he could catch her if he reached out.

"Why? *That* is what I do not understand. What I *cannot* understand. Why would you see me, and no other?"

He did reach out, and he did catch her, wrapping her wrists in his hands. "Because I love you."

The sound she made was one of pain and disbelief, and she twisted her arms in his grip, but he held on. "Brenna, hold. The girl who saved me in the woods all those years ago did so with courage. It was your heart, not your eye, that made you stand up and call him off."

"He ran from my eye. So did you." She pulled again, and this time, he pulled back, bringing her close.

"I was young and did not know better. He was an ignorant fool. But that is no matter. What matters is why you stood up.

95

I don't believe that Odin pulled you up and threw you before my father. You did that. The little girl with the big heart."

She stared up at him, the eyes in question wide and gleaming. Her hair danced in the breeze, kissing her face and flying away, then back again. Vali released one of her arms and brought up his hand to cradle her jaw in it. With his eyes locked with hers, he said, "Brenna. Tell me what you want of me. If it's in my power to give it, it's yours."

"I don't know," she whispered. "I don't understand how to know."

"Do you want me to leave you alone?" He thought he knew the answer. He hoped he did. But the silence after his question grew. "Brenna?"

She blinked and shook her head. "I do not."

"Then I will help you understand." He bent his head and kissed her.

Her lips were full and soft, pliable under his own, and at first he let the kiss be simply that: the touch of lips to lips. Brenna did not respond at all, except that he could feel her pulse quicken against his hand, which still cupped her face.

He moved his mouth over hers, as his body reacted to the silk and sweet of her, to the knowledge that she did want him, even as she remained still. Sliding his other hand over her hip and around to rest on the small of her back, he brought her tightly to him. She came stiffly, almost reluctantly, and Vali began to doubt her interest after all. Perhaps she did not like the feel of him.

But her breath came in quick, shaky bursts against his cheek, and she made a tiny moan that sounded like pleasure, small though it was.

He opened his mouth and brushed her lips with the tip of his tongue, testing her response.

She gasped and jumped from his embrace, and put her hand over her mouth. Vali, stunned, thought he might know where the trouble lay. He caught her hand and pulled her close again, noting the way her chest heaved, the way her eyes had flared wide.

Replacing her hand with his own over her mouth, he caressed the velvety skin with his fingertips. "Brenna. Are you a maid?" Rather than answer, she dropped her eyes from his and tried to free her head from his hold. He didn't let her go.

He had thought her a thrall in all things to Jarl Åke. He had tortured himself with images of her coupling with the old man. As she had snubbed him of late, he had added to his torment the image of her enjoying that coupling. If she was yet a maid? Still innocent of any touch but his own—not even kissed before, as her reaction would seem to suggest?

Ah, then she would be truly his, and he would never let her go.

"Brenna, tell me. Have you never?"

Still she would not meet his eyes, but she shook her head. "No. Who would want me?"

He would. Forever. He wanted her right then.

But they were out in the growing cold, the rocky earth hard and unyielding under their feet, the horses less than a stone's throw away. Vali cupped her face in both of his hands and kissed her forehead, on the small pink scar of the wound he'd treated the first time they'd spoken.

"We should return to the castle."

Perhaps he was drunk with the revelation that she was his, unknown to any other, but he had not anticipated her reaction to his simple statement. He wanted to get her back to the castle, to a warm fire and a soft bed covered in furs. He wanted to honor her, to love her properly. But she gasped as though he'd slapped her, and she knocked his hands free of her. Then she turned on her heel and stalked to her horse, with such fierce intent that the mare shied a little, tossing her head, before settling again and preparing to take her rider.

She thought he was rejecting her.

"Brenna, no! Hold!" He caught up with her just as she had taken hold of the saddle, and he pulled her back to him. "I would have you. I *dream* of it. But I won't take your maidenhead with a rut on the hard ground." He brushed his fingers over her cheekbone. "If you would have me, let me come to you. Don't wander in the dark tonight. Stay in your room and let me come to you."

He kissed her again. This time, she was less rigid but still not responsive. With his lips grazing hers, he murmured, "Open your mouth, Brenna. Let me show you."

She did, and he pressed his lips hard to hers and slid his tongue into her mouth. When his tongue found hers, she jumped and pulled away again. But not far this time, and this time the look on her face was surprise, not shock or suspicion. He smiled.

Then something truly magical happened. She smiled. And it was magnificent. Vali was, indeed, ensorcelled. By a brave, lonely girl with a brilliant, rare smile.

"May I come to you?"

She nodded—and grabbed his tunic in her fists. Pulling him close, she rose up on her toes and offered him her mouth.

He could hardly refuse a gift like that.

~oOo~

Vali had not yet grown used to living in the castle. It was cold and dark and felt more like a cave than a home, even in rooms full of sumptuous furnishings and fabrics. The long corridors lined with heavy doors confused him. More than once, he'd opened a door expecting to find his own bed behind it and had instead found something else, sometimes to his own embarrassment and the true resident's. Once or twice, after a bit too much mead, he'd nearly convinced himself that the rooms shifted behind the doors.

But he knew Brenna's door. She had taken one of the smaller rooms, at the end of a corridor on the east side of the building—about as far from his room as she could have made herself. This was not his first time walking down this corridor at night, the flickering light from the torch sconces breaking up what would have been oppressive darkness. He had trouble sleeping here, as he knew Brenna did. In his own wakefulness, he had seen her wandering. Once, he was ashamed to admit even to himself, he'd followed her back, almost to her room. She'd nearly caught him, too. Twice more after that, he'd gone to her room with the intent of knocking, but he hadn't. He'd wanted her to come to him.

He doubted that she ever would have. Especially knowing now what he knew, that she had no experience of men, he knew she would never have made the move that would have brought them together.

But he had, and now, standing before the heavy oaken door of her bedchamber, he knocked.

After several seconds, as he prepared to knock again, he heard the heavy hasp lift, and the door creaked open. The room was warm and golden with a well-stoked fire. Before that welcoming glow stood a vision in white. Brenna had freed her hair from its braids, and she wore only a loose white gown with flowing sleeves.

"Gods," he breathed. "Brenna."

Looking up at him with wide, wary eyes, Brenna stepped backward and let him into the room. He closed the door, then went to her, reaching out to take her hands that she'd clasped together over her belly. When she tipped her head to watch their hands, her long, fair waves cascaded over her shoulders.

"You are beautiful, shieldmaiden."

She lifted her face and met his eyes, and he pulled her to him and kissed her. As she had by the river, before they'd ridden back, she opened her mouth to him and let her body rest against his, and when his tongue entered her mouth, she let hers slide against it. He groaned and tangled his fists into her thick mass of hair—it was soft, all of her was soft, so much softer than he could have imagined, and as he held her close, he forgot himself and took her mouth with much more force than he'd intended, rocking his hips so that she would feel his need.

Wedging her hands between them, she pushed firmly on his chest until he knew himself again and released her. They were both breathless. Her red lips were all the redder now, and her cheeks had a pinkness made by his beard.

"Vali, I...no one..." She huffed and gave up.

He didn't need more. It had been a very long time since he'd lain with a maid, and he had never lain with any woman for whom he felt so strongly, but he understood. "Forgive me. My need for you makes me rash." He took her hand again and kissed it. "Why don't we begin by showing each other ourselves."

Brenna swallowed, and Vali saw the shieldmaiden rise up in her eyes—this was a fear she could contend with. Taking a step back, she shook her golden mane back from her shoulders and then pulled on a ribbon at her chest. The neck of her gown opened wide, and she shrugged, letting the soft fabric fall to the floor on a whisper.

And there she was, naked before him, her back to the fire. She stood, straight and proud, the shieldmaiden daring him to look. He let his eyes take their fill of her. Strength radiated from her, in her posture, in her long neck and squared shoulders, in the carved contours of her arms and legs, in the flat firmness of her belly and in the slimness of her hips, barely flaring from her waist. There was strength in the savage scars on her leg and her shoulder.

But there was softness, too, in the creamy pale of her skin, in her full breasts tipped with a rosy red like her lips, in the soft puff of dark gold at the join of her thighs, in the silken fall of her long locks, slipping forward over her shoulders and covering her breasts. Perhaps she had been favored by the gods after all.

When he met her eyes again, those wonderful, unique eyes, she cocked her head, like she was waiting for him.

Ah, yes—to remove his own clothes.

He was dressed as he had been when last he'd seen her, in leather breeches and boots and a belted woolen tunic. In safety, he slept without clothing of any kind. Under threat, he slept clothed and armed. To come to Brenna, he'd left his weapons behind. Now he unfastened his belt and sat on a tall wooden chair to pull off his boots. Then he stood and shed his tunic.

Brenna had seen his bare chest many times by now. He preferred to fight bare-chested, and after he'd been wounded, she'd become quite familiar with his back. Yet she watched him avidly, and when he turned from her—unsure why he did—to open his breeches and shed them, too, she came to him, and he felt her hand, small and rough, on his back. She traced the new scar. The skin around it was numb, and her touch felt strange, like faint lightning against his flesh.

He let his breeches fall and stepped out of them. Then he felt her pulling at the leather thong that bound the end of his braid. She pulled it loose and dragged her fingers through his long hair until the braid was undone as high as she could reach. He took over and unwove the hair at the top of his head, then shook it all out.

He turned to find her smiling at him. It took his breath away. Then she looked down, between them, and saw the part of him that showed his need most clearly, and she gasped her breath away as well.

She brought her eyes up to his. "I…I do not…I am…"

He put his hands on her shoulders, under the drape of her hair. She shook like a leaf in a breeze. The shieldmaiden was gone; left in her place was simply a girl, innocent and shy. "Let me take you to bed, Brenna. Let us touch and get to know each other. We need not rush."

When she nodded, he took her hand and led her to her own bed. They lay together, face to face, embracing. Brenna leaned forward and pressed her lips to Vali's chest. The touch sent sparks of heat through his torso and into his loins, and he sucked in a heavy breath and clutched her close.

For a long moment she was quiet in his arms, her body still shaking. Indeed, the shaking had become more pronounced, not less, and he leaned back and caught her chin in his hand. He felt wetness on her skin.

"Brenna?" He lifted her face and saw that she was crying. "Have I frightened you?"

She shook her head at once, and he could see her seeking her courage. With a deep breath and a hard swallow, she said, "No. I am not frightened. Only overwhelmed. I've never...no one has ever touched me with...this."

"With what, my love?"

"With that. With love." A smile, sad and small, and tears topped over again. She ducked her head against his chest, and he held her, his heart swelling.

She was innocent of so much more than coupling. Vali ached to think how lonely and hard her life had been, full of blood and battle but bereft of kindness and love. He could not take her, cause her the pain it would cause her, when even the gentlest touch was new and overwhelming to her.

"You should always be held with love, Brenna. Let me do only that tonight. Let that be enough. Sleep, and when you wake, I will be here, loving you."

Her only answer was to hold him more tightly. And, gradually, to stop shaking.

7

Brenna woke in a dark room, feeling rested and comfortable. Before she opened her eyes, she understood that something was different, yet familiar, and with that understanding came the memory of the night before.

Vali had come to her. She had slept in his arms. She was still in his arms; the scent and feel of him was all around her—it was that which was familiar.

Once before, she had woken with him so close—when she had fallen asleep lying next to him in the healer's tent. That had been the last time, until now, that she'd slept well.

She tipped her head back, and his beard brushed over her forehead. It was soft, much softer than she'd expected, and she let herself shake her head lightly, savoring the touch of it on her skin.

"You are awake," his voice rumbled, quiet and deep, and she froze, feeling abashed. Then he bent his head down so that their eyes could meet, and he smiled.

His eyes were a bright, brilliant blue, the color clear even in the faint light, and this close to him, with the warm glow of the fire reflected in them, Brenna thought they seemed like the faceted jewels that had adorned so many of the prince's treasures. His smile was bright, too, his teeth white and straight and his full lips surrounded by that dark, lush beard.

Perhaps he was handsome, after all.

"Did you not sleep?" Brenna asked, and watched her hand come up so that her fingers could comb through his beard. He closed his eyes with a rough sigh.

"I slept. Though I admit that I watched you as I could. You are beautiful."

He'd said that before; she was more comfortable pretending she hadn't heard him. It wasn't that she thought he was lying to her—it was that she didn't know what sense to make of his admiration. So she dropped her eyes from his and focused elsewhere. Her fingers left his beard and smoothed over the hard, contoured planes of his broad chest, tracing the lines of his tattoos, the rampant bear and wolf.

Many berserkers had ritualized tattoos of a similar sort. The bear and the wolf were their special symbols. The most ferocious of the berserkers, who fought more like beasts than men, the Úlfhéðnar, were thought to be Odin's own warriors. Having seen Vali in battle, Brenna knew him to be Úlfheðinn. She had noticed, too, that he had kept the head and tail of the wolf that had become his main fur, so that the animal itself was slung over his back, in the way of the Úlfhéðnar. He had as much of the Allfather's special notice as she might possibly have.

She traced the bear tattoo over the rounded mass of his shoulder and down his arm, drawing over his scars, lingering in the valleys between each perfect muscle. She was entranced by the presence of him, so big and so firm, and his skin so soft.

Finally, Vali groaned. "Brenna. We lie bare together, skin to skin. I cannot take much more of your exploration. Forgive me." He took her hand and kissed it, then leaned in to kiss her forehead.

When he moved next to turn back the furs and leave the bed, Brenna caught hold of him, hooking her hand around the muscle atop his shoulder. "Don't."

He stopped and looked into her eyes, so deeply. No one had ever seen her the way Vali did. She wondered what he saw inside her.

"What do you want of me?"

She wanted him to make sense of the feelings inside her. She had seen men and women coupling many times; often, she had slept in longhouses full of people or in camps just the same. Their people did not much stand on matters of privacy. But what she had seen seemed ugly, cursory, little different from animals mating. Grunt and sweat and groan. The feelings she had for Vali were not ugly. They were visceral—deep, deep inside her body, in places she'd never fully understood of herself—and they were compelling, making her want things she hadn't wanted to want, but they were not ugly. They were beautiful.

She wanted him to love her.

"I want to understand what it is between us. I want why you came to my room."

"And you're certain?"

No, she was not. She didn't understand enough to be certain. But she knew she wanted to understand. She nodded. "Yes."

He settled the furs back over them and cupped her face in his hand—so broad and strong that he could have smothered her easily with just his palm. "If you will trust me, I will help you understand."

Again, she nodded, and he leaned in and kissed her. No one had ever kissed her but Vali, but even without anyone to compare him to, Brenna knew that he was highly skilled. She was stunned by the sparking sensations that heated her body, simply by the touch of his lips. And his tongue in her mouth! What a thing that was! She could feel, she could almost taste, the small nick in its side, where his father had meant to sever it. Again and again, she found herself teasing at that spot while his tongue explored her mouth.

While she marveled at the kiss, at the way his beard scraped gently at her cheeks, at the feel of his breath on her skin, at the thick silk of his hair caught in her fist, Vali groaned hoarsely, into her mouth, and then his hand left her face. She felt his fingers sweep down her throat and over her collarbone, then down, over her chest.

His hand covered her breast, and Brenna jumped, breaking the kiss with a gasp. It...hurt. Her breast ached under the heat of his palm, and she felt the skin tighten, which only made it...hurt more. But without her bidding, her body arched, pushing itself into his touch, wanting it more. She wanted more. Then his hand shifted, and he drew the pad of his thumb over the pebble-hard point, and she cried out, "Wait!"

Vali went still, but kept his hand where it was. Not even in battle did Brenna's heart beat as hard and fast as it beat now.

"Trust me. Let me help you understand."

When she nodded, he rolled, putting her on her back, his body on hers. She could feel the long, hard heat of him pressing into her belly—her belly that ached low and deep, throbbing downward so that she felt swollen between her legs. Was she ill? "Vali, I don't..."

"You will, shieldmaiden. Trust me." With that, his hand left her breast, moving down, along her side, and he shifted his whole body as if to follow that course. She whimpered, mourning the loss of that strange, wonderful pain in her breast. But then his mouth was on her neck, sucking, his tongue teasing lightly at her skin, his beard tickling, and she whimpered for another reason entirely, and brought her other hand up, scraping back across his shorn scalp so that both hands could tangle in his hair and hold him close.

Every touch of his hand or his mouth made her throb at the place of her womanhood. She flexed her hips, a movement as involuntary as the arch of her back had been when he'd first touched her breast, and he groaned as her body pressed up against him. She felt the vibration of it, and the cool of it as his harsh breath dried the wet he'd made on her skin.

Vali moved his body down farther, and his beard brushed over the excitable bud of her nipple. Again, she cried out and arched up, feeling that not-pain, an intensity too strong to endure.

He stopped and resettled himself so that they were face to face again. Brenna was gratified to see that he seemed stunned, too, and his breath heaved his chest against hers. "You are a revelation, Brenna. Do you trust me?"

Again, she answered with a nod, and again he moved his body down, his skin sliding against hers, and she waited to see what he would do.

When he covered her breast with his mouth, Brenna cried out and twisted away, trying to sit up. Vali stopped and looked up, but held her in place. "Did I hurt you?"

"Y—N—I—I don't know." Now that his mouth was gone, her breast still ached; she could still feel traces of that shocking sensation, and she wanted it. All of this was so confusing. "No. Forgive me."

He smiled—a smile came so easily to his face and looked like it belonged there. When Brenna smiled, she felt the rusty stretch of it in her cheeks. He reached with one hand and combed his fingers through her hair. "Brenna, heed me. What you feel, it's good. It can be bliss, if only you will be easy and trust me. Give me your trust, shieldmaiden. I swear you won't regret it."

This time, when she nodded, she took a deep breath and let it out, as she did before a battle, making her body still and loose.

"Say the words."

"I trust you." She did trust him. But everything that had happened between them since he'd come upon her at the river was beyond her ken. It wasn't in her nature to sit back and allow things to happen to her.

Vali took her breast once more into his mouth and sucked. Brenna drew in a sharp breath as his tongue flicked over her taut nipple, but she made herself lie as still as she could. Once she let herself truly feel what he was doing, she understood that it was not pain—it was as intense as pain, yes, but it was a pleasure far greater than any she'd known, greater even than his kiss, or his mouth on her neck, greater even than his hand where his mouth now was.

Then his hand came up and took the breast his mouth had neglected, and she had to bite down on her lip to keep a scream from finding sound.

She could no longer be still. What he was doing made more feeling than she could contain, and her body demanded to make some kind of response. Pressed between his heavy, broad body and the bed, she could only writhe, and gasp, and moan. She needed. Oh, how she needed. Her belly ached and cramped with need. Of what she had no idea, but when she lifted her hips and pressed her legs and all between them to the firm heat of him, she could feel that succor was near. As she rocked, trying to reach what she did not know, he grunted harshly over her breast, and his fingers clutched her flesh, pinching her nipple and digging into her hip.

Releasing her breast from his mouth, again he moved downward, kissing a trail over her ribs and down her belly. He reached back and pulled her hands from his hair, and the thick hank fell over her like a drape. It was cool; the fire had sputtered to mere embers, and the room beyond the heat of their bodies and the furs that surrounded them had gone dim and cold.

So distracted was she by the feel of his hair and by the touch of his hands on her breasts, still caressing and lightly pinching, making her body arch and twitch, she hadn't realized where he'd been headed next, not until she felt his nose brush through her curls.

He couldn't mean to kiss her there, could he? She had never seen such a thing, or heard of it.

"Vali! What?"

He chuckled, making her moan and twist beneath him. "Shhh. Trust, my love. Wait and see."

She felt his breath against her most private place. He did mean to kiss her there.

At first, though, he did not. Instead, his hands went away from her breasts, and one grasped her hip as the other slid over and up between her thighs. It was his fingers that first touched her there, a place she only touched to clean, or when she had her blood.

She had felt stirrings before, and she had touched herself once or twice, when she was young, but the feeling had been inconsequential, and she had not thought to do so again. The feelings Vali had stirred were of the utmost consequence. Nothing had ever been so important in her life as what she felt when his fingertips, roughened by war, brushed again and again over the point that seemed to ache beyond all measure.

"Vali! Vali!" she gasped, afraid and eager all at once. This was the need, where it would be met. Where it *must* be met. Yet she could sense that all would be different for her when it was.

111

"Ah, shieldmaiden. You are wet with want. I need to taste you." His tongue touched that small point on which her very sanity seemed to balance, and Brenna lost all control of her body and her mind.

She could not say what her body did, because her mind had become the night sky, filled with stars and empty of the world. All she knew was the perfect, consuming, encompassing release, which was all the pleasure she had ever felt, and all the pain, all the love and all the loss, all of life and all of death. All at once.

In the space of several heartbeats, it was over, and she slowly came back to herself, finding her body curled into a curve, rocking hard against Vali's face, her hands pulling his hair. Her breath came hard, heavy, as if she'd finished a fight. Her body, indeed, felt much the same as it did after a battle.

As she relaxed, the touch of his tongue and scrape of his beard made her twitch, and he eased away and lifted his head, smiling.

His beard was wet. Even in the dim room, she could see the gleam of it in what was left of the fire's glow. That was her.

"I make you this promise, Brenna mine. I will see to it that you know well that bliss. You will know love of body and mind and heart. I will love you with all that I have." He put his hands on either side of her body and came up, pushing her back to the furs as he loomed over her. "But first, my love, I must cause you some pain. Not too much, I hope."

He took her hand and brought it between them, until he held it over the wet heat of her sex. His sex was there, too, between her spread thighs. "Feel me, Brenna. Take hold. I want you to know me before I take you."

He curled her hand around his length and groaned when she squeezed lightly and then moved her fingers over him. She had seen other men but had thought little of the sword they always carried. Some men seemed especially proud of their endowment and had, she'd supposed, cause to be, and others less so. Vali was one who could have been proud.

Her fingers arrived at the tip of him, which was much softer than the rest, and his skin seemed looser and moved over the tip smoothly. When, curious, she explored that difference, he groaned and covered her hand with his. "You will unman me. My need is great. Will you let me feel you now? I need the heat of you."

Trying on a smile, she took her hand away. "Please. I want that, too." She wasn't sure whether she could survive another feeling like she'd had when his mouth was on her, but she thought she wouldn't mind at all to die that way.

Breathing a long groan, he took her hand again and brought it back to his sex. "Hold me as I enter you. I want you to feel that with me." Then he took his own hand away and hooked his arm around her thigh, bringing her leg around his waist. When he had her in the position he seemed to want her, he reached between them and took hold of himself and her hand.

His face hovered over hers, his hair dropping over them both. With his serious eyes locked on hers, he said, "Forgive me this, love. There is no other way." Then he pushed himself against the soft, swollen tenderness of her sex—and she lost the ability to breathe.

This was different by far from anything else he'd done. This was an invasion into her body, an impalement. He pulled their hands from between them and propped himself up over her. "It's better if I take your maidenhead quickly, and then the ease will come. I swear it, Brenna."

His words made her anxious. It was stretch, not pain, she felt now—the pain was in her mind somewhere; it was that intrusion that had her wanting to flee him. But she took a deep breath and made herself loose and still. He saw that she

113

had, and, with a nod, he thrust once, hard, his hips slamming into hers—

—and there was the physical pain, sharp enough to make her grunt and gasp. And yet, it was tolerable. Feeling the thick, hard mass of him inside her confused her, however. The pain was already easing; why was her instinct to push him off of her, out of her?

She looked up into Vali's eyes, still locked on her. Each of his breaths came like it had been ripped from his chest, and she could feel his arms shaking at her sides. He flexed gently, moving only slightly inside her, and the feeling under the sting was pleasure, enough that her eyes rolled up.

"Ah, Brenna. Now you are mine." His voice was even deeper than usual and harsh with strain.

That was it, her anxiety. He was claiming her. One thing her solitary life had afforded her was dominion over her body. Even when she had been a slave, no one had breached that boundary. And now she was his. Vali's. No longer her own.

"And are you mine?" she asked, hopeful and fearful of his answer.

He stared down at her, his intent focus on the eye that vexed her so. Shy, she tried to turn away, but he shifted, coming down to his elbows and catching her head in his hands. He pulled her back to face him. His broad, rough thumb traced a light line over her right cheekbone, along the tender skin under her eye.

"I have been yours since you first slept at my side, Brenna," he murmured and bent his head to kiss her gently. "I am bewitched."

A frosty hand clutched at Brenna's heart. There was no thing worse that she could have heard at that moment. With a whimper she couldn't contain, she pushed at his heavy shoulders and fought to be freed. Her movements moved him inside her and made her body flare and seek, yet she fought on nonetheless.

But Vali would have none of it. Making his body stiff and somehow heavier, he resisted her and held her head firmly. When she stopped struggling and glared up at him, frantically trying to keep close her anger lest despair get its hold on her, he said, a smile playing on his lips, "By your heart, Brenna. Not your lovely eyes. By your spirit. And that is no ill thing. I see the woman that you are. I love you."

Before she could make sense of those words, his mouth was on hers again. Then he began to flex his hips, rocking gently in and out of her. Pleasure overtook pain with every slide of his body in hers, and Brenna could make no sense of anything at all.

8

Brenna writhed and grunted, whimpered and arched with Vali's every touch. Even as her mind's doubt and confusion compelled her to question him, her body provided its own answers. He had imagined this—oh, how he had imagined this—but he had not done her justice. In her naïveté, she responded to him like a wanton. When she understood, what delights had they awaiting them?

The rigid naïf at the riverbank was gone. Now, as he rocked his body into hers, the doubting novice was gone as well. She was with him wholeheartedly, body and mind and spirit, forgetting herself as she had when he'd brought her release with his tongue, and she was the greatest gift he had ever known.

She had brought her other leg up and hooked it, too, around his waist, locking her ankles against the small of his back so that he could feel the firm muscles of her thighs pressing against his hips. Her hands clung to his back, her fingers digging in, their short nails scraping his skin. Her tongue moved with his as if she had always known their dance.

She was maiden-tight, her body clenched around his like a scabbard, and the heat of her seared him to his core. Every sensuous slide, like he moved through the thickest, freshest cream, brought him closer to his own bliss. But he would not release his need until she had felt another release of her own, until he knew that the pain he had caused her had been well and truly salved.

With each surge forward, he brought a bit more force, seeking her depths, her pleasure. When she tore her mouth from his and arched her neck, tipping her head far back with a sultry moan, he smiled and pressed his mouth to the pale skin she'd offered him. He could feel her pulse throbbing unstably against his tongue.

"Vali...please," she gasped, her body writhing under his, her legs clamping around him. She had stopped saying that she didn't understand. Now she was wide open to the sensations he could bring her.

He drew his knees up and pulled her up with him until he sat on his heels and she on his lap. She cried out—in surprise at first, and then in pleasure as she landed on his thighs. A groan ripped through him at the new depth, the hotter heat he found at the limit of her body. Holding her tightly to him, he dipped down and caught her breast in his mouth, between his teeth, suckling her as he drove his body into hers again and again. She let go of his back and clutched his head, her fingers catching his hair and pulling fiercely.

She arched backward, so sharply and suddenly that he lost her breast, and her own hips began to flex and rock. Her quiet moans became rutting grunts, and then she went completely still, as inflexible as iron, and her sex clamped around him so completely that she nearly pulled the climax from him.

But he would not spend in her, not yet. She would be his wife before he would. So he bit savagely down on his lip and waited for her to finish. The moment that he felt her body ease, he lifted her off of him. She gasped and clutched, fighting their separation, but he freed himself from her. Before he could take himself in hand, he spent, calling her name in a pained shout, covering her belly with his seed.

He laid her heaving, damp body back on the bed. With a light kiss to her lips, he turned the furs back and sat up.

She grabbed his wrist, her hand closing over his arm ring. "Please don't go."

He rested down again, leaning on his elbow at her side, and brushed tousled, fair hair from her face. "Brenna, it is my wish that I never sleep away from you again. I mean to go nowhere, except to your washbowl. I would clean what I spent on you."

Looking down at her belly, she took a finger of her free hand and drew it through what he had left. With a small, lovely smile, she nodded, and he rose.

The room had gone to a dark chill, and the water in her pitcher was cold. He crossed to the hearth and stoked the remaining embers. When they caught to flame, he laid two small logs on, then went back and poured chilly water into the washbowl, and soaked a clean linen in it. After he wrung it out, he went back to the hearth to warm it, and he laid another, larger log down on the new fire.

Turning back to the bed, he saw Brenna watching him, the firelight glittering in her eyes.

"You are a kind man."

He smiled and crossed the room to sit at her side on the bed. With the furs still turned back, he wiped her belly, sweeping lightly over her skin. She sighed and lay flat, opening herself to him.

Her belly clean, he returned to the washbowl and rinsed the cloth, wringing it out and bringing it back, this time without warming it first. He had taken her maidenhead; she would likely be glad of some gentle cool.

He pulled gently on her thigh, encouraging her to spread her legs, and then he washed her sex. She jumped and gasped as the cool touched her still-hot skin, and then let out a humming breath as he gave her relief.

There was blood on the linen. Only a little, but enough to make his heart hurt. "I am sorry I could not avoid causing you pain. On my life, I want never to cause you more."

"It was not so much. The pleasure was great. There was so much pleasure, I thought I would die."

He dropped the linen to the floor and lay at her side to claim her mouth. She was with him at once, knowing now how they fit, and after mere moments, they were both breathless, and he was stirring again to life. It was too soon to take her again, she needed time to recover, so he pulled away, rolling to his back and bringing her with him. He settled her head on his chest, her glorious hair draped over his arm.

She rested on him, her hand on his belly, stroking softly and keeping him stirred, and yawned prettily. He chuckled and kissed the crown of her head, letting his lips linger there.

"The sun is not yet risen. Sleep, my love. Rest with me."

She sighed, and he felt her body relax utterly.

Vali had never known peace so rich in all his days. He had led a contented life, since he'd run from his father's brutal grip. He had friends, he had honor, he had home and a place in the world. His fellow warriors were his family, his jarl was his father. But lying with this mesmerizing, solitary woman, he had never felt so quiet in his heart before. So full, so complete.

After a long moment, unsure if she were still awake, Vali murmured, "When you love me as I love you, I would make you my wife, Brenna."

"I love you now, Vali." Her voice was soft with comfort.

He turned her face up so that he could see her eyes. "Then marry me."

She smiled that smile that was only his. "I became yours, and you mine, tonight. Of course I will marry you."

~oOo~

"I will go with Orm and Viger to the town," Brenna said and stood.

Vali stood, too. "I would that you would not."

Mirkandi, the town that served as the hub among the three princedoms of western Estland, was likely to be dangerous for any raider. But the villagers now under their protection needed to trade in the town, now, before the winter set in, and later, during the sowing and reaping seasons, when their crops would grow and go to market. They could not hide in the castle like mice.

Vali knew this, of course. It had been his suggestion that they send a small party first and judge the stakes. A large party of raiders would seem to be a raid. But he had not intended for his woman to undertake the risk of that mission, shieldmaiden or not.

Brenna ignored him and slung her longsword on her back. She grabbed her furs from her seat and her shield from the wall, and she stalked toward the door. Orm and Viger watched her, then glanced at each other, then at Vali, then back at each other, and then followed Brenna.

"Brenna! Hold!" Vali took long, quick strides, passing Orm and Viger. Brenna had stopped only a few steps from the door; she did not turn to him until he had her arm in his grasp and pulled. Then, she gave him the full heat of her storied stare.

"Vali, do not. I am not your housemaid to sit quietly in a corner weaving your tunics."

"I know that. But do not do this. We are to be wedded in less than two weeks' time. I would have you live to see it."

"I could say the same. You scout north, into Prince Toomas's lands. Should his men come upon your party—"

"That is why you do this?"

She pulled her arm free of his and took the last steps to the door. "No. I do this because I am a warrior, just as you are, and I know my work." Heaving the door open, she stalked out. After a brief, awkward hesitation, Orm and Viger went after her.

Angry and agitated, he stared at the closed door for a long time, and then he realized the true risk. Yanking the door back open, he ran through the anteroom and out into the castle grounds. Brenna had just mounted her steed, a mare she called Freya. He stopped at the horse's side and held up his arms.

"Brenna."

At first, she gave him that fierce warrior's glare, and then she understood. With a tiny smile, she leaned over, holding her arms out to him, and he caught her. He pulled her off her mount and held her close. "I would not have you go without this," he whispered against her cheek. "I love you, shieldmaiden."

"And I you."

If he never saw her again, at least those words would be the last they would hear of each other.

Reluctantly, he set her down, and she took her mount again, offering him a sincere smile and a pat of her hand over her heart. He returned the gesture and turned back to the castle. He could not bear to see her ride away.

Orm and Viger were mounted, waiting behind her, grinning at each other over the display of affection they'd just witnessed. He walked between their horses and snarled at them. "If she does not return, neither had you better."

That cleaned the dirty smirks from their lecherous faces.

When he came back into the hall, Leif stood alone next to the long table. The others had dispersed.

"Where are Tord and Harald?" Vali hooked his axes through their belt rings and snatched his wolf pelt from the back of the chair that had become his. "I wish to be off."

"They prepare and are collecting Jaan and Georg from the village. I would have them go with you. I think they will make fine warriors and are already our best allies. We should train them up, and they might guide you as they can."

Vali nodded; he agreed. They would need to be ready for war when winter broke, and a warrior with a blade would fare better against a prince's army than a farmer with a pitchfork.

As he headed toward the door again, Leif said, "Vali, a moment."

Vali stopped and turned back, waiting.

Leif walked up to him and put his hands on his shoulders. He was almost as tall as Vali, and they stood near eye to eye. "We are allies and equals. In these weeks here, I've come to think of you as more than that—as a brother. Yes?"

Vali had nothing but admiration and respect for Leif. And affection, too, but he was wary now. "Yes. Brothers."

Leif smiled. "Good. Then as a brother, please hear me. You and the God's-Eye—"

"Brenna." He cut him off. "Call her Brenna. And please, *brother*, do not put your thoughts into words you cannot recant." He knew Leif's misgivings, and he knew they had merit. They had merit, but no matter.

"I must. I see that you are happy. The G—Brenna smiles now, and I have known her long without ever seeing such a sight before. She is a worthy woman. Wed her if you will. None here would stop you. We will celebrate and wish you the grace and goodwill of the gods. But Vali, should your fealties cross, you must think of the risk. Of what you, or she, would do. Would you be sundered from her? Or would you abjure Jarl Snorri and swear an oath to Åke? If you would not, if you would have her renounce her oath, Åke will bring all he can down on Snorri and on you. You would take more from him than a shieldmaiden. Whatever you believe about her gifts, Åke believes her to be the source of his power. He would not rest until he saw your head on a pike at his door. And then he would enslave her, to be sure she never slipped away again."

"You have said this all before. I know you are right. And I know, as do you by now, that it does not matter. I must have her. What follows will be as it will, as the gods wish it to be."

Leif heaved a deep, frustrated sigh and squeezed Vali's shoulders before he dropped his hands. "As you say. Perhaps the gods will ease the way of such a mating for the sagas as Brenna God's-Eye and Vali Storm-Wolf."

"We will make wedding offerings in the hope that it will be so."

~oOo~

Marriage among their people was rarely a matter of love. Even among the poorest of freemen, it was normally a transaction between two men: a man ready to marry and the

124

father of a woman likely to bear him children and keep his house well. Among the nobles, it was little different. Marriage was simply a financial arrangement between families.

But Brenna and Vali had no families, and they brought few material possessions with them but the clothes on their backs and the weapons in their hands. Vali had gold and silver, his portions from all his raids, buried at home, and he expected that Brenna did, too, but they had not discussed it, and Vali saw no need to. Their marriage would be one of love, and there was no other concern of consequence.

They were far away from home, and they were without family but the raiders and villagers who had become their clan. They had no bride price, no holding. Brenna, a shieldmaiden, and a slave before that, had not ever worn the kransen of a gentle maid. She had no women near her who knew their traditions but Astrid, who was nigh as rough and warlike as Brenna herself. Little about her preparations would be in keeping with the wedding traditions of their people.

Vali thought the gods would understand. To every extent they could, however, they meant to keep the gods' ways.

For his part, he had no ancestral sword to offer, and knew she had none, either. They had only their own weapons of war. He need not cleave from his identity as son, because he had broken that tie long ago. But he bathed fully, thinking as he did so of the ritual cleansing away of his bachelorhood.

He thought of Brenna, being bathed by Astrid and Olga and the female servants, standing in the deep tub as they ran hot water over her fair skin, as they washed her long hair, as they cleaned every part of her, and he was glad that he had insisted upon being left to wash unattended, because he had to take himself in hand, spending his seed in the cooling water at his feet.

When he came into the main room of his quarters, he found a snowy-white tunic and new leather breeches tanned so dark

125

they were nearly black, with boots and belt to match, arrayed over the bed he no longer used. He smiled, knowing well it was the work of Olga—she had either made them herself, or she had tasked someone else to do so, but he knew that it was she. Olga had been more fluttery and happy at the prospect of this wedding than had been the bride herself.

He dressed, marveling at the suppleness of the hide and the weighty softness of the finely-woven wool. As he closed the belt, a light knock came at the door.

"Enter," he said, surprised when Olga opened the door and peeked in. "I thought you would be with Brenna."

"I will go back. She has enough with her now. She is well. Too many at once make her..." The word failed her, so she made an angry face, and Vali laughed.

"Yes. I would think women's fuss would make her..." he mimicked Olga's angry face, and they both laughed. "But why are you with me? As you can see, I am able to dress myself. Thanks go to you, I believe, for the groom's finery."

She smiled. "A man should look his best on this day, *jah*? I was able to send for plenty good hide from Mirkandi." Her grasp of their language had grown daily. By now, she was nearly perfectly fluent, though she kept a charming accent. "I come and see if I might weave your hair."

Vali kept his sides shorn and usually kept the long hair in the middle tightly braided, in one or two plaits that started at his hairline and clung to his head until the hair was loose of it, then trailed down his back. Something he could do himself; a slave girl he'd favored when he was young had taught him. Except for what he shaved, he had not cut his hair since he'd left his father, and it fell, when loosed, nearly to his waist. It was dark and thick, as thick as the full head of most men.

He liked fuss no better than Brenna did, but he smiled at Olga. It was his wedding day, after all. "You will not festoon me with winter blossoms, I hope."

"I think not," she laughed. "It will be manly and fierce."

He sat on a nearby chair. "Then weave away."

~oOo~

Leif and Orm met Vali in the hall, where the men all awaited the wedding rites. They grinned at him, then led him into the midst of the group. Just as Vali was about to make a snide remark about their gaping faces, Orm, the oldest of them, spoke.

"I have known you long, Vali Storm-Wolf. You have a fierce heart and a good one. You are a great warrior, spoken of in stories even while you live. You have chosen for your mate a legend. We believe your match will please the gods. We have prepared the offerings to ensure that this is so." Orm turned to the table and picked something up. When he faced Vali again, he had a new longsword, a stunningly beautiful weapon with a dark, intricately woven hilt, in his hands.

"You have no family who would bestow on you their sword, but you cannot be wed without the blessing of Thor, to make your union strong and fertile. So as the family you have, we make a new tradition. We offer you this sword, newly forged and blessed in sacrificial blood, so that your bride might pass it to the descendants of your union."

Moved beyond expression, Vali took the sword in both hands and held it high, bowing his head.

He was ready to take his bride.

Although winter was setting in, there had not yet been snowfall or a hard frost, and their weddings were meant to be outside, in clear sight of the gods. And they were sturdy folk, so none balked, not even the servants unaccustomed to these rites.

The men went out to the grounds and waited, with Vali and Leif, who would preside over their binding, in the center. Behind them, servants held a goat, a sow, and a boar. They would be sacrificed at the beginning of the ritual, and their blood would be sprinkled over Vali and Brenna and the others, to honor the gods and seek their blessing over the marriage.

The women came out from the east door, all of them in white, and Brenna in the lead. Vali caught his breath. Olga had seen to it that she had a dress befitting a bride. Long and pure white shot with gold, it clung to her curves then flared to flow loosely around her legs. The sleeves draped down, over her hands. She was a vision fit for the gods.

More breathtaking than that was the bride's crown she wore over her long, loose hair. It was tall and woven of straw and adorned with flora, exactly as their traditions would have it. That, Vali thought, must have been Astrid's doing. He would not have thought her likely to have offered such a suggestion, but she must have.

As the women walked forward, Harald, the youngest surviving of their men, stepped in front of her, bearing high a gleaming sword with a golden hilt. Their clan had seen to it that Brenna, too, could make their traditions. The gods would be well pleased.

Brenna's smile as she approached him was wide and bright. Vali took her hand and bent down to whisper, "I mean to see to it that you smile like that at least once every day for all the rest of your life."

~oOo~

After a great, raucous feast in the hall, with all of the village in attendance as well, Vali and Brenna were sent up to their wedding bed. They were followed up, nearly chased, by most of their people. As their friends laughed and whooped and gibed behind them, Brenna tripped running up the stone stairs in her long dress, and Vali caught her and swept her up into his arms.

She laughed and threw her arms around him. He had never heard her laugh before. The sound was quiet and stilted, as if stiff from lack of use, but Vali thought it the most beautiful he'd ever heard.

They arrived at their room, which had been hers, and all their friends, their family, clustered eagerly at the door. Vali set his wife down and took her into his arms to kiss her. Their audience cheered with ribald humor. Then he took the flowered crown from Brenna's head and tossed it out the door, into the crowd.

When he could close the door, he dropped the bar across it.

Then he took his wife to bed.

PART TWO
THE STORM

9

Brenna woke slowly, snug under the furs. She stretched and purred as Vali's hand eased up her thigh and over her hip. He almost always woke her this way, his hand under her sleeping shift, smoothing over her skin as if he meant to polish her to a sheen.

"It's nearly dawn, my love. We should rise." He whispered the words at her ear and then drew his tongue along the lobe.

She knew he was right. The winter had come in with bluster and fury, and they'd already endured three long storms. The latest had taken many roofs down in the village, and the castle was full of suddenly homeless villagers and their animals. The day before had brought a reprieve—sun and more endurable temperatures—and they all meant to take the opportunity the gods had given them to make repairs as they could. Those who could read the signs said that this winter would continue harsh and bitter, so they would take their respite when they could.

But the thought of pushing away the furs and stepping out into the cold room made Brenna moan a protest and snuggle back, tightening her bond with her husband's body. He always slept bare, and he was hard; he was always long and hard and hot when he woke. Brenna wiggled her hips against his length until he groaned and clutched his fingers into her thigh. The sounds of his pleasure—that her touch, her body, her nearness could elicit such sounds from him—that was a powerful feeling. A stirring feeling, which heated her blood and made her body yearn.

She opened her eyes; the room was still thick with dark. "We need not rise just yet." As she spoke the words, she reached back, between them, and took him in her hand, sliding her loose fist along his shaft. His hips rocked, and he let out a long, earthy breath.

"You are a wanton, wife."

"Which is as my husband prefers me."

He shifted his arm under her so that he could wrap it across her chest. With his other hand, he picked up her leg and pulled it back to rest on his hip. "Indeed."

Brenna loved this position more than any other she knew—lying on their sides, he behind her, she encompassed by him, he inside her, his hands free to touch every part of her and bring her multiple ecstasies at once. She felt never more thoroughly loved than like so. As he eased into her now, the path smoothed by her need of him, he groaned into her ear.

"You are always ready for me. Wanton."

Chuckling at the end of the sigh with which she'd taken him in, she reached her arms over her head so that she could grab his braided hair. "And you for me."

"Always, yes." The arm across her chest moved, and his hand slid into the neckline of her shift. Further down, the hand that had held her thigh slid up and between her legs. As his body took full possession of hers, Brenna grunted and flexed back.

There was no feeling like this, this joining with another, becoming one. She had thought mating to be nothing better than animal urges, and she had thought the groaning and grunting and heaving to be proof of that. She'd been so very wrong.

The animal urge was there, the inexplicable and undeniable need to have his body inside her body, the way she felt impelled, *compelled*, to pull and bite and scratch as he took her, the way he groaned and growled and grunted and howled and roared—all of that was as animal as ever she'd thought.

What she hadn't known, what she couldn't possibly have known, was the depth of the pull. The expression of the need might have been animal, but the need itself came from somewhere deeper. It came from her very soul. Brenna knew her love for Vali, her need of him in every dimension, would transcend this world and be with her forever.

That was what it was to be mated. Now she understood.

As he rocked into her, and she rocked back, as his fingers teased between the folds of her sex and made her whimper with building bliss, Vali's other hand cupped her breast, and he caught her nipple in his fingers.

That hurt, sharply, and, surprised, Brenna jumped and stilled. "Oh!" She laid her hand over his, the soft linen between them, to stop him.

After two months together, Vali knew her well, and he, too, stilled. "They ache? Is it time for your blood?"

Brenna thought. She had bled only twice before she'd left her parents' home. Upon the first time, her mother had told her to heed the moon to know when her blood would come, but the moon had never seemed to tell her the same thing twice. When she was raiding, sometimes she would go the whole season without blood.

She'd bled once since they'd been in Estland, just after she and Vali had come together, shortly before they were wed. She supposed she was due to do so again. He must have taken note of what her sore breasts then had foretold. It pleased her to think he'd paid such close attention.

"I think yes." She sighed sadly at the thought of going days without waking like this, and without going to sleep in similar ways.

Vali buried his face against the side of her neck and took his hand from her breast, hooking it instead over her shoulder, holding her close. "Then I will take my fill of you now, before I am bereft."

Brenna turned her head, and Vali answered her, covering her mouth with his, plunging into her with tongue and sex alike, driving her need with his own until they grunted together, their bodies tangled and heaving, Brenna's hands gripping his hair, pulling fiercely, Vali's fingers between her legs, rubbing and pinching, his body filling hers again and again, more deeply each time until she thought she could take no more.

Needing more breath that he could give her, Brenna tore her mouth away and sucked in a loud whoop of air. Vali growled deep in his chest, rumbling against her back, and his fingers, so hard and rough from years of battle, pressed down on the node of her pleasure. Brenna cried out again and again, feeling the coming of the loss and gain of everything, the feeling she knew as the peak of her ecstasy.

"Yes, shieldmaiden. Lose yourself to me."

She did. Everything was sparks and light, and then, behind her, at her ear, Vali growled with his release and clutched her tight, and Brenna's peak climbed still higher until she knew nothing but absolute bliss.

~oOo~

She opened her eyes to see Vali hovering over her, his expression a blend of concern and nascent amusement. "Are you well?"

"Yes. Of course. Why?" She lifted a hand and combed her fingers through his long, soft, thick beard.

"In that case, I'm well pleased with myself." He grinned and kissed her hand. "You swooned."

"I did?" She lifted up onto her elbows and looked around. The room was a bit brighter—and warmer; Vali had stoked the fire. And he was partially dressed. She must have swooned—and slept a little after that.

"Indeed. I should be careful not to exhaust you so at the dawn. We have much to do." The amusement left his face, and he furrowed his brow at her. "You are well, though? Truly?"

"Perfectly well. And well sated."

She smiled, and he returned the look and brushed a finger over her cheek. "Not yet a day without a smile like that. My mission is too easy, I think.

"Are you going to be smug and insufferable all day now?" Playfully, she pushed at his shoulders, and he sat back so that she could sit up. Her head swam lightly for a moment; he truly had rendered her senseless.

"Brenna?" He'd noticed. He noticed everything about her. All her life, those around her had made every effort not to look at her directly. Vali hardly looked away from her. His love for her was a heady potion. He had changed almost everything she understood about the world.

She turned the furs back and stood. "You *are* going to be smug and insufferable all day."

He stood, too, and pulled her close. "I made you insensible. Count yourself fortunate I don't announce it in the hall."

Laughing, she punched him lightly in the belly and went to wash and dress.

~oOo~

Although it was warmer and brighter than it had been, it was nearing the heart of the winter, and the temperature was by no means balmy. Yet the work was difficult and physical, and by the time they broke for a midday meal, many cheeks were rosy more from effort than from cold.

Everyone sat at a bonfire in the center of the village, and the women served hot skause and bread and mead. Most of the women, that was. Since her time with her parents, Brenna had not cooked, and since her time as a slave, she had not served. Her effort on this day had been spent helping with the roofs—though much of her work had been herding playful children from trouble while the men chopped wood, hoisted rough beams, and laid the tiered wooden roofing.

Finding herself not hungry, Brenna nibbled at some bread and watched the others. The severe weather and the damage to the village had not seemed to dampen anyone's spirits. Men and women sat around the fire, or milled nearby, chatting and laughing. Young men who had gobbled their meal while others were still being served now sparred in the snow. Children ran and squealed, fleeing Viger, who had become a monster, stomping and snarling after them.

Leif and Olga sat together, chatting. Olga had been teaching Leif the Estland language, and he had been a devoted student. He'd picked up enough that he could speak with the villagers without need of translation. Brenna was envious of his facility. She herself was hopeless with the language, try though she might to learn it. While Olga had become fully fluent in their language, and Leif competent in hers, while Vali and several others had learned enough to make their way, Brenna had picked up only a scant few words and phrases and was still relying on pantomime when she had no one near to serve as interpreter.

Vali had tried to help her, once, but the endeavor had nearly ended in blows between them—the only time they had, since they had come together, had a strenuous disagreement. Away from battle, Vali was an even-tempered, patient, and goodhearted soul. Brenna was discovering a softer nature in her heart as well. But she didn't like to feel stupid, and on that day, she had.

She watched Vali now, speaking with Orm, standing amidst their friends and family. Even as she sat alone, Brenna felt the coziness of companionship. Since they had taken over the castle and built a community with the people here, she had felt every day a bit more normal. Even the raiders who had known her for years had begun to treat her differently—as someone more like them. People spoke to her, and not simply because they couldn't avoid it. In the past few weeks, she had gradually realized that everyone simply called her Brenna now.

Never in her life had that been true before.

Taking a sip of her mead, she pulled a face. Normally, she liked the taste of the Estland mead, but this batch seemed off. No one else seemed bothered, so she took a curious sniff, but when her stomach rolled, she poured it out into the slush of the trodden snow.

Then she stood and went to join Vali and Orm's conversation. Her husband smiled and held out his hand as she approached, and when she took it, he pulled her close and wrapped her in his arms, all without losing the beat of his words. That felt special to her—as if his love for her was so much a part of him now that it needed as little thought as breathing.

As hers was for him.

~oOo~

With the town working together, by midafternoon, the roofs of two stables had been repaired. The decision had been made to focus on the stables first, as the villagers could continue to be sheltered in the castle, but the animals had made that space, meant for a strangely dark and solitary luxury, too crowded and uncomfortable. The raiders were accustomed to sharing their living quarters with livestock; it was a good way to keep warm in harsh winters. But the people of Estland, at least this part of it, lived in tiny huts with nearby stables for their livestock. Many of the stables seemed more comfortable than their homes.

Meaning to work as long as the fickle winter light held, the men moved on to the next roofs. Brenna and Astrid mounted up with Harald and Tord and a few villagers, headed back to the castle. They would herd as many of the animals as they could back, and some of the men would stay in the village to tend them overnight.

Feeling wearier than she had reason to feel, Brenna was glad to be riding to the castle. On Freya, she could rest a bit and refresh herself before they brought the animals back. She drew a long draught from her water skin while she waited for the others to mount up.

They rode with purpose but not urgency, keeping a steady pace, but not so fast that they couldn't speak amongst themselves. Brenna realized that she really was much behind the others in learning the Estland language. Although their party was a mix of raiders and villagers, the camaraderie continued, with people apparently telling jokes and the others laughing. Even Astrid seemed to understand what was being said. But Brenna could only pick up a word here or there, nothing that made any sense outside the joke.

And yet, she found herself smiling, as if good cheer were contagious. She felt a bit lonely, too, left out of the jokes, and that struck her more than it would have a few months earlier.

She decided that she would speak with Olga and put another effort into learning the language.

As they neared the halfway point in their short journey to the castle, Brenna felt suddenly quite ill. She had the thought that the mead must in fact have turned, and then the world shifted sharply to one side, like a ship tossed in a churning sea. In a moment of senseless instinct, she clenched her legs and pulled against the pitch. She felt Freya shy at the contradiction in signal, and then she felt surreal weightlessness as she lost the saddle and fell to the ground.

A blast of pain in her head as she struck the snow was the last thing she knew.

~oOo~

When she opened her eyes again, she was in the bed she shared with Vali. The room had the golden, flickering glow of a fire. It was night. Vali sat in a chair at her side, staring across the bed at the crackling fire, a much bigger blaze than they usually built. The room was snug and warm.

Her head ached horribly, and she lifted her hand to touch the place that hurt the most. There, she found a large knot, both soft and firm. She must have struck a stone under the snow when she'd fallen from Freya.

Her movement stirred Vali, who left his chair and sat on the bed at her side. "Brenna. My love. How do you feel?"

"My head pains me. And my ego as well. I haven't fallen from a horse in many years. I'm sorry to worry you. It's only a bump."

He smiled and lifted her hand to his lips, brushing his beard over her knuckles as he kissed them. "Brenna. Olga believes you are with child."

141

Her head ached, and she felt strange. She heard his words, and understood them, yet they were foreign to her. "What?"

"She asked when last you'd had your blood. I told her what I remembered. The tenderness in your breasts, your lack of hunger, the swooning—Olga says these are signs that a babe is coming to us."

"What?" It was the only word she could think.

He cocked his head. "Love, are you surprised? I sow my seed inside you every day, often more than once. Did you not think we might make a child that way?"

She had not. It had never occurred to her, not even as a dream or a wish. Long ago, Brenna had given up the thought that she would ever know love, much less be a wife or a mother, and the concepts must have decoupled in her mind. Even as the wedding rituals had stressed their descendants, it had been an abstract idea, part of the ritual, not of her life. She had never considered it, and they had never discussed it. "I never thought I would. I gave up hope in my life long ago."

He frowned and cupped his hand around her face. "Well, bring it back. You deserve every happiness, and you shall have it. You are carrying my child, shieldmaiden. The gods smile on us and like us well."

Brenna pushed her hands under the furs and laid them flat on her belly. She had been changed into a linen sleeping shift, so she could almost feel her skin.

A babe. Vali's child inside her. "I want him to have your eyes."

Vali's hands came under the furs and covered hers. "You are so sure you make me a son?"

She was. Though she knew not why, certainty had suffused her mind. She carried a son. "Yes. Somehow, I know it."

Her husband grinned with golden pride. "And he will be strong and perfect, with his own eyes."

Brenna liked that answer, and its thought, very much. "When?"

"Midsummer, Olga says. The ships should have returned by then, but we will wait to sail home until he is born."

At once, like a bolt of lightning, Brenna had another powerful certainty. "Vali, I don't want to go."

It was his turn to be confused. "What?"

"Every good thing that has happened in my life has happened here. I want to stay—to settle here. To make a home."

His hands left her belly, and he stared at her. "Brenna, I am a warrior. I know nothing of farming."

"I know farming. And your father was a smith. You were his apprentice once."

His light frown deepened into a scowl, and he stood abruptly and walked a few steps away, to the end of the bed. "You know the way of that. I want no part in anything of his. I've worked my life to forget that past, and you hurt me to mention it."

She had spoken rashly. "I'm sorry." She held out her hand. "Please come back."

He came at once, this time to the other side of the bed, and stretched out beside her, propped on his elbow. "Can we not make a home among our own people?"

"I have no people, Vali. But here I'm treated as equal. Even those who've known me many years treat me now like Brenna and not the God's-Eye. I know it's you who made them stop calling me that, but now I believe they no longer think it, either." She turned the furs back and covered her belly with her hands again, studying that part of her body as if she could see the child within her. "I am afraid that our child will carry my burden if we live among people who think of me as different."

Looking up again, she turned to Vali, whose eyes were fixed on her belly. It hurt her head terribly to turn her neck as she had, but she stayed that way and said his name, so that he would look her in the face. "It's a hard life, to be different. I wouldn't wish it on our child if I might avoid it."

His eyes searched hers for a long time. Finally, he sighed and shook his head, and Brenna knew a spark of fear.

"I can deny you nothing, Brenna mine. I shall learn to be a farmer."

Relief and happiness swept through her, leaving a warm exhaustion in their wake. "Thank you. I love you." She rested back in the bed and closed her eyes. "No doubt there will be war to make here in Estland, as well," she sighed, feeling darkness coming on in her mind.

Vali settled at her side and pulled her close. With his hand on her belly, he kissed her cheek and murmured, "Enough talk. Rest, little mother. Be strong and well."

10

Jaan surged toward Vali, and Vali sidestepped and brought his sword down on Jaan's, knocking it from the younger man's hold. It clattered to the stone floor, and Jaan shook out his hands.

"Again!"

At Vali's command, Jaan huffed and bent down to retrieve the longsword. Vali kicked it out of his reach, then came in with his own sword, swinging low and stopping just as he made contact with Jaan's ribs. "Now you are dead. Pick it up." When Jaan muttered under his breath words Vali didn't understand, Vali rose up to his full height, more than a head above Jaan's, and made his shoulders as broad as he could. His back caught uncomfortably as he did so; he expected that he would always feel some discomfort under the scar from the wound that had rent him from shoulder to hip, but he ignored it.

"Pick it up." He spoke in the Estland tongue, though Jaan had learned almost as much of his. He had noticed as raiders and villagers spent more and more time together, battened down against the vile weather outside, they were developing a language of their own, a blend of all their words and experiences.

Confronted by Vali's mass and the scowl above it, Jaan swallowed and collected his sword. Vali held back a smile. The boy was a fierce fighter already, but he was intemperate, and Vali enjoyed putting him in his place.

All around them, other men sparred, and the stone walls of the hall echoed with the ponderous clang of forged iron.

They had heaved the big oaken table off to one side and opened the room to serve as a training space, now that the snows piled high along the castle walls and only those with important work outside braved the elements.

Inside, they were warm and comfortable. Most of the men training, Vali and Jaan included, had shed their tunics and were staining their breeches with the sweat that dripped from their bare torsos.

Vali held out his hand and flexed his fingers, signaling to Jaan to come in again. This time, however, as he read Jaan's body's intent to move forward, he said, "Hold!" and Jaan froze, his sword held in both hands, straight out before him.

"Are you Prince Vladimir, a tiny man dancing in a crimson cape?" He thought he'd said the words right.

He must have, because Jaan made a face that only a young man, with the harshest lessons of life yet in store for him, could make: full of contempt and bravado. "I am not."

"Then why do you move like this is for show?" He tapped Jaan's sword with his own. "Held like that, out from you, I can block you here"—he brought his sword down on Jaan's blade, near the tip—"and here"—he did it again, moving inward—"and here, and here"—he was at the hilt now—"and here." The last time, he laid the edge of his sword over Jaan's bare wrist, not quite touching his skin. "Then you fight no more."

Vali held up his own sword and drew his fingers over the tip of the blade. In the manner of his people, the tip was subtly tapered, almost rounded. "See. A blade like this is not meant to leave a tiny spot of blood. Not to..."—he searched for the word—"stab, but to slash." To illustrate, he swung the blade in a powerful, but slow, sideways arc. "No man will stand. Move on the side, not headlong. Perhaps a shield for you."

Jaan grimaced and shook his head. He answered in Vali's language. "You use no shield."

"No. But I am of the Úlfhéðnar, and I have trained and fought long."

"That makes your flesh harder than mine?"

"It makes me harder to hit."

Jaan smirked. "Your back says another thing."

Unoffended by the snide reference to his vicious scar, but unwilling to let the point go unanswered, Vali swung his sword again, quickly and silently, this time aiming for Jaan's neck. He let the blade strike home before he pulled back, leaving a thin seam of red under the cocksure youngster's ear. Caught entirely unawares, Jaan's expression was of shock and fear, and he dropped his sword without even trying to block the attack.

Fierce and stupid, like most young men. Vali shook his head. "You are not ready, pup. I would have killed you many times today. Too much"—Vali came close and grabbed Jaan's crotch, hard, making him grunt in pain—"and not enough"— he let go, made a fist, and thumped the boy on his head. "It will kill you."

Jaan shrugged him off and picked up his sword, this time holding it properly, at an angle, ready to block or to slash. He wanted to go again. He was angry and embarrassed, but he had learned. Keeping his grin to himself, Vali gave Jaan a snarl instead and nodded. "Come then, boy, and show me."

They and the others sparred and bantered through much of the afternoon; then, when all were weary, serving women brought them water, and they sat about, in chairs or on the floor, to rest. Vali watched the men watch the women. Many of the raiders that had stayed behind had been brutal to the captive women at their camp, and a few of them had been slow to come around to the plan to build community with the villagers rather than simply enslave them. Once the leaders among them had understood that Vladimir had treated all his subjects as slaves, they had decided that their likeliest path to a peaceful winter and, should any other prince attack, a victory against him was to make the villagers allies.

And they had. But it meant that the women were not subject to the raiders' whims, and a few men had had to be dealt with when they forgot it. Now, though, months since they'd been left behind, the separation between the groups was almost nonexistent. Even the language barrier had come down for most.

Not for Brenna. She struggled mightily with the language, and Vali thought her skill little improved despite her efforts. The effort and the failure made her impatient and cross.

Vali was impatient, too. She wanted to make this their home. She would need to learn to speak the language of the people here eventually.

Sitting in a tall wooden chair by the fire, his eyes aimlessly scanning the hall, he saw his wife standing in a doorway, and he felt a momentary burst of guilt, as if she'd caught him thinking critically of her. Their eyes met, and she smiled, and then he was simply dazzled.

In the few months since they'd learned she was with child, Brenna had changed. She spent more time with the women, learning or re-learning the skills of the wife: weaving and cooking and home-tending. She had even asked Olga a bit about healing. It was as if the babe had freed the womanly part inside her, a part she had tucked away.

Not much more than a week earlier, Brenna had stunned him by appearing in the hall in a gown and hangerock, her hair twisted into soft, loose braids. Only on the day of their wedding had he ever before seen her in a gown. She had explained that her breeches had become uncomfortable; her belly had grown too much.

Vali could hardly complain. As alluring as he found her dressed in her mannish clothes, her legs so available to be seen, the hide of the breeches snug over her muscled flesh, womanly garb was much more convenient. When the need overtook them during the day, rather than their customary struggle with hide lacings and snug breeches between them both, he could toss up her skirts, loose himself, and be inside her in the space between two breaths.

Lately, that had been quite useful. In the past weeks, freed of the weakness and illness that had plagued her in the time right after they'd learned of the babe, Brenna had become insatiable. She had been enthusiastic and responsive from the night he'd first taken her, she was always ready and always curious to experience everything he could think of, but lately, Vali was fairly certain that she could only be satisfied if he kept her naked in bed all the day and all the night. Truth be told, he was feeling a bit...overextended.

He'd been reluctant at first, thinking it safer to forgo physical love until their child came to them, and for a few weeks, while she felt ill and faint quite often, Brenna had agreed.

And then one night he'd woken with her mounting him, sliding him into herself. She hadn't even bothered to try to wake him—and after she'd found her release, he'd had to grab her hips to keep her from moving away before he could release as well. He wasn't sure she herself had ever fully woken. She'd needed; she'd taken.

That dawn, she'd wanted him again and demanded much of him. He'd spoken later with Olga, worried that he might have been hurting the child, probing around so close. Olga had laughed at him and told him to carry on.

And they had been carrying on.

Still smiling at him, Brenna stepped into the room and walked to him, through the damp mass of men. The small roundness of her belly stretched her blue woolen hangerock so that the lacings on the sides widened noticeably at that point. Vali often found himself transfixed, staring at that pretty swell. His child growing inside his wife. Their love perpetuating.

She came to him as if with a purpose, her eyes never leaving his. When she arrived before him, she kept advancing until she had straddled him, hoisting her gown and hangerock up, baring her legs and boots.

On the whole, their people were physical and affectionate. They lived in congregation with each other, sharing almost everything. They had found the Estlanders' tiny huts confounding and the many walled rooms of the castle bizarre. Privacy was not a need of their kind.

Brenna, his once solitary and suspicious wife, had been markedly more publicly affectionate with him of late, but she had never made such a stark display before. Everyone in the hall noticed. Most kept noticing, staring unabashedly, not even dissuaded by Vali's glare over her shoulder.

Shocked, at first Vali only sat, trying to catch her eyes with his so that he might understand. He went hard at once, of course he did, but he had no intention of taking his wife on a chair in the middle of the well-lit hall, with two dozen sweaty men lazing about around them. Or being taken by her, as more aptly described this circumstance.

"Brenna?"

She bent down and licked his chest, moving up over his shoulder, along his neck, to his ear. "I like the taste of your body after you work."

"Brenna." This time he groaned it. If she kept wiggling on him, he might have no choice but to take her right here. He could feel the heat of her through his breeches, and his body wanted hers as badly as hers wanted his.

"I need you," she breathed into his ear. "I itch for it." She ducked her head and sucked on his throat, burying her face in his beard. Vali could not help but let his head fall back. He stilled her hips, cupping the firm mounds of her bottom in his hands, and stood. As she felt him move, she hooked her arms and legs around him, so that he brought her up with him gracefully.

Trying to ignore the reactions of their audience, which varied from lewd amusement to gaping shock, he retraced her path through the hall and carried her away to their room.

~oOo~

Once in their room, he set her down and barred the door. She kept her hands on him, tracing her fingers over his back while he was turned from her, then plucking at the lacings of his breeches when he faced her again.

Laughing, he caught her hands. She was nearly beyond reason. "What has possessed you, shieldmaiden?"

She calmed and looked up at him. "I don't know. I feel day and night like I need to be close with you. Just now, seeing you training, the way your body…" Her cheeks reddened, and she took a step back. He held her hands fast, or she would have pulled them from his grip. "You think that is what it is—that I am possessed?"

He had not meant to recall for her something that had often been said about her—that her strange eye meant that she might be possessed by the gods at any time. "Only by our child. The fathers among us tell me that how you feel is not so unusual."

"You've spoken about me with others? About this?"

"Love, they've noticed."

Deeply flushed now, Brenna tried harder to pull away, but Vali kept his hold. "There is no shame in it. It pleases me that you want me so, and that you show how you feel among our friends. I only would like to go slower now. While I enjoying tossing your new skirts and taking you quickly on the stairs, now I would lay with you in our bed for a while."

The side of her mouth quirked up. "Have we time?"

It was his turn to pull at her lacings. "We have the time we make."

Loosening her hangerock so that he could pull it over her head, Vali turned and stepped backward toward their bed. Then Brenna stopped, resisting his draw. He cocked his head.

Before he could ask, she said, "I want…"

Rather than try to draw her closer, he stepped forward, coming to her. "What do you want, wife? I can deny you nothing."

"When I sat on you in the hall. Over your legs as I was…"

"Yes?" He could still feel the weight of her on his thighs.

"I could feel you. Pressing against me."

Vali's body clenched with the memory of it, and he groaned and hooked his hand around the back of her neck, under the heavy fall of her loosely-braided hair. He bent and claimed her mouth, finding her tongue at once. She laid her hands over his shoulders and dug her fingers into the muscle there.

When they were breathless, he pulled back enough to ask, "Do you wish to ride me that way?"

She nodded. "Can we? On a chair?"

"Of course. But I want you bare. I want to feel all of you."

Smiling broadly—not yet a day had passed since he'd made her that promise that he hadn't made her beam such happiness into the world—she took a step back and pulled her loosened hangerock over her head. She did it slowly, with her eyes on his. Then she pulled her boots off one at a time and let them drop. Each piece of clothing came off while he watched, and while she watched him watch, as if she were making a show for him, until she stood bare before him, the tail of her braid lying over one round breast.

"Gods, wife. You make me ache."

In a gesture that was becoming habit for her, she looked down and swept her hand over the small new mound of her belly. He found that sight, and the sweet protectiveness and devotion to their child it conveyed, powerfully alluring, and he groaned.

She turned her face up to his. "I ache also, Vali. Sit."

He shed his boots and breeches and sat on a tall-backed wooden chair. The fire had been banked for the day, and the room was chilly, but he was so hot with want that it hardly mattered. He patted his bare thighs in invitation, and Brenna straddled him, wrapping her hand around his shaft to hold him steady as she settled her weight on his lap. She was hot and slick, always ready for him, and he closed his eyes, growling at the liquid friction as her body took him in.

She moaned, letting her head fall back. Her braid dropped from her shoulder and dangled over his hands on her back. He caught the silky rope and wrapped it around his fist, then sat forward, pulling her back, so that he could taste the flesh of her throat, her chest, her breasts.

As he leaned over her, Vali felt her belly pressing against his, their son resting snugly between them. Soon, Brenna would be too great with child for them to couple face to face like this. The thought heated his blood even more, made his need to see her all the more urgent.

She was a sight to behold in her pleasure, a pleasure only he had ever brought her. And now, as her need was nearly beyond her ability to manage it, she was like a wild thing. To hear this woman, his wife, who had been so guarded and inexperienced, grunting and moaning, to see her writhe and flex on him, her muscles rolling through tautness and slack as she climbed to release, to see her beautiful face so intent and enraptured, to scent her arousal in the scant space between them, to taste it on her flesh, to feel her body clenching around his, milking him—Vali had a great deal more experience than she, but he had never felt with any other woman the fire he felt with Brenna. It burned deep, in his marrow. In his soul.

It had been his intent to slow down and savor her, but he wasn't so certain he could manage it any better than she. With a groan of defeat, he caught her breast between his teeth and sucked, pulling the sweet flesh into his mouth, dragging her nipple over the edge of his teeth, knowing well how she would respond. There could be no slow savoring once he claimed her body in this way.

She arched violently backward, taking a loud inward breath, then letting it out. Her hands dug into his shoulders, and her hips trebled the pace of their rocking. Moaning out every release of breath, each one coming more quickly than the one before it, she began to rock so hard that she bounced on his thighs and made it impossible to keep his mouth on her.

Every bounce brought him deeper, closer, but she seemed to have found a level rather than her peak. It took all of his will to hold his own release back. "Brenna!" he gasped. "Please!"

She stopped abruptly and went still, staring down at him, panting, her face flushed and glowing, her loose braid prettily disheveled. With her miraculous eyes locked on his mundane ones, she brushed her hand over his face, combing her fingers through his beard.

"I love you."

He smiled at her whispered words. "And it is the greatest thing I have known in my life that you do."

"Make me see our stars."

It was the way she described her release, and Vali was charmed, as always, by its sweet innocence.

"Hold on to me, shieldmaiden. I will bring you all the stars the gods ever put in the sky." When she hooked her arms around his neck, he changed his hold on her, slid his arms under her thighs, and then stood. The move drove him in deeper, and he grunted with the effort to hold back.

Brenna gasped, and her eyes flared.

"Make yourself loose. Let me move you."

She nodded, and Vali felt her take a long, deep breath and soften her body. Then he lifted her away and brought her back, slowly, rocking his hips at the same time. He saw the fire catch in her and knew that she would peak. Thus freed from his torment, he abandoned restraint and slammed their bodies together until the room resounded with their mingled shouts, and they released together.

Spent, Vali could no longer lock his knees, and he fumbled clumsily to the bed, just managing to lay Brenna down gently before he collapsed at her side. He set his hand on her belly, which swelled and receded with each of her heaving gasps.

Brenna looked down at his hand. "I wonder what he thinks of us."

Vali chuckled and bent to press his lips to the mound where his child lived. "That he comes to a family full of love and will make it even fuller."

~oOo~

"If the winter doesn't break, come summer, I fear we will leave many round bellies behind." Leif sighed and turned from the scene at the back of the room, where young Harald and Sten paid enthusiastic attention to a comely young village woman, whose breasts were bared and whose skirts had been pushed high, and who was audibly content to be on such display.

Leif, Vali, and several other men lazed before the hearth in a room off the hall. They'd never been able to understand the purpose of the room, and none of the villagers understood it, either. It had held only a table carved with strange markings. Now it held furs and mats and made a comfortable place to rest and converse. Smaller than the hall, it was easier to warm, and the hearth was large and welcoming. It had become a room where people went to enjoy company and ease. It felt to Vali more like home than anywhere else in Estland.

Anywhere else but the rooms he shared with his wife, that was. Nowhere had ever been such a home as that.

As her belly grew, Brenna had begun to tire quickly and had taken to retiring early each night. He let her go up alone so that she would sleep. When he went up with her, they rarely slept right away. Her interest in the pleasures of their joining remained voracious.

Though the winter was aging, it had not lost its vigor. Yet another storm had dropped fresh snow nearly to the tops of their boots. The drifts around the castle reached the windows on the second level. They had dug a corridor all the way to the village, so that they could convey supplies to the teams of men who kept the livestock, and so that each team could be relieved for a few days of warmth and comfort in the castle.

Other than that work and training, and repairing damage from the cumbersome heft of the accumulated snows, the men had grown idle and bored. With little else to do, they had been drinking heavily and coupling as often as possible with any woman willing.

The women were much less bored, still tasked with the care and feeding of the group and the tending of the castle, but they didn't seem to mind the lavish attentions being paid them.

At Leif's words, however, Olga's head shot up, and she turned a fierce, dark look on him from where she stood near the fire. Vali was surprised to see Leif catch her look and turn away, abashed. She gathered up her skirts in a huff and stalked back, catching the arm of the younger woman and dragging her away from her admirers and out of the room.

Vali saw Leif's regard follow Olga through the room and out. He knew they'd spent time together; she had taught Leif her language, and he had helped her refine her understanding of theirs, and Olga had charge of the castle, so she spoke often with all of those who had stepped into the lead. But now Vali wondered if there were more to them than friendship and cooperation.

"Are you and she...?" He let those words stand for the whole question.

Leif shook his head. "No. She is a fine woman and beautiful. I care. But we leave soon, perhaps as soon as two months, and I would not take her and then discard her."

There was more in Leif's tone, so Vali said nothing, and waited to see if Leif would say more.

He did. Staring at the fire, he added, "I would ask her to come back with me, but she is too fragile for our world."

"Fragile? Olga?" She was slight in stature, yes. But Vali had seen her put her hands deep into the belly of a man to close a bleeding wound. She had survived the horror their camp had been for the captives, and she had made herself an indispensible part of their life here.

She was their equal—more than that, she was their friend. 'Fragile' was not how Vali saw her. No more fragile than Brenna.

"Her bones are like a bird's. When I put my hand around her arm, I feel I could break her with a squeeze. She is not made for our world."

There was true regret in Leif's voice, and Vali was moved. He thought of how he would feel if he would somehow be separated from Brenna—how he'd have felt even before they had been wed. "You could stay here, with her."

Leif turned to Vali, frowning. "No. Åke will not give up seasoned raiders. He will bring peasants to settle here, and he'll leave a younger son to govern. Ulv, I'd guess, who is smart but too gentle to make a life raiding. His warriors he will send off to find new treasure."

"You speak as if it will be only Åke who returns. I am here for Snorri, remember. I hope the alliance between them has held."

"And if it has not, then you and I are friends no more." Leif looked back at the fire. "And Brenna's position is difficult in any case."

158

He needed say no more; his worries about how Åke would take losing Brenna had been a regular refrain for months.

Vali nodded; it was a thought that lurked always against the back wall of his mind: he had taken Åke's talisman from him. She was no longer the jarl's pet. Now she was Vali's wife. He had married her and seeded her, and she would bear his child. It would be years before she might pick up a shield again. In fact, she might never. Here in Estland, she might always be a farmer's wife.

And Vali a farmer. Love Brenna as he did, willing as he was to see her happy at any cost, the thought of living the balance of his days as a farmer unsettled Vali's heart. Would he be able to make a good home for his family in that way? Would he be contented in his own heart?

They had told no one of their plan to stay, and Vali felt sure that it was news better left unsaid. Not all of the raiders had fully embraced their amity with the villagers, and Leif was right—their friendship balanced on the narrow point of the alliance between two jarls a sea away, two jarls who had warred often. To know that two of their great warriors planned to give up their home could well cause trouble. Right now, in the quiet within this savage winter, the only thing in strife was nature itself. They were at peace; they had friends, a home. His shieldmaiden had found a home, and he would not risk it while he could avoid doing so.

The strife would come. They would need to fight for the life she wanted, the home they had found together. They both knew it, so it didn't need to be said. Not now, not yet.

Vali finished his mead and set his cup away. He stood and laid his hand on Leif's shoulder. "I will see you in the morning. My friend."

Leif nodded, still staring into the fire, and Vali went up to bed.

He missed his wife.

11

"Bring the heddle tighter, or the weave won't be smooth." Olga put her hand under Brenna's and pushed up, encouraging her to do as she'd suggested.

Brenna knew how to weave. She'd been taught, at least, years before. But she loathed it. Nothing in all the worlds was more boring than standing at a loom moving strands of wool together. Her attention wandered within minutes, and then she had a knotty rag that no one would want to wear.

Woman's work was dreary stuff. She didn't mind cooking; that could be made to be interesting—it was even physical at times—and she felt pride when the people she'd fed enjoyed what she'd prepared. But cleaning and weaving? Most days, she'd have happily taken her sword to the loom.

It would be better when the winter was over, and she and Vali could begin to plan their new life. When she had her own home to make and land to work, and a new babe to raise. Now, trapped inside the gloomy walls of the castle, cleaning and cooking—and weaving—for a herd of ungrateful men, Brenna was out of temper quite often.

But she wanted to be good at these things. She knew that her days as a shieldmaiden were interrupted, if not finished. It would be years before she could leave her child and sail away, and she would not wish war on her home so that she might fight near it. She had married, and her husband had planted his seed. Now she was a wife; soon she would be a mother. She wanted to make her name as proudly in those pursuits as she had made it battle.

She could not, however, pretend that her new work was as interesting as her old.

The worst of it was that she had been closed off from discussions and planning—about patrols, about repairs, about preparations for the summer. No one had begrudged her her place as a leader among the raiders as long as her belly had been flat, but as soon as the babe had made himself known, Leif, Orm, all the men—even Vali—had stopped making a seat for her at their talks.

When she'd confronted her husband about it, he had been sympathetic—and unmovable. Her job, as he saw it, was to grow their child. Her attentions should be there, he said, and on learning the language of the place she wished to settle. The concerns of the castle and the village were no longer hers. The people who could do that work should have the say.

And she'd had no strong rebuttal. She'd been relegated to the kitchen and the loom room.

While they worked, Olga and she practiced the Estland tongue, and Olga assured her that she was improving. Brenna didn't believe it, however. When Olga asked her to translate a word, she could usually do it, but when she tried to understand the Estland women around her, she still caught only half of their meaning. At best.

Her mind did not want to know more words than it already knew. Her parents had spoken often of their fear when she was small, because she had not spoken any word until she'd had four years. It had lent credence to people's belief in her strangeness. Perhaps, though, she simply was stupid in this way.

She shoved at the heddle in a fit of pique. "I hate this loom!"

"Say it our way."

Brenna gave Olga her warrior's look, even growling a little, but Olga was unmoved. She simply waited, her expression impassive.

She was fairly certain she understood the word for hate. "*Vihkan.*"

"Say what you said. All of it."

"*Ma vihkan...*" She had no idea what the word for 'loom' was. She had probably heard it, here in the loom room, scores of times, but it wasn't in her head at all. "*Ma vihkan...seda...*"

"*Kudumismasin.*"

Brenna gaped at Olga. How was she supposed to learn a language that could turn a word so simple as 'loom' into that?

Before she could continue her tantrum—lately, she had grown adept at throwing tantrums—the babe kicked her sharply at her bladder, and she clutched at her belly. "Oh!"

Olga laid her hands on Brenna's belly, too. "He moves much today."

Nodding, Brenna smiled down at her rounded midsection. "More even than usual."

It had only been a few weeks since she'd felt the first flutters of his movement, but since then, her belly had gotten noticeably larger and her son moved all the time. Even Vali could feel him now.

"I believe it *is* a son you carry—you cradle him low inside you." Olga put her arm around Brenna's waist and led her to the door. "Enough weaving. Let us sit in the kitchen. I will pour you milk and you can learn more food words. If you know those, mayhap you won't starve."

163

"You are not so funny as you think." Brenna scowled at her friend, who returned it with a wry smirk.

"Funny is what?"

Thinking for a moment as they walked toward the kitchen, Brenna answered, "*Veider?*"

Olga laughed. "Maybe so, if you meant to say I am not strange. *Naljakas* is amusing."

"Your language has too many ways of saying things."

"That is so we always say what we mean."

~oOo~

By evening, the babe pulled heavily on Brenna's back, and she had taken to retiring early, not long after the last meal, leaving Vali to drink and laugh with the other men. She had learned to enjoy the company of others, and even sometimes to join in with their jokes, but she still often found it difficult to be always in the thick of the commotion. All her life, she'd been on the outside edge, and although she had been lonely, that distance had become the thing she understood.

Here, she'd been accepted. Here, she had friends, real friends, people who sought her out and wished to converse with her. People who knew her. It was good. She was happy, for the first time in her life, truly happy. And exhausted. Her moods were sometimes erratic, which they had never been before. Her brain could not keep up with so much energy turned her way.

Olga told her it was the babe, that she would feel steadier and sharper when her son no longer drew on her body so completely. Brenna hoped that was true. She could hear laughter below, and she would have liked to have enjoyed that good humor more, now that she was Brenna and not the God's-Eye.

She had washed and dressed in her sleeping shift and was unbraiding her hair when the door opened and Vali came in. Usually, she was already abed when he came up; sometimes, he came in smelling strongly of mead and fell to bed, and then into a stupor, with barely an affectionate pat of her shoulder.

He was not drunk tonight, however, and Brenna worried that something was amiss.

"Are you all right? I didn't think you'd come to bed so early."

He came to her and laid his big hands over her belly. "You seem pensive tonight. I worry. Are you well?" He rubbed over their son. "Is he?"

His loving attention eased her turbulent mood somewhat. Covering his hands with hers, she answered, "We are well. I'm only...*väsinud*?"

"That is good! Not that you are weary, but that is the right word."

"You condescend." She tried to pull away, but he held her.

"No, my love. I know the language is hard for you. I mean to encourage. I'm pleased that you keep trying. Are you weary because of the child?" He eased his hands around her swell. "It cannot be much longer."

"Olga thinks two months more at least. She counts from when I first felt him. Two months feels long."

The babe kicked as if he were agreeing, and Vali grinned and dropped to his knees. "Hello, my son. Be kind to your mother. She makes you a good place to grow strong." He pressed his mouth to her belly and sucked, drawing the linen of her shift into his mouth.

She laid her hands on his head. "Vali, I would like to ride tomorrow. Not far—only to the village—and not fast. But outdoors, in the air."

"No, Brenna. It cannot be good for you or him. And the winter has been harsh. You are safe and warm inside the castle." He stood and led her to a chair near the fire. Although she wanted to stand toe to toe with him and have this matter out, she was glad to sit. He pulled a chair close and sat before her, holding her hands.

She hadn't given up the fight, however. "Winter is easing. The weather has finally broken. We've had no storm in weeks, and today there was thaw. I will be warm. There has been no threat from any quarter. I will be safe. Warm and safe. I must get out in the world and move around. I must, or I'll go mad."

"The thaw today means ice tomorrow. And how would you mean to mount a horse in your state?"

"I'm no weakling."

"I don't mean that you are weak. I mean that there is a child in your way."

Done with debating irrelevant points with him, Brenna huffed and sat straight. "I don't need your warrant, husband. I am a freewoman. All I need do is wait for you to leave on patrol, and then act as I will."

He dropped her hands and stood abruptly. "No, Brenna. If you make a threat like that, I will put a guard on you."

She stood, too, much more slowly. "Choose a man you like not much for a guard, then, because he will be sorely injured before the day is out. You cannot govern me."

"Why would you take such a risk? With our child? With yourself? You are precious, Brenna. Do you not see?"

"I see that I am locked away, pushed off to the looms, when once I had place at your side. I see that you treat me like a vessel for our son, when once you treated me like a warrior and your equal. I see that *you* do not see *that*." To emphasize her point, she struck him in the chest with the flat of her hand.

The anger smoothed from his brow, and he cupped her face in his hand. "I mean to do none of that. I mean only to love you and keep you safe. But you know that the voice belongs with those who do the work, and you know that you cannot—that you are *unable*—to do the work you once did. You have more important work than that. You also know that it is unsafe, for our child and for you, to mount a horse in the state you are in."

He was right; she knew he was. She wanted to stomp her foot at him, but he was right. So, with a dejected sigh, she gave up and wended her way back down to the seat of the chair.

"Forgive me. I've been in a temper today. I truly do think I'm going mad."

He sat again as well. "You're not going mad, my love. I'm assured that this is part of making a child."

She rolled her eyes. He talked to everyone about her.

He leaned in as if he had a secret for her ears only. "Tord and Sigvalde are taking the sledge to the village tomorrow, bringing supplies. Would a ride on a sledge between two foolish young men suffice to get you out into the world and improve your temper?"

As he spoke, Brenna grinned happily, real relief expanding her chest. She threw her arms around his neck. "Yes! Yes, that would be wonderful! Yes!"

"Still not yet a day without a smile like that. I think I am the one of us with the touch of the gods."

~oOo~

The day rose clear and cold, and the night's chill had turned the previous day's thaw into a glassy shell over all the land. The bright sun in a cloudless sky made stars leap from the sparkling snow into one's eyes. Beautiful and blinding.

They had lost half the snowpack in that single day, and the river rushed loudly, swollen with the fresh cold water of the melt.

Vali, Leif, and a few of the other men planned to mount their intrepid horses and ride north to patrol the land nearest Prince Toomas's territory. They had kept up patrols as they could through the winter, and with the weather warming, they meant to be even more vigilant.

Brenna had woken in excellent spirits, buoyed by the prospect of a day spent in the fresh air. Since she'd been a freewoman, she had spent her winters alone in the woods. This winter trapped inside a stone castle, weeks without real daylight or fresh air, amongst a throng of other souls, and with her belly growing large and changing all she knew about her body, herself, and her life, had taxed her mind more even than she'd realized.

After a waking romp, Vali taking her from behind like a beast and making her scream into the furs, they had joined their people to break their fast.

Now, with the horses for the patrol party saddled and the sledge horse harnessed, Vali had Tord and Sigvalde trapped under his great arms and was speaking to them in earnest. Standing near the sledge, Brenna watched, amused. She expected that the smaller, younger men were being threatened with no end of doom should any discomfort befall her during the day.

He clapped them hard on their shoulders, making them both stumble forward, and then turned and came directly to her, his serious scowl still in place.

"Be mindful, shieldmaiden," he instructed as he reached her and took her hands. "A ride only. Let the pups do their work."

"I will. I'll not be reckless with our child, Vali."

"And yet you would have ridden."

She let loose an aggravated huff. He had made his point. Again and again. "I shall sit meekly in the sledge like the helpless female you think I am."

"Good." He grinned then, and she answered it with a smile. As he brushed his thumb over her cheekbone, he added, "I wish you a happy day, my love. One that brings peace back to your mind. I would that I could join you."

"Perhaps we can go out another time."

"Perhaps."

She knew he was humoring her, and that she likely would not win from him another day like this until after their son was in her arms, but she didn't mind. She was out of the castle and wouldn't see its cursed stone walls again until past midday.

He picked her up with his broad hands under her arms and lifted her high, setting her on the seat of the sledge. As she scooted her cumbersome body to the center, he went to the cargo they would pull and came back with a heavy fur.

"I will swoon from overheating," she complained as he tucked it around her legs.

"If so, you will at least be resting." He leaned in and kissed her, catching her face in his hands and plunging his tongue deeply, stealing, from her lips and from her mind, any further protests.

She traced the nick in his tongue with her own, as she always did, loving that evidence of their first connection. He groaned and broke away, touching his forehead to hers. "Be safe, little mother. My love."

"And you. I love you."

With a press of his lips to her brow, he stepped back, and two pale, anxious raiders came forward to take their places at her sides.

~oOo~

Well cowed by whatever Vali had said to them, Tord and Sigvalde treated Brenna as if she were made of glass, jumping to her aid if she so much as shifted her seat. They were unusually quiet, as well. She had expected to be irritated by their nonstop chatter, but instead she might as well have sat between two posts. Two overly solicitous posts. Despite her normal preference for quiet, Brenna found it awkward to be sitting so near two usually garrulous men who had nothing to say.

The ride to the village was not long; a sledge like this could comfortably make the trip there and back thrice in a day. Brenna decided to pretend she was alone after all. She turned her mind inward, to her thoughts, while she released her body to experience the beauty of the day—the bright sun, the sparkling snow, the brisk cold, and the occasional peep of a bird, the clearest sign yet that the angry winter was stomping off to sulk elsewhere.

Once they got to the village, Tord and Sigvalde became more like themselves. They had friends who were keeping the village and tending most of the animals, and there was a jolly reunion, even though it had only been a week or so since this team had taken over the village. They spent the midday at a cozy fire in a small hut, enjoying skause and bread and mead—and goat's milk for Brenna, who had not been able to abide mead since the babe. Though all the men around her treated her like they might break her, they japed and laughed around her, and Brenna felt contented. The babe had been quiet in the sledge, but he kicked and rolled while she sat among their friends, as if he, too, were enjoying himself.

After the meal, the men unloaded the supplies. Brenna behaved herself and stayed at the fire until Tord came and told her they were ready to be off. Walking back to the sledge, she felt melancholy. Already her good day was ending.

The ride back, however, was much more amusing. Their time in the village had loosened Tord and Sigvalde's tongues, and they bantered back and forth, seeming to have forgotten that a woman sat between them in body while they bickered about one who sat between them in spirit.

"She wants more man than you, my friend. She deserves more."

"And you think you are the one to offer more? I've seen your little maggot that shrinks into your belly in the cold." Sigvalde moved the reins to one hand so that he could hold up his little finger and make it curl down into a nub.

Tord's only response was a rude gesture. When Brenna chuckled, they both looked surprised and then joined her in laughter.

171

"You know less than you think about women if you think what's in your breeches is all that matters," Brenna offered, smirking.

"Ah, Tord. We have an opportunity here that we've nearly missed, to have the God's-Eye give us wisdom about women."

Brenna stiffened at the hated name, but she didn't let it show. It was rare to hear it now, and she knew Sigvalde meant it in jest. So she lifted the brow above her right eye and let him have her God's-Eye glare.

His eyes flared in real shock, and she regretted her failed attempt to join in the joke. But then an arrow zinged past her and buried itself in Sigvalde's left eye. He flew backward, out of the sledge, taking the reins with him.

Pulled sharply off course by Sigvalde's dead body landing on the hard snow, the draft horse screamed and stumbled. As he struggled to keep his hooves under him, another arrow sank into his rump, and he screamed again and went wild.

"Brenna!" Tord caught hold of her arm and tried to shove her down to the floor of the sledge, but she couldn't hide in a runaway sledge. That would get her killed just as easily as the arrows. She fought against his pushing hands, and then they went slack—he'd been struck, too. A fearsomely thick arrow had come through his chest.

He was alive, though, gasping and sinking to the floor. Brenna grabbed for his still-sheathed sword, fighting the violent heaves of the racing sledge, and drew it free.

Leaning over the front of the sledge, trying to protect her child and stay low in case their attackers still followed, Brenna worked to slice through the hard leather of the harness. Before she could get more than halfway through the first strap, the horse, now with several arrows buried in his flesh, stumbled and fell, and the sledge went over, threatening to flip end over end before landing on its side.

Brenna was thrown clear, landing hard on her back. A great gush of liquid came from her body and soaked her legs. She tried to lift her head to see if it was blood, but her head would not leave the snow.

She couldn't move at all. Her breath would not come, either. She stared up at the clear blue sky and tried desperately to make her lungs work. They could not be far from the castle. If she could shout, they might even be close enough to hear, on this bright, still day, with the snow hard enough to bounce the sound.

Just as she managed to suck in an excruciating breath, a man in armor came into her field of vision. He stared down at her and then aimed an arrow at her head.

Brenna saw him note her condition then, and he faltered, blinking. With the arrow still nocked, he dropped his aim. She tried to think of the words she needed to say. "Please—do not harm my child," she gasped in her own tongue. "*Palun! Laps,*" she managed. 'Please' and 'child': the only Estland words she could remember.

He blinked again. Then a male voice beyond her sight shouted words she couldn't understand, and the man above her aimed again.

This time, he let loose his arrow.

12

The patrol was uneventful, as usual, with no sign of any incursion from Toomas's men. The day was fine, a bright, clear day, the cold enough to keep the snow from turning into soup as it had been the day before, but not so frigid that riding was dangerous or even uncomfortable. Not for the likes of them.

Vali was in good humor. Brenna's spirits had been lighter that morning than in weeks as she anticipated an outing to the village, and, although he could not help but send his thoughts her way throughout the day, he was glad he'd been able to offer her a solution to her restlessness. He hoped she and the babe were well. Before they had left, he had impressed upon Tord and Sigvalde the necessity of his family's health for their own.

In the afternoon, as the sun began to sink low toward the earth and bring the heavier cold of evening, Vali, Leif, and the others rode through the castle gate. Immediately, he noticed with some mild surprise that the sledge wasn't on the grounds. The supply run to the village should have returned before them. Perhaps they'd been back so long that the sledge had already been stowed.

As Vali dismounted, Leif said, "Vali." Only that. Vali turned in the direction of his friend's nod and saw Orm coming out of the main castle doors, walking directly to them, his expression serious. Three other men walked behind him, armed and dressed for riding.

Something was wrong.

"We're preparing to send a party out just now," the old man reported as he stood before Vali and Leif. He lifted his eyes to Vali's. "The sledge has not returned."

Without waiting for another word, Vali leapt back into the saddle, as did Leif and the others. He turned his horse and kicked him into a gallop at once. He heard the hooves of other riders' horses following, but he paid them no mind. They would follow or not, but he was going for his wife.

They came across Tord first, just as they left sight of the castle, and Vali tasted the copper of battle rage at the sight of his clansman and what it meant for Brenna.

Tord reeled through the snow, dragging his sword, leaving a red ribbon of blood behind him. He had an arrow through his chest, and when he saw them, he collapsed sidelong into the snow.

Vali jumped from his mount and ran to the young man. "What happened?! Where is she?!" he demanded as he dropped to his knees and grabbed Tord's shoulder."

Tord groaned and spat blood. Gasping, forcing the words from his mouth, he answered, "Beset. Need...help. She's...she...the tree. Halfway tree...covered her."

A pine tree with a massive base marked the midway point of the journey to and from the village.

"Does she live?! Tord, does she live?" His mind flashed him a vision of his wife lying dead in the snow, sinking into a pool of her own blood, taking their child away with her. Leaving him. His stomach rolled. Without meaning to, but unable to help himself, he shook Tord's shoulder, and the boy gave a weak scream. Leif, kneeling at Vali's side, laid a steadying hand on his arm but said nothing.

"Yes...when I...left. Hurt but alive. Can't move. Sigvalde...Valhalla." As Vali shot back to his feet, Tord waved his hand feebly. "Not…Toomas. Flag…the other." Tord closed his eyes and said no more.

Ivan. The one they had discounted as too small and weak to fight them, especially in the winter. They had turned their attention and their resources to the obvious threat from the north, the nearer, stronger, richer, better-provisioned prince, and they had left their southern flank exposed. Indeed, lately they had rarely mentioned Ivan in their planning at all.

None of the raiders who stayed in Estland were real planners. The leaders among them were leaders during battle, not before it. They executed the plans of other men. Of them all, Brenna had been the most insightful strategist, the best planner. She might well have seen what they had missed, but they had closed her out of their discussions because she was with child.

And their blindness had put her in harm's way. Her and the child she carried.

Vali had no time to let that irony sicken him. He nodded and ran back to his horse. As he mounted, he heard Leif tell the others, "They didn't move on the castle. They might have beset the village. Sten, get Tord to Olga. Orm, take the others to the village. Be ready to fight. I go with Vali."

Vali didn't wait. He mounted his horse and he rode.

~oOo~

At the dying horse and the overturned sledge, Vali dropped to the ground, barely taking the time to slow his horse, and ran past the wreckage. He found Brenna, motionless under the fur he'd settled over her legs that morning, lying just beyond the halfway tree.

He dived to his knees as he reached her and pulled back the fur. She was curled on her side, and she flinched hard as he laid his hands on her. Her eyes opened and looked wildly around.

Relief warred with worry. She was alive. *She was alive.* But in the waning light of the day, he could see that her color was wrong—she was pale and blue—and she had been lying long in the snow.

"Vali?"

"I'm here, my love. I'm here."

"Help me. The babe. Something's wrong."

The fur moved, sliding down Brenna's body, and Vali looked up to see Leif pulling it away.

Brenna was lying in melting snow stained red with blood. Her hangerock was stiff with the cold and stained dark as well. There was an arrow embedded in the ground not far from her head, but Vali could discern no wound.

The babe. The blood was their child. Just then, Brenna tightened into a coil and cried out in pain. The sound was weak but still agonizing, and it went on for an eternity. The specter of his brave, stoic shieldmaiden in pain so intense that she would scream made Vali's stomach roll again.

Then she stopped, gasping in a stilted breath, and another, and another. Her body relaxed slightly.

"Something wrong is happening." In her tone, he heard her pleading for his help.

"We have to get her to Olga." Leif had crouched down with them.

"Brenna, can you not stand?"

She shook her head. "My chest. Something is wrong in my chest. But the babe. Something wrong is happening to him. I think he's coming. But it's not his time."

Vali realized then that she didn't know about the blood. "I'll get you to Olga." He slid his hands under her body. When he lifted her, she screamed again, feebly, as if the effort of the scream hurt her more, and a thin trail of blood seeped from the corner of her mouth.

As he stood with his wife in his arms, he met Leif's eyes, and they both, having the same idea, turned to the sledge. No. To right it would take too much time, and to free the harness from the dying—no, dead—horse would take longer. He would have to ride back to the castle with Brenna in his arms.

"I'm sorry, my love. I think I will cause you more pain to get you home."

She shook her head. "No matter. I need Olga. She will fix it."

Leif took her in his arms while Vali mounted. As he leaned down to lift her into his arms again, she made that frail, long scream, her body pulling inward. Leif held her until, again, it eased.

When Vali could again cradle her against his chest, she had swooned.

Leif mounted, and they turned back and raced to the castle.

~oOo~

Olga met him on the castle grounds. She was covered in blood already—Tord's, Vali guessed—but she ran up to him as he handed Brenna to Jaan and jumped from his horse.

179

"To bed! Right away!" Olga's command brooked no argument.

Taking his wife back, Vali nodded and hurried inside. Olga followed, calling out to the women in the Estland tongue. Too focused on Brenna to translate, Vali nonetheless understood that she was calling for supplies and giving instructions.

Once in their chamber, Vali laid Brenna down. She had not woken again on the ride, although a few times more, her body had clenched, becoming like stone in his hold. When he had eased her from his arms, he crouched at the side of their bed and stroked her hair back from her forehead. She was so cold, and her color had the dusky blue of death. But she breathed. He could hear her. He could see the small bubbles of it in the pink froth at the corner of her mouth.

The women were undressing her, pulling off her boots and underclothes. Olga came and wedged herself between Vali and Brenna.

She pulled her hand back and slapped his wife. Hard. Then she did it again. Vali leapt to his feet and grabbed the small woman by the back of her dress. He yanked her back and pushed her against the wall. "What do you do?! She is hurt enough already!"

"Your child is coming. If she doesn't wake and help him, you will lose them both."

He stared down at her, a mix of unfamiliar emotions churning his blood. The most potent of them, the one that weakened his legs, was fear. "It's too soon."

"It is." Olga nodded, her brown eyes fixed firmly on him, and he heard the words she was not speaking. His son would not survive. It was Brenna she was trying to save. "Let me go, Vali."

He let her go.

She stood straight and went immediately to his wife's side. Without facing him again, she said, "Now go. This room at this time is no place for a man."

"I'll not leave them." He put all the resolve he had into those words. He would not be moved from this room.

At that she did turn, and she let those eyes bore into him again. "Very well. Then be useful. She stirs. Come keep her with us."

Vali needed no further exhortation. He nodded and went to his knees at the side of the bed, catching Brenna's cold, slack hand in his. Her eyelids fluttered, and a spasm of pain crossed her brow.

"Be with me, shieldmaiden. You are brave and strong. Open your eyes."

She did, and her head flopped in his direction. "Something's wrong," she whispered, her tongue pushing pink froth onto her lips. "Wrong."

"Brenna." Olga was at his side. "When you feel the pain, do not fight what your body wants. Vali will help you. So will I."

"Olga. It's wrong."

Her voice was so weak, so thready, it was as if she spoke already from beyond this world. Her eyelids fluttered closed again, and Vali clutched her hand. "Brenna! Stay!"

She cried out—that weak, kittenish cry that conveyed so much helpless, hopeless pain—and Olga said, "Vali, lift her to sit up. Now."

He did so, sliding his arm under her back, but when he pushed her upward, she screamed again. "It hurts her!"

"It all hurts her. Ignore that and help her. Brenna! Brenna, heed me. Bear down. Heed your body and bear down."

She did. Her body contracted, her brow pulled tight, and she made a harrowing wail. Olga, with an expression of perfect, serious focus, put her hands far up Brenna's skirts.

Then Brenna went completely slack, and Olga sighed and shook her head. When she pulled back, her hands and arms were bloody.

Brenna's blood. Or their child's.

"Vali, please. It is too late for anything but this way. She must help. Wake her."

He gazed on his wife, so weak in his arms. He was losing her. But he would not, *could* not strike her. So he put his mouth to her ear and spoke to her.

"Brenna, stay with me. Be strong. Fight, shieldmaiden. Find your fury and your fire and come back. Please." He clutched her sword hand and lifted it. "Raise your sword and fight this. No pain can best the God's-Eye. Odin's own shieldmaiden. This will not be what lays you low."

While he spoke, an explosion of thunder rocked the stone walls, and lightning lit the cracks through the narrow windows, shuttered against the cold.

"The gods have seen us, Brenna. Thor has answered. Come now, and do your part."

She woke with a start and a cry, and she bore down. Olga leaned in again. Vali felt mad with the need to take her pain away. A need he could not meet.

As before, when her body eased, Brenna went under. Her head dropped back, and she fell slack in his arms. But this time, Olga didn't pull away, and two of the other women leaned in as well. They were busy under his wife's skirts, between her legs.

He heard a faint sound, like the cry of a mouse.

"*Ta hingab*," one of the women, Anna, muttered to Olga.

"He breathes?" Vali laid Brenna down gently and stood up. "He is born? He lives?"

Still working, Olga made a sharp motion with one arm and nodded to Anna, who lifted a bloody bundle from between Brenna's legs.

Then Olga turned sad eyes on Vali. "He lives. Vali, he will not for long. He is too small and was not done being made. But for these moments, yes, you have a son. There is no shame in turning from this pain. Anna will tend him well until his end."

He did not know the customs of Olga's people in matters such as this, but he knew those of his own, of Brenna's. A child like this, born wrongly or too soon, would be killed or taken out into the woods and left to die. Their world was a harsh one and had no quarter for frailty or deformity.

But that *pain* Olga had spoken of was his son. His firstborn child, who was alive. He would not turn from him. "No. Bring him to me."

"Vali…"

He held out his hands. "Bring him."

Olga nodded to Anna, who, with evident fear, carried the bundle of bloody linens to Vali and set it in his hands. The cord that had bound mother and child together dangled from the bundle, a knot of wool tied around its end.

It was no more than if Anna had laid only the cloths themselves in his hands, so light was his child, who fit easily across his two palms. The bundle moved, and Vali brought it to his chest, cradling it in a way he had not known he knew.

So small. He pulled the cloth back and saw a tiny, perfect face and a tiny, perfect hand. His skin seemed translucent; even in the light of the torches and candles, Vali could see the threads of veins across the back of that wee hand, and over the lids of his closed eyes.

The little face screwed up, and his son made another of those mouse-like cries. At the same time, thunder and lightning shook the sky. Thunder and lightning in winter was rare indeed. A man born on such a night would have his story told. Perhaps it was a sign that, small though he was, his son would thrive.

"Thor is with us tonight, my son. You will be called Thorvaldr."

Vali could feel Olga's eyes on him. He met them and saw her concern. He did not care. His son was alive in his arms and would be named.

"He is called Thorvaldr."

Olga gave him a gentle smile and a nod, then went back to her work. The women still tended to Brenna, who had not woken again. Her color had gone very grey, and her jaw had slackened so that her mouth was open.

"Olga…"

"She has lost a great deal of blood, Vali, and her ribs are…*murtud?*"

It was unusual these days for Olga to have a failure of language. Vali didn't know the word she meant, either.

184

She huffed. "They are injured. This is why she bleeds from her mouth. Bringing the babe did that no help. She must have time to replenish her blood so that she can heal. We will do what we can. If your gods are with you, perhaps they will help her."

Vali held his son and watched the women work to save his wife. He wanted to be near her, but there was no room now for him at her bedside. He didn't know what to do. His heart was cracking apart inside his chest.

He could lose them both on this night. He likely would.

No. They were not alone. They were Brenna God's-Eye and Vali Storm-Wolf, beloved of the gods, and they had brought forth a son.

Thor, he began silently. *I entreat you. Save my family.*

Thorvaldr, his son, made another of those tiny cries, this one weaker than the others. Vali turned his attention to the feather-light bundle and pulled the linens back a bit more. A frail chest, showing each minute filament of rib, throbbed with shallow heaves. As he watched, the pace of his son's labored breaths slowed.

And then stopped.

He stared at that little chest for long moments, willing it to move again, but it did not. The tiny hand lay inert. The son he and Brenna had made together had left them already. His eyes burning and blurring, Vali turned to Brenna, but he couldn't see her through the women tending her.

Would he now lose her, as well?

"Brenna." It was only a whisper, but he couldn't hold it back. "Please."

Lightning struck again, a violent crack of light that brought the thunder of Thor's hammer down at the very same time and left a burning in the air.

"WHAT?" Vali shouted, startling the women. "WHAT DO YOU WANT OF ME?"

Without thinking, he ran to the door and tore it open. Still holding his child in his arms, wrapped in that bundle of cloths soaked in his mother's blood, Vali ran through the corridor, down the dark stairs, through the castle, out the heavy main doors, and into the night.

Snow was falling heavily, in sheets of flakes so large they made the night opaque. The wind blustered from the north and drove the snow toward the south.

Into that storm, Vali ran out to the center of the castle grounds. He pulled the linens away and let them fall to the snow at his feet. Then he raised his arms and held the naked body of his son over his head, toward the stormy sky. "HE IS THORVALDR, AND HE IS YOURS. YOU HAVE TAKEN HIM ALREADY. WHAT MORE WOULD YOU HAVE OF ME? WHAT GREATER SACRIFICE WOULD YOU HAVE THAN MY CHILD? WOULD YOU TAKE MY LOVE AS WELL? BETTER YOU TAKE MY HEART FROM MY CHEST!"

He felt a hand on his back, and he pulled his son to his chest and whirled around with a vicious growl. Leif stood there, stalwart.

"Vali, my good friend. My brother. You tempt the gods."

"I care not! Let them do what they will!"

"Your woman yet lives. You mean to give up before she has?"

With no answer to that, Vali stood and stared, his chest heaving with each angry gasp of icy, snowy air.

Leif held out his hands. "Let me take your son. I will see to it that he is treated with care until you are ready to say goodbye."

Vali pulled away. "Brenna will want him."

"No. It will cause her more pain, when she struggles already with so much. Of this I know. She awaited a child she could nourish. And she is in no state now to say goodbye. Your attention should be with her."

Leif lifted his hands again, and this time Vali set his son in them. He bent and picked up the linens from the snow, and he covered his son's body.

Then he walked back into the castle, through the crowd that had amassed behind him, and went to keep a vigil at his wife's side.

He knew not what he would do if it was a deathbed he went to.

~oOo~

Snow fell for two full days and three nights, burying the castle again. The dawn broke bright on the third morning, and it was the first time the sun had shone since the morning Brenna had taken a sledge ride to the village and their lives had broken apart.

And still she had not woken.

Tord was dead; he had not lived through that first night, but he had told them what he could before he could say no more. Sigvalde was dead. The men who had attacked the sledge had been part of a band of Prince Ivan's soldiers. They had overrun the village, killing the five men there and all the livestock. Orm and his men had come upon the aftermath. Two of the men who'd been in the village had lived long enough to tell them the story.

They had been fortunate. The harsh winter had brought all of the villagers into the castle, and the women and children and most of the men still lived there—all but the team whose rotation it had been to tend the bulk of the livestock.

The harsh winter had saved most of the villagers, and the latest storm, which had brought fresh snow above Vali's knees and drifts up to the second windows, had saved the castle from attack while it was distracted by its losses.

But the storm had ended, and the sun shone again. When Brenna came back to him, Vali would go off and seek the vengeance that his soul demanded.

That morning, while Olga opened the shutters to bring in sunshine and a moment of cold, clean air, Brenna finally opened her eyes and kept them open.

Lying at her side after his own short and fitful sleep had ended, Vali watched her, stroking her fair hair. He saw her come to wakefulness and take a deeper breath. She cut it off with a small grunt of pain and then turned her head and really focused on him.

"My love. My love." He leaned over and kissed her cheek. "How do you feel?"

"I ache," she croaked. She gave him a smile and pushed her hand downward, over her belly, in a gesture that had become habit in the weeks that their son had swelled her.

He watched her true awakening play over her face, and his heart broke yet more.

"Vali? Where? Is he...?" Her voice was rough and unsubstantial, and yet the panic in it cut like a blade.

Olga had come to the side of the bed and was pouring water into a cup. Vali ignored her and kept his focus on his wife.

"He lived for a time, but he was too fine for this world. Thor came and took him away to live among the gods."

She made a face, turbulent with anger and sorrow, and then, in a blink, her expression went blank, and she turned away. Olga offered her a drink, but she didn't heed her.

Vali understood what she was doing, and he would have none of it. He could not survive her cold remove, not now. Not ever again. He reached and took her chin in his hand, forcing her back to face him. "No, Brenna. Do not turn away. We share this loss, and we will share the healing. I cannot lose you, too. I have been sad and lonely and...and afraid. Stay with me. Stay. Please stay." He slid his hand from her chin to her neck and leaned in close, resting his forehead on hers. "Please stay."

She didn't speak, but she lifted her hand from her empty belly and laid it over his hand.

And that was enough to let him know that he hadn't lost her.

"I named him Thorvaldr."

A stifled sob left her injured chest, and she nodded.

Vali scooted carefully closer and gently wrapped her in his arms.

13

Olga cared for her through each day, changing the dressings, helping her deal with her body's needs, washing her, binding her broken chest. Brenna felt—was—helpless and humiliated.

But her friend was steady and kind. Every morning, Vali left her with a kiss to her forehead, and Olga came to nurse her until the night, when Vali came back again and stayed. During the day, he would check on her, but he never stayed long. Other women would come in with questions for Olga or to talk about goings-on in the castle. Olga was in charge, and she continued to manage, even though she rarely left the room during the day, except while Brenna slept.

The first thing she did every morning was to change Brenna's dressings and clean her. There was little physical pain about this, but it was among the hardest things for Brenna to tolerate, with her legs up and her most intimate place bared.

Olga patted Brenna's knee and stepped back, gathering up the bloody linens. Steeling herself against the discomfort that swamped through her whole body with every movement, Brenna straightened her legs.

There was still so much blood. Her son had been born and had died days ago, and yet she bled.

Though Olga assured her that much of her bleeding was normal after a birth, Brenna had lost too much of the blood she needed, and she was too weak to do more than sit up. Even that made her violently dizzy, and pain sliced through her chest.

After she disposed of the bloody linens, Olga washed her hands in the basin and came back. Brenna knew what was next: the worst part of Olga's tender care. Her friend and nurse came to the side of the bed and turned back the furs.

"Come. Perhaps today it will not be so bad."

Sliding her hands under Brenna's back, she lifted, rolling her to her side. Brenna clenched her teeth and bore the pain. There was worse in store.

Olga leaned over her and placed a small fold of linen under Brenna's face. Then, gently, she massaged her back, making long, slow, upward sweeps of firm but careful pressure.

Now Brenna was meant to cough. In her life, she had been sliced with a sword, and she had been hacked with an axe. She had been bashed with shields. She had been punched, head-butted, even bitten. But no pain had ever been so overwhelming as the pain Olga forced on her to heal her. With each cough, Brenna's suffering heart seemed to tear from its moorings and leap into her throat.

The linen under her cheek was to catch the black clots of blood she coughed up. Sometimes, they would come up in a spray, and the coughing would take over and become a fit. That was the worst, more pain than Brenna could bear stoically. On this morning, though, only one clot came up.

When the torture was over, Olga helped her to lie back on the pillows. Then she picked up the cloth and studied it.

"You are healing. Every day is better. There is no longer fresh blood coming, and the old blood is less. Today we will walk across the room and sit by the fire for a while."

Such a small thing, but the thought of it made Brenna weary.

"I'll ask Vali to join us." Olga's voice was kind and encouraging.

Brenna shook her head. She hated for Vali to see her in her weakness, and she knew she would struggle to cross the room—to simply cross the room!—and to sit upright in a chair.

Her resistance to his company wasn't vanity, as much as she hated her weakness. It was the turmoil she saw in him—in his eyes, in the rigid set of his shoulders, the narrow line of his lips. He saw her pain, her frailty, and he became enraged. Not at her, but for her.

He was solicitous and loving with her, and she needed the strength and comfort of his embrace. But he needed vengeance, and every sign that she was not as she had been made his need greater. She could see him choking on his need to avenge her and their child.

She needed vengeance, too. All the good that she had finally found had been yanked away from her, and that could not go unanswered. But she couldn't even stand on her own, so vengeance seemed far away. It was likely that she would be lying abed, in this room, when Vali and the others attacked Prince Ivan. It was likely that, just as the birth, life, and death of her own child had happened without her, the revenge for his loss would as well.

It was a strange thing, to have carried and loved a child for months, and then to have woken one day to find that he simply no longer existed, that there was no sign of him anywhere except the blood still running from between her legs and the milk that swelled and seeped from her breasts. He had a name: Thorvaldr—a good name. But one she had had no part in choosing. The babe she loved was simply gone.

There was not even a marker she might visit when she could. The weather had prevented a burial. Her son had been burned away.

Her heart was broken and her head swam with sorrow, but she did not know how to grieve. Tears were agony. Vali thrummed with fury when he held her. There was nowhere she could turn for solace without causing more pain.

She was alone. Again. For the first time in her life, she had friends and love and a home, and it mattered not a jot. She was still alone.

~oOo~

Despite her wish, Vali came into their chamber while she was sitting by the fire. She dashed a sharp look at Olga, who pretended not to notice and went on with changing the bedclothes.

Her husband came right to her and crouched at the side of her chair, laying his hand over hers. "I am glad to see you up. How do you feel?"

Weak and stiff, sore in every part, and as though each breath dragged itself up from her chest with bared claws. "Better. I'm feeling stronger."

He leaned in and kissed her fingers. "Soon you will be bearing your sword and your shield again."

Not soon enough.

With a long, deep breath, Vali stared into her eyes. Then he stood and took the seat next to her. "We have been planning. I would speak with you about it."

Brenna shifted in her chair, remaining stoic through the sharp discomfort, so that she could face him again. Neither Vali nor anyone had consulted with her since she had been with child. In the days since she had lost him, she had seen few people, and no one, not even Vali, had spoken to her of anything except her own health.

"Please, yes. Tell me."

Rather than speak, he looked up, past her. To Olga. As if he needed permission from her before he would speak to his wife.

"Vali! Please!" The force of her plea rocked her chest and made her gasp. Vali's eyes came quickly back to her, now shadowed under his furrowed brow.

"I don't wish to tax you, Brenna. I want you well."

"I'm locked away again. I'm lonely and sad. That is a worse hurt than any other. Please."

Vali took her hand; then, after another infuriating glance at Olga, he nodded. "We were blind to Ivan, and I wonder if you would have been. You have the clearest sight of any of us. So I would have your counsel, if you feel well enough."

Brenna's pain was, for that moment, forgotten. "Please."

"The snow holds us back. We are buried again, and the new cold has yet to break well. The band that beset the village was on foot—"

"What? What happened in the village?"

She saw it dawn on him that he was telling her something she hadn't known. He squeezed her hand. "Burned. Destroyed. The men there and the livestock are all lost."

Her last full memory of the time before was of laughing and eating with those very men.

She had known that Sigvalde was dead, and she had asked after Tord, who, despite the arrow through his own chest, had tried to help her before he'd realized that he had to go for more help than he could be, so she knew he, too, had perished. She knew that it was not Toomas but Ivan who had sent the men, because Tord had talked while he checked her over and covered her, his voice strained with pain and his fading breath, and he'd said that the colors their attackers carried were Ivan's. Those bits of memory had fallen into shape since she'd woken.

But her memory fogged and then faded away after Tord had left her.

Among the most vivid of her memories, seen again and again in her turbulent dreams, was of a man in armor standing over her, an arrow aimed at her face.

As he loosed it, he had shifted his aim subtly, and the arrow had driven deeply into the ground a scant inch from her head.

He had muttered words she didn't understand, and then he'd turned and called out *Kõik surnud!*

She'd known those words. *All dead.* He had been lying to someone—a superior, most likely. He had saved her.

But what he and his like had done had killed her son. And her friends. Had taken more even than she'd known.

If she ever saw him again, she would look him in the eyes— they were pale brown, like the color of mead—while she carved his heart from his chest. She wanted him to know, to see, that he had saved her for that sole purpose—as his own executioner.

"The whole village is lost?"

"Sadly, yes. It is fortunate that we opened the castle to the villagers, or they might all have been lost. As it is, we will rebuild when the season breaks. But that is when we expect trouble from the north, from Toomas. If it comes before the ships arrive, we are not enough men to fight on two fronts and to build as well—and now it appears that Toomas and Ivan might ally after all."

The three princes had made war on one another again and again, according to Olga and the others. Even so, the raiders had at first considered the possibility that these frequent enemies would ally against an invading horde. Their scouts, however, had found little to suggest that Toomas would bother with such an alliance. Ivan's more distant lands and smaller army, and his much poorer general state, had convinced Leif, Vali, and the others that he was no threat. Toomas, on his own, was a powerful force. He would feel no need to ally with a weak prince he despised.

And yet it had been Ivan who had made the first painful strike.

It made sense to Brenna. He would be the one who would need the factor of surprise in order to succeed. Toomas's men outnumbered them. He could approach them in force and fight them head-on in a show of strength, and would thus wait for the weather that would support such movement.

Their scouting had shown Ivan's soldiers to be fewer and comparatively poorly supplied. If he meant to attack without the benefit of an alliance—and clearly he did—then he would need sneak attacks and ambushes.

They should have been prepared for an attack from the south, but they had grown complacent, after months of quiet, nestled in the silence of the winter's heavy snows.

Brenna noticed that Olga had stopped her work and was standing with a fur covering in her hands, frozen in the midst of laying it over the bed. Her full attention was on Brenna and Vali and their talk. Olga had been born on Ivan's land, and what remained of her family still dwelt there. She had been sent to Vladimir years before, with others of her home village, as part of a truce agreement between the princes.

Brenna motioned for Olga to join them. When her friend sat across from her and Vali, Brenna said, "You worry for your family."

"Prince Ivan will make the village men to fight for him. But he does not train them as you have our men, and even some women, here. I have two younger brothers. They were small when I went away, but they are young men now and will be made to fight. I fear the blades of my new friends letting my own blood."

Vali listened, and he nodded, but he said, "Any man who fights for Ivan is an enemy. We cannot pick and choose, and I mean to see that he has no man left to stand between him and my axe. What he took will be repaid."

Looking down at her hands in her lap, Olga nodded. "Yes. This is the way of things."

Brenna turned to her husband. "What counsel do you seek?"

"I want to ride out now against Prince Ivan. I feel I will tear through my own skin if we wait more. I want to give him his own back. We can strike at night, a small force, with precision, and destroy everything he holds."

"And that, to you, is justice? To sneak like thieves? I cannot believe that Vali Storm-Wolf would be satisfied in that way. I want to see the eyes of the men who took our son from us."

"We cannot wait to fight both Toomas and Ivan. And Brenna, you cannot fight at all."

During this conversation, Brenna had forgotten that she was weak. She had forgotten her injuries and her pain. She had, for these few moments, felt strong and energized. Vali's truth hit her hard, and she remembered it all and felt suddenly woozy.

He pulled her close. "My love?"

"I'm all right." She took a stiff breath and reclaimed her composure. "What does Leif say?"

Vali frowned in irritation, but he answered. "As you seem to. He believes we should mount a direct attack when the weather next breaks. He thinks the snow and cold will chill their plans as it does ours."

"If we lose fighters against Ivan, we will be weaker against Toomas. He is already a greater force than we."

"What are you saying?"

"It is as you say, Vali. We cannot fight Ivan and Toomas and hope to vanquish both. Perhaps when they are unallied, the risk is even greater, with two different enemies to fight. Do we not need the ships and the men they will bring before we face Toomas?"

"We cannot know when they will arrive."

"I cannot speak for Snorri's intent, but Åke will want to come early in the season. We sent great riches home, and he will want to see this land we hold. I think he will be ready to sail as soon as winter is done. And he will relish the chance to do battle."

"Again I ask you, wife: what do you say?"

"I believe you are right. The fight should be brought to Ivan. But not to sneak in the night and destroy—we should do as we did here, with Vladimir. There is livestock we need, and there are villagers, like Olga's family, who might be of use to us. We need only destroy the soldiers and the prince himself. Perhaps we can offer our jarls an even greater gift of two holdings."

She turned to Olga. "Is there a way to get word to your family?"

"I see them only once or twice a year, at market. But yes, I can send word. I know how a messenger might move safely into the village."

"Do the villagers love their prince?"

Olga's smile was twisted and wry. "Only so much as they must show to keep their lives. Vladimir was kinder, and you've seen how he treated his subjects. And my family is not the only that has been broken by Ivan."

"You think to have the villagers rise up as we attack." Vali's voice showed his clear comprehension—and his admiration, as well. He leaned back and looked off into space. Brenna knew he was visualizing her idea, seeing the resulting fight.

"Yes. We wait long enough for Olga's message to get through and to know it has. Then we strike. He might be expecting us, but he will not expect his own people, whom he supposes will fight for him."

"It's good, Brenna. I'll bring it to the others." He leaned forward again and picked up her hands. "But you cannot fight. I'm sorry."

"I understand."

That was what she said. But she could fight. She would. Preparing the message and the plan to support it would take time. Getting the message out and receiving the confirmation would take days. She had time to get stronger. She had time to regain her power.

And she wanted to look those men in the eyes.

That was what she'd meant when she'd said she understood.

That she would fight. That their son would be avenged.

~oOo~

Brenna was abed for the night when Vali came up again. She had forced herself to stay upright throughout much of the rest of the day and had pushed Olga away when she tried to help her walk. Now, she was nearly shaking with pain and exhaustion, and she'd had to fight tears of relief when she'd lain down and allowed herself to rest, but it didn't matter.

Her days of helplessness were over. She was a shieldmaiden, and she would be ready to fight.

Vali stripped to his skin and slid under the furs with her. He leaned on his elbow to kiss her forehead and brush his bearded cheek over her smooth one.

"They like your idea. We should have a plan and a message prepared tomorrow or the next day."

She smiled. "That is good."

"It is. Inaction was driving me mad. I swear on my axe, Brenna. Ivan will pay. Believe me."

"I do." She believed him, and she believed that she would be with him. She knew better than to say so, however. Vali would never agree that she should fight, he would not believe she was strong enough—and at this moment, he would be right.

But she would be strong enough. Even were the fight to be the very next day, she would make herself strong enough. If she died, it would be fighting against the man who'd taken her child.

"You are paler than you were, Brenna. Do you feel weak again?"

"No. Only tired."

He kissed her cheek. "Then we'll not talk. Let us sleep."

She caught his shoulder before he could turn away. Since she'd been hurt, since their son had been born, Vali's attention to her had been loving and gentle. But it had not been intimate. Even lying near her in bed at night, his body bare, he kept a distance between them. That made her loneliest of all.

"Vali, kiss me."

He frowned. "Brenna, you still bleed. And your chest—Olga said—"

She cut him off with a huff. "I know what Olga said. I don't mean for you to be inside me. But will you not kiss me? Do you not desire me any longer?"

The sound he made was strangled and strange, and Brenna didn't immediately understand that it was a laugh.

"Yes, my love, I desire you. I desire you above all else. Even as my heart has been broken into splinters over these long days, I desire you. Seeing your fire when we spoke today had me hard and nearly breathless for you." He took her hand and brought it under the furs, leading it down to his sex, which was hot and thick and rigid. "I am hard for you now. But I am not a beast. I will stay away until you are healed, until you are ready."

She moved her hand over him until he groaned and stopped her.

"You treat me with such care that I feel alone. I'm afraid to show that I'm sad for our child, because you get angry and leave. I'm afraid to show that I'm tired, because you get angry and leave. I'm afraid to show discomfort, because you get angry and leave."

"It's true that anger rides me. It torments me. But I'm not angry with you, Brenna. Gods, no."

"I know that. You're angry about what happened, at the men who did it. You leave to keep that from me. I understand. But you leave, and I am alone, to be sad and hurt and tired. I've been alone enough in my life. I thought having love would mean an end to it."

His bright blue eyes glowed with shock, and regret, and love. "Forgive me."

She took her hand from him and brought it up to smooth over his beard. "Please kiss me."

He did, covering her mouth, cupping her face in his hand, sliding his tongue past her lips for the first time since that bright morning when all was well. She traced the nick in the side of his tongue, and he grunted, as he always did. She lifted her arms, ignoring the pain it made in her chest, and caught his braid in both fists.

He broke away but didn't go far. Looming over her, his breath harsh and shallow, his eyes vivid in the firelight, he said, "I love you."

"And I you." Finally feeling warm again in his love, Brenna dropped the gate in her mind that had held emotion back. "I wish I had been able to hold him."

Vali flinched as if she'd hurt him. But he didn't leave her. "He was so small, Brenna. He fit in my two hands. But he tried to stay. I saw him fight."

His voice broke on the last word, and he dropped his head so that his forehead nearly touched her cheek. Brenna turned her head and pressed her lips to his temple.

Then she felt a warm, wet drop on her neck. A tear.

Nothing could have shown her his love more than that, or given her more strength: to expose his own sadness, his vulnerability, to her.

She knew then that they had both been injured.

And she knew that they would both be strong again. Together.

14

Leif swept a pointed finger over an arc of the wood chips that Orm had placed on the carved table. They had discerned that the table in the room where they took their leisure was etched with a rendering of western Estland itself and marked the physical features of the land and the locations of castles and villages. The market town, Mirkandi, formed the point from which the rest of the land radiated out: Toomas's holding to the north, Ivan's to the south, and what had been Vladimir's holding to the west, along the greater part of the coast. Vladimir's holding, now their own, was the largest of the three.

"Ivan keeps patrol of this area and holds watch points there, there, and there. The woods creep close to the castle wall there. He is vulnerable at the woods. But we only know that the villagers are with us, and how many they say can fight. We don't know the quality of those fighters, or the extent to which they will follow our plan."

Vali leaned forward and moved a few chips away from the larger mound that represented the raiders. He pushed them toward the woods. "Archers into the woods, then. Sten, Hans, Bjarke, and Georg. They cover the villagers, and lead them according to our plan if need be. We have no other need for archers, and the four of them are better useful with bow than blade."

At the grumbled protests across the table, he looked up at the men in question. "I mean no slight by that, my friends. Your bows are mighty and swift."

Leif studied the table, then broke the remaining mass of raider chips into three groups. He counted out the chips as he talked. "Each group takes down a watch point, then moves to the wall. The wall is high, but in poor repair and easily scaled if the guards are distracted. Vali, Orm, and I will lead two score directly to the gates. We ride in as if we are the full force. Astrid and Harald will lead two parties to breach the walls at either side. The villagers breach from the woods." Leif took a step back and surveyed the table. "We'll fall upon them from every direction."

Orm drew a weathered hand over a long grey beard. "If the villagers come in the force they report, they will be like ants in a mound and will overrun the castle grounds. It will be chaos." He smiled. "Brenna's idea is good. To use his own subjects against him."

Brenna should have been in this meeting. In the days since Vali had sought her counsel, she had been out of bed more and more, and the night before, he had helped her down to share the evening meal with the group. She was exhausted by the end of each day, but he could see that she was healing, regaining her strength.

But when he'd told her that they had received word back from Ivan's subjects and asked her to join them in their planning, she had stunned him speechless by refusing. After her protests against being 'locked away' and disregarded, she had declined to join the raiders in the planning of an attack largely predicated on her own idea.

He supposed it was too painful for her to be involved in strategy for a battle she could not fight. He remembered lying helpless in Sven's tent, and he understood her frustration: to be a warrior and cut off from the war—it ate into one's head.

"A leader who treats his people like beasts might come to know their bite."

Jaan had spoken those words, breaking into Vali's thoughts, and the men, and the shieldmaiden, standing around the carved table gave him their full attention. He was young and brash, and he was a villager, a farmer. But over the months that Vali had known him, the young man had become skilled and fierce as most raiders. Vali thought that he would ask him to sail with them. He would leave a father and a sister behind, but that was what young men did: they left their homes and made their own.

"Tell us, Jaan. Will Ivan's villagers bite him?"

Jaan noticed then that he had the eyes and ears of everyone, and he lost some of the cock in his posture. When he answered, he stammered until he recovered that confidence, and he spoke solely in his own language. "I—I—I have always lived in this place. My parents and their parents, and their parents before them, we have all lived here. Vladimir held this land for all my life. He was not a kind man. He plucked girls from the village to become servants in the castle, and those girls were known to…have more…duties…than a girl should have. Brutal duties. And he took the fruit of our toil and made himself rich with it, while every winter we all but starved. The weakest of us often did starve."

He paused and swallowed, the force of it audible in the quiet room. "An invading horde of monsters from across the sea saved us. We know what happened near the coast. Many of us lost family to you on that day. We know how you treated those you held captive—much like Vladimir with his servant girls. We all know. And yet now you are our friends. Because we know you not to be monsters, but fierce and ruthless warriors. And we know you to be fair-minded outside of battle. And because life was difficult under Prince Vladimir, and now it is better."

Again, he paused, but he looked around the table in such a way that Vali thought this pause was for effect. "Vladimir was a hard, unjust man. Ivan is worse. Will the villagers rise up against him if they know they are not alone? Yes. And they will bring all of his injustices back and bury him in them."

~oOo~

Shortly after they had set their plan, Vali went up to tell Brenna that they went the next morning, while they had good weather, and also to see if she was well enough to come down and join the evening meal. The stairwell and corridor were quiet; Brenna had been on her own more these past days, as she needed less care. Even Olga had begun to focus again on her castle-wide duties.

Vali opened the door. Though he had been knocking before he entered since she'd been hurt, because he had never been sure what state he might find her in, this time, he did not.

He froze in the open doorway when he saw his wife, so grievously injured only two weeks before, standing in the middle of their bedchamber, holding her longsword as if to strike.

In the stunned freeze of the moment, Vali saw that she was soaked through with sweat, her sleeping shift nearly transparent and plastered to her body, her hair lank and stuck in swirls to her flushed face.

She was the first to move, dropping her sword to her side and standing straight. Her eyes held his, unblinking and defiant.

Mastering his shock, he stepped into the room and closed the door. "Brenna! What is this?"

He could see that she shook with fatigue and was breathless, but she behaved as if she were neither. Turning on her heel, she walked to the table and picked up her scabbard. She sheathed her sword and turned to face him again before she spoke a word.

"I mean to fight with you."

"No."

Her eyes flared wide at his simple word of refusal, and her brilliant right eye shone especially brightly, the many colors seeming to swirl. "You think to stop me with only that?"

He did. She was in no condition to fight, and he would not put her at risk again—or allow her to put herself there. Crossing the room, he reached out, intending to take her hands, but she stepped back and put a tall-backed chair between them. So he stopped, and they faced each other almost as combatants.

"Brenna, you are not strong enough yet to fight. Look at you—shaking and soaked through, and you were alone in this room. How do you think to fight an armored soldier?"

"I can fight, and I shall." She crossed her arms over her chest like a petulant child.

Unable to fully comprehend that she would be so foolhardy, and that she would simply ignore reason when it was laid before her, Vali didn't feel angry. He was too shocked for anger. "That is your argument? Simply that you will do this thing?"

"I don't mean to argue with you at all. I am informing you."

"And if we ride without you?" It was the only thing he could think to do, short of binding her to their bed. As he asked the question, he began to plan—he would speak with Leif, and they would leave in the dark before dawn.

"Then I shall follow." She sighed heavily, and he saw the wince of pain she tried to hide. "Vali, there is no fight to be had between us. I join your party, or I ride alone, but I fight. This revenge is mine as much as yours. More."

"Enough that you would risk yourself to seek it?"

"Battle is always a risk. And pain is always the price. You have no voice in my decision, husband. I am no longer a vessel for any soul but my own."

"And you care not for my soul, what it would do to me to lose you?"

"I care as much for yours as you care for mine. We are warriors. Our life is risk. I was a shieldmaiden long before I knew you. While it is true that I am not as strong as I could be, you know the strength and fire that comes with a righteous fight. What this man took from us is great. I would not have him take from me the chance to answer it. I would not have you take it from me, either. I fight. With you or alone."

He saw that she was right: there was no fight to be had between them. Certainly not one to be won. She had set her mind, and she was stubborn and resolute. He had only one choice: to protect her in her folly. To love the shieldmaiden she was and to see to it that she found her vengeance and lived to tell the story of it.

"You are not alone, Brenna mine. Never again. If you will not see reason, then I will stay by your side through your madness."

He went around the chair and took the hands he'd reached for before. When he pulled—gently, knowing that no matter her fierce words, her body yet pained her—she came easily into his embrace, still cold and wet from her efforts. He tucked her head under his chin and held her.

"Please do not leave me," he whispered.

"Or you me," came her answer.

~oOo~

That night, Vali woke aroused and gasping. Brenna lay on her side next to him, her hand wrapped around his rigid shaft. He had not had her since she had been hurt, and his need was great. But Olga had told him to stay away until after her first normal blood, which would come some time after the birth blood had stopped. He knew that she still bled. Discreet though his wife was, it was impossible to live in a room together and not know.

It was one of his many great concerns about the next morning: that she would start it already bleeding. Brenna had given him a look of seething contempt when he had quietly mentioned it the evening before, and she had asked him if he believed she had never been in battle during her monthly time, insisting that this was no different. He believed that it was different, but he had let the matter drop.

There was a great deal he did not understand about the inner workings of a woman's body, and he was content with that lack of understanding. His mother had been a healer, and he knew a few things about treating wounds, but she had always shooed him away when women came for help.

He had been but young, only ten years, when she had simply not come home one day. And then it had been only him and his vicious father.

Vali shook that memory away and stopped Brenna's hand. "No, love. It's too soon."

She looked up and smiled, her fair hair falling loose over her face. "I don't mean to take you into me. I would pleasure you this way, if you will let me." To demonstrate her intent—as if he could have missed it—she shook his hand off and slid her loose fist up and over his tip and then back down, against his body, letting her fingers scratch lightly through the hair there and then and down to cup him.

211

Groaning, he brushed her hair from her face. "It doesn't hurt you, to lie like that?" She was on her side, propped on an elbow.

"No. Only tightness, not pain. You worry too much." As she spoke, her hand moved over him, tightening and loosening, as if she meant to milk him.

"I worry the proper amount," he sighed and relaxed, letting her have her way.

~oOo~

He rose before Brenna and dressed in the grey dawn light, keeping a frail hope alive that she might change her mind now that the day was upon them. But she woke as he was preparing to leave the room.

"You did not mean to sneak away, I hope." Her voice was light and teasing, but her eyes were sharp on him.

"Of course not." He went to the bed and kissed her forehead. "I'll see to it that Freya is saddled, and I will be waiting for you." He wanted to ask if she felt well, but he knew how poorly the question would be received, so he contented himself with a survey of her color and deemed it acceptable. For days after their son had died, her complexion had been a ghastly, terrifying grey. On this morning, pale roses bloomed on her smooth cheeks. He kissed one of them and left her to her preparations.

Once in the hall, he helped himself to a bowl of barley porridge from the cauldron hanging over the fire. The commotion in the room was familiar in a way that made Vali feel homesick. They all prepared for battle. They had turned villagers into warriors. There were even two young village women who had braided their hair and donned breeches like shieldmaidens. Astrid had trained them both.

212

So the hall was full of men and women filling their stomachs with warm food and then gearing up for war. The air in the room was heady with the high spirits that came before a fight, a combination of relief from hardened warriors looking forward to the release of the fury that pent up in them when they were idle, and of anxious anticipation from tenderfoots who knew not what they faced.

Vali, a hardened warrior who carried a burden on his heart and mind too heavy for high spirits, finished his porridge and slid his axes into their rings on his belt. He wore a heavy woolen tunic for the ride, but he left it loose over his belt so that he could shed it quickly when the fight came. Even in the chill of this new thaw, he would fight bare-chested, his body unrestrained.

Then he cloaked himself in the skin of his wolf.

Prepared for battle, he went out to the stable, to ready his horse and his wife's.

Leif was there already, leading his saddled horse, a black stallion as big as Vali's bay, toward the open doors. Seeing Vali, he stopped and nodded.

"She is coming?"

"You've known her long. Do you think even I could dissuade her?"

"As I thought," Leif chuckled. "We will all watch out for her. One of us will be at her side always."

"*I* will be at her side."

"Vali, you lead with me. You cannot be sure not to be drawn from her. But she will not be alone."

"I will be at her side, and she at mine. She will have her revenge. And I mine."

The two friends stared at each other, and then Leif nodded. "As is right." He tugged lightly on the reins and moved his horse out to the castle grounds.

When Vali had his horse and Brenna's saddled and out of the stable, he mounted his and waited, staring at the castle doors, holding Freya's reins.

Brenna had named her horse; he did not think any other of them had. She had small, unexpected sentimentalities like this—to name a beast of burden, to dangle string for the near-feral cats and kittens who fed on castle pests, to teach the villagers' children little games and songs. She sang when she cooked. He knew this only because he had walked through the kitchen one afternoon while she was working there. Her voice was frail but true, and of a higher pitch than he would have thought. She had been round with his child then, and he thought she'd been singing to the babe.

Vali swallowed down the hard stone of grief that filled his throat at the memory.

Brenna came out of the castle, and pride pushed his grief and his worry aside. She stood straight and strong, dressed in her boiled leathers, her hair braided in the elaborate way she favored for battle. Her longsword and shield were strapped on her back, and her dagger was fixed to her thigh.

She had lined her eyes thickly with black and had drawn rays around her right eye. The God's-Eye. When she fought, she embraced the name that had been imposed on her.

His shieldmaiden, ready to bring down the justice of the gods on those who had dared to hurt her and those she loved.

All around them, people prepared to ride off—adjusting saddles, tying down supplies, mounting their horses. But when Brenna God's-Eye walked onto the grounds, everyone stopped and watched. They all knew, of course, how she had been hurt, what she and Vali had lost, and they all knew that she meant to fight.

Vali thought that her legend would grow tenfold on this day, especially were they successful. If she rode back to the castle with her vengeance done, then she would be as famous and revered as Brynhildr herself.

She came between their horses and held up her hand for Freya's reins. He handed them down to her. Neither smiled, this was not the time for smiling, but their eyes met and held, and with that look they said all they needed to say of their pride and love and devotion.

She mounted smoothly, with no sign of discomfort. None but the twitch in her right eye. Vali had seen it, he and no other, and he knew it had hurt her to hoist herself into the saddle. But she was a mighty shieldmaiden on a righteous mission, and her pain mattered not.

"Side by side, shieldmaiden. We stay together."

She nodded, and then gave him an almost imperceptible smile, just a tick up at the corner of her mouth. "We save each other. We are destined for it, I believe."

"Indeed we are."

He urged his horse forward, and Brenna did the same, and, with Leif, they led the raiding party through the castle gate.

15

The day had broken clear and cold, but the rising sun brought true warmth with it. As Brenna rode between Vali and Leif, she could smell the change of seasons finally coming. The winter had been unduly long and hard, but summer was at last shaking off its heavy cloak.

Banked snow during the harshest days of the winter had risen at times to more than Vali's height, and drifts had topped the second windows of the castle, and even now the raiders trudged on horseback or foot through snow as high as the horse's knees. It was melting quickly on this day, however, the third in a string of warmer days, and the warmest yet.

By the time they stopped to rest and feed the horses and themselves, they were moving through heavy mud.

Vali jumped from his horse and came to her. When his hands caught her hips as she dismounted, she sent him an irritated glance over her shoulder, but she didn't resist as he set her gently on the ground. Truly, she was sore and struggling. Hours in the saddle, rarely at more pace than a quick walk, and her chest ached enough that every breath caught in her throat. Of more help than simply bringing her to the ground was the comfort of his strong, loving hands on her.

He turned her to face him and then stroked her cheek. "You're pale again, my love."

Rather than deny it, Brenna caught his hand in hers and smiled up at him. "I need this, husband. The power of the need will sustain me."

Searching her eyes, he finally nodded. "Take this time to rest. I will bring you food and drink."

"Thank you. First I need to walk off on my own for a moment."

Understanding that she had personal care to attend to, he nodded again and then bent his head to hers. Standing at Freya's steady flank, Brenna looped her arms around her husband's neck, ignoring the pinch and stretch in her ribs, and kissed him with abandon.

His hands gripped her bottom and pressed her close so that she could feel him grow against her belly, even through their furs and leathers. For that moment, Brenna forgot everything except their love, physical and spiritual.

The kiss ended gradually, with Vali's tongue sweeping over her lips. She sighed and opened her eyes. "I love you."

He touched his forehead to hers. "You hold my heart in yours. Keep it well."

~oOo~

After they ate salt cod and leiv bread and drank water, the mounted raiders tended to their steeds, feeding them grain and cleaning the mud from their hooves. When Brenna leaned on Freya's rump to urge her leg up, a shadow fell over her.

Leif stood at her side. "Let me."

"My horse, my care."

He put his hands on her shoulders and moved her aside. "I am the one who taught you that rule, thus I can break it."

Vali, tending to his own horse, stood and considered them both, then nodded a thanks at Leif.

Brenna thought for a moment on that exchange and then turned to Leif, who had Freya's hoof in his hand. "I believe the two of you are conspiring."

"To protect you from your foolish fire? Indeed we are."

Olga had called her foolish as well. It seemed everyone was in agreement about the loss of her reason. But she was surprised that Leif would not see her way. "You understand, Leif. I know you do. More perhaps even than Vali."

He set Freya's clean hoof on the ground and walked around her rump, keeping his hand on her as he went. Brenna followed, wanting the talk to continue.

Leif had only a few years more than Brenna did. He was no older than Vali, and he seemed younger, with a heavy, long mane of golden hair, a smooth, fair brow, and a full but trimmed beard. Only in quiet moments did his blue eyes take on an older, darker light. She knew his story not because they had been confidants before they'd come to Estland—until Vali, Brenna had not had, nor been, any such thing—but because his tragic story was known all over Geitland, their jarl's seat.

He had been wed young, not long after he'd gotten his arm ring, in the manner that was typical of their people. He had not much known his equally young wife before their marriage, but they had gotten on well, and she had borne him six children. Three had died as babes. A daughter and two sons survived. A fever had taken his daughter just at the cusp of her womanhood. One son had drowned. His wife and their unborn seventh child had been killed by the raiders that had nearly killed Jarl Åke's wife and young children.

Of all his family, only his son Einar had survived. Einar, who had been killed brutally by Prince Vladimir and turned into a horror as a twisted jape at their expense.

If anyone knew loss and the need for vengeance, it was Leif Olavsson.

As he picked up Freya's other rear hoof and began to clean it, his head down, Leif answered, "Yes, Brenna, I understand. I also understand your man, and what he would feel to live without you. It is a kind of wound to one's heart that can never know ease."

"I think I would leave him in a harder way if I had been left at home. I could feel myself dwindle even in these past weeks. I do not know how to give up action for waiting."

Leif set Freya's hoof down and stood straight. He was nearly as tall and broad as Vali, and Brenna tipped her head back to stay face to face with him.

He smiled. "Then we shall see to it that you find what you need."

~oOo~

The sun had moved into the west but was still high enough to give them ample light for battle when Leif and Vali, as one, surged ahead. Brenna had been seeing signs of population in the woods they traveled—most prevalent, a hard pack and grey murk of snow that had been trodden by man and beast alike. They were crossing into the patrolled area.

Leif raised his hand, and the riders and walkers stopped. At another signal, Hans and Bjarke rode up, bows in hand. Leif and Hans turned in one direction, and Vali and Bjarke the other. Brenna knew what they were doing—scouting for the two-man patrol. It would be the archer's job, whichever team came upon the patrol, to kill them quietly.

At the same time, Orm rode up alongside her. "Vali told you how we took your plan?" He spoke quietly.

"Yes. Three groups. The archers and villagers make a fourth, coming from behind. We split now?" With the chance to fight so near, Brenna's body shook off its pain and fatigue. She could feel the drum of the fight already beating inside her chest, making her strong and full of fire.

"Yes. You ride with the main, to the gates. Astrid and Harald lead two groups on foot over the walls. When the scouts return, Hans and Bjarke will join with Sten and Georg and will ride into the woods to group with the villagers."

Behind her, several of the mounted raiders jumped to the ground. Their wide-wheeled cart at the back shed itself of a score more fighters. They grouped with those already on foot, and all divided into their raid teams, as Astrid and Harald commanded.

As she turned and surveyed their force, it did not seem so large, now that they were separating into groups.

"It is a good plan, Brenna God's-Eye."

Brenna turned back to Orm, surprised to hear that name after months away from it. The sound of it didn't grate at her the way it used to. It had become something else during these months at the castle, among her first friends, her first love, her first home. No longer was she everything that people believed her eye was, and nothing else. Now she was Brenna, who was also, when she bore her sword and shield, The God's Eye.

She found that the name fit comfortably now.

The cart driver and his boy collected the riderless horses and led them off into the deeper woods. They would wait for the raiders' return.

They all awaited the scouts' return.

Leif and Hans were first back, bringing their horses nearly face to face with Brenna and Orm's.

"No sign of the patrol. All is quiet eastward."

Waiting for Vali and Bjarke to return, Brenna felt a tightness in her chest that had nothing to do with her injury. Each breath, each heartbeat seemed an infinity.

And then she saw him, and she was dizzy with relief. He rode up, wearing the heavy scowl and snarl that was his battle face, but it softened into a smile as he pulled up his horse. "The patrol was three. We came up behind, and Bjarke took all three down before they could turn." He reached over and punched the man's arm. "I will tell that story all my days, my friend."

Bjarke grinned shyly and then turned, headed toward the other archers. When the four were together, they nodded at the leaders and rode off. They would ride to the woods, staying mounted for the superior coverage that height would offer.

It was time. Leif and Vali sent the teams off on foot, then took their positions at the head of the line of riders. Again, they put themselves to either side of Brenna, and Orm lagged back to the second row. Vali had shed his tunic, and his massive chest rippled with readiness.

No one spoke as they came onto the road and approached the castle gates. Those who had shields pulled them forward. Brenna found strength in that, too, in the familiar and secure heft of her shield.

The gates creaked open, pushed by four men, and a force came through on foot. One rider, in splendid armor, led them all. Brenna scanned the top of the wall for archers but saw none. She did not for a moment think that they had no archers to guard the wall, only that they had been, as planned, caught unprepared. Their task would be to keep the archers from rising to the top of the wall—that was part of the plan for the villagers.

The sole rider spoke, but Brenna's struggles with the Estlander language impeded her full understanding. She thought she heard the word *tulid*, which she knew was a form of 'come,' and his voice had lifted at the end, as for a question, so she guessed he'd asked why they had come.

Leif gestured subtly with one hand, and to her right, between her and Leif, a spear flew past her head. It sank into the mounted soldier's throat.

They had not come to talk.

As the soldier fell, the raiders jumped from their horses and sent them away from the fight. Brenna turned Freya and gave her a sharp slap on the rump, sending her off with a loud, strident *Ha!* The mare ran swiftly with her fellows. In this way, they saved the resource of the horses and ensured that they would not be obstacles in the battle. A horse made good transportation but a terrible weapon.

Then Brenna pulled her sword forward and charged into the fight.

They drove the soldiers quickly back into the castle grounds, and as the raiders cleared the gate, Brenna saw that the villagers were already teeming over the rear wall, jumping onto the straw-covered ground bearing pitchforks and tree limbs, hammers, shovels—the tools of their lives now purposed as weapons for the fight of their lives.

The archers stayed atop the wall and fired down and across the grounds. On either side, Astrid and Harald brought their teams over the walls, all of it timed as if the gods orchestrated from above.

Brenna had no time to look long at the chaos beyond; she was caught in the roiling knot of raiders and soldiers. There was no chance to form a shield wall, no way to gather into a single force. So she focused on the fight before her, using both sword and shield as weapons and both as defense, in the way of her training, a training that was so ingrained in her bones that she needed not think at all. She needed only see, and in battle her vision opened wide and saw all.

She saw that Vali never left her side. Always at her left was his massive, unshielded body, his deep, furious, feral battle cry. Leif was not far, either. In fact, each time she made a move toward the outside of the scrum, she found herself back in the center, surrounded by men she knew. They were managing her, protecting her, and they were stealing her kills as well, taking over every time she made a strike, and blocking strikes aimed at her.

But she fought best from the edges. Fired by a fresh new anger, this at her friends, Brenna screamed and jumped forward, feinting around Vali and past Orm. As she vied with their enemies, she found a way clear of her friends' stifling protection, driving her sword into the soft underarm of a soldier and pushing him through to clear her way.

When she got into the grounds—no less chaotic but slightly looser—before she could pull her sword free, Vali yelled, "SHIELD UP!"

Instinctively, not knowing if he called for her, she threw her shield up high, and an arrow came through it, slicing into her arm.

She yanked her sword from the soldier and brought it around as he fell, striking him across the back of the neck. Then she slammed her shield on his body and broke the arrow free of it.

Vali grabbed her. "You stay with me!" He shook her with each word, and his eyes were wild in his blood-streaked face.

"You hold me back and yourself, too! Let me fight!" Brenna caught sight of a soldier charging up behind Vali, and she bashed her husband hard with her shield, forcing him to the side, then blocked the strike with the same shield as it came down where he would have been. The blast of impact made her wounded arm shriek, the first pain she'd felt in the fight, but she pulled her shield away, lifting up as she yanked, throwing the soldier's sword arm back. Then she spun and took his legs out with a slice of her sword across the backs of his thighs.

Crippled, he fell oddly, to his knees and then backward. His helm fell off as he landed hard, and Brenna saw a face she knew. It had been obscured by his helm and nose plate when she'd last seen him, but she would know his eyes anywhere— pale brown like the color of mead.

The soldier who'd saved her in the woods. One of those who had beset the sledge and caused her to give birth to her son too early. Who had caused his death.

He recognized her, too. Those eyes she knew went wide. "*Halasta minu!*"

She knew those words. He asked for mercy.

Leaning close so that he would hear her whisper even in the din of war, she growled low, "*Ei! Kõik surnud!*"

When she saw that he'd heard and comprehended her, she brought her sword down and drove it into his chest.

She stood and looked for the next fight, coming face to face with her husband. They stared at each other, and then he

225

looked down at her latest kill. When his eyes returned to hers, they were full of knowing.

Then he nodded, and they returned to the fight.

~oOo~

The plan had worked almost perfectly. The back of Harald's team had been caught as they'd come over the wall, and they had lost six to those of Ivan's archers who had made their posts. Eleven of the raiders' villager friends had been lost in all, and two more raiders. Quite a few of Ivan's villagers had perished as well, but they did not yet have a count. Brenna wished that she knew what Olga's brothers looked like, or her father. She hoped that they lived.

Now, while they sorted their dead from the soldiers and killed any soldiers who yet breathed, Leif and Vali had one man who had worn more decorative armor than the others tied to a hitching post. He was a leader of some sort.

Ivan had had few noble attendants and a remarkably small army. It had taken an unabashed, arrogant courage to have mounted any attack on the raiders. He'd managed to do real damage, and would have crippled them, possibly beaten them, if he had been prepared for their retaliation.

Now, though, his holding was theirs, as were all his resources—sparse though they were, his livestock and supplies would help to restock and rebuild the burned village. And, if the villagers agreed, it was Leif's thought to bring the two villages together, reuniting families and consolidating resources.

But first, they wanted Prince Ivan, who seemed to have slithered away.

Vali had his dagger in his hand and was peeling the skin from the last living soldier's arm. At each pause in his screams, Vali asked him the same question: *"Kus on prints?"*

"Ma ei tea! Ma ei tea!" the man wailed, screaming it when Vali cut into him again. *MA EI TEA!"*

I don't know.

When Vali moved from the soldier's arm, which now showed bright red muscle from wrist to elbow, and instead pushed the point of his dagger lightly into his belly, he begged, *"Peatuge! Palun peatuge!"*

Stop.

Vali stopped and asked again, *"Kus on prints?"*

"Tunnel. All köök."

Vali looked up at Leif and then at Brenna. They had all understood that there was a tunnel under the kitchen. 'Kitchen' was one of the first Estlander words Brenna had learned.

Then he turned to Orm. "Keep him alive. We will return. If not with the prince, then"—he pointed his dagger at the soldier—"this one's suffering is not at its end."

Leif, Vali, and Brenna went into the castle and located the kitchen. A portly old woman was still there, hiding under the table. Leif crouched down and led her gently out. "Tunnel?" he asked, his voice kind and soothing.

She pointed at the enormous fireplace. At its side, behind the wood ring, they found a door. It led to a dark, narrow, set of stone steps. Vali grabbed a torch from the wall, and they descended.

They found the prince wedged into a hole carved into the tunnel wall. He had not fixed the door of it properly, because his bulk would not allow the door to close completely.

Brenna thought that if all the princes of Estland were like the two they had fought—a liar and a coward—then this country deserved to be overrun by raiders. These nobles fought their wars on the backs of peasants while they hid in their castles.

Vali dragged Ivan out by the scruff of his neck. The fat man sputtered and babbled, but Vali punched him hard in the face and silenced him well and truly. Then he heaved the round mass onto his shoulder, hunkered down even lower in the low-ceilinged space, and they turned and went back up into the castle and then out onto the grounds.

They wanted an audience for Prince Ivan's demise.

Seeing that Vali bore the prince, Orm opened the soldier's throat and then untied him from the hitching post, letting his body fall to the bloody straw.

Vali bent over and dropped the unconscious body of the prince onto the straw, into the pool of his last soldier's blood. Then he slapped him about the face and head until the man roused.

As the prince sat up, cowering and again babbling, Vali spoke over him in the Estland tongue. He spoke loudly, to the Prince and to everyone else as well. Brenna didn't understand all of what he said, but she picked up a few words, and she understood his body language, so she thought she grasped enough.

He was telling the prince to look at what his mistake had wrought, and that in his greed he had only succeeded in making the enemy that was the end of him and all he had. He was telling the people, she thought, that they were free now to earn their way fairly, and that they could join the villages together.

228

Then he dragged Ivan to his feet, said something else, more quietly, that Brenna did not understand at all, and buried his axe in the prince's face.

~oOo~

They brought their dead back on the cart. By the time the raiders crossed through the gates they had left that morning, the night was dark and cold. The bright of a nearly-full moon had lit their way safely, however, and the chill did not harden into frost.

The gods were with them on this day and night. Brenna would have rather they had been with them on the night of her son's birth, but she was grateful for their aid nonetheless.

She ached badly everywhere. Her chest felt full of spikes. Her lower back and abdomen cramped hotly. Her arm, the new gash as yet unattended, had gone stiff long before. If Freya had not been such a steady mount, and if their mutual trust had not been so complete, Brenna might have had trouble controlling her.

When Vali helped her from the saddle, she could not suppress a sharp groan.

He scowled. "To bed with you. Right now. I'll see to Freya, and then I will be with you."

She did not argue.

She did, however, go to Olga, who had run from the castle upon their return. "We bring you gifts, my friend," she said and took Olga by the hand.

In the middle of the busy mass of dismounting raiders were two young men, dressed in coarse woolens too light for the cold, but under furs offered to them by new friends.

Olga's brothers. All that survived of her family. Both were young men, too young to be bearded but old enough to fight. Their father had not survived the raid. Their mother was long dead.

When she saw them, Olga ran and grabbed them both, sobbing and clutching them to her. Feeling that she intruded to be witness to such a private moment, Brenna turned and went into the castle.

The long walk up the dark stairs to her chamber would, she believed, be the hardest part of this day.

~oOo~

It was long before Vali opened the door to their room, but Brenna had not managed to do much more than remove her boots. She sat by the fire, feeling weary and sore, and listened to the roars and laughter of her friends below, celebrating their victory and expending what remained of their ferocity.

She was out of temper. She had sought vengeance, and she had found it. But her soul was not appeased. Vengeance had not brought her son back. Or their friends.

Vali came and crouched at her side. For the first time, he saw the slice in her tunic and the blood that stained it. He lifted her arm. "You're hurt."

Her arm ached and was stiff, but it was a pain she knew. Too much time had passed for it to be closed, so she would scar, but otherwise, it needed only to be cleaned and covered. She pulled her arm from his searching grasp. "Not badly. The arrow through my shield caught only meat."

"It needs to be cleaned and wrapped."

"And it will be. I needed some time to rest first."

At that, he surprised her with a smile. "I'm glad you're not abed. The women are bringing a bath to us."

Tired as she was, a bath sounded wonderful, and she smiled, setting aside her turbulent thoughts and dark spirits. "I would like that."

He brushed back the hair that had fallen from her braids. "They drink in celebration below, telling already the story of the God's-Eye, who whispered an incantation into her enemy's ear before she cleaved his head away, and who rose up and saved Vali Storm-Wolf with her strong shield arm, as if Odin himself had given her his strength."

"You saved me as well. You would have saved me from all the fight if I had let you."

"I am not threatened by my wife's greatness. They tell my story, too. And yes, I would have, and it would have gotten me killed, I think, to have kept you stifled."

She took his hand from her hair and held it. "We save each other."

"My shieldmaiden. We are destined." He pulled her hand to his mouth and kissed it.

A knock on the door heralded the coming of the tub and hot water. Vali stood and called, "Come!" As the women came in, he smiled down at Brenna. "Now I ask, humbly, will you let me tend to you tonight? I would wash you and ease your aches, and I would hold you tight while we sleep."

The thought of it made tears spring up in Brenna's eyes. She blinked them away before they could fall.

"You save me every day," she whispered.

PART THREE
THE SHIELD

16

As Brenna still slept in the dawn of an early summer morning, Vali lay on his side behind her and watched the subtle lift of her shoulders with each deep, peaceful breath. Her long, fair hair, its waves wild from sleep and from their tumble the night before, trailed over his arm, and he pressed his face into the flax and breathed deep.

He almost always woke before she did, and over the past quiet weeks, he had taken up this waking habit: to lie quietly and watch his wife. To bask in the peace of his love. The peace was hard won and not yet assured, but the love had come surprisingly easy.

After they'd defeated Prince Ivan and claimed his lands, Prince Toomas had sent an envoy; he'd wanted to meet. They had made a peace between them, with Toomas offering resources and assistance in rebuilding the village. He had even offered a daughter in marriage to Leif, but Leif, with no intention of settling here, had declined. Toomas had been insulted, and negotiations had been briefly tense, but when the parties bid each other farewell, a peace was in place.

Any lingering danger would come from their own people, it seemed. Now that the weather was warm and the snow and ice had been replaced by green buds and a rushing river, they had begun to watch for the ships, sending a team of two to the coast every day. It was early yet, but Brenna and Leif both expected their jarl to be impatient, and Vali knew his jarl would not seek a delay, either.

Leif had grown somber; he expected there to be trouble when Brenna and Vali's marriage was known.

The trouble would come, Vali knew, if Åke resisted Brenna's intention to settle in Estland. She had decided that, should he do so, she would forswear her fealty to him. As a freewoman, she had that right, but she would lose all that she had earned while sworn to him. Everything she had was at home, across the sea, and she considered it lost to her already. They intended to start anew here.

Åke would take the loss of her poorly, and he was a ruthless jarl, capable of extreme cruelty. Vali worried for her, and for them. If she had still been with child, or had babe in arms, when the ships arrived, Åke's claim would have been weakened past argument, angry though he might have been.

Knowing this, and simply wanting to make a family with his love, Vali had wanted to get Brenna with child as soon as they were able again to try.

But Brenna would not allow him to sow his seed in her. His desire and her resistance was a constant source of tension between them, a low thrum under all of their interactions. They coupled nearly every day—their need of each other remained great, and their love was deep and true—and Vali had, for the most part, stopped pressing the issue. But he still felt frustrated, and she felt his frustration.

So it was in these moments, quiet, while she slept, that Vali could bask in nothing but their love.

He wanted children with her. He wanted her to carry his child. To have her with child now might protect her in a way he could not: without violence. She refused to see it, refused to acknowledge her full worth to her jarl, refused to believe Åke capable of things she knew full well he was. Instead, she argued that the time was not right, that there was too much work to be done to rebuild the village and to build a new life for them.

The truth, the real, deep truth, he knew, was that she was afraid. She mourned their son and was afraid to try again. He wasn't sure even Brenna herself understood that, or if she did, that she would ever acknowledge it.

He brushed a finger down the length of the jagged scar over her shoulder, a wound that told that she had once been struck with a blow meant to remove her head. She was agile and quick, however, and Vali could visualize the way she had moved to save herself, taking instead a brutal but nonlethal slice. In battle, she was much like he was: single-minded and fiercely brave, without fear and with pure, consuming focus—a way of leaving one's body to do its work while one's mind saw above the fray.

In daily life, though, his shieldmaiden knew fear and doubt.

He loved her all the more for it.

He wanted to put another child inside her. Watching her grow with their son, seeing the mother in her rise up alongside the warrior, had stirred something vibrant in his soul. Losing Thorvaldr had been a pain greater than any he'd ever known, was pain still, but it had not quieted his soul. He wanted a family, children, a home. And he wanted every protection between Brenna and Jarl Åke that he could devise.

He swept her hair from her neck and shoulder and moved close, so that their bodies touched from ankle to head. Pushing his arm under hers and over her firm belly, he slid his hand between her legs while he brushed his beard over her neck and then kissed her, sucking lightly at her skin.

She sighed and stirred.

"Don't wake," he murmured at her ear. "Let me fill your dreams as I fill your body."

While his fingers played through her folds, feeling her body go wet for him, he pushed his knee between her legs and lifted, making way for him to enter her. He did, his passage easy into her ready sheath, and he groaned, overcome with the delight of it. No matter how many times he took her, this moment was always the same: a marveling at their union, at the perfection of her body around his, at his good fortune in finding and claiming a love like this.

"Vali..." The word came as a vague breath; sleep kept her in its hold.

"Shhh." He kissed her shoulder. "Sleep. Feel this as a dream."

As he spoke, he thrust slowly, and she sighed out a deep breath and settled quietly in his arms.

In his heart, he knew that what he planned, what he hoped, was unfair. She wasn't ready. He knew she wasn't. She had not wavered in her resistance. But she was wrong and he was not, and he was her husband. Unfair he might be, but not wrong.

The thought that he might put a child in her now piqued his need, and he felt himself swell and throb as he quickened his pace. His fingers sought and found the bud of her best pleasure, and his other arm folded over her chest so that he could take hold of a full, perfect breast. He held her tight and groaned into her neck with each thrust, need for her taking over any plan he might have had.

She was waking fully, writhing in his arms, panting, beginning to moan, too. As she joined the action, he sped up, driving into her with force, holding her body as tightly to his as he could.

As his finish approached and he pressed his forehead to the back of her shoulder, grimacing through the tense fire knotting in his belly, Brenna stiffened.

"Vali...Vali, wait."

He ignored her, driving even harder.

Now she fought his hold, trying to pull free of him, but strong as she was, he was much stronger. And even through her struggles, he could sense her pleasure, the way she gasped and whimpered.

"Don't. Please don't—please," she gasped. "Vali—not inside me."

Her growing anxiety finally overwhelmed her pleasure and made it more difficult to ignore her. Yet he clamped his arms and held her.

"Vali, please!"

He couldn't. His conscience stabbed at him, and he finally, on the verge of release, stopped. For a moment, they were still, he inside her, they both breathing heavily.

Then he gave up and pulled out. He rolled to his back, still hard and throbbing, and stared up at the ceiling.

"Do you want children with me, Brenna?"

He was angry. He shouldn't have been—disappointed, frustrated, yes. But it was wrong to be angry, he knew that. Brenna didn't deserve his anger, no matter her reasons for resisting what he wanted.

No, she didn't. *He* did. He'd tried to sneak this on her, to foist it upon her, to force something that she didn't yet want.

While he grappled with self-loathing, Brenna rolled to face him. Then she did the worst thing she could have done in that moment. She apologized.

"I'm sorry. I know you want—I'm sorry." She reached down and took hold of him. "I'll bring you to your release this way."

Disgusted with himself, he grabbed her hand. "No."

Too harsh he'd been, he knew. Trapped in a whirlpool of terrible feelings, all directed inward, Vali tossed back the furs and got out of bed.

Brenna sat up. "I do want children with you. Very much. I—only—I'm not ready. Please don't be angry with me."

That was the closest she'd ever come to saying the truth of it. Vali turned back to her and saw his beloved wife, looking rumpled and sad, and felt even worse about himself. He bent over and swept his fingers down the side of her face.

"It's not you I'm angry with, my love. I need to sort my thoughts. Forgive me for my brutishness." He kissed her cheek and picked his breeches up from the floor.

When he was dressed, Brenna was still sitting in bed, quietly watching him.

"I'm going to ride out to the village and get an early start. Will I see you there today?"

She nodded. "Of course."

With a smile and a tip of his head, he opened the door.

"Vali."

He turned back to her.

"I love you."

"And I you, shieldmaiden. In this life and the next. Never doubt that."

~oOo~

Later that morning, after a few hours of good, hard labor, Vali felt clearer in his head. His regret for the morning remained, but he knew what he would do. When he saw his wife and they had a quiet moment together, they would talk. He would give her what she needed—what she told him she needed, not what he thought she needed.

And if Jarl Åke threatened her in any way or refused her what she needed, then Vali would kill him. Whatever the consequences.

Brenna had not yet joined the work at the village, and as it neared midday and the air filled with the savory aroma of the coming meal, Vali took on some small worry. Not for her safety—they were as safe as ever they'd been—but for her feeling. Even in his regret, he'd been harsh and distant to her before he'd taken his leave of her, and perhaps avowing his love had not been enough.

A commotion behind him drew him away from his thoughts, and he turned toward the rise where the freshly-hewn wood beams rested, awaiting their use. Four boys, none old enough yet to be called man, struggled to lift a round, rough beam that had the day before been a tree.

They were not rebuilding the village in the image of what it had once been. For one thing, there were more people now, as Ivan's subjects were joining them and expanding the population—and making it, Vali thought, more of a true town, one that might draw its own commerce rather than be simply a place of dwelling and farming.

For another thing, more of the raiders than only Vali and Brenna had decided to settle here. Orm was staying. Harald had mated with a village girl and was staying, as well as a few of the others. So they were building longhouses in with the Estland huts.

They weren't raiders at all any longer. They were settlers. Vali was finding that an easier adjustment than he had expected— although he had not yet spent much time in the fields.

He walked over to the boys, all of whom backed away as if they were guilty of some transgression. Vali was big among his people; among the Estlanders he was nearly a giant. Even after all these months, many of the young ones tended to goggle up at him, perhaps expecting him to grab one up for a snack—especially those who had been on Ivan's lands before.

"What do you get up to here?" he asked in the Estland tongue, glowering down at the boys, enjoying himself a bit at their expense.

One of the boys stepped forward, shaking back a mop of unkempt dark hair. Jakob was his name. "Sten called for us to carry a beam to him."

The beam was far too large for the boys, all with skinny arms, to carry. Even four could not hope to do more than roll it— and Sten knew it, too. He'd been having his own fun with them, who tended to be in the way more than not.

Vali cocked a brow, not yet finished with his enjoyment. "Then you must do so. Why jape about here while a task is before you?"

"We…we cannot lift it." That came from another boy, Nigul, smaller and younger than the first. Jakob punched him in the arm, making him yell and rub the spot.

"We can. We will."

Vali laughed. "No, you will not." He pushed them out of his way and lifted the beam on his own, setting it on his shoulder. All four boys looked up in awe and wonder.

"You're very strong," Nigul marveled. Vali looked down at the fair-haired child with clear blue eyes. He resembled

Brenna. Vali wondered if his own son might have favored his mother. He closed his eyes until the thought and its ache passed on.

"And you should remember that I am. Go, now, and find real work to do." The boys scampered off, and Vali carried the beam down to Sten's building site.

As he set it down, he laughed. "You think we have too many healthy boys in the village? At least one of them would have broken a limb before they gave up their task."

Sten stepped back from the post hole he was digging. "Usch! Those boys are underfoot. I thought it would take them long to know it was hopeless, and I could get some work done while they tried."

"Why pester you?"

"We are the foreigners, building our strange big houses, and Orm has already scared them away with his grumping." Sten lifted his water skin and took a long drink. "We need to make real work for them. Where are their fathers?"

"Jakob's father was in the village when Ivan attacked, and Andres' father was lost when we retaliated. I think the other boys belong to our team on the coast."

"Ah. Well, mothers, then. Someone to put them out of trouble."

"I will find them work after the meal." As she spoke, Brenna came up from behind and stood at Vali's side.

When he lifted his arm, she tucked herself under it and wrapped her arms around his waist. He was encouraged that the tension of their morning had abated, but still they needed to clear that thrum from between them.

"I am glad to see you. I thought you'd be earlier."

243

"One of the horses injured himself in his stall. I helped tend to him."

"Badly hurt?"

"No. He opened his foreleg, but it's closed now, and he's not hobbled. But he was anxious, and he kicked Dan in the chest. He'll be abed for a day or two. Olga is with him."

Vali nodded at Sten and led his wife away. When they had a private distance from the busy work around them, he cupped his hand around her face. "Forgive me for this morning."

"Let's speak not of it." She turned her head in his hand and kissed his palm. "It is forgotten."

"No, Brenna. I mean to say this: When you are ready to bear my child inside you again, I will be ready, as well. I will wait and not bring it up again, in any way, until you do."

Her eyes brimmed, and she gave him something like a smile—but not the bright beam that he had once so arrogantly expected to bring to her every day. "I know I ask too much. I want what you want. I'm not sure why I hesitate."

"It doesn't matter. What you ask is not too much. We will wait."

"Thank you." She raised up onto her toes, and he leaned down to meet her. Around them, as he kissed his wife, Vali heard the beginnings of the midday meal—the sounds of hammering and sawing ended, and people moved toward the center of the village, where the women had arrayed the food they'd prepared. The sounds of conversation changed from work to leisure.

He pulled back, his hands firmly on her bottom, cupping each firm, perfect mound. "Are you hungry?"

"I am not, but I will sit with you while you take your meal."

The skause and bread smelled fine, and Vali was indeed hungry. But he had more pressing appetites. "Come to the river with me."

"What is there?"

"Privacy. And a bank covered in moss and soft grasses, where I might lay you down and have my way." When a stoniness came into her eyes, he added, "And then spill my seed there on the grass."

Her expression softened. "The river is where we will find privacy?"

"As much as can be found between here and the castle—and if anyone comes upon us, would that be so terrible? To have our love seen that way?"

"Perhaps they could join us." With that astounding sentence, Brenna pulled on his hand, leading him toward the river.

He held back and pulled her to face him. "Brenna?"

She laughed and then shook her head. "No. I wanted only to see that look on your face."

Vali was relieved. The thought of sharing her, with man or woman, tightened his insides uncomfortably. But the thought of being seen excited him. She was generally private, unusually so for their people. He missed the bold days of her pregnancy, when she could barely contain herself, no matter the witness.

And when she wore dresses with skirts he could lift in a rush.

He kissed her hand. "To the river, wench. I mean to make you scream my name so all our friends will hear."

17

Freya turned her head and gave Brenna's hip a push, making her take a step to keep her balance.

"Hush, love. Be brave." She rubbed the salve Olga had given her into the sore on the horse's withers. Freya shifted her feet restlessly, and the skin under Brenna's fingers twitched. The wound was wide and raw, and Freya would bear no saddle for the next few days. "I should have saddled you myself yesterday. I'm sorry."

Vali stepped to the stall door and rested his heavy arms across the top. "How is she?"

"It looks worse, now that it's clean. She must have been in pain yesterday, though she didn't show it." Finished with the salve, she stepped forward and rubbed her horse's nose.

"She is well suited for her rider. Stoic and brave."

Brenna smiled at her husband. Such a fine-looking man he was, especially when he grinned in that way, lighting up his blue eyes and showing the good man under the fierce warrior.

"I thought you had already ridden out." He often rose before her, and he usually got an earlier start to the village. Brenna had been taking up some duties around the castle, helping with the weaving and other domestic needs the new village would have, so she left later in the day.

"I came back for you, wondering about Freya and whether she could be saddled."

"I should not have let a boy tend her. My horse, my care." They had been finding work for everyone old enough to do it, and they had put a few of the younger boys in the stable and out of trouble. The day before, she had allowed Jakob to saddle her horse. Before she'd mounted, she had checked the girth and the blanket, and all had seemed well. Freya had not complained at all.

But when Brenna had pulled the saddle and blanket from Freya's back that night, she'd found an ugly, raw patch, sticky and coated in loose hair, just behind her withers. There had been a fold in the blanket, rubbing her raw all the day.

Now Jakob was hiding from Brenna. She had let him see her warrior face.

"Ride with me, then. My mount can carry us both."

Vali had been riding the same horse, a huge bay, all the time they'd been in Estland, just as Brenna had, but he had never named his. Their people were much more likely to name their swords than their beasts. Yet Brenna felt an affinity for animals, an empathy. She saw them watching and listening. They were not tools. They were beings. They felt pain and knew joy.

And a horse was more than any other—she and Freya were a team. Brenna had let her down.

"Yes, I will." She kissed her equine friend on the nose and left the stall. Before she let Vali take her arm and lead her out of the stable, she scooped up sweet grain and let Freya feed from her hand.

"You spoil that beast," Vali muttered, but with affection.

"No. I respect her."

When they were out on the grounds, Brenna mounted Vali's horse, and Vali came up as soon as she kicked her foot free of the stirrup. Once he was settled, he pulled her back until her bottom rested firmly against him and she could feel the contours of his muscular thighs, as well as the resting ridge of his sex.

They had never ridden this way before, but there were no horses to spare, so Brenna's choices were few. Not that she would have made another choice. To be so close to Vali, to feel his arms around her and the broad shield of his chest behind her, made her feel peaceful and content.

He kept the horse's gait at a quick walk, and the rocking of their bodies against each other soon had Vali hard and Brenna wet. When he bent his head and kissed the skin just below her ear, she chuckled, though it became a moan as his tongue drew a wet line to her shoulder.

"We neglected to consider this complication." She turned her head and nuzzled into his beard.

"I considered this. It is why I came back for you as I did."

"What?"

"Leif offered to send his horse back with me so that you could ride. I declined. I wanted you where I have you now."

He took the reins in one hand, and with his newly free hand reached under her leather top and linen tunic and pulled at the laces of her breeches.

"Vali, we cannot couple in the saddle."

"Were you dressed as a woman, we most certainly could. With your gift tied up in breeches, I will have to content myself with your pleasure. And you will be in my debt."

As he spoke, he opened her breeches and pushed his hand in, over her belly and between her legs. The rough skin of his fingers abraded her most tender flesh in a way she knew well and craved. She sighed and shifted, making way for him.

"So wet," he breathed, the words dancing over her skin. "Touch yourself, Brenna."

She had been resting on his shoulder, her eyes closed, giving over to his touch and the way it made her body clench and shudder. At his request—or perhaps it was a command—she opened her eyes and looked up. He was watching his hand in her breeches.

"What?" she asked.

With the hand that still held the reins, he pulled the tie that gathered her linen tunic over her shoulders. She no longer wore a smaller version of a man's tunic. Vali had hated the way she bound her breasts under it, and he knew that when she wore a hangerock the clothing was cut so that she didn't need to bind herself. He had spoken to Olga—after the fact, she'd learned he had—and her husband and her friend had conspired to have made for her what she wore now, a soft leather top that was modeled after the hangerock but cut short and split up the middle from the waist down. Under it, she wore a woven linen tunic with loose sleeves that was more like her sleeping shifts than any shirt she'd worn before.

The cut of the leather top rested just at the bottom of her breasts and was secured with lacing up the front and straps over her shoulders. She felt nearly indecent in it. She also felt beautiful. It was the perfect compromise between the comfort and practicality of men's clothing and the grace of women's.

Since she had taken to wearing it, other women had made similar designs for themselves. The village was full of women in breeches.

When her tunic was loosened, as Vali had just done, Brenna's breasts were nearly free.

"Take your breasts in your hands, as you do in our bed."

He punctuated that command by pushing his fingers into her. She made the odd, weak noise she made whenever he found a new peak of pleasure inside her, and she put her hands over his and pressed him hard to her.

"I want to see your breasts, wife. I want to see you make them tight with pleasure."

Vali, being more experienced than she in matters of coupling, had always taken charge of theirs, and Brenna enjoyed that. She liked to relax and let him show her things she'd never known even about her own body. But after they had been able to be together this way again, when he wanted to try right away to get her with child again, she had not been able to be so relaxed.

She couldn't explain, even to herself, why she was not yet ready to grow another child inside her. It had to do with more things than she understood—the uncertain timing of the ships' return, the work of the village and all the changes that meant, and something greater and vaguer than either of those. She had carried a child and grown to love him while he was still inside her. She had carried the life and dreams he'd meant for her, and for Vali, for their family and their future.

And then one day, she'd woken and been alone in her body. Her son was gone, his body burned away, as if he'd never existed at all. All she had was the memory of her hopes and dreams for him, and the memory of his tiny body moving in hers.

The thought of another taking his place made her sad and afraid. But she didn't understand why, so she couldn't tell Vali. So she'd left him frustrated, with only frail reasons that teetered on shaky ground.

Dissatisfied with and perplexed by her resistance, he'd tried again and again to persuade her otherwise. Then he'd stopped trying to persuade her and had tried to catch her unawares, exploiting her desire for him and hoping she'd lose herself in it. Her fear was too great, however.

She'd grown wary, waiting for the end of his patience, despite his loving attention to her in all other ways. She'd taken his slowness to begin the build of their own house, always offering instead his assistance with other builds, as a sign that his feelings toward her were fading.

And then, two weeks ago, just when she'd thought she could see the end, he'd apologized and told her that he would honor her need and wait.

Since then, he had begun their house. And she had been able again to relax in his touch.

She opened her tunic and let the early summer air and sun warm her body. Then she cupped her hands around her breasts and closed her thumbs and fingers on her nipples.

Vali's hand moved, coming out of her and focusing again on the small knot where all sensation seemed to concentrate. She flexed and arched as hot bolts of need pulsed through her. She could feel him, hard as iron against her back.

At her ear, her husband groaned. "I may need to take you after all."

"How..." If he could think of a way, then she would not stop him. She had recently discovered a taste for coupling out of doors.

He pulled off the path and stopped his horse near a birch tree. Then he swung his leg over and brought her with him, landing on the ground with her in his arms.

Setting her down by the tree, he stared hard into her eyes and grabbed at her open breeches, yanking them down her hips. Then he dropped to his knees before her and buried his face between her legs. She arched backward, grabbing at his braid to keep her balance. His hands dug into her hips to hold her as well.

Nothing in the world felt the way his mouth on her sex felt—his beard, his tongue, even his breath, it all made her quiver and moan.

He spread her legs as far as he could, and then his hands eased up her belly and took hold of her breasts, doing himself what he had earlier, and so briefly, wanted her to do.

Her release came on her quickly, almost unexpectedly, when he bit down around her bud and danced his tongue over it. Caught in the barrage of sensation, she fell back and would have truly fallen except that they were so close to the tree. Her back hit the trunk, and Vali went on, undeterred, until she squealed and yanked on his hair, too sensitive to let him continue.

When he stood, his face glistened in the sunshine, and he grinned broadly, naughtily. Then while she still reeled, he grabbed her shoulder and spun her around to face the tree. He yanked her hips back and was inside her before she could take her next breath. She grunted harshly as his hips slammed against her bottom and he filled her. The sound he made had no human name.

This rough, feral mating—this was what she had been seeing all her life, in longhouses and raiding camps. She'd thought it ugly and crude, and it had made her cold to the very idea of physical love. Yet now, as Vali shoved her again and again into the birch bark, as it tore loose in her grasping hands, as they both grunted like wild boars, Brenna could think of nothing more beautiful. The feel of it—his body and her body, his need and hers, their love together, under a warm sun—was freedom itself.

When her next climax arrived, she nearly bit the tree to hold back the scream that wanted to tear from her throat. Then Vali pulled out with a roar, and Brenna reached back and took him in her hand, stroking him as he completed.

She had not needed to be vigilant; she could trust him now to withdraw and spill his seed outside her.

They both sagged forward to the tree and rested there, sapped of strength and will.

Vali kissed her bare shoulder and drew his fingers along her scar. "I am complete. Here, with you."

Too overcome to answer with a word, Brenna reached up and laid her hand on his head, holding him close.

They heard the sound of a rider, coming on at a gallop, and both turned and began to settle their clothing.

The rider was Dan, who was one of the team that had been on the coast, watching for the ships. As he pulled up his horse, he glanced at their disheveled attire but said nothing.

"The ships?" Vali asked, tying his breeches.

"Yes. Three. They were perhaps an hour from land when I left, so they have disembarked by now. I left Knut to greet them."

Her clothing arranged, Brenna had stepped to Vali's side. Now, Dan gave her a dark, surprising look and then turned back to Vali. "Vali—they show only Jarl Åke's colors. Snorri is not with them."

Brenna's heart sank. Snorri's men had comprised half of the raiders who had stayed behind and now made up more than half of those who survived. He would not have let Åke sail without him if there were still peace between them, and he would not leave his men to Åke's whim if there were no peace.

If Åke had come alone, then there were only two possible scenarios: either Snorri was on his way, too, and they would face war on the shores of Estland again, this time friend against friend—or Snorri was dead, and Åke had claimed his lands and title.

In that case, Brenna, who knew Åke well, feared for all her friends who were not sworn to her jarl.

Which included her husband.

And might well soon include herself.

She looked up and found Vali's eyes on hers, as she so often did. In their blue depths, she could see that he had made all the same connections and conjectures that she had. He nodded, once, and then turned back to Dan. His clansman.

"Ride to the village and tell Leif and the others. Brenna and I will return to the castle and begin preparations. We'll need to ride to the coast well before nightfall."

From his horse, Dan pulled a face—that dark look that Brenna understood now. He was already seeing enemies where he had seen friends that morning.

Vali reached up and grabbed his arm. "Whatever happened across the sea, it did not happen here. We are all friends. This long, hard winter, we were made family. That has not yet changed. Do not behave as if it has."

The two men stared at each other, and then Dan nodded and rode off, toward the village.

When they were just the two of them again, Brenna reached out and grabbed her husband's hand. "Vali…" she began, but then knew not how to finish.

He pulled her close. "I know, my love. We will weather this storm as we have all the others. Together."

~oOo~

By the time the party from the castle arrived at the coast, the landing party had set up its camp. As the riders dismounted and dropped their horses' reins—Brenna had borrowed Orm's mount, as he had stayed behind to ready the castle in case of trouble—Åke walked out to meet them, with Calder and the next oldest of the jarl's sons, Eivind, just behind him.

As he approached, Brenna looked past him and noted something curious: the new arrivals were all men, and heavily armed. That in itself was not curious; raiders were always prepared to fight. Before the peace with Prince Toomas, they had been holding their plans of attack for when they would be reinforced by the ships' return.

But Brenna noted that there were no women, no children. No crates of supplies beyond the typical for a raid. A party meaning to found a settlement would have brought settlers.

Åke had not.

She could put no further thought to it, however, because he was standing before them.

Despite the days he'd just spent on the sea, Åke was dressed well, as if for a thing, with thick golden chains on his chest and a heavy black bearskin over his shoulders. He was making a show of his power and wealth—his claim.

Smiling broadly, kindly, he opened his arms wide as the riders dismounted, and he went straight for Leif.

"Leif Olavsson! It is good to see you. I have missed you as I might have missed a son of my own blood."

Leif accepted the embrace warmly and then gave a respectful, humble nod. "Jarl Åke. The winter was long. We are glad to have you safely here."

With sharp pats of Leif's shoulders, the jarl turned to Brenna, while Calder and Eivind greeted Leif, their friend.

"And Brenna God's-Eye. My own great shieldmaiden. The ships carried home to us more stories of your exploits for the sagas. And you look very well. Odin's presence has been strong with you this winter, I see." Åke put his hand on her face, drawing his thumb down to widen her right eye. She sensed Vali's tension at the too-intimate touch, but Brenna knew the jarl would do nothing more.

Even Åke did not like to look long at her eye. Brenna had forgotten, during these months away, how it hurt to be thought different and not quite human. As she met Åke's wavering gaze with her steady one, she felt a shaking in her chest.

No, she did not wish to return to the land on which she'd been born, where she was the God's-Eye. Home was here, where she was simply Brenna.

When he waited, bringing his eyes back to hers, Brenna realized that he expected her to speak. So she bent her head in a show of honor. "Jarl Åke."

She said no more, and he stepped back. Then he turned to Vali, and her husband took a deep breath, making himself as tall and broad as he could. He was head and more taller than the jarl.

"Vali Storm-Wolf. You are famed as well, and I am glad to see that your story continues."

"Thank you, Jarl Åke, it does. I would know how fares my jarl, Snorri."

Brenna watched Åke's eyes and saw them narrow in a way she knew was dangerous. But he shaped his features into a sympathetic frown and laid his hand on Vali's arm. "Snorri is drinking with the gods in Valhalla. I am sorry, friend."

Vali remained stiff and straight and did not acknowledge Åke. He was a warrior, not a diplomat. Neither was Brenna. Though Vali was good with words, he struggled to manage his emotions. Leif was the one who always spoke smoothly among them.

After a pause long enough to make it clear that the lack of response had been noted, Åke stepped back and opened his arms to all the riders. "The world is not as it was. But I hope that we will all remain friends. We have much to discuss, I know. For tonight, though, night is upon us. Let us show you our hospitality here in camp, and then we will ride to the castle after the dawn."

He held out his hand to Brenna. "Brenna God's-Eye, join me. I would have your word on the winter."

She took a step toward him, holding her own hand out to Vali. Åke stopped and gave them both a bemused look. "I mean you no dishonor, Vali Storm-Wolf, but I have known the God's-Eye long. I esteem her vision, and I would take a private moment with her."

"I will stay with my wife," Vali nearly snarled.

"We are wed, Jarl," Brenna said at the same time.

Vali seemed jealous and territorial in a way beyond her expectation. Åke was no threat to her, not now, and she doubted that he ever would be. He could be harsh, and the raiders under his command were known to be particularly savage, but he had treated her well enough when she was his slave, and he had freed her when he owed her a debt.

He had put Leif to her training and given her the chance to be the shieldmaiden she was. He would be disappointed to lose her, yes. But he respected her as the God's-Eye, if nothing else. He believed her charmed, and he would not risk the wrath of Odin by harming her.

And now, when she was still sworn to him, he would have no cause at all even to wish her ill.

At their simultaneous statements, Åke lifted his brows in surprise, then collected himself swiftly. Brenna saw that dark narrowing flash through his eyes then, but again, he smiled. "Then good tidings are in order, and we shall drink to the lasting goodwill of the gods. And I welcome the great Storm-Wolf into my clan."

Feeling Vali tense as if to reject Åke's assumption, Brenna squeezed his hand. This was not the time. Not in the dark, at camp, surrounded by men whose loyalty to Åke had not been stretched by a winter in a new home.

Her husband relaxed, and they followed Åke to his tent. Calder and Eivind fell in behind them. Though Brenna knew both men well, she was uneasy to have them at her back.

She caught Leif's eye as they passed, and saw that he, too, was ill at ease.

Another storm to weather. She hoped Vali was right, and they would be standing together when it passed.

~oOo~

The talk in Åke's tent was calm and unthreatening. He called Leif to join them, and they all sat, the jarl and his sons, and

259

the leaders at the castle, facing each other, in something like a circle. The jarl poured mead and offered up a prayer for Vali and Brenna's marriage. They drank, and then he asked them about the course of their months in Estland. He was curious and civil, and he seemed pleased that they had taken over Ivan's princedom as well and grown the holdings in his name.

He offered Vali and Brenna a tent of their own, calling it their wedding tent, though they'd been married for months. When they were bedded down for the night and the camp had gone quiet, Vali lay on his back, fully dressed, his axes at his side.

Brenna sat beside him. She had worn her shield and sword, because she met her jarl as a shieldmaiden, but now they lay near the opening of the tent.

"There is wrong here," Vali muttered, keeping his voice low lest it carry through the cloth walls of the tent. "Åke does not mean to settle. Why did we stay, then? What is it he wants?"

"Calder made the claim. Perhaps the jarls did not want it." She didn't believe the words coming from her own lips. When they had landed in the late summer before, she had wondered why they had moved inland so far, why they had sailed so late in the season. It only made sense if Åke—and, at the time, Snorri—had meant to explore for a possible settlement.

Vali lifted his head and stared at her. "You don't believe that."

She sighed. "No."

"Snorri was a good man, Brenna. He was fair, and he found honor, not glory, in his power. The same cannot be said for Åke."

"Hush." Though she couldn't see through the tent walls, she glanced around, worried, and listened for sounds that someone might be near. "Åke is hard, yes. But he is not bad. He has treated me well. He made me a shieldmaiden."

"First he made you a slave."

"I offered myself as a slave. I was starving and had no other choice."

"You were a child. If he meant to take care of you, he could have done better than that."

"I had had my first blood. He could have done worse than he did."

Vali sat up and picked up the tail of the braid that draped over her shoulder. "We are at risk, my love. You need to see it. Open those beautiful eyes and see that we are but the breadth of this braid from real danger. Snorri is dead. Åke came with three ships full of raiders, and no settlers. He does not have peace in his heart, and those of us sworn to Snorri are surrounded by men he might make our enemies."

The answer was simple and right before them. "You are sworn now to no one, Vali. Snorri is dead. You would not renounce him to swear an oath to Åke now. And then the risk is over."

But Vali shook his head. "I will not swear on my arm ring to him, Brenna. I will not be beholden to him. I have no respect for him."

"He was a great warrior."

"Yet he is no great man."

Brenna's heart began to race. What Vali said—it truly was dangerous, more than she had ever expected. "He claims this land in his name alone. He claims Snorri's jarldom as well. If you don't swear to him, then we cannot stay here. And we will have no place on his ships. We will have nowhere to go."

The thought of losing this home she had found and fought for made her feel a fear deep and cold that settled in her bones.

"As I said, there is danger all around us."

She clutched at his tunic and shook it. "Vali, you must swear. You must! I am sworn. Leif, your friend, is sworn to him. Would we be, were he so terrible?"

"Of course you would be. If you thought there were no other choice, which is why you urge me to do the same now. But I will concede this: I will learn more about Snorri's death. When I do, I will decide if I will offer Åke my fealty—or if I will kill him."

"Vali."

He pulled her close and kissed her. "We'll not find our ground tonight, shieldmaiden. Let us rest, and we'll see what tomorrow brings. I only want you to see. Do you now see?"

"I do."

He lay down again, bringing her with him and settling her head on his chest. "Tell me that you're with me, that we stand together."

She had been willing to forswear Åke when she thought Snorri would have a claim in Estland. She would always choose Vali over any other. But now it meant that she would be truly homeless, more completely than ever before. "I am with you. But I'm afraid."

"Be brave, my love. Believe that the gods are with us."

Brenna thought that if the gods were with them, they would have had their son lying between them.

~oOo~

At dawn, they broke camp and set out for the castle, arriving at midday. Those who had stayed back had prepared for the jarl's arrival—whether that meant good will or ill. Thus far, the mood had been friendly, though Brenna knew everyone felt what she did—a keen watchfulness, just under the surface.

Åke toured the castle and the grounds, then rode out with his sons, and with Leif and Knut, to see the village being rebuilt. He came back full of compliments and ideas, seeming enthusiastic for the settlement and all they had accomplished over the winter.

As the day's light waned, they put out a feast in the hall to welcome the jarl and the ships. Brenna sat between Calder and Vali and scanned the long table, full of raiders and villagers, everyone talking and enjoying themselves. She felt hope.

Noticing an absence among her friends, Brenna leaned to Vali. "Where is Viger?"

Vali, still suspicious, set down his cup and scanned the room as well. "I will see what I can find out."

Brenna laid her hand on his thigh. "No. I'm sure he is fine. He has probably caught Eha for a tumble. Åke will remark if you leave the table before he speaks."

"I do not care."

"But I do. Please. If this might go smoothly, then we must assume the best."

He frowned at her but settled back in his chair. Not long after, Åke stood, and the table went quiet.

"I have seen great things today," he began. "And I have learned of even more. To those of you who gave up a winter warm in the bosom of your families to stake our claim here, I am honored to have had your good service. I know that many of you had sworn an oath to Jarl Snorri Thorsson. He was a great and honorable man, and he died an honorable death. I would be proud and humbled to take your oaths now and call you all my clansmen. The seers tell of a great raiding season coming, one that will fill our chests with gold and our blood with battle."

"And what of settlers for this claim?"

Åke turned to Vali, his eyes glittering with irritation at having been interrupted. "Vali Storm-Wolf asks an excellent question. I cannot spare the raiding ships to carry farmers and seeds, but I will have ships built so that we might settle this good claim later this summer."

"Now is the sowing season, Jarl."

Åke gave up the pretense of good humor and scowled at Vali. "You have made friends of the villagers, have you not? Some of them sit among us at this table. They can sow the fields. What concern is farming of yours, Vali Storm-Wolf?"

Again, Brenna quieted her husband with her hand on his leg. Then she stood. "Vali and I would stay here and settle. This has become a home to us. We are building a longhouse in the village."

She could see that she had shocked her jarl and taken his tongue. For an arduous moment, he stared at her—right at her, not wavering from her eye at all. Brenna stared back, unwilling to be the one who would break.

When he recollected his power of speech, he asked, his voice more quiet than before, "You would lay down your sword and shield, Brenna God's-Eye? You are my sworn shieldmaiden."

"I want to build a family, Åke. I would ask that you let me."

She knew that Vali didn't like her tone of request, but she knew Åke better than he, and a demand would not go far with him.

"I am disappointed. You think this is what Odin wants of you?"

"I do, yes."

Again, he stared. Then he sighed—loudly, dramatically. "I cannot defy the will of the Allfather. And you have brought me great honor, and I would see you happy. If this is your path, then you have my blessing."

Relief nearly folded her knees. "Thank you, Åke. Thank you."

When she sat, she smiled at her husband. "We are safe, and we have our home. He is not a bad man, Vali. He is worth your fealty."

Vali's brow still bunched with wary concern.

~oOo~

Brenna went up before Vali that night, feeling lighter than she would have thought. Though Vali had not yet agreed to swear to Åke, he would see that it was the right choice. They would have their home and begin their life together in earnest.

When their house was built, she would be ready to make another child. The certainty of that truth hit her as she dropped her sleeping shift over her head and then unbraided her hair, standing before the unlit fire. She grinned.

Behind her, the door from the corridor opened with force, and she jumped, prepared to complain at Vali for coming in drunk. She had left him not so long before; he must have been vying with Leif and Orm again in a drinking contest.

But it wasn't Vali. It was Calder.

"Calder, this is the room I share with my husband." That thought almost made her smile, too—not so long ago, the idea of a private chamber like this had seemed bizarre and constraining.

She didn't smile, though, because Calder strode directly to her, his expression blank. She understood that she was in danger with just enough time to glance at the wall across from her, where her sword and shield hung.

Calder swung at her, but she managed to get her arm up and block him. When she tried to run for her sword, her shift tangled around her legs and slowed her down. Calder grabbed for her hair and yanked her back, punching her in the side of the head. His fist felt doubly hard, as if he'd been wearing an armored gauntlet.

The room folded in on itself, and she fell.

While she lay on the floor, trying to make words or any sound at all, still trying to understand what was happening, he punched her again, and again, and she stopped thinking.

18

Vali sat at the table and studied the room. From every perspective, it was a room full of rough men, well fed and well drunk, enjoying a night of leisure. There were fewer women around the castle these days, as the village had been built up enough for most families to have moved in, even if they had to share quarters for a while. They were sowing their seeds and tending their flocks, and there was no time for the trek from and to the castle each day. Now, there were only the women who'd stayed on to manage the work here.

He was glad; Åke's men were rough even with their clanswomen, and Vali had been concerned how the Estlander women would fare among them. But the raiders who had stayed the winter were keeping their newly arrived fellows in check, it seemed.

Still, he was ill at ease. He did not believe Åke would so easily give up his charmed shieldmaiden, and it stuck wrong in his head that he had sailed in three ships laden with raiders to bring the news that he was not yet ready to settle his claim. If he had meant to bring them all home, where had he meant to put them?

Frequently, he had sought out Olga's glance as she moved through the men, managing the meal and the drinks after. She was clearly stressed and weary, and Vali thought she seemed sad as well. He guessed at the reason: she and Leif had grown close over these months and developed a deep friendship. Even under the best of circumstances, the arrival of the ships meant that Leif would be sailing soon.

Vali had suggested more than once that Leif take her home with him. And he'd thought his friend had begun to consider it, despite his reservations about her fitness for their world and his insistence that they were no more than friends.

Then they had brought her younger brothers back from Ivan's land, and any consideration of taking her from Estland had seemingly ended.

Now, Leif sat near the fireplace, with Calder and Eivind. Vali's suspicions of Åke did not fully extend to his sons. Calder was a brutal man, too, as Vali had witnessed. But he had seen enough of him to know that he sometimes felt conflict between his duty to his father and his honor as a man. Eivind was too young yet to have been overly hardened by his father's way.

And there was no better endorsement for Åke's sons than Leif's friendship. So Vali sat at the table and drank his mead and watched the friends talk. Then they stood together and left the room through the back entrance, toward the kitchen.

Vali thought that Leif had shot him a look, but it was gone before he could be sure. Perhaps his wife was right, and his suspicion was unwarranted.

Brenna had gone up to bed not long before. She had found complete ease in Åke's blessing of her desire to stay and make a home here in Estland. He'd seen it in her posture as her jarl had said the words: the breath that had softened her stance and unclenched her hands. She believed that they were safe. She had let her guard down completely.

Unwarranted or not, Vali felt restless in the room now, with Brenna away from him, and neither Åke nor his sons where he could see them. He finished his mead and left the room, headed to his wife.

He had just topped the wide, curving staircase when his good friend Leif stepped out, emerging from the shadow of a side corridor.

"Is there trouble?" he asked, resting his hand where his main axe would have been had he not been in his home and making an attempt, at his wife's behest, not to challenge the jarl.

"Yes, my friend. There is."

Then Leif, still shrouded by the dark of the corridor—why were the torches out?—swung his axe.

~oOo~

He woke in his own bed, with his head throbbing and his arms aching. When he forced himself to sit, he groaned as the room tilted, but he pushed on until he could swing his legs over the side.

No one was with him. Had he been injured, or was he ill? Trying to clear his mind, he dropped his head into his hands and winced when he touched a tender, stitched wound above his ear.

Hurt, then. Attacked? In the castle?

Brenna. Where was Brenna?

He stood at once, and then fell to his knees when the floor pitched sharply under him. With a deep breath and formidable will, he found his feet and stood, wide-legged, until the room settled. As he searched for steadiness, he tried to remember.

Åke was here. Raiders. Calder and Eivind. They'd had a feast. Åke had given them his blessing.

Leif. Leif had attacked him. His friend. He had swung his axe; he must have hit him with the poll side.

And now Brenna was not with him.

"BRENNA!" he shouted and stormed to the door, slamming into the wall when the room slanted again. "BRENNA!"

The door opened and Orm came through, followed by Olga. Even with his double vision, Vali could see that they both looked terrible. Orm had a stitched gash through his cheek, from the bridge of his nose to his jaw, cutting through his grey beard. Olga's lips were split, and she looked as though she hadn't slept in days.

Orm took his arm. "Vali, it is good that you return to us. But sit and rest. There is nothing you can do in this moment."

The horror in Orm's words was so vast that Vali weakened and let the old man lead him back to his bed. "Where is Brenna?"

"You have been two days away. Let Olga tend to you, and then I will tell you all. We need you well, Vali Storm-Wolf."

Olga pushed him to lie back, but he caught her hands in his. "Olga. I need Brenna. Where is she?"

She was shaking. Tears filled her brown eyes and brimmed over. "They took her. I am sorry. I did not know...I did not think he—"

"He? Leif? Leif took her?" It made no sense. When he could get no answers from the crying woman, he threw her to the side and sat up again, turning on Orm. "Tell me NOW!"

"Åke is gone. His sworn men are gone, even those who were with us this winter—those who survived. Leif was with them. Those who resisted Åke's will are dead, or were left for dead. We are only seven raiders here now, all of us wounded. We found you bound in the stable after it was over."

His head pounded and scattered his still-unclear thoughts. It was much like what he'd feared, and yet he could not make sense. "Where is my WIFE?"

"I was there, lying on the ground. They took me for dead, and so I saw. Åke took her, Vali. She was unconscious, beaten, and bound. Calder threw her over a horse and rode off with her." Orm paused and took a long breath. "The ships are gone. She is gone. We are only seven now, none of us whole."

Vali bellowed in shock and rage. And grief. No, not grief. He would not allow grief to have sway in his heart. Grief was defeat, and he would not be defeated. He would get her back. And he would kill everyone who had conspired to take her from him.

Leif, whom he had trusted completely, would go first. He would go slow and hard.

"Who is left?"

"You and I. Dan. Harald. Bjarke. Knut. And Astrid."

"Astrid and Knut are sworn to Åke."

"They were. They resisted his intent to destroy us, and he left them for dead."

Vali stood up and this time shoved the woozy disorientation away with all of his will. "We shall follow them."

Orm shook his head. "Your head is not yet clear, Vali. There are no ships."

"The village has five fishing boats. Surely they can spare one or two."

"And you know that the open sea would break them apart like kindling sticks. We cannot follow, not until we can build a seaworthy vessel, and that will be months."

"NO! NO! THIS CANNOT BE!" What would Åke do to the shieldmaiden who had defied him and dared to make a life beyond his reach? The God's-Eye, whom he considered his own gift from the gods?

Vali's heart raced as if it meant to leave his chest completely. He felt sick at his stomach and consumed by a rage so powerful in its impotence that it drove him to his knees. "BRENNA!"

~oOo~

The castle was eerily quiet with no one else left dwelling in its cavernous depths. Even the raiders who had survived had begun to move to the village.

Alone in any way that mattered, Vali stood in the grounds and hacked at the log that would make the keel of his ship.

He had never built a ship or even worked much wood. He understood the way ships worked on the water, and he knew their composition from stem to stern, but he had never considered why they worked as they did or were composed as they were.

But his father had been a smith, and he had been apprenticed to him in a long-ago life. He had grown up among craftsmen. And he had the will. It would be enough. He would build a ship and sail back to Geitland, even if he would sail alone.

Then he would kill. And then he would collect his wife and bring her home.

Five days had passed since he had woken to find his life and love stolen from him, a week since he had lost her. He felt some lingering disorientation when he turned too quickly, and the throbbing ache at the base of his skull had not left him—but he thought that throb was rage more than wound.

Rage consumed him, waking or sleeping. He could barely speak for the way his fury had made his body taut. Orm, Dan, and the others had tried to engage him in talks and plans, but he cared about nothing but building his ship, finding his wife, and taking his revenge.

Dan and Astrid rode through the gates at a gallop, and Vali stopped his work and his black thoughts and watched them ride up. There was trouble; he could see it on their faces, and he didn't bother to ask.

Astrid spoke, using the blended tongue that they had all picked up, their two languages combined, even when clansmen spoke together. Even Brenna had finally become competent in their communication. "Toomas rides for us. A large mounted force."

"Four score at my count," Dan added.

An army of eighty. Vali sighed, not sure that he cared to fight. His bloodlust was turned a different way.

"We have a peace!" Astrid growled.

"He must have learned that we are weakened beyond resistance." Vali swung his axe down and buried it in one of the supports for the beam he'd been hewing. "He made peace with a force that had bested two of his fellows. We are no longer that force."

"They ride for the village, Vali." Dan gave him a weighty stare.

The village, where his half-built house stood. Where he meant to return with his wife and build a life. Where the friends he had left dwelt.

"Then we fight."

~oOo~

Vali pulled his axe through the neck of a soldier and watched him drop. The road was piled deep with bodies, and the village burned around him, buildings so new the sap in the wood crackled in the flames that destroyed them.

It was another total loss, and the bodies at his feet wore the weave of village linen more than the armor of Toomas's soldiers.

The soldiers slew indiscriminately, taking unarmed women and children as quickly as they took the men who challenged them. Amidst the clang and grunt of combat, Vali heard Astrid's warrior shriek, and the echo of it in the few women who had trained with her.

As he sought his next target, he caught sight of young Nigul, who had only ten years behind him, dangling from the point of a soldier's blade. As he watched, a short iron dagger dropped from the boy's hand. He had tried to fight. Vali roared and threw his axe, leaping after it. When it sank into the soldier's blade arm, Vali was there. He grabbed it, yanked it back, knocked the soldier's helm off with his free hand, and buried his axe in his head.

Nigul, on the ground with the sword through his chest, gurgled and coughed as blood bubbled from his lips and down his chin.

Vali crouched at the boy's side. "It is a great thing to die in battle. You are young to be so honored to sit with the gods in Valhalla. Odin and Thor will be impressed with you, boy."

When the light of life dimmed from his eyes, Nigul was smiling.

Vali sensed movement behind him and, still in a crouch, spun and swung his axe. It buried easily in the belly of a soldier whose armor had broken, and when his entrails began to spill out, Vali dug deep and pulled the mass out with his hands.

He stood and spent a moment to survey what was left of the home he'd chosen. His half-built house was gone, not even enough left to feed the flames that had taken it. No building was left unburned. They were overmatched, two soldiers or more still fighting for every villager.

And then a soldier blew a horn. Vali didn't know their signals, but the soldiers in the village did not stop their fighting, so it was not a call to pull back.

He thought it might well have been a call for another wave. If that were true, it would be an effective means to flatten them completely. They wouldn't even have to dismount.

These soldiers had dismounted, and their surviving horses had massed, as if trained to do so, at the edge of the village. About half of the beasts were dead.

He thought that there were enough living beasts to mount all that remained of his clan and his friends.

They could hold the castle. Its walls were high and solid, and early on they had reinforced it against a possible siege. At least it would give them time to rest and regroup. To make a plan.

"TO THE HORSES! BACK TO THE CASTLE!" he shouted, running through the village. "THE HORSES! RETREAT!"

A familiar voice screamed at his side, and Vali turned toward it, changing his direction without thinking. Olga held a raider's shield in her hands, and she struggled against a soldier swinging a shortsword. She had no other weapon but the shield, but she was blocking his swings well.

Then the shield split in two. As the soldier swung for a killing blow, Vali charged and brought his axe in an upward arc, cleaving the soldier's arm at the elbow. He howled as his blade and forearm fell to the ground. Vali swung again, blood spraying from his axe, and opened the soldier's chest.

Olga stared, wide-eyed, as if the splitting of the shield had split her sense and her courage as well. "Come!" he shouted and grabbed her arm. When he pulled, she fell forward like a statue. So he picked her up and heaved her over his shoulder.

Then he ran for the horses, yelling for his friends to follow.

~oOo~

The soldiers chased after them for a long way, taking yet more of them down. Then they pulled back. When the survivors cleared and closed the castle gates, they were only twelve: five raiders and seven Estlanders.

Olga was among them, because Vali had carried her on his horse.

Her brothers were not.

She had not yet spoken a word. She might not have even blinked. Vali cast his mind's eye back and tried to see in the

276

fray where the young men had been. He had seen them fighting.

He had seen them near where he'd collected Olga. He had seen the older of them, Anton, wielding the shield that had broken in Olga's hold.

"Olga." He put his bloodied hand on her pale cheek. "I am sorry."

She didn't acknowledge him at all. She stood as if made of stone. But they needed their healer.

"Olga. You are needed. There will be time later for grief. Now is for action."

After another long moment in which Vali asserted patience over his battle-manic mind, she blinked and looked up at him. "I have no one."

"Untrue. You have friends. Friends in need. Stay with us. Do not give up."

"Leif did this. He—he made this possible."

"And he will pay. Help me, and I promise that he will pay."

She nodded and shook herself briskly. Then she stalked off to tend to the wounded.

~oOo~

"We have no other choice." Vali leaned forward, his arms on the table. Seated with him were the sum total of the survivors, who had once numbered nearly two hundred, raiders and villagers together. Of the raiders, besides Vali himself: Orm, Bjarke, Astrid, Harald. Of the villagers: Olga, Jaan, Georg, Hans, Jakob, Anna, and Eha. Four women and eight men.

277

"We will die. All of us. Drowned in Ægir's drunken sea." Orm huffed and slammed his cup on the scarred wood.

"We die on the sea, or we die here."

"Fleeing or fighting. I would fight and join my friends and ancestors in Valhalla. My time is long past already."

"You have known me many years, Orm. Do you think I would flee? I mean to fetch my wife and kill all those who called us clan and yet left us to this fate."

"Vali, do you not see? Your vengeance is good and just, but an Estlander fishing boat is not built for the open sea. We will capsize at the first stiff breeze. We will be swimming among twigs if it storms."

"Then we will ask the gods to keep us. As you say, our purpose is good and just. I am named for Odin's son, born to wreak the Allfather's vengeance. I go to save the shieldmaiden who bears his given eye. Do you not think he would ease our way?"

Vali doubted that Brenna's eye bore any mystical import. But her legend said it did, and he knew that Orm and the other raiders believed it. And he was named for Vali, Odin's son, who, in his first day of life, had avenged his brother Baldur's death, as he had been birthed to do. He certainly believed that Odin would see this need for vengeance and know it right.

"The Allfather let Brenna be taken and us all betrayed."

"We will make a sacrifice before we go. Odin will not abandon us. He will not."

Jaan spoke up. "One of the boats was my uncle's. It is sturdy for a fishing boat, and with the women's help, I can craft a sail for it. I need two days, and the beam outside."

The beam that had been meant for the longship that would take Vali back to Brenna. It was fitting that it should be dismantled to be a mast for a wee boat that would have the same purpose. He nodded.

"Even if Toomas makes a siege, we can hold for that long. Most of you at this table would leave your home to sail with us. All of us, I think, call this home now. I make no claim on you. If you would stay and fight, or try to work a peace, or surrender, I understand. But I sail back for my wife. Someday, she and I will return and pick up the life we had begun here."

"That life is dead now," Olga interrupted. "There is nothing left but ash and bone. None of us have anything left here. I will sail with you. My older brother traveled far in his life and had many adventures. I thought his life was the dangerous one. But it was full. Mine has been empty, and yet I have lost what little I had."

"I think we all should sail," Jaan added. "The voyage has a better chance with more hands to row in still winds, and we are not so many that we would overwhelm the boat, even with supplies. Olga is right. None of us have anything left here. We are all penniless orphans."

Vali turned to Orm. "What do you say, old man?"

Orm sighed. "The offering must be great."

"And it shall be." Vali knew what the offering must be.

~oOo~

Two days later, while Toomas's men were camped outside the walls, Vali led Freya onto the grounds. She was a beautiful mare, her coat a rich gold, her creamy mane so long and flowing that it had sometimes tangled in the reins when Brenna had given her her head and let her run.

The mast and sail were ready, and the cart of supplies was loaded. Vali and Orm had ridden out to parley with Toomas's captain, and they would be free to leave the castle and travel to the coast, abandoning all the holdings to Toomas's control.

The twelve were ready to go. Vali knew that they most likely would die on the open water. One storm would break them.

So they needed the gods' help.

While the last of his people stood in an arc, their posture and expressions serious, Vali led his wife's beloved horse to the middle. The mare nickered quietly and nosed at his side, seeking, he knew, a treat. He rubbed her nose.

To him, a horse was transportation. He treated his mounts well because he wanted them strong and healthy and steady, to do the job they were meant to do and to do it well. He had never thought to bond with a beast. But his wife had. She liked animals better than she liked people, and she loved this mare.

It was the greatest offering he could think to make. Freya represented, to him and, he thought, to Brenna, their life here. The freedom and peace they had fought for and nearly won.

He unsheathed Brenna's sword. Holding it up so that the sun shone on the blade and made it glint, he raised his voice and said, "Odin, father of Vali, born for vengeance. Frigg, great mother. Thor, god of war and storm. I am Vali Storm-Wolf, one of the Úlfhéðnar, and I beseech you. Accept this offering and guide us safely over the sea. Our purpose is good and true."

With his hand on the mare's neck, soothing her, he drew the blade across her throat, cutting deeply so that blood washed over his arm. She went immediately down on her front knees, and Vali went down with her, cooing softly at her ear as her rear haunches dropped. When she died, her head simply bowed until her nose touched the earth, and there she stayed, as if she had dozed off.

Emotion surged up from Vali's heart. He cared little for this beast, except that his wife had loved her, and he loved his wife. He bent his head and buried his face in the long, creamy mane.

"Brenna," his whispered, his throat tight and his heart heavy. "My love. Be strong. I am coming."

It had not occurred to him that she might not be alive. He would not allow that thought to take hold in his mind. She was alive, and she was waiting, and he would go to her.

19

A beetle lumbered across the earthen floor near Brenna's face, and she brought her chained hands up and caught it. She ate it quickly and scanned the floor for more. Her first sustenance in days—she had lost track of how many days.

Daylight crept around the door and through cracks in the walls, so she might have used the sun and stars as her guide to track time, but she couldn't account for the periods of unconsciousness that had broken her understanding from the beginning of this ordeal.

Calder had beaten her badly, and they had been at the coast before she'd woken. When she'd struggled against her bonds, he'd beaten her again, and she'd woken to the rocking of a ship on the open sea.

They had not dressed her. She had been dropped on the floor of the ship in her linen sleeping shift, and a fur had been tossed over her. She had been offered occasional drops of fresh water but no food. By the time they had landed at Geitland, she was nearly delirious with cold, hunger, and fever.

Leif had been there, though he had done nothing more than watch her. He had not spoken to her at all. No one had spoken to her. She had tried to speak once and been kicked in the head for it. So she'd spent the voyage in silent misery and grief.

Leif was with Åke, even now. The thought that they had all been betrayed by a man whom they'd trusted utterly, whom they'd loved, who had led them—that thought burned a hot fire of hatred in her soul. Brenna thought it was that fire, that need, which had kept her alive and undefeated so far.

With a rope around her neck and wrists, in nothing but her shift, they had dragged her from the Geitland docks. People throughout the town had come to gape at the God's-Eye so humbled. When they brought her to this dark hovel, they had shackled her neck and wrists. The shackle around her neck was connected by a chain bolted deep into the earth. The chain was no longer than the distance from her fingertips to her elbow. She could not sit up. She could barely move at all. When her body needed to shed its meager waste, it did so where she lay.

Since they'd left her here, no one had come in, not even with water. Although she had no understanding of how much time had passed, although it seemed infinite, Brenna knew it could not have been long. Without water, in her ill, weakened state, she would survive no more than a few days.

She didn't understand Åke's purpose. If it was to kill her, why had he not simply opened her throat? It could not be to reclaim her as his shieldmaiden, because he had abased her thoroughly. And he had, she feared, killed Vali. No, she *knew* he had. She had overheard enough of the raiders' talk during the voyage to know that they had left death and devastation behind them.

Åke knew her; he had to know that she would never bow to him again after this.

So why did she still draw breath? Was it her eye? If so, if he feared Odin's wrath, why was she chained to the ground?

Knowing the answer was irrelevant, she focused her mind on the question even so, because it was something that might be answered. Something that would keep her reason engaged, her sanity, and kept hopelessness and grief at bay. She worked the puzzle and waited for another beetle to cross close enough, until hunger, thirst, hurt, exhaustion, and illness took their due, and she slept.

~oOo~

The creak and drag of the iron hinges and heavy wooden door woke her. The room was full dark; it was night. Hours later? Or days? She didn't know.

Staring into the darkness in the direction of the open door, she waited to see who would come in. Whoever it was bore no torch, but there was just enough starlight to show her a large body that filled the door space. A man, then. Come for what? No one yet had used her to sate their itch, but it was the last abasement she could think of, so she expected it would happen soon. Perhaps that was the punishment Åke had in mind for her—to turn her into a slave whore.

The door closed, taking what little light the starlight had offered. Brenna waited.

Then she heard the familiar slosh of water in an oaken bucket and the drag of a ladle along its side. Her dry throat cramped hard with needful hope.

"Brenna."

Leif's voice killed her hope. If he had come to bring her water, she would not take it. She would take nothing from him. She had not used her voice in days, she had not slaked her thirst in she knew not how long, but she opened her mouth and forced the word "No" from her cracked lips.

She heard the press of his boots on the earth and the slosh of water in the bucket as he came to her. When he crouched before her, he was near enough that she could make out his vague shape.

"I have water for you. And leiv bread. And I would talk with you. You must heed me, my friend."

"I will take nothing from you." The words came as if dragged over loose rock. "You are no friend. I would choke your life out with the chains that bind me if I could."

Again, she heard the glorious and agonizing song of moving water, and then it fell over her lips. Leif was pouring the full ladle lightly over her face. The bliss of the cool water wetting her feverish skin, seeping through her parched lips, drizzling down her swollen tongue, was too much, and a whimper escaped her.

"I understand your hatred. But Brenna, I am your friend still. I am the reason Åke did not kill you. I am the reason Vali still lives—and, I hope, more of our friends. We were too few to defeat him at the castle. So I am trying to keep you alive until we can make you free."

"Vali lives?" Her erratic heart stopped for a moment.

"He does. And so do you. Åke believes I killed him, but I did not. I got him out of the way so that he would live." As he spoke, he held the ladle out to her. This time, she lifted her chained hands and held it to her lips. She would have drunk it all except that he pulled it from her before she could.

"And I? You could not have gotten me out of the way?" Brenna hated the petulance in her broken voice, but this bit of kindness, and this sliver of hope, had opened a crack in her heart.

She felt his hand on her face. When she didn't flinch away, he brushed her matted hair back gently. "Åke would not have left you behind, alive or dead. There was no way for me to hide you. You are his gift from the gods. He was enraged that you wanted to leave him. Please forgive me, but it was my idea that he could make you a slave again. It was all I could think to do to keep your heart beating."

"I will not serve him. Vali will come, and we will destroy Åke and all he loves."

"Vali has no ship, Brenna, and few men. I believe he will come, but not for months, until he can build a seaworthy vessel and gather a force. Until then, you must live. You must give Åke what he wants. Living is the important thing. Perhaps we will find a way ourselves, and you will be free when Vali returns."

As he spoke, he found her hands and placed a small chunk of the flat bread in them. Brenna shoved it into her mouth and swallowed it so quickly that she barely tasted it.

But the flavor lingered, richer and more wonderful than ever leiv bread had tasted before.

"More. Please."

He gave her a drink first, and then another small chunk. "No more, Brenna. It has been long since you've eaten, and you will be ill and lose the good of it. I will come as I can, in the night, and help you. I will try to bring you herbs for your fever soon. But I must be careful. I cannot cross Åke now. Not until we have a way to defeat him. We must both comply until then."

Brenna tried to take small bites of this chunk and make it last. "I cannot serve him, Leif. I have served him well these long years, and yet he would have destroyed everything I love. He might yet have. I cannot serve him, no matter the purpose. I will not."

"If you do not, Brenna, first he will break you—and then, when you break or he loses interest in the breaking, he will kill you. And Vali will come back to grief."

She would simply have to make the breaking of her a challenge, then, and keep his interest until she could take his head.

~oOo~

The water that her jailers gave her was brackish and full of silt. No food was offered. But Leif came in the nights with clear water and bread. He even brought a small bite of meat. And herbs for her fever.

He had come to her three times, and her fever had passed, when one of her jailers—a rotund, red-nosed brute named Igul, whom she'd known of in her earlier days living in Geitland—slammed the door open and let bright sun spill into her dim hole. She blinked in the sudden light and tried to see him.

Usually when he came, he dropped the water bucket before her and made a coarse comment about her filth while he checked her chains. She shrank back against the wall as far as she could. He had a repulsive reputation for his treatment of female prisoners. He had not yet touched her, but she remained leery. She supposed her eye gave her some protection even now. Her attitude about people's superstitions had changed since her life in Estland. Before she had understood that others' fear and awe could be exploited, but she had still wished it away. Now she recognized it as a truly potent weapon and a shield.

She had come to an understanding of herself in Estland, and was no longer her own enemy. Now, she valued the power of her eye, and in her current situation, she was especially grateful to have its protection.

This time, she noticed that the water in the bucket was clear, and instead of a ladle, there was a wad of linen floating in it.

And then a second man came into the hut, his sword unsheathed. Brenna didn't recognize him, but she knew she was in danger, and she shrank back again, the chain tying her to the ground going taut.

Igul reached down and grabbed a handful of her hair, then bent low and got his ruddy face down with hers. "The jarl wants to see you. You're in no fit state for the great hall, so I'm going to clean your filth. I'll unchain your hands, but if you give fight, my friend there will shove that blade so far up your hole you'll taste iron. Do you understand?"

Days with the merest possible sustenance, overcome with ague, and tied to the ground, had left Brenna too weak to fight with anything but her mind. They could do to her body what they would; even if they unchained her completely, she could not have stopped them.

She nodded.

Igul opened the shackles on her wrists, and then released her neck as well. "You move how I say," he grumbled and yanked her by her arm up to her feet.

Brenna's feet and legs exploded in thousands of painful pricks. Her knees promptly gave, and she fell.

Igul crouched low again. "You stand, or I'll shackle your neck again and chain you to the wall." Again, he yanked her up, and this time, prepared for the pain and weakness, Brenna managed to keep her feet.

Then Igul tore her tattered, filthy shift from her body, and she stood naked before these two men and anyone who passed by the open door. With that, Brenna found some last reserve of strength, and she straightened her back and squared her shoulders. She would not cower before these vile men.

When he looked at her face, she caught his eyes and held them, and she took no small comfort in the way his contemptuous smirk faltered in the focus of her right eye, and he looked away. He feared her. Even now.

The water was icy cold, and Igul was brutishly rough as he scrubbed the linen over her body. He was especially cruel—and especially thorough—at those parts of her body he thought his touch would shame her. His fingers, covered in the increasingly soiled linen, probed deep between her legs. He hurt her, and disgusted her, but she stood tall and silent. She would make him pay for this.

When he was finished, he dumped the bucket over her head. Then, while her body was still wet, he dropped a clean, light woolen shift over her head and ordered her to put her arms through.

"You still look like a half-rotted rat, but it will have to do."

He shackled her again, with a longer chain, and the iron sat even more painfully now on her raw skin. Then he pulled on the chain and dragged her out of her prison and into the daylight.

~oOo~

The great hall was nearly empty. Åke sat in his fur-covered seat, his posture relaxed. His grown sons, Calder, Eivind, and Ulv, sat nearby. Leif was with them. And Viger.

Brenna had not seen Viger since before the feast in Estland. She remembered missing him at that feast. Now she wondered if he had been somehow instrumental in the betrayal. He must have been.

She stared long at Viger, until the man felt the heat of her contempt and looked away. Yes, Brenna thought. Viger would know the bite of her blade.

She had neither shield nor sword, of course. But that was a matter of details.

"Brenna God's-Eye," Åke said, drawing her attention to his seat. "How fare you?"

Before she tried to speak, she swallowed to be sure her tongue was not too dry to move. "I am well."

He smiled. "You are strong, there is no doubt. There are few men who would yet be able to stand after so long in your circumstance."

There was no question to be answered, so Brenna remained silent. She stared and waited.

"I bring you here, in private, to save your dignity. I would have you renew your oath to me. That is all I ask. And then you will be released to serve me as you did when first you came to me."

"As your thrall." It wasn't a question. She knew the answer. And it was irrelevant in any case.

"Of course. You think that I would allow you to bear a sword after the way you've disrespected my fine care of you? Trust is lost, Brenna God's-Eye. It must be regained. Perhaps someday it will. But for now, you will return to serve me and mine."

She found her full height. "I will not. I abjure you."

The smug, false benevolence with which Åke had been speaking, and the easygoing posture he had affected, vanished with those words. His expression went dark with violence, and he sat forward. "What power do you think you have to abjure *me*? I am your jarl!"

"No. You are not." Brenna could just see, from the corner of her right eye, Leif reacting in some way. She didn't need to change her focus from Åke to know that he was upset with her. But she would not yield. Let Åke try to break her. He would fail.

For a long silent moment, while tension crackled in the room, the jarl and the shieldmaiden stared at each other. Finally, Åke sat back, affecting his calm demeanor again.

"You will break, Brenna God's-Eye. And I will watch it happen." Looking beyond her, he addressed Igul. "You know where to take her."

As Igul grabbed her chain leash, Leif stood. "Jarl Åke."

Everyone turned and gave him their surprised attention. Åke seemed ready to order Igul to take Leif as well. "You have something more to say, Leif?"

Despite the obvious threat, Leif's voice was steady. "She is the God's-Eye. Do you not invite the gods' displeasure to do her harm?"

Åke answered Leif's question with his eyes on Brenna. "So you say. Yet the gods gave her to me, and she abandoned her oath. She lay with my enemy and wed him. The gods agree that such disloyalty must be punished." He nodded at Igul. "Take her and prepare her. I think the rods will do. Let us see the limit of the God's-Eye's strength."

~oOo~

Brenna knew fear, fear so deep her empty belly felt full of ice, but she didn't fight. She was too weak to win, and fighting to lose looked like nothing so much as desperation. Igul took her into the room where Åke had his questioning done. Justice was meant in their world to be determined at a thing, democratically among the members of the community, but Åke had always meted out certain kinds of justice beyond the notice of his people.

She was stripped again, and then bound prone to a long table, stained dark with the blood of others before her. She knew what Åke had meant when he'd mentioned 'the rods.' Face-down, with her arms and legs shackled and bound to the table legs, she knew what would happen next.

For an infinite time, nothing happened except that the room warmed as Igul stoked the fire until it roared. Then the door opened, bringing with it a quick rush of cooler, fresher air, and Åke came to the side of the table her face was turned to. "You will break, Brenna God's-Eye. You will beg for my mercy."

She stared back and did not answer. No, she would not. All that was left to her was this. She would not break.

"Leif."

There was a stunned silence, and in it, Brenna felt a tiny chip in her resolve. If Leif hurt her, she wasn't certain she could withstand it.

"Åke, no."

"You would deny me?"

"I would ask you, as one who loves you as a son loves a father, please do not ask this of me. I have chosen you and renewed my oath, but it was you who made the God's-Eye my friend."

Another long silence. Brenna focused on breathing, finding her shieldmaiden, the one who knew only fury and not pain.

Åke's voice broke the tension. "Viger, then. Would you deny me as well?"

"No, Jarl. I serve your will."

When the first red-hot iron rod was laid across Brenna's back, just above her shoulder blades, the hot was so hot it almost felt cold, and the pain took a sliver of a moment to assert itself. Then it was completely encompassing, deep and wide, like a vast multitude of beasts clawing and biting their way through her body. She didn't scream. She didn't even have to fight the urge to scream. The pain was so enormous that none of the muscles in her body would work, not even those which would have impelled forth a cry.

The room quickly filled with the scent of her cooked flesh. When Viger pulled the rod up, he had let it cool enough that the skin caught and stuck to it.

Another rod was laid just below her shoulder blades. While it sat there, Åke leaned down and stared into Brenna's eyes. Inside, her mind was shrieking, crying, begging. Her hands clawed at the table legs. But she did not allow her face to tense in any way, or her eyes to drift from his. If there was power in her right eye, she wanted him to know she was using it.

"Again." He stood up and flicked his hand at Viger.

Viger lifted the second rod and laid down a third. By now, her body was so entirely racked with agony that this third rod had little it could add.

The fifth rod nearly undid her, however. Laid across her hips, just below her waist, it found skin tender enough that it broke through the limit of her pain and found a new place, so beyond comprehension that her mind simply stopped. Though her eyes were open, though she could hear, and smell, and gods, she could feel, inside she knew nothing. Only blackness.

"Enough," she heard but did not understand.

~oOo~

When next her mind was clear, she was in her hovel again, this time shackled by her wrists to the wall, face-first. She was still without any stitch of clothing, but that was the least of her concerns.

The pain she had known while Viger had laid red-hot iron rods on her back was a distant memory, dwarfed by the pain she felt now, with her arms raised, both bunching and stretching the tortured skin of her back.

"You are strong and willful, Brenna God's-Eye." Åke was there. Had he waited and watched while she'd been unconscious? "It made you a valiant shieldmaiden. I was proud of you. I despise that you've made me do this. End your suffering now. Renew your oath and serve me. I will bring you into the hall and have your wounds tended as if you were my daughter. Then you can take up the duties you once had. I was not a hard master. Not to you."

"I will not." Her voice cracked with weakness, but she fixed her stare.

He sighed and dragged a pointed finger down the open skin and frayed nerves over her spine. A great explosion of pain— yet another new place—made her gasp and twitch, but she refrained from crying out.

"If you will not serve me as I wish, then perhaps I will give you to Calder. He has always liked your look and asked me more than once to give him leave with you. He will be glad to have my ban lifted. He is unfortunately harsh with slave girls, of course.

"I will kill him if he so much as touches me."

Åke dug into a wound and turned his finger. Brenna could feel the pain stealing away her consciousness.

"Then I think there is breaking left to be done," Åke said and took his hand away. He turned and left, and Brenna opened her mind to the blackness and let it take her.

~oOo~

She felt the painful soothe of healing paste, and heard herself groan, before she knew she was awake. She opened her eyes and shut her mouth, lest Åke hear her vocalize her torment.

She was prone on the floor of her hovel, but laid on a clean straw mat, and unchained. She tried to lift herself onto her elbows, but the pain was too great, and she was too weak.

"Be still, Brenna."

"Leif. You are safe?"

He smoothed cool paste over another burn. "I am, but Åke is suspicious, and he is unhappy with my resistance yesterday."

"Only yesterday?" It seemed as though she had lived a lifetime, or more, since she had been taken from Estland. Each day stretched into years.

"Brenna, please heed me now. There is little more I can do for you if you hold to this folly. I got you these comforts and healing because I argued with Calder that his father might yet risk the gods' wrath by treating you so ill, and he counseled him. But I doubt Åke's restraint will last long. He will not hear me on the matter of you any longer. If you are ever to be free and reunited with your husband, then you first must live now. Yield, Brenna."

The mere idea of giving in to the man who had done this to her, and who had done much more, repelled her. "I cannot, Leif. I cannot be subject to him, no matter what he would do to try to force me."

"I do not mean that you give up. Yield in deed, not in spirit. What opportunity can you have locked in this hut? If you are in the hall, perhaps you will find a chance to fight. But here, you will not. So tell him that you yield. He will be self-satisfied, and you will reap the benefit of that. He will heal you well and treat you like a pet. And there are people here we might bring to our cause. Let them see what Åke did to the God's-Eye, beyond the circle of the thing. Then you might find your chance. But burned and weak, hidden away, you will not."

Even through the shriek of the pain blasting from her back into her mind, Brenna heard the reason in Leif's words. As Åke tried to break her, even if he failed, he would have weakened her beyond the point of any resistance but death. And that would be a victory for him, as well.

Could she pretend to have yielded? Could she behave before him as if she had been tamed, until she was strong enough to show him her bite? Could she wait for Vali and be strong enough to drive Åke to Hel?

Was she that strong?

Yes. She was.

20

Vali leaned against the prow of their little boat and stared out at horizon. In every direction, the world was exactly the same: solid dark grey above, and solid, darker grey below. For days, that had been true. The sky lightened in the day, but not enough to discern where the sun illuminated it. In the night, the world was a perfect, limitless, impenetrable black.

With no clues anywhere about the way they were headed, with nothing to see beyond but the same solid wall, one felt almost as if one were spinning while standing still, and standing still while spinning. It made the mind shift restlessly in its moorings.

Vali bent his head and closed his eyes, forcing his mind to make a picture it could focus on. When the vertigo subsided, he kept his eyes closed and his imagination intent on the vision of Brenna in the Estland woods, sitting at the stream bank, on the day they'd first spoken.

In the peace of that image, he could think.

They had been afloat for days—too many days. They should have struck the homeland already. Instead, there was no sound of bird, no sign of land.

They were lost on the open sea, as Orm had predicted. Even strictly rationed, their stores of food and water would not last beyond a few days longer.

The gods had abandoned them. He would not come for his wife, would not save her, would not see her again in this life.

He thought of the night their son had lived and died. Leif had told him he'd tempted the gods when he'd stood in the storm and called out their cruelty. Perhaps he had.

Leif. Vali's stomach turned at the thought of the man he'd called friend, whom he'd given his unflinching trust, who had betrayed them all—and Brenna most.

Though Vali understood that he would not be the agent of justice for Leif, he hoped that justice would somehow be had.

He turned and sat on the floor of the boat, resting his back against the stem. Before him sat nine beleaguered and disheartened souls, all of whom knew what he knew: they now merely waited for the sea to take them.

They had lost two of their number to the simple price of the sea: Eha and Anna had both succumbed when the toss of the waves had again and again forced even their meager ration of fresh water from their bellies.

Of those who were left—five raiders and five villagers; two women and eight men—all but Olga were experienced sailors of one kind or another, raiders or fishermen. Olga had struggled like Anna and Eha, but she was resolute and far stronger than her slim frame would suggest, and she rallied just as Vali began to lose hope in the voyage.

The boat was small, and had only three sets of oarlocks. When the sea and air were calm, they moved slowly, and even the raiders were beginning to lose the strength to row. Too small a boat, too few rowers.

Not that it mattered any longer.

In this moment, though, his crew was livelier than they had been, resting and even chatting together. Earlier, Orm had thought he'd caught a glimpse of sun behind the opaque drape of clouds, and, though Vali had not seen it, they had put up the sail in a good wind, hoping they sailed westward.

They ran now at a strong clip, straight and true, and that at least had the power of delusion, elevating the spirits of their motley band.

Orm stood and crossed the boat, crouching near Vali. He offered him a water skin. Vali shook his head.

The old man would not be dissuaded. "You have not had your water yet this day. Nor is this the first time you've gone without. I see you giving up your ration and know you think it a sacrifice for us. But you are mistaken. You must remain strong, Vali. Any hope is lost should we lose you."

Hope was already lost, and he knew Orm knew it. But a true warrior fought until he died, hope or no hope. So he nodded and took the skin.

As he let the water drizzle onto his parched tongue, Vali saw the sail drop, from full to dead in an instant. The boat eased to a stop. He handed the skin back to Orm. "Bring the sail down. Now."

Orm nodded and stood. "SAIL DOWN!" he called as he moved to the center of the boat.

While his crew hurried to furl the sail, Vali stood and turned, searching the blank sky for the storm.

There—in some direction, he knew not which, the inky dark of the sea appeared to leach into the grey sky. As he stood there, he watched it move, bringing night on too soon. And then he smelled it, the churning of rain bringing the salt up into the air like a cloud.

He turned and jumped in to help. They had little time to fix the sail as their shelter. For all the good it would do in their tiny vessel, at the whim of gods who did not care.

~oOo~

Until that day and night, they had been spared Ægir's drunken wrath; it had been the one mercy that gods had shown them. But with one storm, that mercy was wiped away. Vali and his small crew huddled under the paltry shelter of their sail, which had of necessity been too quickly crafted and dressed. While the wind and rain howled around them and the storm sank its claws into their vessel, Vali knew the true end of his hope.

Cursing his selfishness, he could not help but entertain one last shred of a wish: that he would find Brenna waiting for him in the next world, holding their son. His wish should have been that she would yet live; it was wrong to wish her dead. But in Åke's ruthless, angry clutches, with no help coming, he believed she would be better off dead.

A wind howled low, through the tunnel of their shelter, and then caught the sail, heaving the boat up, nearly clear of the water. Then the sail was rent from side to side, and they were dropped back into the churn.

Lightning flashed and showed Jakob, who'd stood to try to catch the loose piece of sail, going overboard with a cry.

He was barely a man; he'd had no chance to make his story. Without thinking, Vali followed after him, diving into the frigid water. It was too black, too roiling, too loud for any of his senses to help him find the boy, and yet he dove and rose and swam, closing his mind from its need to see or hear, feeling a sense of clarity in the senseless search.

He no longer knew even where the boat was, but he swam, feeling, with each stroke, each dive, the sea weigh him down more heavily. At least his death would be purposeful and valorous.

Then his hands caught cloth. He pulled and had hold of the slim and solid body of a young man. Jakob. Disoriented and unclear which way was up, he went still and allowed himself to float, hoping that his clothes were not soaked beyond buoyancy.

He felt the direction of his rise and swam that way, holding Jakob in one arm and kicking with all his might. As he broke the surface with a great gasp for air, the rain pummeled him about the face, so hard he almost could not tell the difference between the sea and the air. Then lightning lit up the night and showed him the boat. He swam for it, feeling his muscles—weakened from days with little sustenance or sleep, fighting against the weight of the water—trying to fail, and he turned his mind away from physical matters and set his intent on his mission. This was his way in battle: to become something other than human, something beyond the limits of his body. To be Úlfheðinn.

The night was black again, and he felt Jakob being pulled up from his grasp before he realized that he had reached the boat. Once freed from his burden, Vali felt Ægir, the sea jötunn, tighten his grip around his legs and pull.

He gave in to it, closing his eyes against the black night, bringing up the bright image of his shieldmaiden, on the bank of the stream, frowning down at her reflection. Something in her aspect then had told him everything about the depth of her loneliness and the great capacity of her heart. He thought he had loved her since that day.

He knew he had.

Perhaps she would be waiting for him. If not, then he would wait for her, with their son in his arms.

As his lungs would no longer be denied and sucked in water as if it were air, as consciousness left him, he had the feeling that Ægir grabbed hold of his shoulders and dragged him away.

To Valhalla, he hoped.

~oOo~

He woke choking and vomited sea water over the bottom of the boat. Then his lungs forced him to heave in air in rough gulps. When he had his wits about him, he looked around, but the storm still raged, and he could see nothing until a blast of lightning brought his situation into stark relief. Olga had Jakob's head in her lap. Orm sat near Vali's head.

"Does he live?" he asked Olga. His voice sounded strange and harsh in his head, and no one responded, so he knew he had not been loud enough over the storm. He tried again, forcing a shout from his aching throat and chest. "Does he live?!"

In another flash, he saw Olga smiling at him. Such a strange thing, to see a beautiful woman smile in the midst of such angry havoc.

"Yes!" she called back. "You saved him!"

For what? he wondered. He had not thought before he'd jumped. Perhaps it had been a cruel thing he'd done, saving the boy for a harsher death.

As he himself had been saved, apparently. "Who pulled me out?" He asked Orm, who was nearest by.

Another bolt of lightning showed Orm frowning. "No one. None of us could have. We thought we'd lost you, and then you pulled yourself into the boat."

But that was impossible. Even in the storm, the wale was too far from the surface of the water, and he had been in soaked furs and leathers, exhausted and malnourished.

He thought of that moment of release, feeling Ægir pulling him away.

Perhaps it had not been Ægir taking him, but someone sending him back. One of the gods? Brenna?

Vali did not know. But he believed it to be meaningful. He should have died. He had not been saved by his crew, and he could not have saved himself, not alone.

Even as the storm raged, heaving the small boat over a foaming sea, Vali felt hope rekindle in his chest.

~oOo~

The storm ended during the night, and dawn brought the sun. For all the crash and heave of the storm, for every time it picked them up and threatened to slam them upended into the water, the little boat had held. The sail was in tatters, so their prospects remained grim, but they had survived, and Vali took that, and the return of the sun, as good omens.

With the sun, they could at least head again westward with certainty. He no longer had any understanding of where they might be, or if west would even bring them to land, but west was the direction they knew of as home.

Then he heard the most beautiful sound he had ever heard in his life. At first, he would have sworn before the gods that it was the soft, husky trill of Brenna's laugh, right at his ear, but then sense took over, and he knew he'd heard something outside his mind's fantasy. He froze, with his friends still deep in the exhausted sleep that had taken them over almost as one when calm had returned to the water, and listened hard.

He heard it again, faint and distant: the cry of a gull. Rising to his feet and clearing the remnants of the sail shelter, Vali stood and scanned the horizon, turning all his hope toward the west.

And yes—he stared until he was sure. The western horizon broke and became jagged. Mountains.

"LAND!" he shouted, but his voice failed him. He tried to swallow, but was too dry. Finding a skin, he squeezed a few drops into his mouth and tried again. "LAND! LAND!"

Within scant moments, everyone was moving, even Jakob, who had hit his head on the boat as he'd fallen overboard. They had the ruined sail unlashed and the oars locked in, and Vali, Bjarke, Hans, Jaan, Astrid, and Harald began rowing with a strength Vali would not have believed they still had.

It took hours, and they rotated the crew twice, as much as they could. Vali stayed at the oars, as did Bjarke, the next biggest and strongest, both of them taking the middle oars.

The sun was full in their faces when the land stopped being a growing hope and became truly discernible. Vali paused in his strokes and scanned the coast. He scanned it again, the other direction.

He knew where they were.

The storm had corrected their course—or perhaps had done one better.

Bjarke, taking on the drag from Vali's neglected rowing duties, said, "Vali?"

Vali turned to his clansman and smiled. "Look. You see where we are?"

Bjarke looked. Now everyone had stopped rowing. It was Orm who voiced what those who would know—only Vali, Bjarke, Harald, and Orm—understood.

The old man pointed at the thick brush of green atop the cliff that had marked Vali's first view of their salvation. A dense, familiar forest. "That is the Wood of Verdandi! We are home!"

Olga turned to Vali. "Home?"

Vali grinned and began rowing again, feeling strength charge into his body. All the rowers followed his lead. "Not where we meant to be. Well north of that. But to those of us pledged to Jarl Snorri Thorsson, this is our homeland."

She frowned. "But is this not also Åke's land, then? Is that how it would be among your people? That the victor would take the holdings of the vanquished?"

"Yes," Orm answered. "But our people warred with Åke long before that hollow peace was made. And he has slain an honorable and beloved jarl. If he has kept these lands, it will have been with force. Our home is far removed from Åke's seat. He will not have a large presence here. Vicious, yes, but not large. If he holds it, we can break his hold. The return of Vali Storm-Wolf will galvanize a resistance."

"The gods brought us to an army, Olga," Vali added. "We will go for Brenna and find our vengeance, and we will do it with a host of warriors at our backs."

The gods had not forsaken them after all.

21

Åke had lied, and Leif had been wrong. Neither of these truths had surprised Brenna.

She had yielded, but Åke had not taken her into the hall and healed her as if she were his own daughter. He treated her not like a pet, but like a beast.

He had left her in her rank hovel. But he had lengthened her chain and left her her straw mat, and he had ordered Igul to treat her wounds—which he did, cruelly but effectively enough. And he had fed her water and leiv bread, enough to survive on. It was so much more than she'd had since she'd been taken from Estland that she even began to gain strength on mere bread and water.

When Åke determined that she was sufficiently healed, she was put to work. Not in the hall, at her old duties with his family. Instead, she was sent to the most menial women's work. She slopped the beasts and slaughtered them. She cleaned the pots and scrubbed the linens. On days of rain too heavy for anything but the most essential outdoor work, she was put on the dye vats. After a wet spell, her hands were dyed a rusty red like old blood, and she had not yet been able to wash it fully away.

She did her work, and she lived her life, chained. Åke didn't trust her—Brenna knew it was fear he truly felt—so, ostensibly to mark her out and prevent her from running or fighting, he had left the iron shackle around her neck, having the smith seal it closed. A long length of heavy chain dragged from it. At night, she was chained down in her hovel. During the day, she looped it around her waist like a belt over her rough slave's shift.

The heavy iron dragged on her throat and rubbed her skin raw. For days, her blood had stained the otherwise undyed wool of her shift. Then the skin began to heal. Someday, it would toughen, and the weight and rub of the shackle would be familiar. Then, when she had grown used to it, she would truly be a slave again.

Unless she could find a way to get free.

As had been the case the last time she'd been in thrall to Åke, those who had to work with her, or in her vicinity, did so with evident nervousness. This time, they were more afraid, and Brenna had heard enough of their mutterings amongst them to know that they feared that their jarl was failing a test of the gods.

They all knew the stories of the gods walking among them, or even possessing men and women's bodies, and those who believed her eye was a gift from Odin, rather than a curse from him, now believed that he would never have allowed his shieldmaiden to fall so low without a godly purpose. They cast their average eyes sidelong at her, watched her throw slop and muck waste, saw the heavy shackle and her blood-stained shift, glimpsed the healing burns on her back, and perhaps even saw the resolve in her expression, and they tried to make distance between themselves and whatever fury Odin might bring down upon their jarl.

Brenna was, again, alone.

Leif kept his distance. She understood; he had made himself too vulnerable in his efforts to save her life, and he would be no good to her if Åke killed him. So all they had managed in the time since she had begun to work was a rare moment of eye contact. Until Brenna was allowed back in the hall, she couldn't see how they would manage more.

That was her first task: to be brought into the hall again. She knew that she had to remain quiet and seemingly humbled so that Åke might want to gloat. She had spent years in his hall, and she knew him well. He believed what he'd said to Leif, that Odin was on his side, and he would see his success in breaking her as a testament to his vast power and righteousness.

If she could somehow prove herself unbroken at the right moment, with the right audience, she might erode his support. It could not be only slaves who worried about the God's-Eye and if Odin might be unhappy with her abasement. If his freemen saw that she had kept her power, from wherever it came, they might think twice about their fealty to Åke.

And that might make a chance to kill him.

~oOo~

She accomplished her first task several days later, on the day of the thing. The freemen of Geitland and the surrounding villages came together at a thing to right wrongs among them, to administer justice, to oversee transactions of property, to witness young men get their arm rings and swear to the jarl, to plan the next raid, and then to feast.

Brenna had expected a massive attendance, since Åke had usurped Snorri's lands as well, but she saw few new faces in town. Åke had either decided to leave his new holdings in its people's own hands, or he was cutting them out of the power of the thing. The latter seemed more likely than the former. If she could get into the hall, she might know for sure.

In the late afternoon, Vifrid, one of the house slaves, ran up to Brenna as she carried full pails of water from the well, hanging from a yoke across her shoulders. Fetching water was one of the more difficult jobs Brenna had. The yoke pressed down on the shackle and dug into the tender new flesh of her topmost burn, and she nearly always had to pull up her shieldmaiden to make it across the town.

The burns no longer caused her excessive pain, in general. They were tender, and they protested when she stretched the skin too far, but after the maddening agony of the first week, almost any other pain was bearable. The yoke pushed at that limit somewhat.

The worst part now was the itch. A constant buzzing just under her skin. Most of the scabbing had fallen away, and Brenna had hoped that the itch would abate thereafter, but as yet it had not. It made her cross and impatient, not that that mattered. No one spoke to her, except to give her commands, so she had no cause to be genial.

But Vifrid came running up so quickly, while Brenna was focused on keeping the yoke still so that it would not dig more than necessary into her wounded back, that the two women nearly collided. Water sloshed from the buckets, and the yoke rocked painfully.

"Usch!" Brenna snapped, hurting and annoyed. She didn't have to be obeisant to another slave.

Vifrid ducked her head, "Apologies, Brenna God's-Eye. Forgive me. You are wanted in the great hall. Jarl Åke calls for you himself."

He meant to make of show of her, she was certain.

"I will take the yoke," Vifrid offered, still not meeting Brenna's eyes.

"My thanks." Brenna lifted the yoke over her head and set it on Vifrid's ready hands.

Then she walked toward the hall, with her back tall and straight. She didn't bother to check her appearance. She wanted all to see the extent to which Åke had tried to debase her. She might not get her vengeance on this day, but she could lay the ground for it.

~oOo~

Åke sat with his family and closest friends and associates at a long table at the head of the hall. Long, but less great tables accommodated most of the rest of the freemen and freewomen. Others sat around the edges of the hall, dining at their laps.

The atmosphere was bright and jovial, as always during such a feast. Brenna came in from the kitchen and found a place in Åke's line of sight to stand until she was summoned. While she waited, with her head canted at a downward angle in supposed supplication, she scanned the room, looking for potential friends or true ones.

Leif was seated at the head table, but at an end far from Åke, rather than amongst the jarl's children. He was yet being punished for his interference on her behalf, though it was obviously only a punishment and not a true loss of favor. He didn't see Brenna right away, and she took a moment to study him and settle in her mind that he truly was her ally.

He, too, seemed watchful, scanning the room and taking in its mood. She waited until his eyes met hers. After a pause, with a subtle tip of his head, he let her know that he was with her.

Just to have a single known ally in this room made Brenna feel immensely powerful. She was not, she knew that, and she could not be rash. But this was the first chance she'd yet had to even understand the field of the battle she meant to fight.

The hall had begun to go quiet as people around her recognized her. Even with her eyes downcast, they knew her. She was the only of Åke's slaves to be thus shackled, and the story of the God's-Eye's fall would have been traveling already.

When the quiet became noticeable, Åke saw her and stood, and with that, the last of the conversation stopped. Staring at her as if his eyes alone could hold her in place, he lifted his hands, and Brenna knew he meant to give a speech.

"My friends. We have done good work today. Our world is in balance, and our strength and power grows ever greater. Now we prepare to raid again, and for the first time all three of my grown sons will raid. I sought the seer's counsel before the thing, and he told me that we have the eye of the gods and will soon see the seat of Geitland begin a long era of greatness."

As a cheer went up at that, Åke swung one arm forward and flicked his hand at Brenna. "Come, girl," he said, and the hall quieted again, watching Brenna walk around the edge of the room, her chain rattling dully, until she stood behind the jarl.

He grabbed the chain where it hung down her back and yanked her forward. Then he spoke again.

"I know that there is talk that I tempt the gods' wrath with my treatment of the God's-Eye. But know this—I do not forget what power she holds. It is she who forgot. Odin gave her to me as my thrall. I raised her up and allowed her to fight for me, my smiths made her sword and shield, and she gained great renown on the shoulders of my good care. Then she turned her back on the will of the gods and abjured me."

Now he grabbed her hair, in its long, simple, dirty braid, and jerked her head up so that her face was visible to everyone in the hall. "Do not fear her. She is nothing more than a vessel. Her power is Odin's power, and she sought to claim it for her own. It was she who tempted the gods. Her degradation is their justice, not mine."

Brenna opened her eyes wide and watched the people staring at her. Åke was convincing them, she could see it. If they truly believed that he acted within the will of the gods, then her chance to find allies here dwindled to nearly nothing.

But they were raiding again. That would take the strongest among his men away—and all three of his grown sons. And Vali might still be coming. She would not give up hope. Even now, as Åke pulled sharply on her braid and her chain, driving her to her knees before him, she did not lose hope.

When she knelt, he shook her chain. "The gods are with us, my friends. We go to greatness!"

As the hall erupted in cheers, Åke yanked Brenna back to her feet. "Go back to your slop, slave," he snarled in her ear. Then he pushed her away.

As she walked back to the door, she sought out Leif, whose eyes were already on her. He looked immeasurably sorry for her. So she turned her warrior's face on him—only for a moment; now was not the time to show anyone else that she had not been broken—and he blinked in surprise, then gave her a nod.

She was strong enough for all of this. She was not done fighting. She would never be done fighting, not until she could drive Jarl Åke's head onto a pike.

~oOo~

That night, after Igul chained her down in her hovel, he stayed crouched in front of her. She met his leering stare and knew what was in his simple mind. The jarl's words had taken away his fear of her.

He pushed her down on her mat and tugged roughly at her shift, exposing her below the waist. Then he untied his breeches and dropped his soft, sour-smelling heft on top of her. Chained to the floor as she was, there was little she could do except stare at him and imagine the vengeance she would someday claim.

But his floppy worm wouldn't stiffen. He pushed it at her pathetically for a while and then grabbed her hand. "Take me in hand, slave, and if you try anything, I'll find a branch to do you with instead."

She yanked on him, resisting the strong urge to pull until it came off. His rank breath filled her head as he panted in increasing frustration, but still his little man wilted.

When he took hold of her jaw, she knew what next he intended, and she was not willing to lie still for that, no matter the price of her rebellion. She twisted her head free. "I will bite it off."

Igul punched her hard in the face, and blood gushed from her nose. Then he punched her between the legs, and Brenna was shocked by the pain that flowered into her belly and through her chest. It stole her breath.

He stood then, and Brenna remained still, despite the blood washing down her throat and the fire churning up her belly and chest.

"No food or water for you," he grunted as he closed his breeches. And then he left.

Brenna rolled to her side, pulling her legs and arms in against the pain, and choked up blood onto the dirt.

When she had her breath back, she put her hands to her face and, with a quick and practiced motion, reset her nose. It wasn't the first time she had done so in her violent life.

She was strong enough for all of this. She was.

She was.

She had to be.

22

Two hundred and thirty men and women in three longships. Vali had his horde.

In Karlsa, they had found a small contingent of Åke's men making themselves at home in the great hall. With the help of locals unhappy with the interlopers, Vali and his friends had dispatched them, taking no new losses despite their weakened condition.

Then they had taken a few days to heal and regain their strength, and to persuade Vali's clansmen to take on the jarl. Finding allies eager to demand an answer for the death of Snorri, they had taken a few more days to prepare their ships for war.

Two days again on the water, and now Geitland emerged from fog before them.

Vali stood at the prow of the main ship, his chest bare, his axes in their rings at his hips. The sails were full, showing the colors of Jarl Snorri Thorsson, and the warriors and shieldmaidens behind Vali stood. As they neared the docks, they began beating their shields with their weapons.

Let Åke mistake them not; this was no peaceful visit.

Scanning the town, Vali saw that Åke was slow to respond to the coming threat. Their ships were nearly at the dock before armed men appeared in force on land. Archers fired first, and at his call, Vali's warriors threw up their shields.

He stood where he was, unshielded, his axes at his hips. When an arrow came at his chest, he caught it and threw it into the water. No other came near him, despite the thunder of arrows hitting the shields behind him.

He did not release his archers to respond, though in each ship they stood ready, arrows nocked.

Another volley from the shore, and he heard the grunt and splash as one of his men was struck. Still, he did not release a response. He could sense the restlessness around him, but he knew his plan.

As soon as the water was shallow enough, warriors jumped from the ships and surged to the shore. Åke's archers did not release a third volley. The force on the shore stood pat, waiting.

Vali had his ship brought right to the dock, and he jumped onto the slatted wood as soon as the vessel came abreast of it. Unaccosted, he strode toward land while Åke's men stood with their weapons raised and watched him.

He scanned the crowd but did not see Brenna or Leif. The first, he meant to save; the latter, he meant to kill.

When he stepped onto land, he stopped. "I challenge Jarl Åke Ivarsson to single combat!"

As he spoke, his force made land and stood in a thick row across the town's shoreline. For the first time in ages, Vali was not outnumbered.

He scanned the crowd again, this time not looking for particular faces, but seeing all the faces before him, and he understood. Åke had sent his ships out. His most powerful fighters were off raiding. The town defense would fold quickly to the invasion. Vali had won already.

But perhaps his plans for Leif would have to wait. Leif was a powerful raider, and no jarl would keep such a warrior back from a raid.

In the meantime, Vali doubted that the old jarl would have weathered a second voyage in the same season, so he knew he would have at least that revenge.

Again, he called out, "I challenge the jarl! Here and now!"

The town was almost perfectly silent. Vali stood, alert, and waited. Then the crowd facing him—which was as much populated by townspeople as by fighters—split in two, and his former friend, Leif Olavsson, walked toward him, dressed in his boiled leathers, his sword in his hand. He had been kept back after all. Curious.

Viger walked with him, standing just behind and carrying Leif's shield. Vali spared a moment to sneer at the smaller man. Viger had been part of their betrayal, too. But Viger had not been so great a friend as Leif had, and so Vali's need for vengeance against him was less. He would be content if Viger died, no matter how.

Vali pulled his axes, and at that, his fighters shifted into even greater readiness.

Leif stopped. "Vali Storm-Wolf. Jarl Åke accepts your challenge and sends me, Leif Olavsson, as his champion."

An acceptable response according to their ways, especially considering Åke's age, but Vali found it craven. If he was strong enough to perpetrate horrors, he should have been strong enough to answer for them on his own. "I will gladly kill you, Leif, for the hurts and betrayals you have made against me and mine. But I will see Åke on my axe this day, whether he stands like a man in combat, or dies a coward's death instead."

Then Leif did something Vali thought exceeding odd: he smiled. "I understand. I would offer another plan."

Without any other warning, Leif turned hard and brought up his sword. He slashed Viger's throat so quickly and cleanly that the dying man stood, still holding Leif's shield, blood washing down his chest, for a long, stunned moment before he fell.

By the time he did, Leif had turned back to Vali. "I am your friend, Vali. Always have I been."

Vali had no time to make sense of that turn, because Leif's move against Viger had incited Åke's men to fight. Chaos churned around them, and Leif was already fighting for his life.

Vali charged up into the fray.

~oOo~

The defensive force Åke had kept home from the raids was no match for Vali's horde of angry warriors seeking redress. The townspeople fought or ran, as was their wont, but Vali held his people off from chasing the runners down. They had no need to decimate Geitland. Vali made it his primary mission to seek out any of Åke's men who had been in Estland with them. He found none besides Viger and Leif—and seemingly Leif had not betrayed him after all.

But he *had*. He had taken Vali out of the fight and allowed Brenna to be taken. A true friend would have alerted him to the danger and fought at his side—as he was doing now. Vali had been so full of black rage for so long that he could not believe in Leif's assertion, even as they fought side by side and slaughtered Åke's men. As he hacked and slashed, he had no time to sort it out. But he kept his eye on Leif and never turned his back.

As the number of enemies dwindled and he could turn his attention from the fight, he grabbed Leif's arm. "Brenna?"

Breathless and splashed with blood, Leif nodded. "It has gone hard for her here, but she lives, my friend. She carries a mighty warrior's heart in her chest. She was at the stables this morning."

Vali's heart sagged as relief pushed despair from it. Brenna was safe. He nodded. "First, Åke. I will not risk him escaping or doing more mischief. I will wear his entrails around my neck."

They ran together toward the great hall. Orm, Bjarke, and Astrid saw them and ran up as well. As they approached the door, Vali surveyed the area and knew for a certainty that they had won. He did not think more than a few of Åke's force had survived.

Before he opened the door, he turned to Astrid. "Brenna is at the stables. Will you bring her to me?"

Astrid gave Leif a poisonous glare and then nodded at Vali. "I will. Watch your back." She spat at Leif's feet and trotted off with her axe in her hand.

Astrid had been sworn to Åke, just as Leif and Brenna had. She had been left for dead in Estland when she'd resisted Åke's cowardly, clandestine departure. Vali thought there could be no clearer condemnation of Leif's complicity than his clanswoman spitting at his feet.

He would decide what to do about Leif later. For now, he opened the doors to Åke's great hall and stormed into the dark.

The hall was empty but for a few goats and a couple of cats. He had expected Åke to be protected, but there was no one at all, neither fighter nor family, in the hall. Vali ran back to the private quarters and found no one. Had the coward already run and escaped?

If so, Vali would not be far behind. He turned to Leif. "Is this yet another betrayal?"

"He was in his seat when I left, Vali. On my arm ring, I swear."

"The arm ring on which you swore to Åke?"

Leif made a frustrated sound. "I am with you. I kept you alive. And Brenna, too. It was the only way."

Brenna. Without another word or hesitation, Vali stormed back out into the daylight and ran for the stables.

All around him, he saw frightened townspeople, mostly women and children, hiding just inside their doors, or under wagons. But they were all safe now. He could hear that the fighting was over. All that was left was the collective moan of the injured.

Just outside the stables, Astrid stood in tense readiness, her axe raised. As Vali came up to her, he saw what held her at bay—and a fury immense and white-hot soared into his head. He roared loud and long, until his breath and voice gave out.

Åke had Brenna. He held her before him, one hand around her slim throat. His other hand held a long, jeweled dagger, its point pressed into her flesh, under her ear, already deep enough that a thin line of blood trickled down, disappearing behind the shackle she wore.

She was shackled. A heavy chain sagged from it and was looped around her waist like a belt. She was filthy and skinny, her face badly bruised, and Vali could see the damage that vile iron band had done to her lovely, pale throat.

"Brenna!"

Brenna's eyes locked on his, but when she tried to answer, Åke pushed the blade in a hair deeper and snarled, "She is mine!"

Vali tried to stay calm and find his next move. "She is not. She is mine—my wife. More than that, she is her own. And you will pay for all the harm you've done her."

"No. I will have your word that my family and I may leave Geitland well-provisioned and unharmed, or I will put this dagger into her brain." He pushed it in a little deeper still. Much farther, and he would kill her. Vali tried to see his way to save her.

Then Brenna turned her head in Åke's grip. The movement made the blade slice her neck, and her blood poured from the wider wound. With that very blood, her life force leaving her body, she freed herself. It made Åke's hold on her and on the dagger, both, slip, and then Brenna simply dropped to the ground.

Vali wasted no time. He swung his main axe with another mighty roar and planted it in Jarl Åke Ivarsson's head. He fell at once, a look of dumb surprise frozen on his face.

While the jarl's body still twitched, Vali dropped to his knees and gathered his wife in his arms. "Brenna!" Leif handed him a length of linen, and he pressed it to her bleeding neck. That shackle—he wanted to bring Åke to life again so that he could end it more painfully.

Brenna laid her hand over his. "Vali. When Leif told me you lived, I knew I'd see you again in this life. But I wanted to kill Åke."

Vali chuckled, and the sound seemed oddly choked to his ears. "It was my turn to do the saving, shieldmaiden."

She smiled. "I don't think it was."

Her blood had soaked through the linen. "You need a healer."

"It's not mortal. I have survived worse." She clutched at his arm. "Olga?"

Crouched at some distance from them, Leif, too, sharpened his attention at that name. Vali didn't look at him. "She is well. In Karlsa."

"Karlsa?" Leif asked. "She came with you?"

Vali ignored him and directed his answer to Brenna. "There is nothing left in Estland. For her or any of us. But enough of that. We have all the time in the world to tell our stories. You need healing and rest."

But his wife shook her head and pushed him until he let her sit up. She took the linen from him and held it to her own throat. Then she turned to Leif. "I want Igul. I want him alive until I have my hands on him."

Leif nodded but said, "Brenna, Vali is right. You need strength. If he still lives, we will put him away for you, but you need care first."

She fought her way up to her feet; Vali's jaw clenched at the rattle of the chains on her. "No. I need the smith to take this cursed thing off of me, and then I need Igul and Viger chained to that table."

"Viger is dead. I opened his throat." Leif seemed suddenly abashed.

Holding her hand to her bleeding throat, bruised and scarred, filthy and weak, shackled in iron, Brenna cast a look of regal disdain on Vali and Leif both, as they crouched at her feet. "Have you left me no vengeance of my own? If Igul is dead as well, perhaps I'll take it out on your hides instead."

Then she walked out of the stable with her back tall and her shoulders square.

Her braid lay over her shoulder, and Vali thought he saw a scar across the top of her back. Yes, they would tell their stories, and soon. He retrieved his axe from Åke's head and spat in the dead man's face. There would be no Valhalla for him. He had been a great warrior once, but he had died a coward. Hel could have him.

~oOo~

He stared at the raw, red flesh around Brenna's neck. Now he knew that it was the least of her injuries, by far. To remove the shackle, the smith had opened her soiled shift and pushed it down to her waist, and then Vali had seen the ladder of vicious burn scars, still tender and pink, from her shoulders to her hips. Since then, his stomach had tossed violently with a fury he could not assuage.

Åke had died far, far too easily. So had Viger, who had been the one to burn Brenna, Vali now knew. He and Leif had taken her vengeance away from her. He had been single-minded and arrogant, thinking of the wrongs done to Brenna—which he'd only imagined, and were in fact much worse than his mind had conjured—as if they'd been done to him. He could have disabled Åke and left his death to her, but it had not even occurred to him. He had acted out of rage and need.

Leif had caught Igul, however, and he would not be so lucky as the others. The fat punisher was chained, supine and naked, to a massive table in a room made for bad intent.

Once Igul was in custody, they had convinced Brenna to take a moment for herself first. Now—unshackled, tended to by the healer, bathed, braided, and dressed in a gown and hangerock more befitting the great woman she was—she rolled up the sleeves of that gown and picked up a small dirk from a table at the side of the room, on which were arrayed a number of brutal tools.

When she had instructed that Igul should be stripped of his clothes, Vali got a sick feeling in his stomach about the kind of wrongs Brenna meant to right in this room. But he stood aside and remained quiet; he would not interrupt or interfere.

Brenna had wanted Leif in the room, as well. Vali felt jealous and territorial; he didn't like that there was ease between them when Leif had caused so much of the damage they were repairing today. Brenna's trust in the man spoke to the truth of his friendship, perhaps, but her body told the story of how much she'd suffered because Leif had let her be taken.

Igul shook, making his chains rattle, but he had not yet spoken, neither word of challenge nor of plea. When Brenna came to the table, standing at his hip with the dirk in her hand, however, he grunted out a "No."

Brenna stared at the blade. "I told you once I would bite it off, but I have no wish to have that diseased thing in my mouth. So a blade will do instead."

Vali's fists clenched so hard that he felt blood wet his palms.

"No," Igul said again, panic adding an edge to his tone.

When she put her hand around his flaccid worm, Igul lost his bladder. She paid that no mind and severed his member with a quick flick of her wrist.

Igul screamed, his mouth wide open as he yelled until his air gave out, then took a great gasp and yelled again. Brenna dropped what she had taken from him into his mouth, and the sound of his agony was reduced to muffled gagging.

She turned and laid the blade on the table where she'd picked it up, then went to the bowl and washed her hands. When she was clean again, she dropped her sleeves.

Brenna turned to Leif. "Will you see this to its end?"

Leif tipped his head in a terse nod. "I will, Brenna. Shall I keep his head for a pike?" She had insisted that Åke and Viger's heads be displayed at the docks.

She stared down at the suffering, dying man on the table. "No. He is not worthy. Cart him out to the woods to rot."

At Leif's agreement, Brenna came to Vali. Feeling more emotion than his chest could contain, he brushed his thumb over her cheek. So pale and thin, so bruised, and yet still so beautiful to him. His shieldmaiden. "Brenna."

She laid her hand on his chest. "I knew you'd come. I knew our story was not ended."

He pulled her into his arms and kissed her head. "And it never will be. I would like to find a place to be alone with you." She stiffened, and Vali shoved back the fresh surge of rage at what she'd been subjected to. He bent his head and put his mouth to her ear. "Not for that. I would only hold you and talk with you. I have missed you, shieldmaiden."

"Take the jarl's quarters. They are yours now, Vali," Leif said.

Surprised, Vali turned to Leif, forgetting that he didn't trust him. "What?"

"You killed Åke," Brenna answered. "You invaded and vanquished him. No one will challenge you for the seat. You are now jarl."

Of course. But he didn't want that. This was not his home. He was not a leader, not off the field of battle.

The sudden new direction of his turmoil must have been apparent on his face, because Leif smiled. "We can discuss such matters later. For now, be with your wife. You fought hard to rejoin her, and she fought hard to be waiting."

Friend or not, Leif was right. Vali took his wife's hand and led her out of that room of death.

23

Brenna let Vali lead her into and through the empty great hall. So rarely was it empty that its dark quiet seemed eerie and unfamiliar to her, even though it had been long since she had been a welcome presence in it.

When they crossed into the jarl's private rooms, she stopped. Prevented by her hesitation from going any farther, Vali turned and squeezed her hand. "What is it?"

"Hilde? Turid? The children?"

Åke had had three wives, who among them had given him twelve children. His first wife, Torunn, had died birthing Ulv, the third son. After her death, he had taken Hilde to wife. When she gave him only daughters, he'd brought Turid into their bed.

Six of Åke's children were grown. The three sons, Calder, Eivind, and Ulv, were off on the raid. None of the three had yet married. Hilde's three oldest daughters had all been married away. At home still were six children—four daughters and two sons. The boys, Turid's only issue, were the two youngest—one a babe still at the breast, not much older than Brenna and Vali's son would have been, and the other just toddling.

The oldest of Hilde's child daughters was eleven. When Brenna had first served Åke as thrall, she had become close to Hilde and her daughters. Saving their lives had freed her from that servitude—so she had thought at the time. She remained fond of them, even of the little ones she had never tended.

Now that Åke was dead, his family would have been killed as well. It was the way, but it hurt her heart nonetheless. She hoped it had been quick.

Brenna looked up at Vali. "What of his wives and the children?"

Vali cocked his head and then led her to a nearby chair. When she sat, he crouched before her and took her hands. "Åke sent them out of town, but they were stopped on the road and returned. We hold them in a house at the edge of town until we can decide what should be done. What would you do?"

"They have not been killed?"

"Is that what you would advise?"

Confused, she frowned. "The children are likely enemies. Their mothers would nourish that. That is our way."

"No, Brenna. It was Åke's way. He was brutal and impatient in all things. My jarl, Snorri, would have said that if we kill everyone who might someday be an enemy, there will be no one left alive to be a friend."

"So, what then would you do?"

He picked up her hand and kissed her fingers. "I would offer them sanctuary here and allow them to remain as freewomen to make their way."

"Hilde is a proud woman. She will never be subject in the home she once ruled."

He sighed. "Then I would offer them supplies and let them find a new home."

"And if she and Turid sow hatred in the hearts of their children? There are already three strong sons who will soon come home to a Geitland greatly changed."

"Calder and his brothers we will contend with when they return. We will be prepared in a way they cannot be. As for the hatred of a suckling babe, that is a concern for the future. Only a seer can know so far ahead."

Remembering something Åke had said only a few days before, at the feast after the thing, Brenna chuckled.

Vali smiled in response. "What amuses you, my love?"

"Åke said something before the raiders left. He had been to the seer, who told him that he had the eye of the gods, and Geitland was about to enter into an era of greatness. He thought the prophesy meant that he had the gods' blessing to do to me what he did. But he was wrong. Bringing me here was his ruin. And *you* are the jarl who will bring greatness to Geitland."

Vali stiffened and stood. "I don't want it, Brenna. This is not my home, and I am no leader. Estland is lost to us. I would return to Karlsa. That is my home. I would bring you there and become the farmer you would have me be."

She stood, too, and took his hand again. "But you *are* a leader. Even here with me now, talking about Åke's family. Your words, and your thoughts, are wise and true. Your actions are purposeful and righteous. You heed the counsel of those you trust. And people trust you. They admire you. They follow you. I think you are a great leader already."

He shook his head. "I don't want it. I want to go home."

Brenna found herself charmed at how much her great, brave, strong husband sounded like a homesick boy. The thought that the little home they'd almost made for themselves in

Estland was gone made her feel homesick, too. She had no other place she had ever wanted to be a home.

She certainly had no love for Geitland, where she had twice been a slave, and where she had been abused and abased. Karlsa was far north, farther than she had ever been, but she thought she could love a home that Vali loved. Perhaps his people would treat her as a woman, as he himself always had.

She had an idea. "Split the jarldom with Leif. Restore the territories—we will go north, and you will take Snorri's seat in Karlsa. Leif can take Geitland. This is his home."

Vali stalked away, almost to the luxurious bed, then stopped and turned back. "You trust him? After all of this?"

"I do. He is our friend. He saved us both."

It was odd to be standing in this room, still appointed with the personal effects of Åke and his family. She found herself distracted by a piece of half-finished needlework resting on a chair not far from where Vali stood. Such an innocent, domestic thing on this day of violence and upheaval.

Vali's focus was sharp, on the other hand. "No, Brenna. He betrayed us. He let us be overrun in Estland. He let you be taken. He let you be hurt!"

"Vali. What else should he have done?"

"He should have warned us. We could have fought Åke there. He should have *protected* you!" He slammed his fist into the palm of his other hand to punctuate his last sentence.

"He did."

Her husband stalked back to her and cupped his hand around the side of her neck, his thumb brushing lightly over the skin her shackle had made raw. "No. He did not."

She pulled his hand away and held it. "He made himself a shield between me and the worst Åke would have done to me. He made sure I could live and fight."

"I want to know everything, Brenna. Everything that happened to you. I want to know it all."

She had no intention to indulge his fruitless curiosity, and she had even less desire to relive their time apart. "No. You have seen the scars and wounds. That is enough."

He flinched at that. "And nothing else?"

She knew what he was really asking. Even if he had not imagined it already, allowing him to see the way she had killed Igul would surely have put the thought in his head. "No. Nothing else. Igul tried, but he could not…temper his sword. When he tried something else, I threatened him, and he beat me instead. A fair trade."

Rage still lit Vali's eyes. "I cannot forgive Leif. It is because of him that Åke had you. I cannot forgive him, and I do not understand how you can yet call him friend."

"I have known him long. He trained me in the ways of the warrior. I *know* him, Vali. He is our friend. Perhaps we would have made different choices, but his choices were made in love and loyalty. His choices put him at risk, as well."

Vali glowered, and then shook his head again. "He is not my friend."

With a sigh, Brenna gave up that approach. She stepped up to him and closed her arms around his waist. "But might he be your ally?"

He embraced her as well, gazing down into her eyes. Then he bent his head and pressed his lips to the bruised bump on her nose. "You trust him."

The words didn't have the lilt of a question, but she answered them anyway. "I do. With my life."

"Then I will heed your counsel. If Leif will take the seat here, you and I will go to Karlsa and lead there together. We will be allies with him." He curled his finger under her chin and held her head up. "But he is not my friend."

It wasn't true, but Brenna wouldn't fight that losing battle. "I understand. I hope one day you can find forgiveness for him."

He brushed his fingers over her throat again and shook his head.

~oOo~

"All of Åke's lands are rightly yours, Vali. It was your axe that killed him. It is you and Brenna he most wronged."

Vali only glared across the table at Leif. Before the three of them sat brimming cups of mead and a platter of meat and fruit that had made Brenna's mouth flood when Vifrid had brought it out, but thus far only she had partaken of anything. The men vied tensely, silently, on either side of her.

They had already called Hilde and Turid in and offered them sanctuary in Geitland. Hilde had turned them down flat, with her chin held high. Turid looked surprised, and torn, but she dipped her head and deferred to Hilde. The women and their children would be given a horse and cart, a driver, and a week's provisions. They would leave town at the dawn and find their own life.

"Vali," Brenna said, prompting him to calm himself and speak. He glanced at her and then sat forward and finally took a drink from his horn cup.

336

"I do not want this seat. I want no part of it. I hate this place with all my heart. You have Brenna's trust, and she has mine, so we offer this arrangement instead."

"To split your land in twain would split your power as well. Are you sure you want this?"

"I have little interest in power. But what I have would be split only if you are not my ally. Are you not?"

Leif sighed and dropped his head as if it had suddenly become heavier than he could manage. When he looked up, he said. "I am, Vali. I am your friend and Brenna's. Always will I be. I will accept this arrangement. Geitland and Karlsa will be allied as long as you wish it so. If you agree, we can have the rituals here, tomorrow, and you and your clansmen can be on your way north."

Brenna cut in then, leaning in to put herself as much between the men as she could at the table. They couldn't leave yet. "The raiders will return, three ships full, and Åke's sons will find their father dead and their family displaced. Calder is much like Åke in his rashness and quick anger. You need the warriors of Karlsa to hold this town. You need us here until that battle is won."

Leif turned to her. "You are the God's-Eye, Brenna. Calder knows your import to his father, and he heard the prophesy. He will believe that Åke's defeat is your doing—which is not far from true—and he will blame it on the power of your eye. You should be far from here when he returns."

Brenna bristled. "You would suggest that I cannot fight him and win?"

"As you are now, after these weeks enslaved? I would say that you are not as strong as you should be. And I would say that you have fought long and hard enough, and Åke has caused you harm enough." He turned to Vali. "This is my peace offering to you. Go, and take your wife away. If Geitland is to be mine, then I will hold it."

Vali nodded.

"Vali! We cannot!" Without the Karlsa warriors, Leif would be as weak as Åke had been.

Husband and wife stared long at each other. Brenna tried to make him see, with only the power of her gaze, that it would be wrong to leave so soon.

He returned his attention to Leif. "I will speak to my people. If they will stay and fight with you, then we will leave them and the ships, if we might take one of your karves back ourselves." Swiveling his head back her way, he added, "But Brenna, we are leaving. I will take you from this place as soon as I can."

She sat back and crossed her arms over her chest. "And if I will not go?"

A frown shadowed his blue eyes. "Then I will put you over my shoulder and carry you away."

"As Åke took me?"

Vali reared back from that verbal slap. It was Leif who spoke. "Brenna. Please. I will gladly take the help from any other who would stay, but I want you to go. I have seen what this ordeal took from you. Go and build your home and life. I will hold Geitland. If I do not, it will be because I was not worthy to be jarl."

Brenna sat between these two strong, valiant men. Her husband and her friend, one angry and the other contrite. She turned to Leif. All at once, she understood how very tired she was. How sore and weary she was, how close to broken she had been. She had woken that morning in thrall, shackled to the ground. The night of that same day had not yet gone fully dark, and everything had changed. Vali was with her again. Her enemies were dead. And she was wife to a jarl.

"You are worthy." Her voice broke, and tears filled her throat and stung her eyes. She swallowed hard and held them at bay.

Leif reached across the corner of the table and squeezed her hand. "Then let me prove it."

~oOo~

That night, Brenna and Vali took a small house that Åke had kept for esteemed guests. They had allowed Åke's wives and children to sleep in the jarl's quarters, under guard, before their departure the next morning.

Elsewhere in town, buildings burst with people, as did the hall itself. But the year away in Estland, with their private chamber, and her solitary captivity here, had made it difficult for Brenna to find ease when a great many people were around her. So she and her husband had found a place to be alone.

The candles were already lit and the bed prepared. There was food and drink at the ready, too, and a low fire smoldered in the pit. Brenna went to it and stared down into the red embers. Trying to make sense of all that had happened on this day made her mind spin and her eyes ache.

Vali stood behind her and began to pull loose the ties of her braids. She closed her eyes and savored his gentle touch as he slipped his fingers through the woven strands until her hair fell loose around her shoulders. Then he swept the mass aside and reached over her shoulders to unfasten the brooches of her hangerock.

A small, sharp pinch of anxiety tweaked her heart, and she put her hands over his. "Vali, I…" Too many abuses had

339

been perpetrated on her body. She did not think she was capable of accepting an intimate touch, no matter how loving or gentle. Not yet.

"I don't mean to couple with you tonight, my love. But I would see your body, and sleep bare with you. I want nothing between us. Too much has been between us of late. Whole seas and more." He kissed her head. "Please. It will be as it was on our first night. This, too, is a first night for us."

Reminded of the beauty of that night, when Vali had held her, when he had given her all that she needed and asked no more of her than what she could give, when he had kept her close while she wept for the sheer shock of feeling love, Brenna dropped her hands and let him unfasten the brooches. He unlaced the sides of her hangerock and pulled until it fell to the floor around her feet.

She did not stop him when he took off her gown and her underclothes. She stood still and quiet while, behind her, Vali took in the whole of her scarred back.

His voice was tight with sorrow and anger when he spoke. "Ah, Brenna. What they did to you. Forgive me for taking your vengeance from you."

She nodded. Åke was dead. And Viger. And Igul. She was free, and Vali was with her. It was enough. She had found no satisfaction in vengeance against Prince Ivan in Estland. It had not filled the hole the loss of her son had made. There were holes that simply could not be filled. "I do."

Then he drew his finger down her spine, crossing each tender scar. There was no pain to his touch—not of a physical sort, at least. But Brenna felt pain of another sort well up from her heart and fill her head. She had focused all these weeks on surviving, on being strong, on not breaking, on waiting—for her chance, for her freedom, for Vali—and she had built a shield of the strongest oak between herself and her feelings.

With his rough fingers gentle on her damaged flesh, Vali blasted that shield into splinters.

"Vali," she cried, and in that sound she heard all the desolate emptiness she had refused to let herself feel. "Vali. Vali. Vali." She couldn't stop saying his name. Even when tears overcame her and made her sob, still she repeated it, like an incantation. "Vali, Vali, Vali."

"I am here, my love. My wife."

He turned her and gathered her up in his arms. For a long while, he simply stood in the middle of the room, cradling her against his chest like a child, while she clutched him and wept. Then he went to the bed and laid her down. He took off her shoes and then stripped off his own clothes. When he joined her, he pulled her close, drew the furs over them, and tucked her head under his chin.

She cried herself to sleep in his embrace.

When she woke with a start in the middle of the night, he was there, and he eased her back to sleep. Each time.

When she woke in the morning, he was there.

He was there.

~oOo~

In the great hall, the next afternoon, the warriors and townspeople gathered to drink and make merry. After a tense beginning, on the words from Leif and Vali, speaking jointly about their plans to restore the balance of their worlds, an easy friendliness had taken over. Almost all of the Karlsa clan had agreed to stay and fight; those who spoke in favor of it spoke of finishing their vengeance in Snorri's name. Those who did not agree to stay said that they would not see their new jarl leave unattended.

Then they had made sacrifices in order that Leif and Vali's jarldoms would prosper.

And now, they feasted.

Brenna, still feeling the unreality of the changes in her circumstances, sat quietly in a corner and watched as Vali and Leif were toasted and congratulated, as men and women made petitions to them both. Vali seemed supremely uncomfortable as the subject of so much deference. But he would be a great jarl. He was a good man and wise. A strong and fierce warrior, storied among all their people. Compassionate when he could be and decisive when he had to be. The seer had seen clearly. With Leif and Vali holding two of the most important seats in all their world, a great era was most certainly dawning.

He caught her eye at every chance, and took his first opportunity to extract himself from the crowd and join her in her little corner. He pulled her from her seat and took it, then pulled her onto his lap. Smiling at the possessive gesture, she hooked her arm around his shoulder and let her hand play with his braid.

"Is this what it will be like always?" he grumbled as they watched people search for and find him. They would not have this private moment much longer.

"When you want solitude, you will have to make it, I think."

A disgruntled sigh was his only answer.

Sitting alone, Brenna had been thinking. Since she'd woken that morning with his arms around her, in a comfortable bed, in a cozy room, she had been thinking. Since she had dressed in a beautiful, brilliant blue dress, braided her hair, and slid hooks through her ears dangling elaborate blue stones, she had been thinking. While she watched her husband and good friend each claiming a jarldom, she had been thinking.

About the future.

She had never been to Karlsa. She had never seen the home that Vali meant to bring her to, but she felt easy in the knowledge that it waited and was good. A home.

Now, in the ebullient throng of the great hall, sitting on her husband's muscular lap, feeling his need of her against her bottom, she leaned down and put her mouth to his ear. His hands grasped her more tightly at even that innocently intimate touch.

"I am ready to bear another child."

He jerked away and stared hard at her. "Brenna? But last night—"

"Last night I needed what you gave me, and I feel cleansed today. You always give me what I need. Now I need to make our home and family. I want your seed in me."

His eyes were so intense—they seemed to hold more magic than hers ever had. He cupped her cheek in his hand. "I would not rush you."

"I know. You give me what I need. I need this." She turned her head and touched her lips to his palm. Then she stood and held out her hand.

He furrowed his brow. "Now?"

"Would you rather not?"

"You are sure?"

"I am."

A grin took over his handsome face. He stood and grabbed her hand. "Then I am as well."

24

Brenna sat at the side of the bed, her body bare, and unwound her braids. She stared at a point on the floor, lost in thought. While he undressed, Vali watched her, his chest aching with love—and with the lingering, impotent rage he could not seem to master.

Written all over her fair skin was the story of her suffering since she had been taken away from him. She was skinny, her ribs, collarbones, and cheekbones so pronounced they made shadows on her skin. Her knees and elbows were scraped, her legs and arms bruised. Bruises marked her everywhere. Her nose had been broken and still bore the marks of it, and the skin below her eyes was a riot of colors, from beating, exhaustion, and starvation. Her wrists were raw from wear of the shackles. Her neck—her neck. She would bear the choker of Åke's abuse for all her life.

And her back. Vali had demanded that Leif tell him of that torture, in detail. Hot rods laid on her back. Laid there and left to cool while the flesh cooked away beneath. When he'd first fully seen the long, vicious furrows the rods had left behind, Vali had nearly been undone by his fury and grief. But he had been with her, and she had been vulnerable, saying his name again and again, weeping, needing his strength and his calm. So he had swallowed back his rage and given her what she'd needed.

Leif had stood there in that room and let it happen. He had stood there and watched. Vali cared not about his reasons. No true friend would have stood by. Brenna said she understood. She trusted him. She even said Leif had *saved* her, *shielded* her.

But Vali gazed down at his beloved wife, at her battered, starved, burned body, and knew that he would never forgive the man who had let her be taken, who had stood by and let her be enslaved and abused.

Never.

"Where are your thoughts?" Brenna asked, and Vali brought his mind back to the room to see her smiling up at him, her hair loose over her shoulders.

He was glad to see her smile, though it wasn't the brilliant, beaming light he had promised her, on their wedding day, that he would bring forth from her every day. The smile she gave him now was dimmed around the edges by all the griefs and trials they'd had since then.

"I could ask the same of you." He went to the bed and knelt before her. Lifting her hands, he put his lips to the marks around her wrists. "You were lost in thought as well."

She turned her hands and laced her fingers with his. "My head seems to spin whenever it's quiet around me."

He frowned up at her and searched her face. "You should rest, and we should wait to make a child until you have recovered."

Brushing her fingertips over his drawn brow, she shook her head. "That was not my meaning. I feel well. I feel strong. I'm merely finding it sometimes difficult to adjust to the changes that have happened over these two days. I was in chains yesterday. Today, I wore a gown finer than ever I have before." She shook her head lightly, making swing the blue stones that still dangled from her ears. "I wear *jewels*."

When she released one of his hands and moved to pull an earring from her ear, Vali stopped her and reclaimed hold of her hand. He had not ever noticed that her ears had been pierced, but earlier in the day she had slid the hooks into her lobes without trouble. "It cannot be the first time you've worn jewels in your ears. Why else would they have been pierced?"

"Glass beads. These are stones. Precious. And not mine." They had been Hilde's. So had been the dress she'd worn. "I don't know how to be a woman of precious stones and fine clothes."

"Only the circumstances have changed. You have not. You are a beautiful woman, Brenna. More than that, you are a great woman. You are a warrior. Whether you be dressed in rough clothes or fine, in wool or furs, in linen or leather, in chains or jewels, it makes no matter. That is what Åke did not understand. Even in that shackle, you were no slave. You have never been anything but the woman you are."

She smiled and leaned in until their foreheads touched. "You tell a fine tale with pretty words."

"If I do, I have you to thank for saving my tongue to tell it."

"Your tongue does other pretty things as well." She kissed him, darting her tongue out to tease at the corner of his mouth. Just a feather-light touch, but it made Vali's blood sing. Yet she was so battered. Åke had not broken her, but he had surely tried.

"Are you certain?" he breathed, brushing his lips over hers. "I have no wish to hurt you."

"I know, and you never have. I want to feel your loving touch. I want to feel the bliss you bring me. I want to bring you bliss. I want to put this all behind me, behind us, and make our future."

She pushed away and slid backward on the bed, making room for him to join her. "Make me see our stars."

He took her in his arms and loved her slowly and gently, keeping her body as close to his as he could manage, keeping his eyes fixed with hers all the while. The sweet, delicate sounds of her pleasure assured him that he caused her no harm, and when she clutched him tightly and dug her fingers into the muscles of his back, her breaths growing frantic and deep, he let himself become more forceful and turned part of his attention to his own pleasure as well.

When she released, her eyes rolled up in her head and her body went fully tense, curled up against his and twitching, and the intense power of her pleasure almost brought Vali to his. He slowed his thrusts, holding deep inside her, until she had felt all of her bliss.

Then she relaxed, and she gazed up at him with a sated, wanton grin. She pushed on his shoulders until he understood. With a grin of his own, he rolled to his back, and she rode him to his finish. As it struck him, he roared and rolled again, returning her to her back just as his seed surged forth and filled her.

Vali dropped to her side and held her close. As they lay together in a gasping tangle, Brenna asked, "Do you think we made another son tonight?"

He brushed the damp strands of her fair hair from her face. "I don't know. And in this moment, I don't care. I am with you again. You have my love, and I yours. We are making our future, whether we've made a child or not."

~oOo~

Her sleep these past two nights had been fitful, full of dark dreams. Vali knew because she started awake again and again, her eyes wide and her body ready to defend itself, and for a few moments she stayed in that wary state, until she would blink and know that she was with him and safe. Then she would ease slowly back to sleep.

They were leaving early the next day for Karlsa, in the little karve, with a small crew of his clansmen—including Jaan, who was by now as much a part of his clan as any other. Georg and Hans had elected to stay and fight Calder. They both had had family in the coastal village when the raiding ships had first landed, and had grudges against Calder from the first raid. They had made peace with Vali and the other raiders who'd stayed, but Calder had done his damage and then left, until he had returned to do still more.

Vali had a grudge against Calder as well; it was he who had first beaten and then stolen Brenna in Estland. But his need to get her far from this place was greater than his need to see Calder's head rotting next to his father's. He would leave Calder to Leif.

And if they two—who had been, after all, good friends all their lives—ended up allied, if Leif betrayed Brenna's trust yet again? Well, he did not have Vali's trust. So Vali would be prepared, and he would take them both down.

He had already begun to plan.

"You are lost in thought again," his wife whispered. Her head was pillowed on his bicep, and he smiled down at her.

"I am thinking about our voyage today. Are you rested?"

"I am. But I'm still worried about leaving Leif to fight Calder alone."

"Not alone. Two hundred of our men will stay and fight with him."

She nodded but said nothing more.

"Brenna, I would speak with you about something. Leif and I spoke last night in the hall, and I would extend our journey somewhat. We are in agreement that we should visit the jarls between here and Karlsa, to ease their minds about events here and the way our world has changed."

All of that was true. He and Leif had spoken on that matter, and they had agreed that Ivar and Finn, who had apparently—and rightly—been unhappy with the way Åke had bound them in, holding lands on either side of theirs, should be offered the respect of a visit to hear about Åke's demise.

But Ivar's seat was Halsgrof, the town of Vali's birth. Brenna, too, had been born in Ivar's territory. They had met in the woods outside Halsgrof. He wasn't sure how she would feel about returning so close to her birthplace. She had run away from there long ago and never returned.

"You and Leif spoke and agreed on this?"

"We did. Don't make more of it than there is. I am willing to consider him an ally. Nothing more. We agree on this point."

And Vali intended to forge bonds with both jarls during these visits, bonds that he might draw on should Leif turn from their alliance.

Undeterred, Brenna smiled. "It's a sound plan, and I am glad you agree. Each time you agree with him, there is less for you to be suspicious of."

He didn't wish to be distracted by talk of Leif. "How would you feel about returning to Halsgrof?"

Her smile faded; she clearly had not made the connection until now. "Oh." She looked away, thinking, and then brought her eyes back to his. "How do you feel? You lived in Halsgrof itself. What about your father?"

"Love of mead and hatred of everything else took my father long ago. I have no strong feeling about Halsgrof." He smiled. "Except that I met you there, and you changed my life."

"I would like to see that old tree again."

He didn't understand, but she'd said the words in a way that seemed almost private, so he didn't ask her to explain. Instead he pressed the point of his own concern: "Would you wish to seek out your mother?"

Brenna frowned. "I'm not sure if she yet lives. My parents were already growing old when I came to be."

"If Dagmar Wildheart had died, surely the news would have traveled."

"I suppose." She sighed and rested her head again on his arm. "I did love her, and she me. She meant a terrible life for me, but she meant it well. I'm not sure. I will decide while we're in Halsgrof."

"Well enough. If you are rested, I would begin our preparations. I'm eager to put Geitland at our backs today."

Raising up on her elbow, Brenna smiled at him. "Must we rise just yet? I am eager, too, but not only for the voyage." She brushed her nose through his beard, and then, as if he might somehow have missed her meaning, she tucked her head and drew his earlobe into her mouth.

Vali chuckled and pulled her over so that she straddled him. "You are my wanton wife. And I am already risen."

~oOo~

Vali and Brenna stood on the dock with Leif, beside their laden karve. The men who went with them were all on board.

"Fare you both well," Leif said. "I will send word after Calder's return. If I can, and if I would be welcome, I will sail to you and tell you myself."

"Of course you will be welcome." Brenna then lifted her arms and threw them around Leif's neck. Vali could see that Leif was as surprised as he was by such an impulsive display of affection.

When Leif returned her embrace, Vali felt a queer mix of jealousy and doubt. Not doubt in Brenna, but in his own feelings about Leif. Brenna was stingy with her personal affections. To see her so unreserved in her faith in and affection for Leif did make Vali wonder if he were too harsh regarding the man.

But then she stepped back, and he saw her neck. She made no attempt to hide her new scars; they were, to her, battle scars and no source of shame. But they reminded Vali of what their 'friend' had, at best, made no attempt to prevent. No. Brenna had had a blind spot about Åke; she might well have the same blindness about Leif.

Leif held out his hand to Vali, who took it after enough pause to convey his disdain.

"I regret any part I had in all that befell you both, but I did all I could think to do to save you. I would have us friends again. If it is proof you need, Vali Storm-Wolf, proof you will have."

Vali nodded once, and took his hand back.

With that, Leif gestured to a young man behind him, one Vali did not know. That young man stepped up and brought a bundle of white linen forward. He held it out on his two hands, and Leif unwrapped it.

352

The longsword that Leif and the other men had presented to Vali on the day of his wedding. Meant for Brenna to hold in safekeeping for their descendants. Vali watched as Leif took the sword and handed it to her. He could see the emotion roiling in his wife's eyes.

"Thank you," she said, her voice soft with feeling.

Leif smiled at her and then turned to Vali. "Åke took it to claim as his own, as he took Brenna. I only return it to its rightful place."

Vali was moved; to himself, he would not deny it. The sword was important, a symbol of the strength of his union with Brenna. And, as well, a symbol of their friendships in Estland.

But he was not so moved that he was blinded to the scar circling his wife's throat or the furrows in her back, or deafened to her cries in the night. As Leif had said, he had only returned the sword into the hands from which it never should have been taken. As Brenna never should have been taken.

So Vali simply gave Leif another single nod. Then he turned and helped his wife onto their boat so that they could leave Geitland and its new jarl behind.

~oOo~

As they had expected, the other jarls had been prepared for battle with Åke and were relieved to find instead a small karve docking at their shores, with a new jarl and the balance among them all restored. That the new jarl was Vali Storm-Wolf, who was wedded to the God's-Eye, was all to the better.

Vali took his opportunity with Finn and then with Ivar, when each wife had drawn Brenna off for womanly chat, to judge their feelings about Calder. Both considered Calder a shadow of his father, and bore him little affection. Then Vali made the kind of statements that would indicate that, should the alliance break between Geitland and Karlsa, Jarl Vali would be their true friend.

Jarl Vali. Such a strange sound those words had together.

It was a delicate balance, to persuade a man both that the alliance was sound and peaceable and that, were it not, Vali would be the stronger friend, but Vali had always been good with words.

When Brenna and Ivar's wife, Alva, returned, Vali moved the conversation to a more neutral topic and then stood to take his wife's hand. She wore leather breeches and tunic on the karve, but in the jarls' halls, she had reverted to more elegant, womanly dress—all of which had been taken from the belongings Hilde had left behind. Vali would be glad to get his wife to their own hall, where clothes might be made new for her.

"We would like to walk the town on our own for the afternoon, if we have your leave," Vali said, pulling Brenna close.

Ivar, an old, grandfatherly man with a snow-white beard, the braid of which lay over his vast belly, yet still hale and astute despite his years, smiled and laid a gnarled hand on Brenna's shoulder. "Of course. I remember you both as young children. You were strong then and you have grown into legends. It pleases me that I may call you friends and equals now."

"May I ask, Jarl Ivar...does my mother yet live?"

Ivar made a serious face. "Dagmar Wildheart. Yes, I believe she lives. She has not been to Halsgrof in many a year, but I am certain word would have come to me if she had gone on from this world. Do you know nothing of her?"

"No. I have had no word since my father died, long ago."

"Brenna God's-Eye. I'm sure it has been difficult to live with such a gift as Odin gave you. I saw with my own eyes how you struggled as a child, and I imagine that what I saw was little more than a flash of understanding. I realize why you might have run away. But you have done your mother a grave injustice all these years. Perhaps you are now my equal, but I am much older than you, so I speak the wisdom of age when I tell you: to lose one child is a great agony. To lose them all—I cannot imagine that pain. To lose one while she lives? Even gods have been driven mad by such a loss."

Vali sensed Brenna's back straighten in self-defense, and he wasn't surprised at the edge in her voice when she answered, "I know the pain of losing a child."

Ivar's expression softened. "Then I am deeply sorry for you both." He turned and held out his hand to Alva, who came near and took it. "But perhaps knowing that pain, you might find compassion for her?"

"Thank you for your wisdom, Jarl Ivar." Brenna's tone was chilly. Knowing her the way he did, Vali understood that Ivar had made a much greater impression than she would admit.

~oOo~

She was quiet as they walked through Halsgrof toward the woods. Vali noted the smithy, but he barely looked. That was not his father's shop. The sounds and smells of it turned his stomach, but that was always the case, whenever he neared any smithy anywhere. It was a phantom memory, without fists.

Once in the woods, near the shoreline, Brenna paused at a great old tree. Vali took no special meaning for the place, but his wife crouched at a small nook in the base of the tree and stroked it as if she expected the bark to feel her touch.

"It's so small."

He crouched at her side. "I don't understand, my love."

"When we came to town, my mother and father would send me away while they did their business. Mother would give me a bit of hacksilver for the sweets-monger, but I never used it. I hated going there, where all the children were. Adults were fearful or suspicious, but children were mean. So instead, I would come here, and tuck myself down into this nook. I would spend the afternoon almost asleep, my eyes closed, telling myself stories about what my life would be like. I imagined myself to be a great shieldmaiden and voyager. I even imagined that I might be jarl someday myself."

"And you achieved all of that."

She smiled. "You are jarl, not I."

"I would hand the title to you in the space between two beats of my heart."

"No. I don't want it. When I was a girl, all I saw was the wealth and comfort. Now I know what goes on behind. And I don't speak well with people. I will stand with you, but it is right that you are jarl." She stroked the tree again. "I cannot believe that I ever fit into such a tiny space."

"You were very small when first I saw you. You grew tall and strong since, but then, I took you for much younger than you were."

"I was in my little nook when I heard you and your father. You and he were there."

She pointed to a stand of pines not far off, and suddenly the memory of that day struck him in violent, vivid detail. He shut his eyes and shook his head at the force of it.

"Vali?"

The memory of his father's abuse, and of his own terror as his tongue was yanked forward, and as the knife bit into it, gave way to the sound of Brenna's young voice, loud and sure, full of righteous fire and fury.

"Vali?" Brenna laid her hand on his arm, and he opened his eyes.

That small girl who'd save him from the horror of that day, who had saved him from so much more, was the great woman at his side now. A storied shieldmaiden. His wife.

"I love you, Brenna God's-Eye."

Usually, she flinched when that name was used, but this time, she smiled—the first full, brilliant smile he had seen from her since they had been reunited. "And I love you."

He slid his hand into her hair and made a fist, knotting the tresses with his fingers. "I love you. I love you. I love you." He kissed her.

Over and over, he repeated those three words, punctuating each repetition with a kiss, and as he did so, he took control of her. He laid her down on ground soft with moss and fallen pine needles, and he pulled her finely woven gown up her strong, scarred, beautiful legs.

There in the woods where they'd first met, he loved her deep and long.

~oOo~

The next morning, Ivar happily lent them two fine, strong horses for the ride to the village of Brenna's birth. The occasion of riding horseback provoked Brenna to ask about Freya. Vali considered telling her that the mare was safe, but instead he told her the truth.

Her eyes glittered with sadness, but she nodded. "It was a good offering. The gods were with you, so they saw her worth."

Vali believed that as well. For all they had suffered—for all Brenna had suffered—now they were together and strong, and they had set right more than merely their own lives.

Perhaps they were about to set right one thing more.

It was past midday when they approached a tiny cluster of buildings. Brenna's posture changed, as if she were trying to see more clearly.

"This is your village?"

"It is where I was born, yes. Up that hill there, deep in the woods, is where Oili lives. If she still lives. She was an old woman when I was a child. She is a healer and a völva—it was what my mother meant for my life. But if my eye is Odin's gift, and if any power at all comes from it, it is not the power of the sight."

"No. It is the power of the spirit. Your spirit is stronger than anyone I've ever known, shieldmaiden. You have a godly spirit."

She turned to him. "Then you do believe my eye is inhuman?"

"I believe it does not matter. However you came to bear Yggdrasil and all the colors of the worlds in your right eye, whether it was a gift from Odin or an accident of birth, your spirit is a mighty thing. If your eye is the way that people see your greatness, then so be it. Perhaps that was all the gift Odin thought you needed: no mystical power, merely something to set you apart."

She cocked her head, thinking about his words, and then she smiled. "I like to think of it that way. That feels right. All my life I've struggled to understand, but that feels right."

They had been riding as they'd spoken, and Brenna had led them off to the east, toward the wooded hill. They neared a small homestead that seemed to have fallen on hard times. None of the village seemed prosperous, but this stead was in dire need of repair.

Brenna nudged her horse forward and took the lead. She pulled up just outside a door. Before she could dismount, the door opened, and an old woman stepped out. Her hair was a dull, greying blonde, woven into a simple braid over her shoulder. She wore an oft-mended woolen dress and worn leather shoes. But she stood tall and straight, a simple woolen shawl over her shoulders.

Was this Oili, the old völva?

She stood in the doorway and stared up at Brenna, her eyes wide and her mouth agape.

Vali noticed that her eyes were the exact color of Brenna's left eye—the clear blue of summer sky.

This was Dagmar Wildheart.

At the same moment Vali knew her, she fell to her knees. "Brenna."

Brenna dismounted and held out her hand. "Mother."

Dagmar Wildheart, a storied shieldmaiden in her own right, reached up and clutched her daughter's hand, but she did not

359

rise. Instead, on her knees before her only living child, she wept.

~oOo~

There had been no effusive exchanges of apologies between these two strong women, no heartfelt cries of mutual love. Brenna had asked her mother to stand, and Dagmar had composed herself and stood. They had embraced stiffly, and then Brenna had introduced her mother to Vali.

Then they had gone into the derelict house, and Dagmar had offered them a meager meal.

Vali sat back and watched them as they navigated their reunion. What was clear to him, in this dreary house, seeing mother and daughter face to face, was that Brenna was the stronger of the two. Dagmar might have fought trolls in her youth, she might have fought in Jötunheim and killed giants—the stories would have it so, at least—but she had been broken. She had lost her children, and she had lost her husband, and she had given up that which was her own self and closed what was left off to rot along with this house.

Vali didn't think there was any loss that would cause Brenna to give up herself.

Clearly, Dagmar would die here; she was waiting to die here. Without knowing why he did so, Vali suggested that she go with them to Karlsa. Both women agreed with little resistance. Brenna gave him a surprised glance, but then she nodded and reinforced the idea. By the time they retired to the straw mat on the floor, they had decided that Dagmar would leave her single goat and her five chickens for Oili, and they would pack up whatever belongings she wished to keep and ride for Halsgrof and the docks the next morning.

~oOo~

The next morning, Vali opened the door while the women were still dressing and came face to face with a tiny, ancient hag with wild white hair.

"Hello," he said, surprised.

"You are the wolf," said the old woman. "And the storm."

"And you are the völva." It wasn't a leap to guess that she was Oili.

"You brought the God's-Eye home, and now you mean to take the Wildheart away."

He wondered if the old woman ever used anyone's name. "I do."

"That is good. Her heart has not been wild these long years since. She has more story to tell, but it won't be told here."

He felt Brenna's hand on his back and sidestepped so she could come through. The old woman gasped, her toothless mouth wide, and rushed up to Brenna, reaching with her spotted, clawed hands. Vali lunged between them. "Watch what you do, old woman."

"It's all right, Vali," Brenna said. "She means no harm." She pulled on his arm until he stepped aside again. He felt a bit ridiculous, shielding Brenna from an ancient woman barely as tall as his elbow, but she was a völva, so who knew what she might be capable of.

"Hello, Oili," Brenna said and held out her hand. The old woman grabbed it and turned the palm up. She brushed her shriveled fingers over it, frowning down as if in great concentration, muttering to herself all the while. Then she gasped again and stared up into Brenna's face.

361

Letting go of Brenna's palm, Oili stepped close and laid her hand, as flat as she could make it, on Brenna's belly.

"Your womb quickens and fills again. You nurture a great warrior, Brenna God's-Eye. Songs and stories will be made for her. Her light will be bright and warm as the sun."

As Vali watched, his heart pounding with growing joy, Brenna laid her hand over Oili's on her belly. "I am with child?"

"Not often do the gods let me see so much so clearly. It will not be an easy carrying, but if you are strong, she will be. You will need your mother with you. Go north and make your home. You and the wolf will fill it full with daughters and sons, until the day your family is complete."

Brenna shook her head and dropped her hand from Oili's. "It can never be complete."

Oili patted her cheek. "Your boy of thunder waits for you, God's-Eye. The gods keep him well until the day you join him."

With that, the völva stepped back and reached into her patched hangerock and pulled out a small, soft leather pouch on a cord. She took it from her neck and held it out to Brenna. "Give this to your mother. Tell her I thank her for the goat and chickens."

Then the old woman turned and shuffled away.

For a few stunned moments, Vali and Brenna watched her go. Then Vali went to his wife and knelt before her, laying his own hands on her belly. She was still so skinny.

"Do you think it is true?" He leaned his head against her.

Brenna laid her hands on his head. "Oili is a true völva. Think of all she knew of us. Yes, it is true."

He stood and took hold of her chin. "She said it would be a hard carrying. I would keep you safe and comfortable. I would have you let me take that care. Please."

"She said I should be strong, and that our daughter would be. Don't try to make me weak. But I promise to be careful. And I promise to try to be patient with you and your care."

He grinned. "That is enough. Now I want to get you home. To our home."

His magnificent wife cupped his face in her hands and beamed up at him. "You are my home, Vali. I need no other."

EPILOGUE
THE SUN

SOME MONTHS AFTER

Oili had not overstated the difficulty of this pregnancy. From nearly the moment Brenna's feet touched Karlsa soil, she had been sick and sore. The babe rested high, and as she grew she seemed to crush Brenna's lungs and stomach so that she could never catch a full breath and she struggled always to keep any food long enough to nourish them both.

Olga and Dagmar had both fussed without cease, and Vali had nearly gone out of his head. Brenna had been weak and ill enough by the end that she accepted any and all care offered to her. The truth was that, even knowing the prophesy, she felt sorry for herself and struggled to keep her spirit.

She had found it easier to stay strong when she had been shackled in Åke's dark hovel.

She worried endlessly that Oili had been wrong, or that there had been some twist in the words of the seeing that would take her happiness away. Prophesies were slippery, their import subjective. She thought of how Åke had taken his last prophesy. He had thought it meant his great success, but instead it had meant his ruin.

While she had struggled and suffered, Karlsa prospered. They had been welcomed as heroes, and there had been a great celebration when Vali reported that not only had Åke been defeated, but Vali himself was their new jarl.

Then, mere weeks after Vali, Brenna, and Dagmar had landed in Karlsa, just as the first snows of winter lay over the ground, many of the warriors who had stayed behind in Geitland arrived, reporting that Calder and his ships had returned, and that Leif had killed Calder in single combat. Eivind and Ulv, with the rest of Åke's raiders, had been given the chance to swear fealty to Leif and save their heads. Eivind had refused. Ulv had sworn to Leif.

The era of greatness that the prophesy had foretold had dawned.

But Leif had not yet come. Despite Leif killing Calder, his best friend since childhood, and taking Eivind's head, Vali saw his reluctance, if that was what it was, to come north as further evidence that he was no true friend. When Brenna suggested that Leif had a new jarldom and a new peace to make strong, and that in any case, the emerging winter was no time to travel when one would have a return trip as well, he remained unmoved. He kept stubborn hold of his anger and distrust, and Brenna knew that the ice between them would not be moved unless the two men could again be face to face.

Now, though, in the next summer, Brenna had more pressing concerns.

As another tightening racked her body and Dagmar helped her to sit up while she bore down, Brenna hoped that the prophesy about their daughter was true as she understood it.

The pain was like nothing she'd ever felt. She'd done this before, but had no memory at all of giving birth to her tiny son. This was worse than anything, worse even than the hot rods. More than that, it was *work*, more work that she had strength for, after months and months of bringing her food up.

She was much better at the work of the warrior than she was at the work of the woman. That had always been true. It made her worry about how she would mother her child.

Her strength gave out before the pain did, and she screamed.

"Gods! Help her!" Vali yelled.

Dagmar set Brenna back on the bed and stalked over to her husband. "Get OUT, Vali! You do her no good!" She shoved at his chest.

In this moment of respite, Brenna lay and watched them, trying to find her strength.

She saw Vali put his hands up as if he meant to shove her mother back, but then he stopped. "I will not leave them! I will not!"

Between Brenna's legs, Olga said, "He is incorrigible, Dagmar. We can put him to use. Vali, take over for Dagmar. Dagmar, I need you here." Brenna's mother moved to the end of the bed, and her friend smiled up at her. "I know this has been long and hard, Brenna. Your daughter is a greedy girl, and she took all you gave her. She is big and strong, and you will need to be strong to push her forth. Remember what your seer told you."

As another wave of pain crashed over her, Vali crouched at the side of their bed. He helped her to sit up. "Brenna, look at me. See me."

She locked her eyes with his, those brilliant blue lights. Finding her shieldmaiden, she bore down, grunting with effort and agony, and he smiled.

"You bring forth a great warrior today. Like her mother. And her mother before her."

Brenna nodded and bore down.

~oOo~

"Her name is Solveig," Brenna said on a yawn.

Lying at her side, their daughter sleeping between them, Vali said, "That is a fine name. 'The way of the sun.' Yes. She is our sun and our way, I think." He brushed his fingers over the soft, pale down that was her hair. "She is the most perfect thing I have seen ever in my life."

They were alone in their quarters, all the fuss and mess having been cleared away. It was just them, their little family, snuggled together in their own bed.

Brenna kissed the back of her daughter's head, then stayed there to breathe in the magical scent of her. It tugged at her heart in some way. That scent made her breasts tingle and her womb ache. It was as if love itself had a scent. She no longer worried about what kind of mother she would be. From the moment her daughter had been placed in her arms, she knew that she would do everything in all the worlds to raise her strong and content.

On the back of her right shoulder, Solveig had a birthmark. Just a tiny, dark red mark, no bigger than the tip of Brenna's first finger.

It seemed to have the shape of a rayed sun.

"She has your eyes." Feeling tired and happy and unbearably cozy, Brenna snuggled closer to her babe, under the furs. Her body was beset by myriad pains, and her bottom felt enormous, but she had never been more comfortable in her life.

"She has her own eyes," Vali answered, leaning over to kiss Brenna's temple. "She is magnificent. Like her mother." He kissed her again, and she sighed. "Sleep, my love. I will be here when you and Solveig awaken."

"You are mine," she mumbled, feeling sleep ease over her shoulders.

"Ever will I be," her husband whispered at her ear.

Susan Fanetti is a Midwestern native transplanted to Northern California, where she lives with her husband, youngest son, and cats.

Susan's blog: www.susanfanetti.com
Freak Circle Press blog: www.freakcirclepress.com

Susan's Facebook author page:
https://www.facebook.com/authorsusanfanetti
'Susan's FANetties' fan group:
https://www.facebook.com/groups/871235502925756/

Freak Circle Press Facebook page:
https://www.facebook.com/freakcirclepress
'The FCP Clubhouse' fan group:
https://www.facebook.com/groups/810728735692965 /

Twitter: @sfanetti

Made in the USA
Monee, IL
28 March 2022

93718718R00203